THE CAPTIVE CROWN

'The same obstinate, self-righteous Jamie Douglas, I see! Your father has been much concerned for you.'

'When last I saw him he was more concerned for . . . others!'

'Perhaps. He has had time to reconsider, however, and to decide that you were not wholly at fault.'

'But I am still a landless outlaw.'

'And must continue to be so, until the sentence is withdrawn. Which means, until you make your peace with my nephew Robert of Albany.'

'That I will never do.'

'Then you must accustom yourself to being landless and an outlaw, Jamie. For *you* will never beat Robert. And he will never relent.'

The Captive Crown

The third volume of the
House of Stewart trilogy

Nigel Tranter

CORONET BOOKS
Hodder and Stoughton

PRINCIPAL CHARACTERS
In Order of Appearance

SIR JAMES DOUGLAS OF ABERDOUR (JAMIE): Illegitimate eldest son of the Lord of Dalkeith.

SIR ALEXANDER STEWART OF BADENOCH: Eldest and illegitimate son of the late and notorious Earl of Buchan, Wolf of Badenoch.

ALASTAIR CARRACH MACDONALD OF ISLAY: Brother of Donald, Lord of the Isles.

WILLIAM DE SPYNIE, BISHOP OF MORAY.

LADY ISOBEL DOUGLAS, COUNTESS OF MAR: Countess in her own right. Sister of late 2nd Earl of Douglas.

MARY STEWART, LADY DOUGLAS OF ABERDOUR: One of Robert II's illegitimate daughters. Married to Jamie.

MARIOTA DE ATHYN (or MACKAY): Mother of Sir Alexander Stewart of Badenoch. Late mistress of the Earl of Buchan.

LORD JOHN STEWART OF COULL AND ONELE: Second son of the Duke of Albany.

LADY ISABEL STEWART: Sister of the King. Former Countess of Douglas, now married to Edmonstone of that Ilk.

JAMES DOUGLAS, LORD OF DALKEITH: Former statesman and wealthy noble. Father of Jamie.

SIR JAMES DOUGLAS, YOUNGER OF DALKEITH: Half-brother of Jamie. Husband of the Princess Elizabeth.

SIR ARCHIBALD DOUGLAS OF CAVERS: Illegitimate son of 2nd Earl of Douglas.

ROBERT III, KING OF SCOTS: Great-grandson of the Bruce.

RICHARD II OF ENGLAND: Deposed by Henry IV. Called The Mammet, in Scotland. Possibly impostor.

ARCHIBALD, 4TH EARL OF DOUGLAS: Son and heir of late Archie the Grim.

SIR JAMES (the Gross) DOUGLAS OF ABERCORN: Brother of above.

HENRY WARDLAW, BISHOP OF ST ANDREWS: Primate.

SIR JAMES SCRYMGEOUR: Hereditary Standard-Bearer, and Constable of Dundee.

ROBERT STEWART, DUKE OF ALBANY: Next brother to the King. Governor.

GILBERT GREENLAW, BISHOP OF ABERDEEN: Chancellor.

DAVID, EARL OF CRAWFORD: Lord High Admiral, and chief of the Lindsays. Brother-in-law of the King.

SIR ANDREW LESLIE OF BALQUHAIN: Powerful Mar laird.

SIR ALEXANDER FORBES OF THAT ILK: Powerful Mar laird.

JAMES I, KING OF SCOTS: Surviving son of Robert III.

HENRY IV, KING OF ENGLAND: Usurper.

MURDOCH STEWART, EARL OF FIFE: Eldest son and heir of Duke of Albany.

EDMUND HOLLAND, EARL OF KENT: Great English noble.

ROBERT DAVIDSON, PROVOST OF ABERDEEN: Merchant and shipmaster.

IAN BORB MACLEOD, YOUNGER OF DUNVEGAN: Heir to chief of Siol Tormod.

ANTON DE VALOIS OF BRABANT: Brother of the Duke of Burgundy.

JOHN DE VALOIS, DUKE OF BURGUNDY: French prince, and Count of Flanders.

ISABELLA OF BAVARIA, QUEEN OF FRANCE: Wife of King Charles VI.

CHARLES VI, KING OF FRANCE: Insane.

BERNARD, COUNT D'ARMAGNAC: Powerful French noble. Father-in-law of young Duke of Orleans.

HENRY BEAUCHAMP, EARL OF WARWICK: Great English noble. Envoy to France.

HECTOR MACLEAN OF DUART: Great Highland chief; son-in-law of Donald of the Isles.

SIR ALEXANDER IRVINE OF DRUM: Grandson of Bruce's Armour-Bearer.

SIR ALEXANDER KEITH OF GRANDHOLM: Heir to the Knight Marischal.

PART ONE

SIR JAMES DOUGLAS, lately of Aberdour, Stoneypath and Baldwinsgill, and now a landless fugitive, reined in his sturdy, broad-hooved Highland garron on the heather ridge and, shielding his eyes against the mellow October sunlight, gazed southwards over the wide and fair vale of mid-Strathspey, golden, scarlet and olive-green amongst the blue mountains. In a land of colour, with the heather fading from purple to brown, October was the most vivid of all months, the chromatic range and vehemence of the turning leaves almost unbelievable to Lowland eyes.

The Douglas was not on this occasion thinking about all that far-flung brilliance — or at least not Nature's overwhelming contribution. It was man-made colour that he looked for, and had no difficulty in finding. For a couple of miles at least beside the wide, silver river, moving colour rippled and surged and gleamed, a great host — and by the flicker of sunlight on steel, an armed host, thousands strong, only a small proportion of it mounted. Yet it was moving fast, eastwards, down-river, and with a decided air of purpose about it all. It was further on by some miles than the man had looked for it. Nodding to his two companions, running gillies in ragged tartans, he kicked the barrel-like flanks of his shaggy mount, and set off at a trot, slantwise downhill, his gillies loping long-strided, tireless, at his sides. Parallel with the falling Tulchan Burn, they dropped from the wide heather wilderness of Dava Moor.

It took him some time to reach the head of that long column, passing company after company of kilted clansmen, Mackintoshes, Macphersons, MacGillivrays, Shaws, Cattanachs, MacQueens, MacBains and the like, armed with broadsword, dirk and Lochaber axe, most naked to the waist, leather targes slung over lean, sweating shoulders, the fastest-moving infantry in Christendom, going at the slow-trot which ate up the miles. They were almost opposite Ballindalloch, on the other side of Spey, before he saw the leadership.

Under a single great banner in front, the Stewart fess-chequey impaling the green-and-red of Badenoch, a group of chiefs rode, proud of bearing, eagles' feathers in their bonnets. Amongst them, more modestly garbed than most, was Sir Alexander Stewart of Badenoch, acting Justiciar of the North, and nephew, although illegitimate, of the King of Scots, Robert the Third.

At sight of the newcomer, this young man pulled up sharply. "Jamie! Jamie Douglas!" he cried. "God be praised — yourself, by all that is blessed!" He reined his horse over, alongside to Douglas's, and embraced his friend, from the saddle, there before them all. "Back from the dead — or nearly! Jamie — we feared for you."

The other grinned, embarrassed, his dark and rather sombre good looks lightening up. His was a less forthcoming nature than that of the sunny Stewart's, but he was no less pleased at the reunion.

"Alex!" he said. "It is good."

They were so very different, these two, in more than their greetings. Both now in their early thirties, where Jamie Douglas was swarthy, stocky, strong-featured, of medium height, Alex Stewart was fair, slender, tall and of a fineness of feature which was almost beauty, but redeemed from any hint of weakness by the firm line of mouth and jaw. He did not look as though he was the eldest son of the late and notorious Wolf of Badenoch; but then Alexander, Earl of Buchan, himself had *looked* good, too — the Stewarts having a tendency that way.

"You have come from Lochindorb? How long? How long have you been there, Jamie?"

"Almost two weeks. I near came west, seeking you — but reckoned that Mary and the bairns were entitled to their husband and father for a space. And you with your battles won."

"To be sure." The other turned. "You will know most of these my friends — the Mackintosh, Cluny Macpherson, Shaw of Rothiemurchus, MacGillivray Mor, MacBain of Kinchyle, the Cattanach?"

One by one the chiefs bowed from their saddles, or inclined stiff heads towards the Lowlander, and he nodded back. Mac-Gillivray, at whose side he had fought at Glen Arkaig, reached out to grip his hand, and murmured greetings in the Gaelic.

Then Stewart swung on another smaller group, distinguishable from the rest only in that they looked fiercer somehow, and wore winged helmets of an antique aspect.

"And here you see others of whom you have heard and even drawn sword against, but have not met, I think — Alastair Carrach MacDonald of Islay and Lochaber, brother to Donald of the Isles. And sundry of his captains."

Jamie stared. "Alastair Carrach himself? Here? Your prisoner?"

"Say that I have persuaded him to return with me to the scene of his indiscretions, to the city of Elgin. To express suitable regrets to the representatives of Holy Church there, for having caused fire at the canons' manses, and other parts of the town — as befits a Highland gentleman! Even from the Isles!"

The Islemen gazed back at the newcomer expressionless, from almost uniformly pale blue eyes, the Scandinavian Viking admixture in their Celtic blood very evident, not so much as a nod amongst them. Yet this Alastair, and of course his brother the Lord of the Isles, were likewise grandsons of the late Robert the Second, their mother the Princess Margaret who had married John of the Isles. The present monarch, Robert the Third, had some strange kinsmen.

"Guidsakes!" Jamie muttered, striving to repress a grin at the audacity and wry humour of this son of a father who had himself burned the same Elgin and its great cathedral almost to the ground, in malice, now imposing penance for a lesser deed on the Lord of the Isles' brother. "*You* well won your campaign, then, Alex!"

"Say that we brought matters to a decent conclusion. You, unhappily, were less fortunate I gather, Jamie?"

"I served a fool as commander," the other said briefly.

"Yes. Archibald Douglas something lacks the style of his proud line. But — tell me as we ride on, Jamie. I am eager to hear what went wrong with the English invasion. You will come with us to Elgin?"

As they resumed the march eastwards, Jamie gave his friend a typically cryptic account of the late abortive Scots campaign in Northumberland ending in the disaster of Homildon Hill five weeks before, under his chief, Archibald, 4th Earl of Douglas.

"Mismanaged from the start," he said. "Ten thousand men wasted. No discipline. Angus, Moray, Murdoch of Fife, with no

11

experience of war amongst them. They conceived it something between a tourney and a Border cattle-raid, where it was meant to be a vital counter-invasion stroke. Within hours of crossing Tweed, hundreds, possibly thousands, dispersed, looting, driving home beasts. I advised a hanging or two, but the Earl Archie would not. Folly all the way to Newcastle. Besieged that town, hoping Hotspur was inside — as only a fool would have been. I went seeking him. Found him at the head of Derwent, far to the west. Meeting a large force of mounted archers from King Henry's army on the Welsh March."

"Ha — archers! And you had none?"

"Aye. I took the word back to Douglas, at speed. He had wearied of sitting round Newcastle, without siege machinery, and was retiring north. Still burning, looting, burdened with cattle — untold thousands."

"I can guess what happened, friend."

"Wait you. The Percy got in front of us, in the Vale of Till. Barred the way. A great force. To win round, westwards, we had to ford the Glen Water. I took my father's Dalkeith men, four hundred, and held the approaches to the fords. When I regained the host it was not where we had arranged, but crowded up on top of a hill. Homildon Hill."

"Go on, man."

"Safe from Hotspur's cavalry, up there, yes. But a higher hill rose just to the east — Housedon Hill. A deal higher. And within arrow-shot."

"God's mercy — a death-trap!"

"That is what it was, yes — and thousands died, to prove it. Nor could strike a blow in return. I pleaded for a break-out. Down, in wedge-formation, through the encircling cavalry. Douglas refused. And he fell, at last, leading a foot-attack on the *bowmen*! The blind folly of it! After that, I led what I could off the field — nine hundred or so. Downhill, in wedges, through the cavalry. To escape. Leaving the rest — Douglas and the others. Two brothers of my own. That was Homildon Hill."

Stewart considered him. "Folly, yes. We heard that it was a great defeat. But not all this of folly and weakness. Douglas did not die?"

"None of the earls died. Nor my brothers. But all were wounded, and captured. Many brave men did die. Whereas I — I escaped with a whole skin! And pay the price now."

"You mean . . .? You are blamed? For surviving?"

12

"Blamed, yes. Damned as a craven and a traitor! The man who fled the field, leaving all to their fate. His chief, even his own kin. Worst of all, leaving Albany's son and heir, the Earl Murdoch of Fife! I am a hooting and a hissing, in the South. Albany has seen to that. Even my own father miscalls me, for failing to bring home my brothers."

"But this is crazy! You, of all men!"

Jamie shrugged. "Crazy or no, I am now a landless hunted man. Outlawed. My wife and bairns dependent on others for their bread."

"Then your misfortune is my *good* fortune, man! For I need you here in Badenoch, as never before."

"You mean, because of Drummond's death?"

"Wha-a-at! Drummond — dead? Sir Malcolm?"

"Save us — did you not know? Have not heard? I would have thought that you must have heard of it. Been sent word . . . ?"

"No. When? When was this? When did he die? How?"

The other cleared his throat. "See you, Alex — this is a bad business. I had not thought to be the bearer of such ill tidings . . ."

"Scarce so ill as that, Jamie! Sir Malcolm is, was, no friend of mine, as you know. His death will make for . . . changes. But . . ."

"Changes, yes. For you, I fear, Alex." His friend's discomfort was not to be hidden. "You see, *you* are getting the blame for it."

"Damnation — me? How could that be? I knew naught of it. He was slain, then?"

"Slain, yes — after a fashion. Your lady-mother says that you sent a small force, under your brothers, to keep watch on Drummond when Donald of the Isles struck, and you yourself marched to deal with the Islesmen."

"Yes. You mean . . . that it was my brothers who slew Sir Malcolm?"

"Who knows? But somebody did. The word is that he was taken unawares, as he rode between Kildrummy and Kindrochit, in Mar, by a band of caterans. Carried to some remote hold in those mountains. And, and there fed neither food nor drink. Until he starved to death."

"Christ God!" Shocked, appalled, Stewart involuntarily drew rein, to state. "Starved . . . ?"

"So it is said. Like the Duke David, your cousin. And you are being blamed. Can you wonder? If your brothers did it — and

13

you sent them. Your fondness for the Countess, his wife, is well known."

"But, but . . ." He paused, as the implications of it all began to dawn on him. "Saints of mercy — so evil a thing!"

"Evil, yes. I grieve to bring you such tidings. Your brothers have told you nothing of it?"

"I have not seen them since I left Lochindorb with my main force. They do not much find it necessary to inform me of their doings! But if they have done this thing, I, I . . ." He swallowed. "God pity us all, they shall suffer for it! It would be Duncan, of course. Andrew and Walter are hard — but would not do that. And James, new wedded, is still at Garth, in Atholl, not concerned in this fighting. It would be Duncan, if any. He has a devil in him. Like, like . . ." He did not complete that, but Jamie knew that he was thinking of his father, the Wolf.

"See you, Alex — perhaps your brother thought to do you a service?"

"A service! This will damage me as nothing else could. All the Southern Highlands, Atholl, Breadalbane, Angus, Gowrie, as well as Mar itself, will turn against me. Malcolm Drummond, *An Drumanach Mor*, was a great chief, head of a large clan, connected to other chiefs by marriage and kin. The King's goodbrother. To starve him to death will never be forgiven. Every chief will look askance at me — even those who follow us now. I can no longer remain the King's Justiciar of the North. A service, you say!"

"Yet he may have considered it so, in ignorance — your brother. To have Drummond dead, for you — caring not how, freeing the Countess of Mar from her loveless marriage. For you . . ."

"Fiend seize you, man — how can you say such a thing! This is beyond all — to murder the husband in order to gain the wife!"

"Others will say it, Alex — nothing more sure. Mar is a great earldom. For you to gain some control of it, your brother may have seen it as worth a murder! When he could name it an act of war, the realm threatened by Donald's Islesmen, and Drummond in secret league with them."

"And what, think you, will Isobel say?"

The other did not risk an answer to that, and they rode on together, silent.

When at length Sir Alexander spoke again, he said, "Say

14

naught of this, Jamie, meantime — until I know my own mind in the matter." He smiled a little, ruefully. "When I said that I needed you as never before, I scarce knew how much it was to be! If you will hold to me, still?"

"Think you I would not? Forby, *my* need is as great as yours. We are both in trouble. And more like to win out of it better together than apart!"

"So say I, friend . . ."

* * *

Branching off the great Spey valley at Rothes, to head due northwards, they camped for the night in the mouth of Rothes Glen. The Douglas, who did not speak the Gaelic, could not have much converse with the assembled chiefs, but heard from Alex Stewart that evening, by the camp-fire, an account of his campaign against the Islesmen's invasion — how he had caught up with them at Elgin, defeated them whilst they were in disarray at the sacking of the city, chased them right across the Highlands to Moidart, where they had left their galleys, and defeated them again as they were hastily embarking, capturing most of the leadership. Unlike his father, Alex made a point of maintaining excellent relations with the Church authorities, and he was taking Alastair Carrach back to Elgin to make some sort of reparation.

With their accustomed speed, astonishing for an infantry host, they covered the ten miles between Rothes and Elgin, in the fair Moray plain, in just three hours — having sent faster messengers ahead to warn the Church and burgh authorities. The city, The Lantern of the North, awaited them with evident suspicion and alarm, behind closed gates, Highland armies of any sort being held in grave doubts by the plainsmen, and justifiably. Their cathedral, after all, the finest in the land, was still being rebuilt after the Wolf of Badenoch's burning of 1390, a dozen years before. But the Church dignitaries, led by the Bishop of Moray himself, William de Spynie, were moderately forthcoming, having had many dealings with Alex Stewart, who had done his best to redeem his father's offences. They were waiting to greet the Highlanders at the Panns Port, the same southern gateway at which, as the Wolf's prisoner, Jamie Douglas had waited that day, twelve years before, for sunrise to herald the attack on the city.

"Ha, my lord Bishop," the Stewart called, dismounting. "A

15

good day to you and your people. The better for being the Eve of the Blessed Saint Kenneth. I have brought you for your forgiveness and absolution, I hope, a sincere penitent, one Alastair Carrach MacDonald of Islay and Lochaber, who, having offended against Holy Church, is now concerned to redeem that offence in due and suitable fashion. With some of his brother's island chieftains."

"Indeed! You say so? Then you rejoice us, Sir Alexander," the Bishop replied, carefully. "We always welcome the penitent — provided he is truly so. And, h'm, prepared to make required and adequate restitution." The prelate, a heavily-built, square-jowled, florid man, inclining to fat but with eyes shrewd enough for a horse-dealer, sketched the sign of the cross vaguely over all.

"Ah, yes — that is important, my lord. I think our friend Alastair here, will prove sufficiently repentant. And . . . open-handed! You agree, Alastair?"

The Islesman stared blankly, expressionlessly. He had the thin down-turning moustache and tiny beard, which, with the pale glitter of his eyes, effected a sort of smouldering savagery which might send shivers down the impressionable spine. He did not speak.

"I hope that you may be right," the Bishop replied, a little doubtfully. "You do not intend to bring all these men into the city?"

"No. They will wait out here. A few of my colleagues only. The Mackintosh, Cluny Macpherson, MacGillivray Mor, Shaw of Rothiemurchus . . ." He named the chiefs of the Clan Chattan federation, who offered little more acknowledgement than had the Islesman — and whom the clerics eyed with equal wariness. "And here is my friend Sir James Douglas of Aberdour, of whose fame you will undoubtedly have heard."

"Ah, to be sure — we have heard of Sir James. And but recently! You have come north quickly, sir. The last we heard of you was in . . . Northumberland!"

"Then I hope that you are *well* informed, my lord," Jamie said briefly.

"Holy Church is always that," Alex observed. "Where, my lord Bishop, do you wish this little, er, celebratory office to take place?"

"Why, in the cathedral, Sir Alexander — where else? Thanks to your generosity, and that of others, it now has a roof again. The Lady Chapel is all but complete. We shall go there."

16

Leaving most of the force outside the town-walls, the leaders and prisoners rode inside, with the clerical party, a mob of citizens following on, some jeering once it became known that their oppressor, MacDonald, was present. The Bishop glanced back at Alastair Carrach, and spoke, rich voice carefully lowered.

"Sir Alexander — what do you propose? The word you sent was that you held this MacDonald, had brought him to repentance and would fetch him here to make restitution. What would you have me do?"

"Why, do what the Church does with penitents of substantial offence, my lord. No doubt you will have seen fit to pronounce some suitable anathemas upon him? You will have some form of ceremony for lifting it? I seem to recollect my esteemed father taking part in some such exercise at Perth, once!"

"H'mm." The Bishop looked away. "Perhaps. And reparation? Restitution?"

"*I* shall vouch for that. We captured much booty with the Islesmen."

"Ah. Some may well have been stolen from Holy Church."

"Then it shall be restored. With a sufficiency of further compensation."

"Very good. Suitable, commendable, my son." The other glanced sidelong at Alex. "And, ah, timely. Aye, timely, I think."

"Why that?"

The prelate cleared his throat. "Later might have been . . . different. Difficult."

"I do not understand you, my lord. Later?"

"In the matter of the unhappy death of Sir Malcolm Drummond. So very unfortunate. No sure word has reached us yet. But, when it does, Holy Church may be placed in a position of some awkwardness, Sir Alexander."

"You mean, as regards myself?"

"I fear so, yes."

The Stewart drew a deep breath. "I had nothing to do with the death of Drummond, my lord Bishop," he said flatly.

"Ah, to be sure. Excellent. I would not have expected it of you. Indeed, no. But . . . until that is established, before all men, you will understand, Holy Church cannot be seen to accept gifts and service from one whom men may think of as a murderer. And whom she might be called upon to, h'm, excommunicate! You will perceive our difficulty, my friend?"

"I perceive that you have been listening to idle tales, my lord Bishop. I was in the west, dealing with your unfriends here, in Moidart, when Sir Malcolm Drummond died."

"How fortunate. But the caterans who took him were your men, were they not? Led by your own brothers? And so, it might be deemed, under your command?"

Tight-lipped, Alex reined up at the great west portal of the cathedral, still smoke-blackened. "I do not myself know what took place," he said. "I have not seen my brothers. But . . . you said, my lord, that my coming here today was timely? In these circumstances, why?"

"Do you not see, my friend? Because thus far it is only hearsay. Mere reports — which Holy Church need not heed. Meantime we may accept your good offices, this excellent restitution, still deeming all to be well. Later it could be *too* late."

"Ah, yes. I see it. I see that the Church is glad to receive what I have to give — so long as it is sufficient — whether I am a murderer or not. So long as she may. *Before* she excommunicates me! Timely, indeed!"

"That is less than just, sir. The Church must not countenance sin. But she can and should exercise charity towards the alleged sinner, until the sin is proven. Just as she will exercise clemency towards this MacDonald repentant who has so shamefully used her."

The Stewart, dismounting from his garron, did not have to answer that.

Jamie Douglas had listened to all this with grim interest, a little distracted by the emotions aroused by this his return to Elgin Cathedral, after twelve years. When last he had been here, this great and noble fane was spouting smoke and flame, its stained-glass windows exploding, coughing, choking Highlandmen staggering out clutching its treasures, not to save but to steal. Alex Stewart had been there then, too, at his side, as guard, deploring his father's savage fury but unable to halt it, almost as much a prisoner as he was himself. Now they were here in almost opposite roles; they were the captors, not the prisoners.

Ordering their captives to dismount, they followed Bishop Spynie within. Scaffolding and workmen's gear festooned the vast building outside and in; but one of the side-chapels was almost wholly rebuilt, and here they were led.

The clerics disappeared into a vestry, and Alex arranged his party to face the candle-lit altar. The Islesmen were not bound but kept hemmed in by a sufficiency of guards to ensure their security. They remained strangely impassive, almost as though they were the merest onlookers at the proceedings.

The Bishop and his assistants emerged, resplendent in full canonicals, in glittering and jewelled magnificence. For the first time the MacDonalds' eyes betrayed interest, calculating the worth of all that finery. The prelate took up his position at the altar, and turned to them.

"In the name of Almighty God, the Father, the Son and the Holy Spirit," he intoned impressively, "we are here to receive back into the outspread arms of Mother Church a repentant sinner such as is beloved of our Lord Christ. Although his sins be as scarlet they shall be whiter than snow." He paused. "Sir Alexander Stewart of Badenoch — you have one such great and penitent sinner here present?"

"I have."

"Name him."

"Alexander MacDonald of Islay and Lochaber, known as Alastair Carrach, brother-german to Donald, Lord of the Isles and son of the late John, Lord of the Isles and the Princess Margaret, eldest sister of our Lord King."

"This is he who entered this city by force with an armed host, slew many, burned many houses including the property of Holy Church, the manses of the canons of this cathedral, and so didst grievously sin against the Holy Ghost?"

"The same."

"And he does now heartily and sincerely repent him of the said great sins, confesses his grievous fault before Almighty God and all present, and is prepared to make due, ample and fullest recompence and restitution, here before God's holy altar and in the sight of all men?"

"He is."

"Bring the said Alexander MacDonald forward."

Alex, his hand on the Isleman's shoulder, climbed the three steps nearer to the altar, the other allowing himself to be pushed forward, grinning now.

Noting that grin, the Bishop frowned. "Alastair of Islay and Lochaber," he said sternly, "do you understand? Do you fully and truly repent you?"

"*He* says that I do, whatever. And Stewart is an honourable

19

man, is he not? So it must be true!" Alastair Carrach had a most gentle, lilting, West Highland voice, in notable contrast with his reputation and appearance.

The prelate looked uneasily from one to the other, and cleared his throat. "You must say it yourself, man. Another's word is not sufficient — even Sir Alexander's."

"I will be saying whatever he wishes, Clerk. Words cost a deal less than the ransom I am paying."

"Ransom . . . ?"

"He means reparation and sacrifice, my lord," Alex said evenly. "In good measure."

"Ah. Yes. Yes, indeed. That is important, to be sure. Deeds rather than words. Yet words are necessary also. Repeat after me these words. 'I do confess before Almighty God and these present . . . '"

"I do confess before Almighty God and these present . . ."

" 'That I have sinned . . . ' "

"That I have sinned — as who has not?"

"Repeat *my* words only, my son."

"So long as they are *your* words, whatever!" That was cheerfully said.

"Be silent, sir!"

"Very well. I am silent."

"Repeat, 'I have grievously offended against the laws of God and man.' "

Silence.

"I say, 'I have grievously offended against the laws of God and man.' "

"No doubt, Clerk."

Alex Stewart coughed. "My lord — he has come here, and confessed that he has sinned, before God and all present. Moreover he has agreed to make fullest restitution and reparation. I respectfully suggest that this is the heart of the matter, and that the rest is less vital. Would not absolution now serve the case sufficiently — and save us all further delay?"

"H'mm." The Bishop frowned again, eyed the Isleman's arrogant amusement, and sighed. "Very well. It may be that you are right." He raised his beringed hand high. "In the name of God the Father, God the Son and God the Holy Ghost, I absolve you, Alexander, of your grievous sin. And, and . . ." by way of postscript he added, ". . . and may God have mercy on your soul! Amen!" And turning, with the briefest of nods to the altar, he stalked off to the vestry-door, and through. Hurriedly, in some confusion, his subordinates followed him.

Alastair Carrach barked a single hooting laugh, and then relapsed into his accustomed uninterested silence.

A move was made, out into the open air, relief showing on not a few faces.

Before the west portal was now drawn up a train of laden pack-horses. Stewart gestured towards it.

"Alastair Carrach's booty — or most of it," he murmured to Jamie. "An offering for the Bishop. He will be round to inspect it in but moments, I swear!"

"Why?" the other demanded, low-voiced. "Why this . . . play-acting? So, so like your own father's folly at Perth?"

"Good reasons, friend. It is the best way to deal with Alastair. In a day or two it will be all over the Highlands that he has come and made humble abasement before Holy Church at Elgin, and yielded up his booty — a deal more hurt to his name and reputation than sustaining a couple of small defeats. It is sheerest mummery, to be sure — but no matter. *I* learned that after my father's case. His repentance was the greatest mockery — yet the word was accepted far and near that he had humbly atoned. Nothing so infuriated him, that I can recollect. Keeping Alastair a prisoner will not serve my cause. I do not need ransom moneys. Better that I should send him back to his brother, unwanted, with this tale of atonement and grovelling, however untrue. And I make the Church my still better friend. I think that I am going to need the Church's friendship, Jamie!"

Bishop Spynie did indeed put in a prompt appearance at the west front of his cathedral, to set about examining the baggage-train with an expert eye and considerable diligence — an eye that lightened and brightened as he peered and poked into each pannier, package and bundle. There was the spoil of a score of churches, villages, townships and communities there, some undoubtedly from Elgin but most from otherwhere. Holy Church, however, was clearly glad to accept all, with no awkward questions about former ownership.

"Very good, very good!" The prelate beamed on all. "This is most . . . suitable. A worthy atonement. Most commendable. It will be cherished, I assure you — much cherished. And *your* faithful love of Mother Church not forgotten, Sir Alexander."

"Then, I pray, remember it, when you hear further slanderous reports about me, my lord Bishop. Which my unfriends will put

21

about, I have little doubt. Now — if you will tell me where you wish this treasure bestowed, we shall take it there and then be on our various ways. My people have marched far and fast to deliver it here, from Moidart. They would return now to their glens . . ."

So, presently, the Highland host turned southwards again from the Panns Port of Elgin, and soon began to break up and disperse, each contingent hiving off to take the shortest route back to its own clan territory amongst the great mountains of the Monadh Ruadh, the Monadh Liath or Braemoray.

Riding by Dunkinty, the now quietly thoughtful commander of it all turned to Jamie Douglas. "My friend," he said, "I think, before I return to Lochindorb, that I should pay a privy call at Kildrummy in Mar. There is much that I would learn there, if possible. If you can bear to be parted from your Mary a day or two more, I should be glad of your company. How say you?"

"You want me? *There*, Alex?"

"Yes. Two heads could be better than one. And yours could be cooler than mine, in this."

"Very well . . ."

Presently Stewart halted the rump of his force. He spoke, in the Gaelic.

"Alastair Carrach — here I leave you. From henceforth, you and your friends are free men. The Mackintosh will provide you with an escort to Moidart. Go you back to your Isles, and tell your brother not to trouble us again."

The Islesman eyed him searchingly. "This is no trick, Stewart? No ransom? No further conditions?"

"None. Save that you and yours spare us your attentions in future. And tell Donald the same."

"You are a strange man, Cousin. I cannot think that you are a fool. Yet . . ."

"Think me fool if you wish. But for the rest, recollect how many times this fool has fought you, and won! Now — go in peace."

The other's strange eyes glittered as he turned away.

II

WITH A TINY escort of only half-a-dozen gillies, all mounted now, the two friends made their unobtrusive way through the empty hills dominated by pointed Ben Rinnes, across Glen Fiddich and over the high desolation of the Cabrach, and so by the Mounth of Clova into the great province of Mar. On the second day they rode down to the upper Don at Lulach's Stone, and up a side-valley to the ancient earldom's principal fortalice of Kildrummy.

The castle was set on a neck of high ground between ravines, overlooking a wide prospect of the fair vale of Don, a commanding and splendid site. They were not permitted to approach it unobserved and unchallenged. But the guards knew Sir Alexander well, and sent back word — so that the newly-widowed Countess of Mar herself was waiting for them at the drawbridge end as they rode up.

Alex threw himself from the saddle and all but ran towards her. Then he seemed to recollect himself, and slowed, to halt and bow.

"Isobel!" he said, eyes searching her face.

She nodded, wordless, the faintest smile on her reddened lips.

It was not often that Alex Stewart showed uncertainty. He bit his lip. "I . . . I am sorry, Isobel," he said. "An evil thing. I grieve for you."

"Need you?" she asked. "Since I do not grieve for myself!"

Isobel Douglas, Countess of Mar in her own right, was a handsome and splendidly built woman, now in her early forties, her powerful femininity nothing diminished by maturity. She certainly gave no indication of distressed widowhood; but then, she and her husband, the Drummond chief, had gone their separate ways for long.

Alex, who had been in love with her for years, although

23

fifteen years her junior, all but bounded forward again, to take her substantial form in his arms. "My dear!" he cried.

She returned his embraces and kisses heartily, careless of the watchers, although with just a hint of mockery perhaps, mockery of herself as well as of the man. Then over his shoulder her eyes caught Jamie's, and, fine brows raised, she pushed the other away firmly.

"I see that you have brought my heroic fellow-Douglas with you again, Alex — his heroism now, sadly, a little tarnished, we hear! I am ever a mite wary when you bring him here — for I judge it to mean that you need his help against me!"

"No, no — not so, Isobel! You, you much mistake. Jamie is your good friend, no less than mine, I swear . . ."

"Liar!" she said, but not harshly. She had a deep, husky voice which had its own unsettling effect on susceptible men.

"If I am not welcome, my lady, I shall remove myself," Jamie said stiffly.

"Tush, man — be not so thin-skinned! We are both Douglases, are we not? And can speak plain. I do not believe the tales of you, running from this battle. You will tell me the truth of it. Come you . . ."

Kildrummy Castle was a mighty and extensive fortress, larger even than Alex's Lochindorb, perhaps the greatest in all the North-East, the key to the most important of the Mounth passes between the Aberdeen, Mearns and Angus plain, and Moray, the Spey, Findhorn and Ness valleys. It was a strange place for a woman to control, even such a woman as Isobel of Mar. And she did control it and its vast dependencies, and had done all along, never having elevated Sir Malcolm Drummond as Earl of Mar in her right, as she could have done. Very much the Countess, she made a better lord for Mar than it had had for generations.

Alex made one or two attempts to introduce the subject of Sir Malcolm's death, before the Lady Isobel took it up, as they ate.

"My husband was a strange man, and not one *I* would ever have chosen to wed," she observed. "And I cannot in honesty claim that I mourn him greatly. But his was an ill death to die. He deserved better than that."

"It was devilish!" Stewart agreed. "If it was as Jamie tells me. Locked in a cell, without food or drink, until he died. Is that true?"

"Sufficiently. He starved, that is certain. Locked in the small, remote hold of Badenyon, in the mountains."

24

"And . . . who did it?"

"The question comes strangely from you, my dear, does it not? It was a band of your caterans who took him, when he was riding back to Kildrummy from his new-building castle of Kindrochit in Brae-Mar, conveyed him to Badenyon, and held him there."

"Isobel — I knew nothing of it. Nothing. I tell you! You cannot believe, you cannot think . . . ?"

"No, I cannot, Alex. Do not distress yourself. I know well that it was none of your doing. You have your faults, my dear, but you are not a cold-blooded killer! Nevertheless, your brothers led the party, all aver, in your name. There is no question of that, is there?"

"I sent a company under my brothers, yes — to watch your husband, in case he joined forces with Alastair Carrach in Donald's invasion — as we feared. But this . . . !"

"Why should they do it? Thus? To slay him, I could understand — if they deemed him enemy. But starvation . . . ?"

"God alone knows. But if it *was* my brothers, it would be Duncan. He has a devil in him. He hates, as none of the rest of us can."

"What reason had he to hate Malcolm?"

"I do not know. None, that I can think on."

"Could it be that he somehow blamed Sir Malcolm for Prince David's death?" Jamie put in. "Revenge. It was the same death. Could there be any link? Even in mistake?"

"David was my husband's nephew, his sister's son. Why should he wish him dead?"

"Who can tell? But . . . Duncan Stewart must have had some reason for this shameful deed. Does nothing at all come to mind, Alex?"

"I have racked my wits. The only link between them, that I know of, was when Duncan led that great raid into Angus and Gowrie after our father's excommunication, when he won the victory at Glasclune. Sir Malcolm Drummond was prominent in gathering and leading the host which assembled against my brothers then — his Drummond country, to be sure, was overrun. I was in Uncle Robert's prison at Falkland at the time, so know not all that happened. But there may have been some incident. And Duncan never forgives. And so took this opportunity for revenge."

"It scarce sounds sufficient . . ."

The Countess shrugged. "I cannot think that it had aught to do with David Stewart's starving, at least. There is no least connection. Nor even with Malcolm's other nephew, the young James . . ."

"James? The new heir to the throne? What of him, Isobel?"

"Only that there was some talk of the King sending him up here to Kildrummy, for safety. From his Uncle Robert of Albany. He is at present in the care of the Bishop of St Andrews — but it seems the King still fears for him, and would find more secure lodging, out of Albany's reach. No doubt he fears a second death in the family — and then Albany himself is next heir. So there was talk of sending him up here, to bide with his uncle. But . . . I do not see why this should cause your brother anger?"

"No. No — there is nothing there to concern Duncan. Or any of us."

"Well — it is done now, and cannot be undone," the woman said. "In time you will learn, no doubt — and take what steps are necessary. But that is not important, meantime. What *is* important is that we should seek to counter the ill effects. For they will be grievously ill, Alex — as, I vow, you well understand."

"Yes. It can make shipwreck of my whole state and position. I can no longer remain Justiciar. It gives my Uncle Robert of Albany what he needs against me. I could well be outlawed. Sir Malcolm, being the Queen's brother, uncle to the heir to the throne, will enable Albany, as Governor, to accuse me almost of treason! And being chief of Clan Drummond, I will have all the Atholl, Gowrie and Stormonth clans against me. Chiefs everywhere outraged. Not to speak of this great earldom of Mar!"

"Leave Mar to me. Malcolm never had much say or sway over my people. What concerns me most are the accursed churchmen. Excommunication. If they excommunicate you, Alex, it could cost us all dear."

"I think, I *hope*, that I have the Church my friend. Unlike my father! We have just come from my Diocesan, the Bishop of Moray. Any excommunication would have to be imposed by him. I would say that he is sufficiently . . . sweetened."

"Good. Then they cannot prevent us marrying, my dear," she commented, matter-of-factly.

His indrawn breath was audible. Although Jamie Douglas barely heard it, for his own.

"Lord, Isobel — we, we cannot think of that! Not now!"

"Why not? There is now no . . . impediment."

"But — save us, do you not see? It is impossible. This was one of the first evils of it all that came to me. So long as men blame me for your husband's death, I cannot wed his widow. It would be said . . ."

"Said that you had had him slain, to wed me? Perhaps. Some might say that is the height of love, indeed! There will be talk, to be sure. But talk there would be, anyway — how Sir Alex Stewart had wed a woman almost old enough to be his mother . . .!"

"Isobel! You are but a dozen years older."

"Fourteen, my heart. Important years. And I might have had a child at thirteen — I was sufficiently keen! So, talk there will be. What signifies a little more talk?"

"No. But this is different. It cannot be, my dear. Not until my name is cleared. Our good repute would be gone — both. You must see it. I will not be named as the man who murdered to gain a bride! We could have no true marriage that way."

"For how long must I wait, then? *My* time is shorter than yours! I cannot delay for years, whilst you establish your innocence to your fullest satisfaction."

Jamie Douglas coughed. "It may be that I should leave you . . . ?" he suggested.

"Do not be a fool, man!" the Countess jerked.

"No, Jamie — do not go," Alex urged. "We need cool wits to try unravel this tangle. You can see the problems. Can you aid us towards an answer?"

"Me? No." He did not know whether this of marriage was his friend's wish, or only the Countess's. Alex had never mentioned the word marriage to him. He was careful. "Save to agree that it would be folly to wed, in such case. Even those who accept you as innocent would doubt it then."

"I would not have guessed that Sir James Douglas would have been so concerned for what folk thought!" the lady said.

"Since what folk may think determines how they may act and speak, it could be important, lady. *I* know that, to my cost! And Alex's position is delicate."

"Why so delicate?"

That man had difficulty, with the features he had, in ever looking really apologetic; but he did glance at his friend uneasily. "He is less than securely based, Countess. Albany, the Governor, hates him. He was his uncle's prisoner once, who was forced to

27

free him, against his will. The Duke never forgives nor forgets. This matter will be a joy to him — if he ever wins joy from anything! Then, his son Murdoch, Earl of Fife, now prisoner in England, has long been Justiciar and Lieutenant of the North — in name. He dared not come north to take up his appointment — nor greatly wanted to. So Alex has been *acting* Justiciar since his father died, for both the Prince David of Rothesay and this Murdoch. But only acting. Now, with Murdoch Stewart captive, Albany is bound to appoint someone else — and it will be someone more strong, you may be sure." That was a long statement for Jamie Douglas.

"That matters not, Jamie," Alex put in. "Since I shall resign the office anyway."

"No doubt. But have you considered what a *strong* man, sent up here as Lieutenant and Justiciar, could do? To *you*! If you have lost the support of the clans through this slaying of Sir Malcolm?"

"M'mm. You think that I could be endangered? My own self?"

"It is the first thing that your successor would attempt, I'd say. Seek to be rid of you. And you are not strong in manpower, Alex. So long as you had the clans behind you, you were strong. But you have few men of your own. This is not Stewart country. Up here you are incomers. Lochindorb is a strong castle — but it can raise no large forces. You are Lord of Badenoch, yes — but only *de facto*, not *de jure*. For, like me, you are a bastard. The Crown has never confirmed you in your lordship. You have never been summoned to parliament as Lord of Badenoch. Which means, I fear, that Badenoch will remain yours only for so long as you are strong enough to hold it!"

There was silence at the table for a few moments.

"You are a damnably gloomy counsellor, Sir James!" Isobel of Mar exclaimed.

"No — let him continue," Alex said. "He has the sort of sober head we much require. And he is right in what he says. It is all true. Go on, my friend."

"As I see it, until you clear your name of this murder, with fullest certainty, you are in dire danger. Not yet, perhaps, but in a short while. Even though not excommunicated, you will be outlawed — as I am. Albany will see to it. That means any man may attack you, with impunity. And be rewarded for doing so. My father made it mightily clear to me, I assure you. So, either you clear your name swiftly, gain strong forces to your side, in some fashion — or go into hiding. That, or leave this your country meantime."

"You make matters accursedly stark, Jamie!" the other commented grimly. "What, then, is your advice?"

"Clear your name. And quickly."

"But how, man — how?"

"How much do you love your brother, Alex?"

"Eh? You mean . . .?"

"I mean, find him. Hold an open trial. Whilst you are still Justiciar. As is your duty, indeed. And hang him, if proven guilty."

"Lord God!" Stewart breathed.

"There speaks Douglas!" the Countess nodded. "And I am a Douglas, too! This time, I agree with him."

"No," Alex got out. "Not that. Not hang."

"Yet, as Justiciar, you have had to hang many, have you not? And if he was other than your brother you would hang him?"

"I cannot, I *will* not, hang my own brother." That was flat, final.

"I feared as much. Then the choice must be other. Which?"

"I do not know. What can I say? Where can I gain forces to my support, whilst this hangs over me?"

"That, at least, is easy of answer," Isobel of Mar said. "Marry me, and I will make you Earl of Mar, in my right. None can gainsay my right to do so. Then you will have all Mar at your back. And little lack men to your support."

Both men looked at her, and then at each other. Alex swallowed.

"You would do that for me, Isobel? After . . . this? What you would never do for Sir Malcolm?"

"I never loved Malcolm Drummond," she said simply. "My father chose my husband, not I."

"But . . . but . . . I thank you, my dear, with all my heart. But I could not do it — accept the earldom. The thing is not possible."

"Tell me why not?"

"Isobel — the same objection as to our early marriage. Men would accept it as all but proof of guilt. It would be believed that you yourself were party to it — to Malcolm's death. That must not be — such calumny."

"If I am prepared to risk such calumny, why should you balk

29

at it? Were you Earl of Mar you might snap your fingers at Albany, Alex."

"I fear it is less simple than that," Jamie put in, "so long as Albany controls parliament. Earldoms require to be confirmed by the King in parliament. King Robert is but a cypher. A saint perhaps, but weak, a recluse, leaving all to his brother Albany. To think that he is the great-grandson of the Bruce! Albany, the Governor, is strong, ruthless, cunning. I know, who have been fighting against him, suffering his ill-will, for years, ever since he had the Earl James Douglas, my master, murdered at the Battle of Otterburn. I vowed . . ." Jamie Douglas cut himself short. On the subject of Robert Stewart, Duke of Albany and Earl of Fife and Menteith, he was perhaps, preoccupied, prejudiced — and knew it. "I say Albany would counter Alex's confirmation in the earldom," he ended.

"I fear that is true, my dear . . ."

"That would only affect your right to vote in parliament, sit on the Privy Council and the like. In the North you would still be Earl of Mar, in all that matters."

"No, Isobel — my thanks, but no. We must work this thing out otherwise. Somehow. Perhaps another time we shall see more clearly. When we are less weary and our wits are sharper . . ."

They left it there.

Later, Jamie discreetly declared himself ready for his couch and retired sufficiently early to leave the other two to each other's company.

*　　*　　*

Although the Countess Isobel tried very hard to make them stay longer, Alex Stewart pointed out that matters for his urgent attention were piling up, and after their second night at Kildrummy insisted that they must be gone. He wanted to interview his brother Duncan before either of them was very much older, for one thing. The lady accompanied them for some way on their journey westwards.

Some sixteen miles on their way, at the summit of the Glenfenzie pass over the Gairn Mounth, she drew rein, on the watershed between Don and Dee.

"Far enough, Alex," she said. "I think that you are being foolish. But men are often that, to be sure. You will come back to me, I prophesy, before long — no longer so proud as to

30

refuse what only I can give you. Until then, God go with you."

"It is not pride, Isobel — or not merely so. Our reputations are at stake in this — both of them. And your good name, as well as mine, is important to me. But . . . I thank you, my dear."

"Thanks I do not ask for. But — remember that I am forty-two years of age. I see time something differently from you. You can be Earl of Mar whenever you wish. But . . . you could leave it too late! And there will be others on that hunt, I think!"

He frowned at that, despite himself.

"I expect to hear from Robert of Albany, any day!" she went on. "He can scarce marry me himself — although I suppose he could dispose of that poor creature of a wife, as he has disposed of others! But he has another son — other than Murdoch, prisoner in England — unmarried. Or other nominees for my earldom — that you may be sure. Do not give him too long."

As she turned back, they rode on very thoughtfully.

"I had not thought of that," Jamie admitted. "Of Albany." His friend did not reply.

Long and hard riding brought them to the upper Dee, and into the mighty mountains of the Monadh Ruadh, where that great river rose. Beyond Linn o'Dee they left the river, to follow up a lesser stream, the Geldie, south of the main massif of the mountains. By its birchwood side they camped, and next morning rode up, westwards now, to the bare moorland and peat-hags of its watershed, and so down the infant Feshie beyond, with all the spread and colour of upper Strathspey opening before them, back into Badenoch again.

The Feshie's lovely dozen-mile valley brought them at last to the pine forests of Rothiemurchus and the tree-girt Loch-an-Eilean with its island-castle. With Ruthven, at Kingussie, Castle Roy in Strathnethy, Drumin in Strathavon, and others, it was one of a series of strategically placed strongholds set up by the late Wolf to control the huge province of Badenoch, each under the captaincy of one of his bastard sons. Jamie had been brought here twelve years before, as captive, when its captain had been Rob Stewart, a half-brother of Sir Alexander's. Now, apparently, it was the seat of Sir Duncan.

Nevertheless, it was Rob Stewart himself who rowed over for them, when they shouted across the still waters for attention, the echo resounding from the close-thronging hillsides. The

31

Earl of Buchan had knighted only his five sons by Mariota de Athyn, to constitute the ruling family of Badenoch, illegitimate as they all were.

"Duncan is not here," Rob Stewart informed. "Has not been, for long."

"No? Where is he then, Rob?"

"I do not know. Somewhere in the South." This was a stolid and somewhat surly individual, no typical Stewart.

"The *South*! Duncan? Surely not?"

The other shrugged. "That is where I was told he had gone."

"But . . . why? Where? Duncan hates the South, the Lowlands. He has no friends there. This is crazy! When did you last see him?"

"Three weeks past. More. After, after . . ."

"After the Drummond business? You were there?"

"I had naught to do with it, Alex. It was none of my doing."

"Perhaps not. But it was *somebody's* doing. And you did not stop it."

"No. See you, Alex — I was at the *capture* of Drummond, yes. We all were, Duncan, Andrew, Walter, Tom. Duncan was the leader — he always is. We took Drummond to a small tower called Badenyon in Brae-Mar. But we left him captive, under guard. We went eastwards then, deeper into Mar, to Kildrummy country. Then south towards Atholl, looking for any muster of fighting men, as you had ordered . . ."

"And Duncan with you?"

"He came with us at first. Then he left us, saying that he had other business."

"But, if he was in command . . .?"

"He handed over to Andrew. Saying that he had private business. And went back."

"Back? You mean . . .? What business?"

"He did not say. You know Duncan. He keeps all close, gives little away. I have not seen him since that day."

"You believe that he it was who killed Drummond? Or ordered him to be starved to death?"

His brother looked distinctly alarmed, glancing at Douglas. "I did not say that, Alex. I know no more than I have told you. When we left Drummond, locked in that hold, he was well enough. An old man getting, mind . . ."

"And being fed?"

"I know not. I tell you, I had naught to do with him."

"And you think that Duncan went south, afterwards? When Drummond was dead?"

"Yes."

"Who told you?"

"Gillies here said it, Seumas and Colin."

"Alone?"

"He took two gillies only."

"Then he was going secretly. Why? Why kill Drummond? And why go to the South? Duncan, of all men?"

"The one because of the other, belike?" Jamie suggested. "Flight. He fled from *your* wrath."

"But . . . that would mean . . . ? No — Duncan has no friends in the South. He has never crossed the Highland Line — save with a drawn sword. He knows none . . ."

"You are wrong, Alex. Duncan does know someone," his brother said. "A man was here, some months back, two months, more. Here at Loch-an-Eilean. A Lowlander. He stayed for three days. Lindsay by name."

"Lindsay? You mean, from Glen Esk, in Angus?"

"No. Not that airt. I thought at first that he came from the North, some place — for his style was Lindsay of Ross. But no, it was from the South . . ."

"Ross — not *Rossie*?" That was Jamie, almost with a bark. "Lindsay of Rossie? Sir William?"

"He was a knight, yes. William Lindsay . . ."

"Dear God!" the Douglas exclaimed. "Lindsay of Rossie is one of Albany's jackals! He and Sir John de Ramorgnie were mainly responsible for Prince David's death at Falkland. By starvation!"

His friend stared at him. "Albany!" he whispered. "Mary-Mother — not that! Not my uncle Robert!"

"If Lindsay was here? What brought him all this way? A Fife laird."

"What was he doing here, Rob?" Alex demanded.

"I do not know. He was here when I came, one day. Duncan told me nothing. Said that he was a friend, that is all."

"Why have I not heard of this Lowland visitor?"

"Duncan said . . . better not say anything."

"A plague on you, Rob! *I* am Lord of Badenoch, not Duncan! You know that I require to be told of every stranger who crosses into my territories. Saints give me patience! A

33

Lowland knight, a creature of the Governor's — and I knew naught of it!"

His half-brother scowled. "Duncan is a hard man to counter."

"And so am I, by God! As you, and others, will learn!" With an obvious effort Alex controlled himself. "Forgive me, Jamie. I am sorry." He turned back to his brother. "Duncan captained this castle. For *me*. Yet he has left it, without my authority. And put you in command? Of this, at least, I ought to have been informed."

"You were in the West," Rob said heavily. "Busy."

"You could have sent a messenger."

Silence.

"I see that I shall have to put my own house in order!" Alex said grimly. "You will hear more of this, Rob. Is Andrew at Ruthven? And Walter?"

"They are both at Drumin, with Tom. Or were."

"Indeed. What do they there?"

"I know not."

"No? Then, if you have nothing else to tell me, we shall leave you, meantime. I shall send for you to come to Lochindorb, in due course."

As they rode on, northwards now through the great forest, minds busy, Alex said, "I shall have to take my brothers in hand, it is clear. If I may no longer control the North, as Justiciar, I can at least control my own family. We are going to require a united house, I think!"

"*Can* you?" Jamie asked bluntly. "As I remember them, they are all hard, strong men."

"Ha, my friend — but perhaps you have not seen *me* at my hardest and strongest! Moreover, I have a hold over all of them. Our father, in his wisdom, left all the lordship to me, its castles, lands and privileges — did not break it up. He knew them, you see!"

"And knew you! But, Alex — this of Albany? How think you? Could he have had anything to do with Drummond's death?"

"The good God knows! The thought had not so much as come into my mind, before this. Why should he?"

"Why should any? Save *you*! But — they were unfriends. Drummond had a grudge against Albany, over the unentailed lands of Douglas, which were prevented from coming to his wife. And this is the same death which he caused his other

34

unfriend to die! And you also are an unfriend — and this strikes at you! This link with Lindsay of Rossie must mean something. Why should one of Albany's men come all this way into the Highlands to see your brother?"

The other shook his head.

"I wonder . . . ? You remember what the Countess Isobel said? About the King considering to send the young Prince James into his uncle's care at Kildrummy, for safety? Safety from Albany, to be sure, who slew his brother. Could that have to do with it?"

"You mean . . . ?"

"I mean that only young James now stands between Albany and the throne, should the King die. And he is a sick man. The King greatly fears for the boy's safety, that is evident — and has him put in the care of Bishop Wardlaw at St. Andrews. He appears to feel that insufficiently secure, if he thought to send him north. Albany could be proving that his arm can stretch as far as that! To teach others not to interfere, to offer sanctuary to the prince. And to dispose of Drummond, the King's last remaining close friend. And embroil *you* whom he hates and fears."

"Save us — you would make Robert Stewart the Fiend Incarnate, Jamie! Even he could scarce be so devilishly clever as that."

"Why not? Think how he had the Earl James Douglas slain — and the slayer's mouth closed. And the mouth-closer slain likewise! All by others' hands. Your Aunt Gelis at least, believed that he had her husband, Will Douglas of Nithsdale, assassinated equally cunningly, in Danzig. He had his nephew David starved to death at Falkland — and parliament to absolve him afterwards. Think you this would be too much for him?"

"I do not know. If Albany is in this, then all is changed, and we require to look a deal more closely at many things."

"Yes. It may not be so. But, I say, we would be fools to overlook that it is possible . . ."

III

LOCHINDORB WAS AN extraordinary place by any standards. Deep, remote within the high heather and rounded hills of Braemoray, almost ten miles from any real village or community, a wide green amphitheatre opened in the prevailing brownness. In the floor of this lay a loch two miles long by half-a-mile wide, with only a scattering of trees around; and towards its centre a single island. Following the irregular contours of this, the walls of a major castle arose in stark masonry, the massive and lofty curtains enclosing a sizeable area, with heavy squat drum-towers at the angles and what amounted to a township of subsidiary buildings within — greater and lesser halls, dormitories, kitchens, armouries, barracks, stables, store-rooms and a chapel. There was even a garden, ladies' pleasance and orchard within the perimeter walling, little to be looked for in this wilderness. A cluster of thatch-roofed cot-houses, cabins, byres and the like formed a castleton on the east shore opposite the island, where there was a stone jetty — with the ferry-scow always berthed at the castle side. Cattle grazed the enclosing braesides up to the heather-line.

To the uninformed it might seem a strange, indeed a pointless place to site a powerful castle. But, in fact, it was a highly strategic situation, in a position to command almost every important route from the fertile and populous Laigh of Moray to upper Strathspey, Moy, Strathdearn, Strathnairn, the Great Glen and the Highland West. Edward the First of England had recognised this, during the Wars of Independence, and here, in then Comyn territory, had built up a small clan-chief's fortalice into this great stronghold. And Alexander Stewart, Earl of Buchan, had perceived its potentialities and made it his head-quarters for the domination and control of the North-East, transferring here from Ruthven or upper Speyside the principal seat of his vast Lordship of Badenoch. Here he had installed Mariota de Athyn, his famous concubine and chief mistress, daughter of the chiefly house of Mackay of Strathnaver; and here were reared their five sons and one daughter. At Lochindorb Alex Stewart now reigned in his stead, the Wolf eight years dead. Illegitimate, he could not inherit the earldom of Buchan, or even be *de jure* Lord of Badenoch; but *de facto*, he ruled a huge territory as lord, and governed all the North-East as acting Justiciar and Lieutenant for the late heir to the throne, David, Duke of Rothesay, so far not effectively replaced save by the absentee Murdoch of Fife.

That castle could never be approached unwarned, and well before they reached the landing-stage, a boat had put out to come for the travellers. In it, with the rowers, was a young woman and her children, a boy and girl, aged eleven and nine. Their shouted welcome echoed from all the enclosing hillsides.

It was Alex who called back, waving his bonnet, laughing, Jamie Douglas not at his best in scenes and occasions — unless drastic action was called for. He grinned affectionately at his wife and youngsters, however, and at his friend's demonstrative greetings.

"Mary!" the other cried. "Had I wife as comely and excellent as you, I swear that I would never leave home! As for these two, Lochindorb would be a poor place without them."

"Let us hope that you continue to think so, Alex," Mary returned. "For it seems that you are burdened with us for no little time yet."

"Would that my other burdens were of such sort! That, at least, is good news. We will make Highlanders of you all, to be sure, in time!"

"You are kind . . ."

Jamie, although less forthcoming verbally, was nowise backward in embracing his wife appreciatively. And she was of the sort a man much appreciates within his arms, warm, eager, shapely, big-breasted and all woman. The Stewarts had a tendency towards beauty of feature and person, and this illegitimate daughter of the late King, sister of the present monarch, and aunt, after a fashion, of Sir Alexander himself, had the family excellences in full measure, without some of the more notable failings. Less actually beautiful than one or two of the princesses, her half-sisters, she had a lively attractiveness none of them

37

could rival. Her children had to tug and squeeze their father with some vigour to gain their due share of attention.

The Lady Mariota welcomed them at the castle landing-stage, another attractive woman although now in her fifties, handsome, large, forthright, of a natural and far from unpleasing lustiness of character and bearing, which reminded Jamie at least of the Countess of Mar, in some measure. Indeed, it might well be that something of this was in part responsible for Alex's preoccupation with so much older a woman — for he greatly admired his mother. Not that there was anything the least motherly about Isobel of Mar.

Although Mariota de Athyn, or Mackay, was known throughout the kingdom as a notorious courtesan, and concubine of one of the most spectacularly wicked men that even Scotland had ever produced, king's son though he was, she gave little impression of that role; but rather of an assured and effective chatelaine, respectable as any in the land. She had, indeed, been as good as wife — and a good wife — to the Wolf, who had never lived with his wedded spouse, the Countess of Buchan and Ross in her own right. Undoubtedly Mariota had been the best influence in that wild man's life, had given him a fair home amongst his innumerable dens, and brought up their family in as normal, domestic and stable a fashion as had been possible in the extraordinary and testing circumstances. If some of her sons behaved like their father on occasion, that was not altogether her fault.

She was demonstrably happy to see her favourite son safely back from the wars, whilst greeting Jamie with almost equal affection, and an added womanly appreciation wasted on a son. The two young men might have their problems, but they had priceless assets in their womenfolk.

That evening, round the fire in Mariota's own private chamber, the real heart of that great fortalice, what amounted to a council-of-war developed. Alex told them what he had learned at Kildrummy and Loch-an-Eilean, and explained Jamie's theory of Governor Albany's possible involvement. The women expressed their inevitable doubts, if not actual disbelief, and even when these were in some part countered, remained by no means convinced.

"Jamie is prepared to believe anything of Robert," Mary Stewart declared. "He will attribute every evil to him. He is a hard and twisted man, and has done much ill in his day, but I

38

cannot conceive him as black as Jamie thinks, nor possessed of so long an arm."

"Myself, I cannot see that Drummond's death and Alex's downfall could be so important for him. To go to these lengths," Mariota said. "It all would have taken a great deal of planning and working out, beforehand."

"As did the murder of Earl Douglas. As did your . . . as did my lord Earl of Buchan's excommunication plot. That is the kind of mind Albany has," Jamie asserted. "How he works. You cannot deny it, Mary."

"No. Not his devious, malicious mind. It is his purpose and need, in this, that I doubt."

"Let us leave the matter open, then," Alex put in. "Accept only that Robert Stewart *may* be concerned. But if he is, then we must tread a deal more warily. Possibly be prepared for further blows."

"No doubt," his mother said. "But — first things first. What is most important, Alex, is to establish your innocence in the eyes of men."

"Agreed, yes. But none so easy, is it? With Duncan gone, who is going to believe my denials?"

"You cannot perhaps *prove* who did it, in law. But you can perhaps make it clear that *you* did not. Knew naught of it. You are still Justiciar. Before you think of standing down, Alex, hold a trial. Before a great company . . ."

"I agree," Jamie said. "I have said as much."

"How can I, when there is none to stand accused?"

"You have other brothers, besides Duncan, my dear, who also led that company. My own sons, yes, but they have served you ill, done nothing to aid you in this. You must use them to clear your name."

"You mean . . . ?"

"I mean take Andrew and Walter into custody. As Justiciar. Charge them with the murder of Drummond. In your Court. They will, pray God, be shown to be innocent. But they must be made also to establish *your* innocence, before all. Then they can be set free. Mary and I have talked much of this. We believe this is what is required."

Alex frowned. "A sore, hard business that. To arraign my own brothers. They will not love me for it!"

"They will understand," Mary said. "Besides, they *owe* you this, at least. You must do it, Alex — for their sakes, as well as your own. If you go down, to be a mere outlaw and Highland freebooter, *their* state and security is also endangered. All our safety."

"But . . . who will take heed of the findings of such Court? In my own Court, absolving myself and my brothers! All will scorn it, as a merest device."

"No," Jamie intervened. "There is much point to this, I think. It *has* to be your Court, as Justiciar. The highest Court in the North, dispensing the King's justice. No other would serve — the sheriff's or other. The King's good-brother has been slain. It is the King's Justiciar's duty to seek out and try the guilty — none other's. So you must remain Justiciar until then, at least. Although some may scoff, none can controvert such trial. *You* will not seem to be on trial, moreover . . ."

"It will be assumed to be but covering my own fault, nevertheless. As Robert Stewart did after David's murder, at the Holyrood trial."

"Then sit with others in judgement. Say, two others. A triumvirate. Men of repute. Your Bishop? He would serve in this. And would show that you had the power of the Church behind you — a considerable matter. And some other. It would be a duly lawful trial. And whatever Albany might say, or do, its decision could not be questioned in *law*. Any more than his could, at Holyrood. So he could not use parliament against you, at least. That would prevent outlawry, meantime. A sound move, Alex."

The other nodded. "Perhaps you are right. Who could I ask to sit with me? The Mackintosh? Chief of Clan Chattan . . .?"

"A pity that Thomas, Earl of Moray is prisoner in England," Mary said. "Another nephew of the King, he would be of the right stature."

"I can think of what would carry more weight still," Jamie said. "A representative from Mar! The Countess Isobel could find you one, I swear. That would look notably well."

At this mention of the Countess, Mariota stiffened. Her son went on hurriedly.

"I will think on that. But — after? What then? We find Andrew and Walter not guilty. And myself, by implication, more so. If we have established Duncan's probable guilt — what to do? He has disappeared."

"You will have to order his apprehension and arrest, in the King's name," his mother declared steadily. "You can do no

40

less, as Justiciar. Since, it seems, he has left your jurisdiction for the South, you will not be able to enforce it. He will stay away. But, better that than hanging, God knows!"

"And Robert of Albany? What will he do?"

"Who knows? But you will be on the watch for him."

"Albany will surprise, nothing is more sure," Jamie asserted. "But . . . I fear for your Duncan. If he deserves it! When Albany has finished with one of his tools, he does not usually live to tell who paid him!"

"We do not *know* that Robert paid him, Jamie," his wife pointed out. "We do not even know that Duncan did this thing."

The men had to admit that this was so, and that they had only suppositions to work on.

They could plan no further meantime.

*   *   *

It was nearly two weeks later, of a fine autumn early afternoon, that Jamie Douglas fished assiduously for salmon in the swift run of amber water where the quite major Dorback Burn issued from the foot of Lochindorb. He had been at it for almost three hours, without so much as a nibble, and had been telling himself and all the watching hills that it was a hopeless waste of time, that it was too bright a day, that the water was too clear, that it was the wrong hour, that his lures were quite useless, and that he should give it all up and row back to the castle while still he retained his sanity — this for over an hour, when his young son David came paddling across the loch in a basket-and-hide coracle, to announce breathlessly that his father was required forthwith, that there were visitors arrived and he must come.

Jamie produced the required grumbles about being disturbed at his well-earned recreation, but packed up his willow-wand and line the while, ignoring his son's interested queries as to how many fish he had caught, and gingerly embarking in his own frail craft for the paddle back to the island. Alex Stewart was away at Elgin, making arrangements for the great trial to be held there. Jamie's son, splashing alongside, insisted that his father was to go to the castle, not to the landing-stage on the shore opposite, where a fair-sized company could be seen to be waiting.

Mariota and Mary met him just within the castle gateway, out of sight of the waiting visitors, and for once the former displayed unwonted agitation.

41

"Jamie," she said, "you must deal with this, whatever. I will not have that woman in my house! She ought not to have come here. Send her away, Jamie. She is not to come here."

Bewildered, he looked from one woman to the other.

"It is the Countess of Mar," Mary said. "No doubt to see Alex. She will have to be told . . . not to come out here. And you know her, Jamie."

Her husband moistened his lips. "You say I have to turn her away? From this door? Having come all this way from Kildrummy? A great lady, like Isobel of Mar. Alex will not like this, I think!"

"Alex is not here. And I would not have her in my house if he *was* here. You may tell her so!" the normally generous and imperturbable Mariota de Athyn said.

"But . . . but this is going to be most difficult, trying," the man protested. "I have partaken of her hospitality, more than once. As has Alex."

"*I* have not! And would not! Send her away." And their hostess turned and swept off, back across the courtyard.

The man stared at his wife.

"I am sorry, Jamie — but I can prevail nothing with her," Mary told him. "I have tried. She hates the Countess, and her influence on Alex."

"No doubt. But to turn her away from the door! One of the greatest in the land. And new widowed . . ."

"What has either to do with it?"

"Sakes — if you do not see it!" He shook his head. "Women!" he exclaimed. "This countess could throw the whole of Mar behind Alex. One of the most powerful earldoms in the realm. Or . . ."

"By the sound of her she will do that anyway! She has her claws in Alex, for her own designs. Now — go across, Jamie, and tell her that the Lady Mariota is indisposed and unable to see her. But that Alex is at Elgin, and if she goes there she will see him. She will understand very well."

"That she will! Alex *loves* this woman, Mary. Has done for long."

"Then he will see her the sooner — at Elgin! Go you, Jamie."

"If I go, you come with me."

"That is foolish. I can do nothing . . ."

"You can do as much as I can. You can speak to her as a woman. And this is woman's work! Come."

So they both were rowed across the four hundred yards of water to the main landing-stage.

The sizeable party, perhaps fifty strong, was dismounted and waiting there. The Countess was easily distinguished, the only woman present, seated on a log with every appearance of patience for so proud and forthright a character. She was dressed in a travelling cloak and man-style tartan trews, cut on the cross to cling to a substantial but shapely leg, and wore a feathered bonnet with an air. Standing beside her was a young gallant, also with an air to him, features vaguely familiar.

"Who is that? A Stewart, I swear!" Mary Stewart said.

"I do not know him. Yet I should know that face, I think."

As they landed, the Countess exclaimed, "On my soul — I wondered whether all had died a death in yonder hold! And now it is Jamie Douglas and Mary Stewart! Has Alex taken to his bed, or what?"

"I am sorry, my lady, that you have been kept waiting," Jamie said, bowing stiffly. "Sir Alexander is not here. He is presently at Elgin."

"Elgin? A plague on it!"

"He has been gone two days. And we do not expect him back before two more."

"Ah. Unfortunate."

"Yes. The Lady Mariota, I fear, is indisposed and cannot receive you at the castle."

"Indeed? You mean . . . ?"

"It is a pity that you have been thus delayed, Countess — when you could have been on your road to Elgin," Mary put in. "Still a long road, I fear."

"Ah. I see. Yes, I see." Isobel of Mar smiled. "That makes the position entirely clear! Alex should have been more . . . explicit, in his letter."

"Letter . . . ?"

"Why, yes. Alex sent a messenger, with a letter, asking me to find someone, some representative of the earldom of Mar, to sit with him as judge, in the trial anent my husband's death. I have bettered his suggestion — eh, John?" And she turned to her lounging companion.

"As to that, who knows?" he said. He was a tall, well-built and good-looking young man in his early twenties, with fair hair, long features and fine eyes. He laughed — and clearly he laughed easily. "Sir Alexander may find me young, for justiciaring."

"Alex is none so old himself, boy," she said. "Unlike my aged self!"

"You have the secret of endless youth and delight, Isobel," he said — and this time he did not smile, strangely enough. Indeed his fine eyes smouldered.

"Flatterer!" she returned. "And you so young. Who taught you, I wonder? Not your father. Nor yet your brother Murdoch, I vow!" She looked at the others. "Perhaps you do not know each other? Although you, Mary Stewart, should know, one would think. This is the Lord John Stewart of Coull and Onele, in Cro-Mar. Known in Mar as Brave John o' Coull. And whether he is notably brave or not, he is sufficiently bold — that I can vouch for! Second son to the Governor of us all, the Duke of Albany!"

To say that Jamie and Mary caught their breaths would be an understatement. Utterly taken aback, they stared, at a loss for words.

The young man bowed elaborately, smiling again — but at Mary rather than at the Douglas. "I believe that I may be privileged to name you Aunt!' he said. "Like all too many another, I fear!"

"Johnnie Stewart!" she gasped. "Can it be true? I have not seen you since you were a child-in-arms."

"No. I was reared far from Court. My mother, daughter to the Marischal, enjoys the barony of Coull and Onele, in the valley of Dee, in Cro-Mar. It has become my home and in-heritance. My mother was never greatly enamoured of Court life, and retired there."

"So that is where your mother took . . . refuge!"

"Exactly, Aunt!"

The Countess Isobel laughed. "The Stewart family never ceases to surprise! Sir Jamie — does it not surprise you? But . . . how think you this one will serve the Justiciar as second judge?"

That man took moments to answer. To have Albany's own son as co-judge in this case was so improbable-seeming as to be almost inconceivable. If he could be relied upon to co-operate and assist in the project of establishing Alex's innocence, his adherence would be invaluable — for Albany's hands would thereby be much tied, since he was hardly likely to denigrate the judicial findings of his own son, or not publicly. It would give vastly greater validity to the entire exercise. On the other hand, he would be in a position to wreck all, should he so elect, if he sought to play his father's game. He would well recognise this — for he looked to be no fool. Yet the Countess Isobel was no fool either, and she had chosen him. So she must believe that he would be good for Alex's cause, rather than Albany's. He, it seemed, had been reared much apart from his father — indeed, Jamie had scarcely ever heard him referred to, or indeed the Lady Muriella Keith's other, younger children; only Murdoch, the son by the Governor's first wife, the Countess of Menteith in her own right, was seen much about the father. Albany was neither a man with much use for women, save for what they could bring him, nor yet for family life. So the Duchess Muriella had to make her own life. And this John of Coull might possibly make a useful ally.

As all this flashed through Jamie's mind, he nodded. "I think notably well," he said. "Provided that his intentions are . . . kindly disposed."

"I think that my lord's intentions are kindly — towards myself, at any rate!" The Countess's tone and glance were significant, archly so.

"H'r'mm. Yes. To be sure," Jamie muttered. If Alex ever eventually married this one, he was not likely to lack problems.

The younger man grinned cheerfully.

Mary spoke. "Nephew John, how think you your father will see this?"

"He can scarce object to me assisting the King's Justiciar, Aunt."

"You think not? *Acting* Justiciar, only!" Mary amended.

"To be sure. But then, if my brother Murdoch is in truth Justiciar — as I believe he was appointed? — then, since Murdoch is a captive in England, is it not the more my duty to assist his . . . deputy?"

"Your father may see it otherwise, perhaps."

"Then my father will have to communicate his pleasure, or displeasure, to me — which he does but seldom, God be thanked!"

Mary's faint smile at that held a hint of admiration; and Jamie decided that this Stewart was certainly no fool or simple innocent — which made him consider the Countess the more thoughtfully.

"So now you would have us ride to Elgin? Without further . . . delay?" the lady asked.

Jamie coughed. "Yes. That is best. Alex should hear of this at the earliest. I will ride some way with you. Put you on the best road. By Glen Erney, Dallas and the Lossie, to Kellas and Pittendreich. It is near thirty miles. But there is the Valliscaulian Hospice of St. Michael at Dallas, where you could pass the night."

"You are thoughtful, my friend!" She turned to Mary. "You will convey to the Lady Mariota my concern for her health? Should we inform Alex to return with all haste to his mother's side?"

"That will not be necessary, I think."

"Ah — I am relieved to hear it! Tell her to take good care of herself. We older women must not over-tax ourselves!" And the Countess snapped imperious fingers for her groom to bring forward her horse.

Jamie exchanged glances with his wife, and hastened to collect a mount for himself from the castleton stables.

*　　*　　*

Elgin, as well as being the chief town of Moray and the diocesan centre, was also in theory the official seat of government for all the North-East and site of the principal royal castle. So, for maximum effect, Sir Alexander Stewart chose to stage his great trial there, on a day of early November, in the said royal castle, on the modest height of the Lady Hill towards the west end of the town, a place he seldom used, like his father before him. It was, in fact, no impressive stronghold, old and in disrepair; but it had a large old-fashioned hall and an indefinable air of authority about it.

From an early hour, whenever the town's gates were opened for the day, folk had been flocking into Elgin — for Alex had sought to publish the word of it far and wide. The townsfolk were out in force also. Only a limited number could gain admittance to the hall, of course, and these mainly burgh, chiefly and lairdly representatives and churchmen; but the crowds could wait outside, see the principals arrive, and hear what was relayed to them from within.

Jamie, Mary and the Lady Mariota were installed at the side of the dais-platform, where they could see all, yet remain hidden from most of the hall by the serving screens. Unfortunately they were not hidden from the Countess of Mar, who sat by herself directly opposite at the other side of the dais — to the marked

46

embarrassment of Jamie at least. *She* did not seem concerned at her isolation, any more than did Mariota or Mary, women being a law unto themselves in such matters, but rather mildly interested and amused by all that went on, the jostling for position in the body of the hall, the bickering, greeting and general stir.

It was all well managed. A trumpeter blew a flourish, and a herald — really more of a Highland sennachie than a Lowland pursuivant — strode in and announced in ringing tones but a musical Highland voice that all should be upstanding for the entry of His Grace the King's Lord Justiciar of the North, the excellent and right puissant Sir Alexander Stewart of Badenoch, Braemoray and Kinneddar, supported by the Lord Bishop of Moray, Master William de Spynie, and the Lord John Stewart, of Coull and Onele, sworn Justiciars Extraordinary. God Save the King's Grace!

He was a little early, but no matter — the stir at the naming of the third judge was sufficient to keep tongues wagging until Alex paced in, with the other two behind.

Alex, who usually dressed in Highland fashion, was today clad in his finest — actually old court clothing of his father's, crimson velvet, silver filigree and cloth-of-gold, slightly tarnished but not too obviously so. The Bishop was magnificent in his most gorgeous cope, stole and mitre, aglitter with jewels; John Stewart, much more modestly garbed, carrying himself with confidence enough for any. Seen together there was a distinct family resemblance between the Stewart cousins.

Three throne-like chairs from the cathedral were placed in the centre of the dais. The triumvirate sat. After a few moments pause, Alex lifted his hand, and the trumpeter blew a single blast for silence.

"My lords spiritual and temporal, chiefs, barons, tacksmen, freeholders, burghers of this city, and people here assembled, leal subjects of the King's Grace — hail!" the Justiciar called, clearly, still sitting. "I, Alexander Stewart, *Alastair mac Alastair Mor mac an Righ*, acting His Grace's Justiciar, do hereby declare that His Grace's lawful and superior Court of Justice in this northern part of his kingdom, is now duly in session. Let any who may question that authority stand forth."

Silence.

"So be it. I do declare that I, and my colleagues here before you, the Lord Bishop William and the Lord John of Coull and Onele, will hear, question, consider and make and pronounce judgement, with open minds, firm purpose and honest hearts, on the evidence to be put before us, as we value our immortal souls — so help us God!"

"Amen!" intoned the Bishop.

"I agree," said Brave John of Coull.

"That ensured, I now declare to all that in order that the King's justice be done, it is necessary that we herewith consider and enquire into the recent and horrible murder of Sir Malcolm Drummond, Knight, Lord of Cargill and Stobhall, *An Druma-nach Mor*, Chief of Clan Drummond of Strathearn and Gowrie, husband of the most noble Countess of Mar and the Garioch, and good-brother of the King's Grace. Which horrible and shameful murder, said to be by starvation, took place within our jurisdiction, to wit, within the hold of Badenyon in Brae-Mar, on a date unspecified between the Feast of St. Barnabas the Apostle and that of St. Palladius, Bishop and Confessor, in this year of Our Lord, fourteen-hundred-and-two. To which end we now make due inquisition."

He paused and turned to the herald, a brother of the Mackin-tosh, now to double as prosecutor.

"You, sir, have in custody two suspects whom it is conjectured may have committed this grievous murder and offence?"

"Yes, my lord. Two. Sir Andrew Stewart of Ruthven and Sir Walter Stewart of Glenavon. A third, Sir Duncan Stewart of Loch-an-Eilean, is not to be found, and believed to have left the territory under the jurisdiction of this Court."

"Yes. We note the third name. I hereby now state and affirm that these accused, the said Andrew, Walter and Duncan Stewart, are brothers-german to my own self. But that it is my simple and undoubted duty to put them on trial for this shameful offence against the King's peace and his lieges. But in case any should question my honest purpose and impartial judgement in this matter, I have empanelled two further honourable and un-prejudiced judges, who have no least connection with the accused, to ensure a right verdict. Should there be disagreement amongst the judges, the vote of any two shall prevail. Is all understood? Then — bring in the accused."

The buzz of exclamation, comment and speculation was loud in the hall.

Mackintosh went out, and returned with the two young men. They stalked in stiffly, proudly, heads high, with nothing of guilt, fear or uncertainty about them. A couple of years between them,

48

they were very much alike, although one had reddish hair, the other golden-fair. Although both bore an evident family resemblance to Alex, it would be wrong to say that either was *like* him, in the way that they were like each other, likeness, implying similarity of appearance or impact, being quite absent. They were stockier, rougher, less fine-honed versions of a superficially similar model, that is all, features good and regular but somehow blurred in comparison, expressions entirely different, with a distinct air of intolerance and arrogance. These, one could well believe, were truly sons of the Wolf of Badenoch. Jamie Douglas, seeing them anew after a long interval, perceived them as somehow liker to Alastair Carrach MacDonald than to their eldest brother. All were grandsons of King Robert the Second, of course — as was John of Coull.

The pair strode rather than were led, to the side of the dais, where they inclined brief nods towards their brother — none could say that they bowed — and so stood. They did not so much as glance at the crowd.

Mackintosh, at a nod from Alex, spoke. "Andrew Stewart, Knight, and Walter Stewart, Knight — you are hereby charged that on a day between the Feast of St. Barnabas the Apostle and that of the Blessed St. Palladius, you both and in concert, with your brother Duncan Stewart, Knight, did lay violent hands on Sir Malcolm Drummond of Cargill and Stobhall, the King's good-brother, whilst on his lawful occasions, did convey him to the lonely hold of Badenyon in Brae-Mar, and there did ill-use him so grievously that he died, and so did murder him. What say you to this fell charge?"

"No," Andrew, the elder, answered briefly.

"You deny guilt? Both?"

"Yes."

"Do you deny taking Sir Malcolm, when about his lawful affairs, and conveying him to this Badenyon?"

"No."

"Why did you so do?"

"We did so on the King's business."

"The *King's* . . .?"

"Yes."

"Explain yourself, sir. How the King's business?"

Andrew had clearly taken upon himself to act spokesman, with whatever brevity. "Donald of the Isles had invaded this country. Alastair Carrach was sacking and slaying, had sacked

49

this city. Drummond was known to be dealing with Donald. It was feared that he would rise, to aid Alastair. We were sent to see that he did not."

"Who sent you?"

"I did," Alex intervened. "As King's Justiciar and Lieutenant it was my duty to seek preserve the King's peace. I had reason to believe that Sir Malcolm Drummond might support the Lord of the Isles in his revolt. I sent a strong company, under my brothers, to keep watch on Sir Malcolm, and myself came to the relief of Elgin and the countering of Alastair."

"The accused then, my lord, were sent to *watch* Sir Malcolm Drummond — not to slay him?"

"That is so."

Mackintosh turned back to Andrew Stewart. "Do you agree? That your orders were to watch Drummond? Not to slay him?"

"Yes."

"Then why did you slay him?"

"We did not."

"You do not deny that he was slain? In that remote hold in Brae-Mar. Locked therein, given neither food nor drink, and starved to death?"

"It may be so. But it was not our doing."

"Whose, then?"

Neither of the accused spoke.

"You must answer my question, whatever. If you did not slay Drummond, who did?"

"We do not know."

Mackintosh glanced at the judges.

Bishop Spynie spoke. "Is it your plea that you knew of the slaying but were not party to it?"

"No. We knew naught of it."

"But you were at the taking of Sir Malcolm and the immuring of him in this hold?"

"Yes."

"How then can you claim innocence for his death?"

"We knew naught of it. We left him there, well enough."

"Ah. So someone else was responsible for this starving? After you left. When you were not there?"

"Yes."

"Who?"

Silence.

John of Coull spoke. "Who commanded your company, Sir Andrew?"

For the first time the other looked uncertain. "There, there was no true commander," he said.

"No commander? Of an armed force? How many men?"

"Three hundred perhaps."

"Someone must have been in command."

"We were all brothers. In command."

"Who, then, was the eldest?"

"I was," Andrew admitted. "But . . ."

"But you were not in command?"

The other prisoner, Sir Walter, raised his voice at last. "Our brother Duncan is . . . forceful," he said.

"Ah. So, in effect, Sir Duncan it was who commanded? In fact if not in name? Sir Duncan, who is now missing."

"I can confirm, my lords, that Duncan is the most vehement and headstrong of our family," Alex put in. "Therefore I seldom give him overall command."

"But was it not he, my lord, who led the great raid on Angus and Gowrie some eight years back?" the Bishop asked. "And won the Battle of Glasclune and other fights?"

"Yes. He is an able fighter, strategist — and bold. But . . . headstrong."

"Did Sir Duncan, then, order the apprehension and immuring of Sir Malcolm Drummond?"

Walter nodded.

"And you left him at this place, in your brother Duncan's care?"

"No. We all left, Duncan with us." That was Andrew again. "We rode for the Kildrummy country. To discover whether forces were massing there, to the aid of Alastair."

"Leaving Drummond in this hold — the name of which I misremember? Alone, without food or drink? You left him to die?"

"No. We left him under a small guard. With ample victual."

"So — you are saying that it was these men of your guard who abandoned Sir Malcolm and left him to die?" The Bishop now considered himself as chief inquisitor.

Silence.

"Answer, sirrah!"

It was Alex who eventually spoke, and there can have been few who did not sense the reluctance with which he did so.

51

"I heard tell that Duncan left you, however, the next day. Turned back. Is that so?"

"Ye-e-es."

"Back to Badenyon?"

"I do not know."

"But you *understood* that is where he was bound?"

No reply.

"Later, the guard you had left returned to you?"

"Yes."

"And what did they say?"

"I do not exchange idle gossip with gillies!"

"A plague on it, man . . .!" Alex stopped himself. "Your pardon, my lords. I forget myself. Andrew Stewart — I charge you to answer my question. Do you not see? If you seek further to shield Duncan your brother, *our* brother, you condemn these your gillies. Without cause, it may be. Innocent men. For either he, or they, would seem to have starved Drummond to death. Answer me on two points. How long until the guard returned to you, in the Kildrummy area? And what did they tell you when they came?"

When Andrew continued to scowl obstinately, Walter spoke. "I will tell you — and thereafter *yours* is the responsibility, Alex, not ours! Mind it! They came in five days after we left them. And said that Duncan had sent them back to us."

Something like a sigh rose from the packed hall.

"So now we have it," the Bishop said. "Sir Duncan sent them back. So he went there, after he left you. And was still there when these left. No man will starve to death within five days. And Sir Duncan was left alone with the prisoner, the man he had insisted on taking and imprisoning. *Was* he alone?"

"He had his own two running gillies only," Walter said.

"And these are now where?"

"Neither he, nor they, have been seen since."

"I agree that no man is like to die after only five days without food. Or even water," John Stewart of Coull said. "So it seems that Sir Malcolm Drummond was caused to starve to death thereafter — by Sir Duncan Stewart. But why? What was his reason for this barbarous act?"

When none answered that, the young man went on, "He must have had cause for so ill a deed. Some hatred, or some score to pay. Such a thing is not done for simple enmity or malice."

52

When still he obtained no response from any, he turned to Alex. "My lord — have *you* any notion as to why?"

Thus directly challenged, that man spoke carefully. "I do not know. So far as I am aware, he never met Sir Malcolm before. He fought against him at Glasclune — but so he did against many another. If indeed he is guilty, he must have had a reason unknown to me. Unless . . . he was put up to it by another."

"Who would so do?"

"Your notion is as good as mine, my lord. But it would require to be someone who hated Drummond and would benefit by his death. And possibly who would wish to injure *myself*, by seeking to implicate me in this evil thing."

There was a stir at that.

"And have you no notion at all, my lord, as to whom that might be?"

"I shall make it my business to find out!" Alex said grimly.

"It may be that the accused could tell us?" the Bishop said. "Do either of you know? Or have any notion?"

Both stared at him, wordless.

"You must answer," Mackintosh told them.

"No," Andrew said.

"No," Walter said.

The prelate frowned and puffed. "Insolent! This is an outrage!"

Alex intervened. "My lord Bishop — I think that they probably speak but the truth. If *I* do not have such information, it is unlikely that they will have it. Duncan keeps his own counsel. If it is some secret matter, an intrigue, they will know no more than I do. Moreover, I think, interesting as this knowledge would be, it is scarce our present duty to discover. We are here, are we not, to seek find out *who* murdered Sir Malcolm — not why he did so? That would be valuable to discover, and I shall endeavour it. But meantime we have a decision to come to. Do we require further questioning of these accused?"

The Bishop puffed.

"Are there further witnesses?" John Stewart asked.

"Not that I know aught of. Or can conceive of. Perhaps the accused can tell us that — if there are others who might inform us in the matter, to their advantage? Andrew? Walter?"

The brothers both shook their heads.

"The only other witnesses who could take us any further, it seems to me, are the two gillies Duncan Stewart took with him

53

back to Badenyon," Alex went on. "And these, it appears he has likewise taken with him to the South. No others could speak to the actual death of Sir Malcolm."

"I agree," John of Coull nodded. "Which makes our decision here simple, does it not? We cannot declare finally who murdered Drummond — but must say that it would appear to be Sir Duncan Stewart of Loch-an-Eilean. We *can* say that it was not the doing of the two accused here before us, however. Nor does any responsibility rest with the higher command of the Justiciar's forces."

"I thank you, my lord. A clear exposition of the situation. And you, my lord Bishop?"

"The same. Save that I would have it recorded that we here recognise that the reason *why* this shameful murder was committed should be discovered, as of vital importance, in order that we may learn who, if any, was behind Sir Duncan Stewart in the commission of this crime."

"Agreed. The clerks will record that — although I fear that it may be difficult to ascertain. There is one further matter which I would wish to have established before all, before we dismiss the accused — and which they can tell us. This involves myself, in person. I would have it established what were my orders to this company I sent to Mar — since it bears on the matter. All three brothers I summoned together at Lochindorb before sending them off. Do you agree with that?"

The pair nodded.

"Do you also agree that you were ordered to *watch* Sir Malcolm? And if he had a fighting force raised to aid Alastair Carrach in his invasion, you were to seek prevent such force from joining up with Alastair? Only that. No word of arresting Drummond."

Again the nods.

"I would have you confirm that, in speech. Before all. For it is important. Did I give any order for the arrest and imprisonment of Sir Malcolm Drummond? Or that could be held to mean that? Andrew?"

"No."

"No," Walter declared.

"Very well. I declare now, in the name of the King's justice, that Sir Andrew Stewart and Sir Walter Stewart are hereby found to be not guilty of the murder of Sir Malcolm Drummond, and are free to leave this Court. And further declare that we find that the murder would appear to have been committed by Sir Duncan Stewart of Loch-an-Eilean, now fled furth of this jurisdiction. The reason for the crime being presently unknown, and to be fully enquired into, in the furtherance of justice — by order of this Court. Also that the said Duncan Stewart be found and apprehended, by all means possible. In the name of the King's Grace." He paused, and stood, waving to his companions to remain seated. "That concludes the business of this Court. There is, however, another matter of His Grace's business and concern which it is my duty to declare. In the present circumstances, with my own family and name involved in a grave matter contrary to the King's peace, I deem it right and proper that I should no longer continue in the office of Justiciar and Lieutenant of the North. Accordingly, I herewith declare that I demit and vacate that office of the Crown, so that another may be appointed thereto. This decision I shall communicate to the King's Grace, at the earliest."

There was a considerable stir and clamour in the hall, in which even the two co-judges took part. Clearly this renunciation was not popular.

Alex held up his hand for quiet. "On this I must insist," he said strongly. "The King's justice must be accepted and maintained as fair, honest and unprejudiced — this is above all important. My present state could cause some to doubt that. Therefore I must stand down. But I shall continue to see that the duties are carried out until His Grace's royal will in the matter is known and implemented. This is my decision. God save the King's Grace!" He turned. "My lords . . .?"

The herald, accepting his cue, signed to the trumpeter, who blew strongly. The justiciars strode off. After a moment or two the prisoners, finding nobody any longer interested in them, strolled away likewise, slightly bemused but keeping up a proud front.

It was some time before Jamie Douglas could see Alex Stewart alone. "You took a step wrong there," he asserted. "Unnecessary, I say. You should not have stood down."

"I had to, Jamie. For my good name's sake, this was something I had to do."

"You are too nice in your judgement, man. As all present would tell you."

"All present, perhaps. But it is not on account of these that I am standing down. It is on account of many folk much further

55

away. For my name's sake in the South, before the Council and parliament. You must see it?"

"I see that the North will suffer grievous loss. And to whose advantage? But . . . you have done it, now. Although I do not see any replacement for you arriving for sufficiently long, or being acceptable to the folk here. We shall see." He shrugged. "For the rest, it was well done. Skilful. Albany's son was a great help."

"Yes. A useful young man. But worth watching, I think, nevertheless."

"Perhaps. But today, excellent. The trial went very well."

"You believe so? To me, it seemed that there were many holes left to be stopped."

"Some, perhaps. But small holes only. Not sufficient to sink your boat. Save, it may be, for one. The matter of who might be behind Duncan."

"Yes. That I perceived. It was . . . difficult."

"You leave it open, to be discovered. So that it could be Albany, yes. But, equally, it could be *yourself*! And more believedly, for many. There was nothing established, back yonder, which proved that you did not give Duncan *secret* orders to slay Drummond. You could have done, more readily than could Albany, or other. And you had a motive, all will recognise, in seeking to gain the Countess. Albany will not fail to perceive it — and exploit it, I fear."

"I know it well. But what else could I have done? Stating so before all would not have aided me — but only brought it to people's minds. Other than by standing down, I can see no way to show my honesty. Can you?"

"No. None. But it is a grave weakness."

"One we must needs accept. Now, Jamie — will you escort my mother to the Bishop's town-house? And Mary, of course. I must see Isobel alone, for a little. If I can get John of Coull prised loose from her!"

"The price to be paid! He is much taken with her?"

"As to that I care not. Many men are. But she — she now appears somewhat taken with *him*! Little more than a stripling! It is . . . unsuitable."

"She but uses him, I think, into provoking you, Alex — into marriage. She will use any weapon to her hand, that one! And she has not a few!"

Alex Stewart frowned at him, unseeing, for a long moment, before stalking off.

IV

JAMIE DOUGLAS GAZED southwards to the Lothian coast with mixed feelings. He had not thought to see that coast again for long — nor was certain that he wanted to, in the circumstances. But it was good to see his home country again, after ten months of the Highlands, especially in early July when Lothian looked so very fair. And, of course, the object of his hazardous journey was in itself unhappy — to attend at his father's death-bed. He had, to be sure, done this twice before, in the last eight years — as Mary had not failed to point out; but from his brother's letter and urging, this time it was really serious. And he was fond of his father who, considering the fact that he was only a bastard, had always treated him exceedingly well — until that last meeting. It would be a shame and a sorrow to part on the poor terms of that day ten months ago.

The skipper of his ship, the *Fair Maid*, of Dysart, carrying hides, tallow and wool from Invererne, the produce of the Priory of Pluscarden, to the metropolitan warehouses of St. Andrews, had agreed to carry his passenger the extra distance as a favour to his ecclesiastical charterers, and to set him down at the little haven of Aberlady, the port of Haddington. Here, in the cowled black robe of a Benedictine friar, if questioned he would be on his way to the Priory of Luffness nearby, where he had reason to believe the Lindsay prior would aid him. It was a dangerous procedure, of course, for an outlawed man; but the country between Aberlady and Dalkeith was largely Douglas-owned. Even so, he might not have risked it — or, more accurately, Mary would have forbidden his coming — had the Church authorities in the North not told Alex Stewart that it would probably be comparatively safe. Always amazingly well-informed as to what went on all over the kingdom, they announced that another major invasion of England was being arranged, astonishingly enough, allegedly to avenge Homildon Hill, and that Albany himself was leading it. This had seemed scarcely believable to Jamie, but the churchmen insisted that reports described musters in progress all over the Lowlands, and the Governor making sundry but definite statements of intent. The Earl of Douglas was said somehow to be involved — although how this could be, when he was still a prisoner in England, was not explained. At any rate, the indications were that it would be as good a time as any for a fugitive to risk a visit to the South, with all in authority otherwise preoccupied. Holy Church was seldom wrong in such matters, and Jamie had decided to take the chance, arguing that he owed it to his father. His wife was less sure, but had reluctantly acceded.

He was duly landed at the jetty at the western mouth of the great Aberlady Bay, friar's robe carefully donned and cowl up. To seek to hire or borrow a horse would be but to draw attention to himself; wandering friars seldom went other than on foot. Not being challenged in any way, on disembarking, he had no need to make for Luffness Priory. He calculated that it was about a dozen miles to Dalkeith — but that would not kill him. In the Highlands he had got into the habit of large walking. Admittedly there was a Douglas property at Kilspindie, close to Aberlady, and he might have got a horse there; but he decided that it was not worth the risk of identifying himself.

By Longniddry and Seton and Tavernent he went, then, glad enough to stretch his legs after the constrictions of his four days in the vessel, through the July afternoon, admiring with new-seeing eyes the full stackyards, golden-turning rigs and sleek cattle, as compared with the thin and scanty crops and lean beasts of the Highlands. Folk working in the fields, rigs and orchards, pigs rooting in the woodlands, poultry everywhere, mills clacking, salt-pans steaming, coal-sleds being dragged — these were sights little seen in the North, and reminded the traveller more keenly than anything yet had done that he was indeed an outlaw and fugitive, that such scenes, formerly part and parcel of his life, were now to be noted and remarked upon.

Along the long and quite lofty ridge of Elphinstone and Fawside, wearying a little now but with the wide valley of the Esk opening before him whilst still the Forth estuary gleamed and glittered on his right, he trudged. Dalkeith lay in the

Esk valley four miles up from its confluence with the firth at Musselburgh.

He came to his old home with the sinking sun, a great sprawling palace this, compared with Lochindorb, Loch-an-Eilean or even Kildrummy, scarcely a fortress at all, although it had grown out of one, in green parklands where the North and South Esk rivers joined. But there was still a gatehouse and drawbridge — although Jamie could scarcely remember the latter ever being fully raised. Not until he felt its timbers sound hollow beneath his feet did he remove the cloying monkish robe.

He was well received, at least. The great house seemed to be full of relatives, kinsfolk and friends, drawn to the old lord's bedside. The first he saw was his one-time master's widow, the Lady Isabel Stewart, sister of the King and former Countess of Douglas, now nearing fifty but still a beautiful woman.

"Jamie!" she cried, and ran to him, arms outstretched. "How good to see you! Good, yes. It has been so long." She embraced him and kissed him eagerly, almost hungrily. "My dear! So you came? From those barbarous Highlands!"

Embarrassed, he shook his head. "Scarce barbarous, Isabel. I, I have received much kindness there. You are well? You look well. But . . . my father? How is he?"

"Better, Jamie. A deal better, I am glad to say. More himself. He supped a bowl of soup this morning. All of it . . ."

"Better! Himself — and supping soup!" the traveller exclaimed. "And I, I have put my head into a noose to come all this way . . .!"

"No, no, Jamie — you will be well enough. We shall look after you, my dear. Robert is not here. He has gone to the Border, with a great host. A strange business, that is not like Robert. But let us thank God that he is gone . . ."

"Jamie! A God's good name — Jamie himself!" That was his brother Will, last seen falling under the hail of arrows on Homildon Hill. "The saints be praised! Give me your hand, man — if the Lady Isabel will release you for a moment!"

Jamie actually flushed. "The Lady Isabel is my good-sister, Will," he asserted. "I . . . ah . . . it is well to see you on your feet, looking little the worse. You are well again? Whole from your wound? And back from captivity."

"We have been back a month and more. Paid for in good siller! Lord — I had not known that I was worth so much money! That Hotspur drives a hard bargain. The wound healed

59

well — quicker than James's. An arrow through the shoulder, passing neatly between lungs and gullet. We Douglases take a deal of killing!"

The James whom Will referred to was his elder brother, legitimate heir of the house. Jamie, older than both, but illegitimate, had been brought up at Dalkeith with the others, the old lord making little distinction between his offspring, lawful or otherwise. But, of course, when it came to inheritance and title, the lawful James must prevail.

Will at least seemed to bear no ill-will for being left by his half-brother on the stricken field of battle.

"And James? I received his letter, to bring me here. But he said naught of his own health . . ."

"He had two wounds. One in the neck which is not yet fully healed. And one in the thigh. But he is well enough. Come, we will find him . . ."

"I had better see my father first. Having come all this way . . ."

"Oh, the old one is well enough, likewise. He will not die this time! We thought that he would, mind you — it was near enough."

Between his brother and the Lady Isabel he was escorted to his father's chamber.

Father and son were almost equally reserved at their greeting. The last time they had been together it had been a difficult interview, with the old man blaming Jamie for having deserted his half-brothers on the battlefield, and forcing him to resign his baronies of Aberdour, Stoneypath and Baldwinsgill to his full brother Johnnie to save them from being forfeited on account of his outlawry — making in fact a pauper of him. Now they eyed each other warily in that over-heated bedroom.

"So, I am not dead yet, you see!" the Lord of Dalkeith croaked, almost defiantly. "Your journey wasted!"

"I rejoice to see you so much the better than I had feared, my lord."

"Aye, perhaps. But James should not have sent for you. Even if, if . . ."

"To be sure he should. It was right and proper."

"You come at the risk of your neck, boy."

"I have risked my neck many a time for less good cause, sir. How do you feel? In pain?"

"Not now. Two days back I took a turn for the better, God

be praised." He made a to-do of coughing, all but dislodging his nightcap. "Son — do you not bear me a grudge?"

"No, my lord — no grudges."

"Can we not be done with this my lording? See you, boy — I perhaps spoke you more sorely than I should have done, that day. I, h'mm, I regret it. I have thought much on it these weeks, lying on this bed. And I believe that I may have been over-hard on you."

"It is forgotten."

"Not by me, lad — and not, I think, by you either! It is not the matter of resigning your lands to Johnnie. That had to be. Only so could they be saved from forfeiture. It is the blame I laid on you for leaving your brothers on yon field. Now that they are ransomed and returned to me, I can see it differently. They have told me how it was . . ."

"As did I, if I remember rightly!"

"Yes, yes. But they confirmed your tale of the Earl Archibald's folly — more than confirmed it. Folly indeed. And they tell me more. Of what you did before — the ambush in the valley, the scouting deep into Durham, the warnings. The seeking to halt the reivings and break-up of the army. *You* told me none of this."

"I scarce had opportunity, I think, or desire to."

"No. Perhaps not. I was . . . less than kind. But, we will say no more of it. You won your way here without trouble? None sought to take you?"

"I came by sea, from Invererne to Aberlady, then walked, in a friar's robe. How much danger am I in, think you?"

"Who knows? You are still outlawed. I have tried to have it lifted, but without success. If Earl Archibald had been ransomed, *he* might have prevailed on Robert Stewart — since he ever needs Douglas aid. But *I* can not."

"The Earl — why is he not ransomed, then? You were gathering the money?"

"You have not heard, in your Hielands? A strange business. I . . . I . . ." The old man was getting distinctly breathless. "James . . . will tell you, lad. I . . . I canna speak for over-long. A strange business — but ask James. He has more wits . . . than has Will. Come again . . ."

Jamie's priority, however, was to the kitchen, for food and drink, not having eaten adequately for a considerable time.

It was there, at the long table, that his limping brother James

61

found him presently, with their uncle Sir Will Douglas of Mordington.

"Jamie, boy — for an outlaw and next to being a damned Hielantman you look surpassing well!" the older man cried. "You look like a gipsy — but then, you never did know how to wear clothes!"

"And you, Uncle, grow fat!" he was told succinctly.

"Jamie — I fear I have brought you a long way, and at some hazard, for little purpose," the heir of Dalkeith greeted. "Our father has made one of his recoveries! Which, of course, is excellent," he hastened to add. "But we much feared for his life."

"You did what was right. Although Mary was not for allowing me to come!"

"Aye, women ever fear the worst. But — I am sorry, Jamie, about all this. The outlawry. The miscalling. The ill repute. You have received much ill-usage. Even from our father, he tells us. It was shameful. You, of all men!"

"Quite right," Sir Will agreed. "I did not believe a word of it."

"Many did, and still do. Albany would find it all a useful stick to beat me with."

"Aye. He did not take long in proclaiming you outlaw." Sir James shook his head. "God, Jamie — I wish that we had heeded you, that day on Homildon Hill, Will and I. Had not followed the Earl Archibald down the steep, like, like . . . what were they? Pigs, of some sort . . . ?"

"Gadarene swine, you mean?"

"Aye — the Gadarene swine. It was just as stupid — and hopeless. And if we had stayed back with you and Johnnie, much of all this might never have happened. You might never have been outlawed, and our father saved a deal of siller!"

"I still might — since the Earl Murdoch of Fife, Albany's son, would still have fallen and been captured. And it was *that* his father could not stomach — not that I left the Earl Douglas and yourselves on the field." He shrugged. "What happened to Murdoch Stewart?"

"He was wounded, and captured too, with Angus and Moray and the rest. Angus the most sore wounded . . ."

"Was he, Fife, with you at Hotspur's Alnwick Castle?"

"No. The traitor, my uncle Dunbar, got his hands on these others. Moray of course was his own brother's son. Where they are now, God knows."

"These are not ransomed yet, then? Any more than Douglas himself? Yet our father collected the siller. What went wrong? He said to ask you."

"It is a strange business. And has had stranger results."

"By the powers, it has!" their Uncle Will agreed. "There is something fell odd going on."

"Over the ransom moneys?"

"Not that," James Douglas said. "Or not that I have heard. There are two parts in this, Jamie. The first we knew of, before ever we were released from Alnwick. Henry, the English king, sent word to Hotspur — and no doubt to Dunbar and the others too — that all important captives from Homildon were to be treated as the Crown's prisoners-of-war and not ransomed. Hotspur was fell angry. He does not love Henry Plantagenet anyway, and this he took as a great insult. Henry said to send all important prisoners to him. Hotspur refused to do this. Us he let go — having our ransom. But he did hold up the Earl Archibald's release. I take it he did not consider us important!"

"Yet your wife is the King's daughter."

"He knows how little important is the King in Scotland, today!"

"What is Henry's purpose in this?"

"Lord knows! Always it has been the captor's right to ransom prisoners, the victorious commander to have his choice."

"But that is not the best of it, man," Sir Will interrupted. "Tell Jamie about this of Albany — and Cocklaws."

"Aye. Hotspur, see you, is up to some strange ploy, with Albany. He has invaded the Middle March, with a large force, and sat down around the Tower of Cocklaws — and taken the Earl of Douglas with him . . ."

"Cocklaws? Should I know Cocklaws?"

"Well may you ask! It is nothing but a small Border peel-tower, near your friend Archie of Cavers' house, held by Sir James Gledstanes of that Ilk, vassal to Cavers. In a strong position on a ridge in Teviotdale, yes — but no great fort or stronghold. But there they are . . ."

"You are saying that Hotspur, with Douglas, and a great force, are besieging this little Teviotdale tower? Only that? Why, of a mercy?"

"Answer that, boy, and you are more clever than we are!" his uncle said. "But there is more than that. Albany has assembled a great army, and gone to relieve this rickle o' stanes!"

Jamie stared.

"He has fifty thousand men and more," his brother went on, "said to be going to invade England. In answer to Homildon. And to force the release of his son Murdoch, whom Henry is holding fast. But first, to save Cocklaws! Have you ever heard the like?"

"No. It sounds to me nonsense. Albany does not embark on adventures like this. He does not lead armies — not alone. Who has he got with him?"

"None of any note. The Marischal, his good-brother, Sandilands, Ramorgnie. No true soldiers."

"There is more to this than meets the eye, then. There always is, with Albany. But — Hotspur? This, of Cocklaws, is as unlike him as the other is of Albany. And you say the Percy has our own Earl with him?"

"Yes. That is the word. God knows why!"

"Could it be something to do with the ransom? Hotspur seeking to get past his King's command? There will be much siller involved, for the Earl of Douglas. And the Percy with his own ransom money to make up, when he was prisoner here after Otterburn."

"Who knows? Father has collected near on twenty thousand gold nobles. He thinks that Hotspur and Albany are in league, some way, in this."

"But against whom? It could be Henry. I can conceive that Hotspur might engage to hand over the Earl Douglas to Albany, at this place, Cocklaws, at a play-acting engagement, in which Douglas seemed to be recaptured — so long as he got the moneys. Twenty thousand gold nobles is a vast sum. But you say, do you not, that the money is still here? Albany has not got it?"

"No. Father still holds it. And has had no further word."

"Strange indeed. Unlike both Albany and Hotspur. But . . . there must be an answer. Suppose, suppose Albany was doing this on his own behalf? Making his own bargain with the Percy. Using his own money — or the realm's — to buy our Earl's release? What better way to bind Douglas to him? He much needs the power of Douglas. Might he not think to buy it, thus?"

"It could be, yes. But . . ."

"Would he need fifty thousand men for that?"

"No-o-o. That is true. Much more than is needed for such

64

demonstration. But it could be that — and something else as well. This of invading England? That sounds but little likely. You have no further word on that?"

"Only that it is supposedly in return for Homildon."

"Not Albany's way. And what happens now? What is Albany at, at this moment?"

"We have heard nothing for three days. There are but few Douglases with his array. The last we heard was that his force was in Tweeddale, near Melrose. Making but slowly south for Cocklaws."

"I cannot believe in this. There is something false, somewhere . . ."

The lady of that great house put in an appearance. Jamie's relationship with the Lady Egidia Stewart had always been a little uncertain, in name as in nature. His father's second wife, and he but a bastard, she was scarcely his stepmother, any more than her predecessor had been. She was Mary's aunt, after a fashion, a sister of the late monarch, Robert the Second; but this did little to regularise their mutual positions. She *was* stepmother to his half-brothers, and great-aunt to James's wife; and with children and grandchildren by her two previous marriages, was at the centre of a tangle of relationships indeed.

"So — the wanderer returns!" she greeted him crisply. "And looking none so ill, considering the company he keeps, and a diet of oatcakes and braxy sheep — or so they tell me! Thank God I have never had occasion to set foot in those ungodly Hielands! It is good to see you, boy." That last was high praise from Lady Egidia.

"I find the Highlands a deal kinder than the Lowlands, my lady," he told her. "And the King's governance better carried out than here!"

"Ah. By which you mean that outlawry is not enforced there — since all are more or less outwith the law, anyway?"

"If by the law you mean the Duke of Albany's decrees and wishes, then perhaps you are right!"

"Aye — you still harp on that string, boy! I would have thought that you might have learned more wisdom, by now."

"By wisdom, do you mean that I should agree with evil when it seems to be winning?"

"The same obstinate, self-righteous Jamie Douglas, I see! Your father has been much concerned for you."

"When last I saw him he was more concerned for . . . others!"

"Perhaps. He has had time to reconsider, however, and to decide that you were not wholly at fault."

"But I am still a landless outlaw."

"And must continue to be so, until the sentence is withdrawn. Which means, until you make your peace with my nephew Robert of Albany."

"That I will never do."

"Then you must accustom yourself to being landless and an outlaw, Jamie. For *you* will never beat Robert. And he will never relent."

"The King could remove the outlawry, for all is done in his name. There *is* still a king in this realm!"

"*Could*, but will not. John was always timorous, and afraid of Robert. Now he quakes at mention of his brother's name. Not for himself, for he wishes that he was dead. But he still has one son, you see — the child James. So long as James is there, his father will do as Robert says."

"But — this is monstrous!"

"No doubt. But it is reality, boy — Scotland, in this year of our Lord! There is none to challenge Robert now."

There was silence in the great vaulted kitchen for a little.

Jamie changed the subject. "Johnnie — he is not here? How is he?" he asked his brother.

"He has all but recovered from his wound, likewise. He was here until two days back. Then he returned to Aberdour."

"Aberdour . . .!"

James coughed. "Yes. He has been dwelling there, in your absence. Our father thought it best. In Fife, in Albany's territory, with so many of his people nearby — Lindsay, Ramorgnie and such. Safer to have the new laird there in possession . . ." His voice tailed away.

"I see." A pause. "At least I am glad that he is recovered."

"Yes. He is . . . much grateful to you."

The Lady Egidia smiled.

*   *   *

Jamie stayed at Dalkeith for a few days, in case his father had a relapse, never venturing beyond the immediate vicinity of the castle. But, not a particularly patient man ever, he quickly wearied of inactivity and being cooped up. There was still no reliable news from Teviotdale and the Border as to Albany's army, though there were rumours innumerable. The Lady Isabel

Stewart wanted him to accompany her on a round of her properties, as he had done in the past, in the interests of better management and vassalage, her present husband being slothful; but the others all agreed that this would be unwise, hazardous, since most of the former Countess of Douglas's lands and jointure properties were in the Borders, and that was the last place for Jamie to venture to in present conditions — though Isabel asserted that he would be entirely safe with her, the King's sister. In this instance, the outlaw was well enough content to accept the advice of the more cautious — since he had tentative plans of his own, and in quite another direction. He would not stay immured in his father's house like some captive, but would make a discreet and modest journey northwards rather than southwards, and in only his own company, dressed in his friar's robe again. He would go to Aberdour.

There was considerable attempted dissuasion for this course, too. But he was determined. He would return to Dalkeith before he went back to Badenoch. But meantime he had affairs to see to.

So, through the good offices of the Sub-Prior of Newbattle Abbey, illegitimate kin of his father — the abbey was only a mile or so away, and largely indebted to the Dalkeith Douglases for support — one fine July morning, dressed in the Benedictine habit, Jamie joined a monkish party *en route* for the ecclesiastical metropolis of St. Andrews in Fife. There was a constant coming and going between the abbeys and religious houses and the metropolitan see, on account of the vast trading operations of Holy Church, for which St. Andrews was the clearing-house. Newbattle specialised in two very valuable products, coal and salt. Fortunately it was a vessel loaded with sacks and baskets of the latter commodity which carried the travellers across the Forth, from the monks' saltpans at Salt Preston, eight miles up the estuary from Aberlady; the coal-boats made for less pleasing travel. The salt was destined for the burgh of Dysart, almost directly opposite across a dozen miles of the firth, where there was a major industry, again largely Church-run, of salting and casking herring supplied by the many little Fife fishing harbours, for export to the Low Countries and France, one of the country's most important trading assets.

The clerical voyagers were set down at Dysart then, after a breezy passage, where jennets were supplied by the Benedictine Priory of St. Dennis for their onwards journey to St. Andrews. Jamie, refusing the offer of a mount as tending to be conspicuous, resumed his role of wandering friar and set off on foot westwards the ten miles to Aberdour, by Kirkcaldy and Kinghorn.

It made a strange home-coming, that late afternoon — for this little castle above the silver sands of Aberdour Bay *was* his home, in a way none other could ever be, where he had brought his bride thirteen years before to set up house, where their children had been born and reared, where the happiest years of his life had been spent, where they had planted and improved, fashioned and built, farmed and husbanded. And now, abruptly, it was his brother's house, and he came to it in stealth.

Aberdour Castle was a typical oblong stone keep, massive and thick-walled, of four storeys and a garret, with parapet-walk and cap-house, set within a small curtain-walled courtyard containing lean-to outbuildings, with a chapel nearby older than the castle, the whole surrounded by gardens, orchard, farmery and fields, a quite ancient barony which had belonged to the Anglo-Norman families of Vipont and Mortimer before the Douglases acquired it fifty years earlier. It was a fortified house rather than any major stronghold, standing upon a defensive site above the ravine of the Dour Burn, back from the shore. There was no moat and drawbridge, although a tiny gatehouse did guard the arched entry to the courtyard. The massive gates were shut and barred at night, but seldom were even guarded by day. Jamie walked in unchallenged, save by a barking deerhound which he did not recognise. He rasped the tirling-pin on the open keep door. He was surprised that it was a fresh-faced young woman who came in answer, she, like the dog, unknown to him.

"Yes, father — and how may I serve you?" she asked, pleasantly enough.

Jamie had forgotten his monkish habit, rather. "Ah . . . yes . . . I seek John Douglas," he said. "Is he here?"

"To be sure. He is down at the bee-skeps, seeing to the clover-honey. We must see to such things whilst the good weather lasts, father. But — come you in, and I will send for Johnnie."

"My thanks — but I will go see him, myself."

"But . . . you do not know where to go?"

"Yes. I, I have been here before." He realised that she was looking at him curiously. Perhaps he did not sound very like a cleric. It came to him also that she had called his brother Johnnie, not the master or the laird; and had said that she would send for him, not go for him.

In a corner of the old orchard, behind the chapel, he found Johnnie and two other men at the sticky business of extracting the clover combs from the skeps and spinning them in drums to run the honey out. He had thrown back his cowl now, so that his brother recognised him at once — the two helpers likewise, men of his own.

"Jamie!" Johnnie cried. "God be good — it is yourself! Here's a wonder. How good!" He came to embrace him, sticky hands and all.

John Douglas was his full brother. They were sons of a Dalkeith steward's daughter whom their father had fallen in love with in his youth, but whom the heir to such wealth and power could by no means wed — especially as he had been betrothed from an early age to the daughter of the then Earl of Dunbar and March. The young woman had died after the difficult birth of Johnnie, and the bereaved father had insisted on rearing the boys in his own house, making little difference between them and his later and legitimate offspring by the Lady Agnes of Dunbar. So Jamie was the old lord's first-born and indeed, until recently, favourite child, however unlawfully begotten — although he could never be heir. Johnnie, however, was very different in appearance, as in nature, a tall, sandy-haired happy-go-lucky extrovert, more like his half-brother Will, lacking any great depth of character but excellent company. It was now ten months since Jamie had brought him back, wounded, from the fatal field of Homildon.

"You are well? Fully recovered?" Jamie asked, always stiffer than he intended to be on these occasions. He also sought to make recognitions towards the two other men.

"Yes, yes. Arrow-wounds heal quickly — if they do not kill you! And you, Jamie? How do you manage? In those Hielands, in mist and snow and floods, among Erse-speaking savages? We often speak of you. Feel for you."

"I am much beholden!" his brother jerked, more stiffly than ever. "But — it is not like that. The country nor the people."

"How does Mary abide it?"

"She abides it very well. Alex Stewart is a kind host and good companion. We live passing well."

"So long as he is your *friend*! Can you trust him? After what he did to Drummond."

"So you have swallowed that tale also! It is false. Put about by Albany — if indeed the killing itself was not Albany's planning."

"Oh, come you, Jamie — you were ever crazed about the Governor! He is a hard man — but scarce so ill as you would have him."

"It is good to have your word for that!" the other snapped.

"M'mm. I, I can but judge by what I know, not what I, or you, may fear, man. He has never done me any hurt."

"No. Indeed, he has served you passing well! You would not be sitting here, so snugly, in Aberdour, were it not for Robert Stewart and his sentence of outlawry upon me!"

Johnnie shot a sidelong glance at him. "No. But . . . that is . . ." His voice tailed away.

His brother drew a deep breath. "I ask your pardon," he got out. "That was ill said."

"It is all yours still, you know, Jamie," Johnnie said uncomfortably. "I but hold it for you."

"Not so. In law the barony, all three baronies, are yours. I signed all my rights away. Our father said it was the only way. And better to you than to James or Will, who have plenty."

"Even so, when you are free of the outlawry, you can claim it all back." Thankfully he changed the subject. "Tell me, Jamie — how got you here? How did you win through? I never thought to see you. Did none seek to hold you?"

"I came by ship . . ."

As they walked back to the castle, Jamie paused. "Johnnie — that young woman who answered the door when I chapped — who is she?"

The other shrugged, a shade uneasily. "Ah, that was Jeannie. Jeannie Boswell, of Balmuto."

"So?"

"She . . . ah . . . we, we like each other well. Balmuto is a barony, some few miles inland. As you will know."

"I know Balmuto, yes. And the Boswells thereof. But Jeannie I know not."

"She is the youngest daughter. Old Boswell died. His son's wife now rules at Balmuto. She and Jeannie do not agree. A hard, managing woman."

"So Jeannie has come to live with you?"

"Yes. I needed a woman about the house . . ."

"But you are not wed?"

"No. I . . . ah . . . no. I fear that our father would not approve. He desires me to marry some heiress, with lands and siller. You know how he is about such things. Jeannie has nothing."

70

"So you live with her but do not wed her."

His brother frowned. "See you, Jamie — it is plaguily difficult. I have just had all this property put in my name. I do not wish to offend my father. He is old, and like to die, soon. No time to wed against his wishes . . ."

"Lest he disinherits you? Overlooks you in his will?"

"There is that, yes. But it would be an ill time to hurt the old man."

"Oh, yes. And Mistress Jeannie? Is she not . . . concerned?"

"She is prepared to wait, until, until . . ."

"Until my lord dies! She is very understanding, compliant!"

"We understand each other. Sufficiently to wait."

"Ah, yes. But I vow that you have not waited for everything!" The other grinned. "You know how we are made!" he said.

Jean Boswell was somewhat abashed when she learned of the visitor's true identity, not unnaturally, and Johnnie became almost boisterous in seeking to put her at ease. Jamie, for his part, knew a certain sympathy with her, despite the pangs it gave him to see her acting mistress of his Mary's house and home — which she did seemingly with fair competence. Presently he found that he was liking the girl. She was bonny, straightforward, and clearly doted on Johnnie. He reckoned that his brother could have done a lot worse for himself, whatever might be their father's verdict.

He explained that he had come to Aberdour mainly to recover certain personal belongings, especially of Mary's, which they had left behind them in their hurried departure, certain clothing, some jewellery and one or two items of furniture, household goods to which she was particularly attached. Also some treasures of the children. The small items he could take with him, when he went; but the heavier things would have to be packed for despatch by ship from Dysart to the Moray coast.

Johnnie and Jeannie declared themselves only too glad to see to this, if he picked the items out for them.

He had to admit then that this was not the only reason for his quite risky visit. The fact was that he had certain enquiries to make, in Fife. Sir William Lindsay of Rossie's house was situated not very far away, in the Eden valley near Auchtermuchty; and while Lindsay himself would probably be away with this odd expedition of the Governor's, being a creature of Albany's, there might well be information to be gleaned at Rossie anent a possible Highland visitor to that establishment.

Jamie explained briefly about Sir Duncan Stewart of Loch-an-Eilean.

The couple heard him out, intrigued and excited, Johnnie declaring that he would be happy to go and make discreet enquiries for him. But Jamie asserted that this was something that he must do for himself. Only he knew the right questions to ask, and what to look for. Besides, there were dangers in this, and he was not going to have them involved. He was quite definite about that. But Johnnie could assist, in a minor way.

So next morning, in the guise of a groom, he rode behind his brother northwards across Fife, against the grain of the land, climbing gently, past the barony of Balmuto, Jeannie's home, through the Carden Forest, to cross the River Ore at Cluny and on to Leslie, mounting towards the spine of the great peninsula. Dipping down beyond into the broad vale of the Eden, at Dunshalt, some score of miles from Aberdour, he dismounted, leaving his brother to turn back the four miles to Falkland, where was Albany's main Fife seat, there to ask only certain carefully rehearsed and discreet questions; whilst he himself donned his friar's robe and cowl and started his walk towards the estate and small castle of Rossie some two miles to the north-east, on the edge of its wide and shallow loch, which he had to circle.

There was no village of the name, but a millton and small castleton, half-a-mile apart. At the first, where a stream entered the loch, Jamie ascertained from the miller that the laird indeed was from home, gone south with the Governor; but that his lady was there. He explained that it was not Sir William Lindsay himself that he sought, but for a friend who he believed might be in Sir William's company. Had the laird taken a party with him on this Border expedition?

He had indeed, the miller said — had not their own son gone, and a score of others. But his reverence's friend would be of the gentry, no doubt? In which case he could not help him, knowing nothing of what went on at that level. He should go speak with Sir William's steward.

Carefully avoiding the said steward, Jamie made for the castleton cot-houses, where he changed his tune somewhat, adopting a travesty of a sing-song Highland lilt, and declared that he was seeking a kinsman who had, he thought, come here some two months before, from the Highlands. Had anyone seen a Highlandman, a gentleman mind, visiting Rossie?

The place had the usual low-browed alehouse, and the slut who ran it hooted at this quest for a Hielant gentleman. There was no such thing, she asserted loudly, and the reverend father-in-God ought to ken it. The only Hielantmen who had crossed her door these many months were two black-avised, half-naked caterans with not a word of Christian speech between them, drunken hairy rascals that she had put to sleep in her henhouse.

Jamie sadly averred that these could be no kin of his, to be sure. He was after looking for a tall, fair-haired, fine-looking figure of a young man, who could speak with as good a Scots tongue as himself. He was turning away, at the woman's skirled laughter, when a thought occurred to him.

"What were they doing at Rossie, these two *borachs*?" he asked, mildly.

"Och, waiting just," he was told. "Idle. Naething to do but idle themsel's. And get between a decent woman's feet."

"To be sure. But why, here?"

"Waiting for their maister, what else? Up at the castle. Some freend o' the laird's, who had to be taken to Falkland to see the Duke."

"Ah. And this master? Was *he* tall and fair?"

"Och, I but saw him once — a guid-way off. Yon kind dinna frequent *my* hoose, reverence. A right tall swack lad, he lookit. But nae Hielandman, mind. Na, na — nae bare-shankit heathen yon, but a decent Christian gentleman by the looks o' him."

"You did not hear the name of this Christian gentleman with the Highland servants?"

"Fegs, no — the laird took him to Falkland, that's a' I ken."

"And after? Did he come back from Falkland? And then go south with Sir William, in the Duke's array?"

"As to that, I dinna ken. But he and his billies went when the laird did — Goad be thankit! I canna tell your reverence mair."

Thereafter Jamie risked a brief call at the kitchen premises of Rossie Castle itself, enquiring for a mythical visitor named MacAlastair, of some weeks back. And when knowledge of such was denied by the domestics, went on to ask if any Highlander had been there recently, whatever the name — again to draw a blank. It seemed that these good folk classed all Highlanders as bare-kneed wearers of tartan who spoke only a barbarous tongue and were definitely non-gentle. Mention of the tall swack gentleman that the laird had taken to Falkland produced

73

no name; evidently Lindsay had not named him to any — perhaps in itself significant? The only point gained from his somewhat dangerous interrogation was that the gentleman had had a strangely soft sort of voice. Further Jamie dared not go. To ask to see Lady Lindsay would have been too hazardous. Apart from the fact that she might possibly have recognised him, from some Court appearance, he would have to uncowl his head before her and reveal that he had no tonsure.

He had to be content, then, with what he had learned — or, not learned but garnered and deduced. The probability was that it *was* Sir Duncan Stewart who had come to Rossie with his two gillies, had been taken for interview with the Duke of Albany, and thereafter had gone with Lindsay and the rest on this peculiar Border expedition, presumably more or less anonymously. There was no proof, but it all made sense and had a likelihood about it.

Reasonably satisfied, he retraced his steps to Dunshalt, where he found Johnnie waiting. As he had feared, his brother had failed to glean anything of value at Falkland. The place was too large, with far too much coming and going at the ducal castle for any but the most kenspeckle callers to be noted by the citizenry — and clearly Duncan Stewart would avoid being that.

They turned homewards, and rode as far as the burgh of Leslie before night overtook them, where they put up in an inconspicuous change-house, Jamie very much the groom again.

Two days thereafter, he set off on his return to Dalkeith, promising to say nothing to his father or brothers about Jeannie Boswell of Balmuto.

*   *   *

The journey back was less expeditious than had been the outwards one. First he was delayed at Dysart, waiting for a suitable vessel. And when eventually he found a skipper who would take him across Forth, they were held up grievously by contrary winds, reaching almost gale force, causing the craft twice to put back to harbour. It was all highly annoying when, between the driving rain-squalls, he could actually *see* the Fawside and Edmonstone ridges cradling Dalkeith, from Dysart.

When at last he reached his father's house, it was to find all in a state of some excitement. There was news from the Border, and from further afield still — astonishing news. Hotspur Percy was dead. And the Earl of Douglas was wounded once again, and more prisoner than ever — Henry Plantagenet's prisoner this time.

In the old lord's bedchamber Sir Archibald Douglas of Cavers, who had brought the news, Sir Will of Mordington, and the brothers James and Will, were in voluble discussion when Jamie was ushered in. All talking at once, it was some time before he gained any fuller information than these salient points.

"By the Mass — quiet, will you!" he burst out, at length, scarcely respectfully. "You, Archie — since you seem to be the fount of this — you tell it, of a mercy!" Bastard though he might be, not to mention landless outlaw, the others involuntarily acknowledged him to be the strongest man there by doing as he said.

"It was a ploy, Jamie — a trick. The whole Cocklaws business," Sir Archibald of Cavers, illegitimate son of the murdered hero, Earl James of Douglas, declared. Three years younger than Jamie, he had been knighted at the same time, after the fateful field of Otterburn. "When Albany arrived at Cocklaws — and he had taken his time, by God — it was to find Hotspur and the Earl Archie gone. Gone by many days ..."

"Gone, where?"

"Gone back to England. And not just to Northumberland, but south, far south. To Shrewsbury, no less."

"Shrewsbury? But, that is on the Welsh Marches!"

"Aye, so I am told. So Albany and his fifty thousand sat down around Cocklaws — a small Border peel-tower! The most crazy-mad thing any Scots army has ever done, I swear! It is only a mile or two from Cavers, mark you. And there they waited, idle. Idle save for stealing my cattle, for their pots! When I went to see what was to do, there was some fool story that Hotspur had made a knightly compact with Albany that if he had not come to claim it again by the first day of August, Cocklaws would revert to the Scots. And with it his claim to the whole earldom of Douglas! He was claiming, mind, that King Henry had given him the earldom, as reward for winning Homildon — an English king gifting the Douglas earldom! The bairns-play insolence of it!"

"Scarce bairns-play. That was Henry's way of mocking the Percy, whom he hates — and deriding Scotland. That is *all* he gave Hotspur for the victory — the earldom of Douglas, if he could take it! To support this English claim that their kings are Lords Paramount of Scotland. The old story. But — why Cocklaws? A small place, of no importance, not even one of the Earl Archibald's own houses. Gledstanes thereof is a vassal of *yours*, is he not? Even if he had assailed your Cavers, there would be more point to it . . ."

"That is just it! He, Percy, did not *want* a fight. As he would have got at Cavers, foul fall him! It was just a ploy, a play-acting, an excuse."

"To what end, man?"

"All was but excuse to assemble an army. And to have Albany assemble one also. Against *Henry*."

"Guidsakes!"

"Hotspur had turned rebel! He is kin to Roger Mortimer, who has better right to the throne than Henry the usurper. He and the Percy have ever been unfriends."

"But would Albany play this game? Aid Percy's revolt? He was to invade England — behind Hotspur, from Cocklaws?"

"That is what is claimed. The reason for the entire strange business. Cocklaws was but an excuse for both sides to muster large armies without causing Henry to take fright."

"I see, yes — I see. Yes — and I vow that there is more of Albany's twisted mind behind this than the Percy's! Only — Albany would stand to gain the more, that is equally certain! What — beyond a share in the possible defeat of Henry? And gaining his son back, and the Earl Douglas? There will be more than that?"

"Who knows? To show him as a successful commander, perhaps? And he could do with that, by God! But, if so, it was not to be."

"You mean, this of Hotspur's death? What went wrong?"

"There was a great battle at this Shrewsbury, they say. Hotspur was slain. Our Earl fought gallantly, leaving Hotspur's van. Indeed he all but captured Henry, but fell, wounded once more. His usual luck! Dunbar fought on the King's side. But Henry won. The Earl is *his* prisoner now, and the revolt over."

"And Albany?"

"Cannily, Albany had not moved from Cocklaws. Possibly he never intended to. When this word reached him he sent a small force to make a demonstration over the Border, whilst he packed up his pavilions. He is now on his way home, with his fifty thousand — having cleansed Scotland of the English! And not a drop of blood shed!"

"Aye — that sounds like Robert Stewart!"

"And by the same token, Jamie, it means that *you* were better on your way!" his father intervened, fairly strongly for a man who had been at death's door so recently. "Once Robert is back in these parts, it will not take him long to learn that you are in the Lowlands. For he has spies everywhere — even in Dalkeith, I have no doubt. It is an ill matter to send you from my house again — but it is for your own good."

Jamie nodded grimly. "And . . . sundry others! But, yes — I will go. Forthwith. Besides, since you look like to live a while yet, there is naught to hold me."

"Yes. God willing. You saw Johnnie?"

"To be sure. All is well with Johnnie — passing well. Quite the laird!"

"Good. I have had the Sub-Prior over, from Newbattle. He is seeing to ship-passage for you to St. Andrews, then on north-wards. He will see to all."

"You waste no time, my lord!"

"It is for the best, boy. Robert Stewart must not get his hands on you. It will not take him long to reach Lothian. Is there aught that you require? Gear? Siller? James will see to it . . ."

Jamie nodded.

V

JAMIE DOUGLAS HAD become very much a travelling man — as
of course befitted a landless adventurer. Hardly had he won
back to Lochindorb, via the port of Nairn, in mid-August,
than he was off again, south by east, for Kildrummy, in haste.
The Lady Mariota had a touching faith in his ability to influence
Alex Stewart for good, wisdom, moderation — something he
found hard to understand. And on this occasion, Mary abetted
her, despite her husband's late absence in the South. And those
two women represented a daunting coalition.

It seemed that some ten days before, a messenger had arrived
from the Countess of Mar, with a letter — a letter which, whatever else, had the effect of setting Alex by the ears. He had not
divulged its contents to them, but had hastily summoned together some two hundred armed men and marched off with them,
without delay, in the direction of Mar, merely saying that he had
urgent business to attend to. Mariota, of course, was convinced
that it was some new deep and nefarious plot of the Countess
Isobel's, to the detriment of her son's repute and well-being. He
was a fool about this woman, if in little else. That she was bad
for him, the veriest child could see. Mary evidently agreed with
this last, at least. Jamie was considered to have more weight
with Alex than had anyone else. He must go after him, therefore,
to Kildrummy or wherever he had gone, to seek dissuade him
from major follies. Let him remind the former Justiciar that,
since he had obstinately insisted on resigning that office, he no
longer had the right to range the country with large bodies of
armed men. It was a blatant breaking of the King's peace, and
could give the Governor just the excuse he required to declare
Alex forfeit and outlaw.

So here he was riding the now quite familiar route, by mid-

Strathspey, Glen Livet and the Mounth passes, with Tom Durie, the Aberdour steward's son, and two running gillies as escort, a man on an urgent errand to do he knew not what.

He had no certainty even that it was Kildrummy that Alex had made for; but it seemed sensible to call there in the first instance. On the second day of his journey, therefore, after passing the night at Invernahaven in the Braes of Glen Livet, he crossed the watershed of the Ladder Hills and slanted down Glen Buchat to the wide valley of the middle Don. And even from a distance, it was fairly evident that he did not require to go further than Kildrummy. For, camped around the castle on its mound was a sizeable force, the blue smokes of its cooking-fires ascending on the golden evening air. The music of bagpipes, thin and high, made it clear that it was a Highland host, too.

In the castle itself he found himself welcomed with a heart-warming enthusiasm by Alex, if with less obvious delight by the Countess, as he joined them at their meal at the dais-table in the great hall. Alex seemed to look on his arrival as perfectly normal and to be expected, and was anxious to hear all his news from the South. It took some considerable time and conversational tacking before Jamie could work round to the reason for Alex's presence, with an armed force, at Kildrummy.

"Sir Jamie is agog, Alex," the Countess said, at length. "He has been sent here by your mother expressly to save you from my clutches — if he can! He is at a loss to know what he is at or where to begin! Have pity on him, and tell him what's to do."

"Is that true, Jamie?" the other asked, shaking his fair head. "Did my mother send you?"

Jamie Douglas was no expert prevaricator. "She would have me to come, yes. But myself I wanted to see you, Alex, at the earliest. I have much to tell you, concerning Albany . . ."

"We can tell you something about Albany, our own selves!" the other interjected. "For that is why I am here."

"You say so? Is his arm stretching up here, then, from the Borders?"

"He has a long arm, yes — if a crooked one!" His friend toyed with his goblet. "He uses men, and women, like inanimate things, tools, weapons, dirks — aye, dirks!"

"Go on, my love. To the point," the lady urged. "Or must I?"

"Aye. You will recollect our, our indebtedness to John Stewart of Coull, Jamie — or mine, at least — at the trial? And you may possibly know that he greatly favours the Lady Isobel here?

Well, my uncle Albany is damnably well-informed, it seems — even when on his expeditions. Learning of this, he has sought to turn all to his own advantage. He has sent the Countess word, as Governor of the realm that, in the realm's interests, powerful earldoms cannot be allowed to languish in weak women's hands! As bound to be coveted and fought over by the unscrupulous and power-seekers. He therefore sends his regrets at her husband's unhappy death, and proposes, for the Countess's comfort and protection, no less than the realm's weal, that she should be wed forthwith to a suitable and reliable candidate — to wit, his own son John Stewart of Coull! Who would thereupon become Earl of Mar, and ensure the Countess's safety from adventurers, the well-being of the earldom and the best advantage of the kingdom. The said John would also be appointed Justiciar of the North."

"So-o-o! That sounds like Albany, yes. Clever, I swear — yes, clever! John Stewart, I take it, will be far from loth!"

"To be sure," the Countess agreed, smiling. "Even at my age!"

"That is the devil of it!" Alex said. "John does not greatly love his father, and might well disobey him on occasion. But not in this instance! He had already proposed marriage to Isobel."

"A pleasant youth, my dear."

"Aged twenty-two years. Half your age!"

"But offering marriage — where you do not, my so-elderly Alex!"

"Isobel — be serious, of a mercy!"

"I am, my love — since it is *my* life that is being disposed of, is it not? It seems that married again I must be. The Governor insists!"

"He has no power to force you, has he?" Jamie asked.

"Not directly, no. But indirectly he can do much to . . . persuade! He could have the Privy Council declare the earldom of Mar to be improperly managed, and a danger to the realm. Because the earls of Scotland are, in a sense, lesser kings, as regards the *Ard Righ*, the High King, the Crown has certain concern in their disposal . . ."

"He would do that if *I* was to wed you, and become Earl of Mar!" Alex interposed.

"Perhaps. But then, you could muster my forces, and your own, and oppose any interference from the Council or the Crown, which a mere woman can scarcely do. Also, using the King's powers, he could take away sundry of my lands and revenues. He might even take me into custody—he has done stranger things than that! It might be less trouble to marry his son!"

Jamie looked from one to the other, Alex visibly upset and concerned, the Countess almost seeming to enjoy herself, playing her double game blatantly.

"What is the reason for the armed force you brought with you, Alex?" he asked.

"That is to show Albany that two can play his game. That we know what he is at. I am showing him that he is too late. That I am taking over this castle and earldom."

"You mean . . . ?"

"He means, Sir James, that he prefers to do this, to seem to take by force what he could gain in free gift! A strange man, is he not? Was ever a woman thirled to so unnatural a lover! He must rape and ravage where he might sweetly enjoy!"

"Isobel! A God's name — how can you speak so!"

"I speak in figure, of course! Sir James will understand? Alex is prepared to come and take over my house and heritage by force, rather than to marry me and gain it lawfully. Can you understand *that*? He scarce flatters a woman, does he?"

"That is not the way of it at all, Jamie! I will rejoice if I may wed Isobel — one day. But not within but a few months of the murder of her husband, whom my unfriends declare that I starved to death. Surely that is not difficult to understand? My name and fame and honour demand it . . ."

"Name, fame and honour — how very much a *man's* notion of marriage!" the woman mocked. "And not every man! *I* see our union otherwise. Concerned with warmer, tender things."

Jamie cleared his throat. "I still do not understand this of your force outside, Alex. What are they here for?"

"They are here to seem to take over this castle by armed strength, man. Is that not clear enough? To serve warning to Albany, John of Coull and any other, that *I* am in possession. That I, by *force majeure*, have prevailed upon the Countess of Mar to make over to me, by charter hereafter, her castle, property and earldom, in default of her own issue. I would have believed that sufficiently plain." That was said in a forced voice and manner so unlike Alex's normal as to cause Jamie to blink. He looked at the Countess, who smiled.

"The lady agrees . . . to this?" he got out.

"It was the lady's suggestion."

"Only as but a poor second choice, my dear. If you had agreed to marriage, right away, none of it would have been necessary. But, since you are so concerned with your honour, I proposed this alternative. Although I cannot see how honour is enhanced . . ."

"It is *your* honour that gains by it, woman!" That was almost exasperatedly said. "Do you not see? *Will* you not see? Yours. To be sure, you see — or you would not have suggested it! This way your name is preserved. You have been forced. But it will give John Stewart and his father pause. And any others with designs on you. They will recognise that they will have to come in force, be prepared to fight, to gain you and your earldom now. After, in due course, if you still will have me, we can wed."

"In due course! How long is this sorry woman to wait upon your honour?"

"Give me a year, Isobel. Twelve months. Then the thing can be done with some decency."

"Your description of our nuptials, Alex, might not content *every* woman! When Brave John would wed me tomorrow! But . . . if you insist . . ."

Jamie stared from one to the other. "Dear . . . God!" he said. And, after a pause. "You understand what this will mean? You fully realise, Alex, that it will give Albany most ample opportunity and cause to outlaw you? If he so desires. You will be declared cateran and brigand."

"By some, no doubt — but they would say that anyway. Others will see it differently. As I shall inform the Privy Council. I, as recent Justiciar, see it as necessary to preserve the King's peace, here in the North. I have had word of attempts to be made on the earldom, to coerce the Countess. I need not mention John of Coull. But it is necessary to protect the Countess. The earldom of Mar, in wrong hands, could be a grievous danger. It can raise many thousands of men. *I* have had no word from the Governor. Until I am replaced as Justiciar, it is my duty to safeguard and ensure the King's peace — thus."

"M'mm. I fear not a few will see it much otherwise, Alex!"

"That is how *I* see it — which is what signifies, at this present!"

"I cannot think it wise . . ."

"Then what do you propose instead? Out with it, Jamie."

Helplessly that man shook his head. "Since it cannot be lawful, how can you claim it your duty as former Justiciar?"

"Ah, but it is lawful, Sir James," the Countess said. "If *I* agree to it. The earldom is *mine*, and all within it. If I give Alex a charter of it all, duly signed and sealed, the thing is lawful —

for all is within my gift, meantime. Although it grieves me to say it, marriage is not *necessary*. A countess in her own right — or indeed an earl — can bestow the earldom on whom she, or he, may designate, resigning it into other hands. The King must confirm, yes. But for the King *not* to confirm would require an especial hearing before parliament. Albany himself would be the last to contest the legality of this, for *he* gained the earldom of Fife thus, not marrying the Countess thereof, who was his brother's widow. Robert Stewart was already married to the Countess of Menteith — gaining *that* earldom from her; but he prevailed upon the unhappy Countess of Fife, by what means has never been made clear, to make over Fife to him. She was known greatly to dislike him. That, indeed, is what gave me the notion for this."

"It was *your* notion, then?"

"To be sure. Think you I would allow this to be imposed on me?"

Jamie shrugged. "You both know more of it all than do I — the legality. But I do not like it."

"You mean, the Lady Mariota de Athyn will not like it, Sir James? And you to fail her in your mission!"

"No. That is as may be. It is myself who sees it all as dangerous. For Alex. Even if not unlawful. It will take him long to live this down — if ever he does."

"What is the alternative then, Jamie?" his friend insisted. "If I do not this, and do not marry Isobel forthwith, Albany will make all endeavour to have his son wed her. With all the resources of the kingdom behind him."

Jamie could not say that this might be no such bad outcome, that the Countess was not the wife for Alex, that John of Coull might indeed make none so ill an Earl of Mar. His friend loved and wanted this woman. And needed, or conceived himself to need, the manpower and resources of her earldom to retain his position and safety in the North. He spread his hands eloquently.

"This charter — is it to be something of a deed of gift? A marriage contract for the future? Will it specify marriage hereafter?"

"It does not. It is already drawn up and ready. We have considered it well. It is no marriage contract, nor betrothal document. Isobel honours me by resigning all her properties and powers into my hands, without stated condition. It will seem as

83

though I had forced it upon her, by main strength and armed might. But I would liefer have that than be named as the man who had foully slain her husband in order to marry her. I cannot make it more clear."

"You make it entirely clear, my love!" the lady said, grimacing.

Jamie held his peace.

"Now — what have *you* to tell us about Albany's doings in the South? And your own position now?" Alex demanded, as though thankful to change the subject.

"My own position is that I am still outlaw, and my brother sits snug in Aberdour Castle! But says he will give it back when I am a free man again — if ever. As to Albany, I tell you sufficient to show that the man is cleverer even than *I* had thought! He used Hotspur Percy as excuse to raise a large army — which he had little intention of using. He seemed to avenge Homildon, by driving the English from Scots soil — without a sword drawn or a drop of blood shed! He put himself in a position to gain greatly had Hotspur triumphed in his rebellion against King Henry, mustering to possibly aid the revolt. But when the Percy was slain and the revolt failed, he was able to return quietly home with his army, never having so much as set foot on English soil. Whatever Henry may suspect, he has no case against Albany. He comes back, position at home strengthened — and at no cost."

"On my soul, perhaps I should indeed embrace the man as a good-sire, so clever is he!" the Countess exclaimed. "You sound almost sorry that there was no bloodshed, Sir James?"

"No. Only that he can fool the realm so cheaply."

"Is that not part of the art of kingship? For Albany is king in all that matters. I think that he might have made a fair enough king — better than his brother or father, at least. For if he had done all this, as king, you would have been the first to praise him, I swear!"

"No," Jamie denied. "Not so. It would still have been chicanery, deceit. My father also says that he might have made a good king. But I say that is wrong. A deceiver, a man dishonest, without scruple, can never well rule a kingdom."

"There I differ with you. Kings must often be all these — since state craft itself is partly thus. We cannot judge rulers as we do other men."

"Whether we can or no," Alex intervened, "at least we are further warned how cunning is the man we are seeking to

84

counter. To be better on our guard. Did you learn anything, Jamie, of our especial business? Or *mine*, of Duncan?"

"I cannot prove it, but I believe that he went south with the Governor, in Lindsay's train. I am fairly well persuaded that he went from here to Rossie, in Fife, as we thought that he might, to render his report on Sir Malcolm Drummond's death, was taken to Falkland to see Albany. And later went with Lindsay and his men in the Border adventure."

"And then . . . ?"

"I heard nothing more. I did not linger to await the Governor's return!"

"To be sure. So Duncan is now of my, and his, uncle Albany's party! And a further danger to us all."

"And to himself, I think. Albany's tools are apt to have short lives!"

* * *

Next day Jamie was shown the charter which the couple had drawn up, and the two copies which the castle chaplain was making of it. In effect, it delivered the earldom — although not the title and powers of Earl of Mar — into Alex's hands, to manage as he saw fit, and to retain for so long as it was not required of him by any heirs of the Countess's body. Since, at forty-four, she had had no offspring, despite indubitably a considerable variety of bedding, the probability was that this clause would remain inoperative. But it gave the impression that the heritage of future generations of the ancient line was being considered. The original paper, duly witnessed, was to be retained by Alex, whilst one copy was for the King's consideration and the other for Albany. The timing and method of delivery of these two documents to their appropriate destinations was the subject of considerable debate.

The hope was that the monarch, feeble as he was, might be given his in secret and prevailed upon to endorse it before ever Albany saw his own copy or heard what was to do. Obviously this would not be easy to achieve. To get the paper down to Turnberry Castle in Ayrshire, the recluse King's retreat, unsuspected, would be a problem in itself; whilst to have it smuggled into the sovereign's presence, behind Albany's myriad spies and minions, and get it out again, endorsed, would be no mean feat. But that was what was required if the project was to have fullest effect.

Out beyond the lowered drawbridge-head, looking over the

stirring scene of the Highlanders' camp there, in the mellow autumn forenoon sunshine, watching the Braemoray and Badenoch clansmen at their strenuous amusements, tossing cabers, putting heavy stones, wrestling and the like, Jamie Douglas made up his mind, although reluctantly.

"It will have to be myself," he declared. "I do not see how any other could achieve it. Only through one of the princesses can the King be reached. The Lady Isabel best. She hates her brother Albany sufficiently. On none of the others could I prevail, I think."

Alex looked at him. "I am not sufficiently hypocrite, Jamie, to pretend that I had not thought the same, myself. It is a scurvy fortune that it should have to be *you* who should make this hazardous venture, you not myself. But I have no especial links with the princesses, nor with the King either — although he is my uncle. I scarce know him, or them. Nor do I know the Lowlands as do you. Neither am I a Douglas, with a Lowland voice. I will come with you, but it is you, I fear, who must achieve the business."

"Yes . . ."

"That would be folly, Alex," the Countess said. "For you to go, also. Dangerous and needless. Besides, your place is here. This mission might take a considerable time, and who knows what could happen here in the North the while? Do you not agree, Sir James?"

He nodded. "I do. It would achieve nothing — but good company for myself."

"Two heads can improve on one, on occasion."

"Perhaps. But I have learned that a single wandering friar can go far, unchallenged. But two such are seldom seen together. That would attract notice. No, I am better alone, Alex. You must see it?"

"Your Mary will not like this."

"Mary will understand very well. She is as concerned for your cause as I am. We are your guests, after all."

"I had not thought to have you pay for your lodging thus, man!"

"No. But it is something only I can do. Or attempt — since I may not be successful. God knows. Give me a few days at Lochindorb with Mary and the bairns, and I am your man."

"I mislike it," the other said. "But I see no other way, with the smell of success to it . . ."

VI

TEN DAYS LATER, therefore, the travelling man was on his
way again. This time, out of much thought, he was following a different route, despite the fact that he now had the
east coast sea route all but perfected, for secret travel. He
reckoned that the major danger-point of his venture might well
be in getting away from the royal castle of Turnberry after his
mission was completed — should he ever get that far. He might
have to leave in haste. In which case experience of unobtrusive
flight by the *west* coast could be valuable.

So, instead of journeying eastwards to find a ship at one of
the Moray ports, he headed south-westwards by upper Strathspey and down the great rift of the Laggan valley, across the
watershed of Scotland, making for Lochaber in the first instance,
and then further south to Appin. Alex insisted on accompanying
him on this early stage of his journey, with a score of gillies —
for Lochaber was ever a dangerous place for raids by the Islesmen, not major invasions like Alastair Carrach's but constant
petty incursions by individual bands who looked on this area as
their legitimate prey, much as the Borderers did the English
Marches. He would take him to the Priory of Ardchattan, in the
Benderloch district of South Appin, whence it was hoped that
onward transport would be available.

It was early November but still colourful autumn in the warm
Highland West, with the weather open and the rivers not yet
running full to make travel difficult. Nothing of course enabled
them to avoid the constant great detours made necessary by the
long sea-lochs which constituted the principal obstacle to travel
in this land; but Alex knew the terrain well — since in theory he
might lay claim to be Lord of Lochaber, this having been one of
his father the Wolf's many titles — and he was able to take many

short-cuts by little-used passes and drove-roads, by causeways through peat-bogs and by ferry-scows. The latter were usually run by churchmen, with adjacent hospices of a sort for travellers, even in this wild country, and Alex's policy of keeping on good terms with the Church was again proved wise. They were not attacked by any, Islesmen or others.

They turned due southwards in the Braes of Lochaber country, crossed Spean, and took a lonely climbing drove-route through the empty mountains by the Lairig Liacach and Mamore to Loch Leven. Avoiding the terrible wastes of the Moor of Rannoch they went west through Duror of Appin, made the circuit of Loch Creran and came at last through Benderloch to great Loch Etive and the Firth of Lorn.

Ardchattan was one of only three Valliscaulian monasteries in Scotland. But since the largest was at Pluscarden, near Elgin, and Alex had taken the precaution of obtaining a letter of introduction from the Prior there, of old acquaintance, they were well received. The Priory was situated on the northern shore of Etive, not far from the great castle of Dunstaffnage, the keepers of which, since the Bruce's time, were Campbells. Alex was uncertain as to this potentate's allegiances, and was not disposed to linger long in the vicinity. He handed over Jamie to the Prior, stayed but the one night, and departed early the next morning after an affectionate and rather anxious farewell.

The Valliscaulians were great tillers of the soil, stock-breeders and wool-growers, and much of the produce of their, and their tenants' farms granges, tanneries and mills had to be sent to the South to obtain the revenues desired by Holy Church. As a consequence there were frequent shipments sent from the loch-side pier, especially in the autumn when the various harvests were over and before the winter storms closed a dangerous seaboard to prudent mariners. This was Jamie's objective in coming here.

A vessel had sailed, unfortunately, not long before their arrival, and he had to wait for five days for another to come in and be loaded. But the brothers, despite their notably rigorous discipline — much more so than other Orders — were not too demanding as to his falling in with their regime, as for instance in eschewing meat and rising an hour before dawn. They were not permitted to venture beyond the monastery precincts, and this applied to Jamie also — but this aided the secrecy of his presence. For an impatient man the time passed but slowly, and the visitor was left in no doubts that he was not cut out for a monastic life. But the brothers, a score of them, were friendly, and he was not ungrateful.

Eventually, covered again in his black Benedictine robe and cowl — the Valliscaulians wore white — he took leave of his hosts and boarded the *Brigid of Lennox*, of Dumbarton, with a great train of pack-horses unloading wool-sacks, bales of hides, and skins of cured leather. The vessel flew two large banners of a white Paschal Lamb on blue, the flag of the priory — which, he was assured, would alone save it from the attentions of the Lord of the Isles' galleys and the independent pirates who infested the narrow Hebridean seas. The Church's judicious admixture of tribute and anathema appeared to be effective insurance. Jamie found that a fellow-passenger had been rowed across the loch from the south shore, a Campbell merchant on his way to Glasgow; but this proved to be an uncommunicative individual prepared to keep his own company — which suited Jamie.

They had to judge their sailing time exactly, for the narrow mouth of long Loch Etive was guarded by an extraordinary submarine waterfall, which at certain stages of the tide made the passage quite unusable. Even when the timing was right, the negotiating of the Falls of Lora was quite a navigational hazard in a large vessel, and the sense of plunging downhill was alarming to the novice.

Jamie had never sailed the Sea of the Hebrides before, and he found it all a notable and even exhilarating experience and quite the most colourful journey he had ever undertaken. Had the weather been otherwise, of course, all would have been very different, he recognised. But in slight north-easterly airs and mainly clear pale-blue skies, they tacked and twisted in sparkling waters over a long, lazy swell, round islands innumerable, great and small, where seals basked and seabirds circled, past foaming skerries and towering stacks, through narrow sounds between steep mountainsides, below mighty cliffs, skirting gleaming white-sand beaches decked with multi-hued seaweeds and shallows showing every shade of blue, purple, amethyst and green. They were never far from land, had to make wide circuits and detours to avoid tidal overfalls, races and even whirlpools, and were subjected to sudden and disconcerting down-draughts from flanking hillsides and hidden valleys. More than once they sighted lurking galleys, long, lean, evil-looking craft, low-set but with soaring prows and sterns, under a single great square sail and with serried ranks of oars. But though some pulled near, possibly to check on their flag, none molested them.

The third day out they rounded the dreaded Mull of Kintyre, graveyard of shipping, on a shining sea as innocent as a baby's smile, and sailed up into the sheltered waters of the Clyde estuary between the Isle of Arran and the Ayrshire coast, Jamie actually able to see the King's castle of Turnberry, his ultimate destination, in the passing, with mixed feelings.

Beating north-eastwards now, directly into the breeze, it took them a full day and a half to reach Dumbarton. Jamie had scarcely seen the Campbell merchant throughout, for he had remained seasick in his berth most of the time — possibly the reason for his unforthcoming attitude. At the busy Clyde port they disembarked, and the cargo was unloaded for transhipment to smaller craft for the pull up-river to Glasgow and the Bishop's warehouses. Jamie made discreet enquiries at the port as to shipping likely to be sailing northwards again in a week or two, and was concerned to learn that the traffic was practically over for the season, few shipmasters being willing to risk a voyage round the Mull of Kintyre after mid-November. The cargoes and few passengers for Hebridean waters during the winter months must go by the sheltered route through the Kyles of Bute and up long Loch Fyne to Tarbert, there to land, cross the isthmus, and await another craft to carry them onwards into the Western Sea — or else travel on by land. This was normal practice — and clearly a wandering friar was expected to know it.

Jamie took passage on one of the many small craft plying the Clyde between Dumbarton and Glasgow, some fifteen miles.

He had never had occasion to visit Glasgow, and found it a small place of crowded narrow streets and twisting wynds, yet set amongst the gardens and orchards of the rich senior clergy. It was much smaller than Dumbarton, clustering round the great cathedral, with its soaring wooden spire, which tended to dwarf all else. Clearly all here was the Bishop's — at present one Matthew Glendinning, uncle to Jamie's colleague at Otterburn, Sir Simon Glendinning (but better avoided, nevertheless) — from the eight-arch stone bridge, to cross which all had to pay toll, to the strong castle or palace near the cathedral, from the expensive pilgrim shrines to the seminaries for training priests, from the leper hospital to the great rows of warehouses and stores by the riverside. It was not so large or impressive as the ecclesiastical metropolis of St. Andrews, but it gave a greater impression of dedication, notably towards amassing wealth. It did not seem the sort of place to look for aid against the ruling power.

Jamie was tempted to turn directly southwards here, to make for Turnberry, some fifty miles away — so much less difficult and hazardous than crossing Scotland to the east coast again, first. But he recognised that this would be foolish and might well bring his whole project to naught. He even toyed with the idea of making for Nithsdale, which was not so very far south-east of Turnberry, to seek the widowed Lady Gelis Stewart there, the youngest and former favourite of the King's sisters, on whom once he himself had doted. But, although she hated Albany sufficiently, blaming him for her husband's death — though this was doubtful — she was known to have become very strange, practically a recluse, seldom leaving her house. Even though she might agree to go with Jamie to Turnberry, he felt that he could not rely on her to carry out a difficult task of persuasion. It would have to be her sister Isabel.

So the next morning he left Glasgow, for the east, with staff and satchel, great walking ahead of him, since there was no alternative, a very energetic and determined friar. Deliberately he avoided the direct routes between Glasgow and Linlithgow or Stirling, where the Governor's influence might be expected to be strong and informants numerous, keeping well to the south, following up the Clyde valley as far as Cambusnethan and then taking to the higher and little populated lands of Upper Lanarkshire, country he knew but little but judged would be of small interest to Albany. Putting up at remote inns and humble change-houses, philosophically accepting the grim conditions as no worse than many he had encountered on sundry campaigns, and now carefully eschewing religious establishments or hospices where his sham status and lack of tonsure would be obvious, he pushed steadily eastwards in poor weather now, mainly in a thin cold drizzle, averaging around twenty miles each day. He spoke to few and met with no sort of challenge save the physical. Three days after leaving Glasgow he was well into Lothian — but upland Lothian. He crossed the Pentland Hills by the high pass of the Cauldstane Slap, and came down into the valley of the North Esk.

Now he had to traverse populous country, where he was

known. On the other hand, he knew every inch of it, where to go and what to avoid. Carefully he kept away from Dalkeith, and by roundabout ways presently arrived at the servants' door of the House of Edmonstone on its long ridge two miles to the north-east. Here he could throw back his cowl at last, for all knew him well. Asking for the Lady Isabel, he was thankful to learn that she was at home — which was by no means always the case.

His princess sister-in-law received him joyfully — as he had had little doubt that she would, for she had been almost too fond of him for many a year. He liked her too, but found her no rival to his Mary, and was a little embarrassed by her frank displays of affection. She was some fourteen years older than he was, but that was not the sort of thing to worry any of the Stewart women. Her present husband, Sir John Edmonstone of that Ilk, was no inhibiting factor, for he was elderly, lazy and seldom sober, though amiable enough. It had been only a marriage of convenience.

"Jamie! Jamie!" she cried, flinging her arms around him. "I was desolate, thinking not to see you again for an eternity! And now here you are back to me so soon. I can scarce believe it. Did you not return to your Hielands?"

"I have been and come again," he assured, stirring somewhat in her embrace.

"For an outlaw, my dear, you come and go in remarkable fashion!"

"I choose my paths carefully. Your husband, is he well?"

"He is, I believe, as he prefers to be — unconscious! Have you come from Dalkeith?"

"No. I came straight here. From the West — from Glasgow, which I reached by ship."

"Ah! Then I cannot suppose that it is any poor attractions of mine that have drawn you here across wide Scotland, Jamie?"

"I . . . ah . . . no. Leastways, not only that, Isabel. I need your help."

"Yes. You are ever honest, if naught else! I conjectured that was it. But . . . what can I, a weak woman, do to aid so determined an outlaw?"

"You can help in a further countering of your brother, the Duke Robert Stewart."

"Ha — you say so? For that I am seldom loth! Come to my room, Jamie, and tell me whilst you refresh yourself."

He explained Albany's plan to marry his younger son to the Countess of Mar, and Alex Stewart's plan to stop it. The Countess was Isabel's sister-in-law, also, the late Earl James of Douglas's sister.

"So-o-o! Isobel Douglas would have your friend and my nephew, Alex, Earl of Mar?"

"Yes. *She* would have him that now, wed him out-of-hand. But he will not. Declares it too soon after her husband's death. So they have conceived this plan — to forestall Albany. The Countess has made over the lands and powers of her earldom to him, in advance of marriage, in trust, by charter. And he brought a force of his Highlanders to sit around Kildrummy, to seem to invest it, to seem to force her in the matter. To aid her good name . . ."

His companion emitted what, in anyone less lofty and attractive, could have been called a hoot. "Anyone who knows Isobel of Mar would conceive it a deal too late for that!" she declared. "Alex need not be so nice!"

"So *she* says, also! But he is determined — and I well understand his mind. He is a man ever seeking to make up for the ill fame of his father."

"No doubt. But this arrangement will but injure his repute without aiding hers."

"So I told him, but he would not heed me. Forby, it is done now. The misfortune of it is, being an earldom, any such charter needs the King's assent. I have two copies of it here in my satchel. Somehow to gain the royal signature before Albany can stop it."

"And I am to persuade him?"

"I can think of none other who could."

"I do not know that I may be able, Jamie. John is a man lost, now. Drawn in on himself. Caring nothing for what goes on outside the walls of Turnberry Castle — unless it affects his son James. Now that the boy is at St. Andrews Castle in Bishop Wardlaw's care, his father appears to have nothing to live for. David's murder struck him hard, on top of Annabella's death. Now he leaves all to Robert. And prays, always prays!"

"How in God's good name does he match that with his coronation oath? To love and cherish, to rule and govern his people justly and well?"

"Do not ask me, Jamie, for I do not understand him. He never wanted to be King. He is a poor creature, weaker even than was his father. A saint without a saint's strength!"

"But . . . you will come? And try?"

"For you I will, Jamie. Not for Alex's sake — who seems to be a fool! And certainly not for Isobel Douglas's! But for you — and to spoil Robert's plans, I am willing to attempt it."

"I thank you. Alex has shown me, and Mary, great kindness. And he is no fool, I assure you. Of all the Stewarts he has the most good in him, I think. The most able and honest . . ."

"He need not be a paragon to be that!" she said. "But . . . perhaps you are right. When must we go?"

"Soon, Isabel — the sooner the better. We must act before Albany can."

"Act! You make it sound as though all we need do is go to Turnberry! How am I to persuade my brother to sign this paper? It is no clearly just cause. Indeed, it smells but ill, does it not? He will say that it is an unholy alliance, belike. Scarce made in heaven . . .!"

"Say that the other would be worse. Albany's son, John of Coull, is but twenty-two years. Only half the Countess's age. And he is to make him Lieutenant of the North and Justiciar, if he becomes Earl of Mar. Little more than a boy." Jamie paused, uncomfortably, his inconvenient and essential honesty not to be submerged thus. "Although I liked him well enough, and believe him able," he ended, lamely.

"The King will say that is naught to do with him, the Governor's business."

"We believe Albany was responsible for Sir Malcolm Drummond's murder. Like others. It would be an evil thing for his son to wed the widow."

"You think that . . .? Another murder?"

"It looks that way. We cannot prove it, once more. Albany covers his tracks well. But . . ."

"Then *I* cannot prove it to my brother, either. He will but wring his hands and hope it otherwise!"

Jamie frowned. "There is one thing that we might try," he said slowly. "Something that Alex suggested. I do not greatly like it. But it might serve. Playing on the King's weakness — to get behind his guard. You spoke of this about the Prince James. Alex, like many another, believes the boy to be in great danger — from Albany. The only life between him and the throne, now. St. Andrews Castle and the good Bishop are not strong enough to protect him, if Albany decides to remove the lad. Alex suggested that he might offer to have the prince up in Badenoch, at Lochindorb. He would be safe there, beyond the Highland Line. If the King is anxious for his remaining son, he might be thankful to have it so. Alex is his nephew too, after all."

"You mean, offer this to my brother in exchange for his signature?"

"Scarce so crudely as that! But . . . if Alex was Earl of Mar, and with the power of the earldom added to his own Lordship of Badenoch, he could offer a more notable and safer refuge for the heir to the throne than any bishop's palace. None would take the boy out of Lochindorb Castle unbidden, that I swear!"

"So might my brother fear! Delivering his darling, and all the power that would give, into the hands of the Wolf of Badenoch's son! Myself, I would hesitate!"

"Would you leave your son at St. Andrews Castle? With Albany as threat?"

"No-o-o. Oh, I do not know, Jamie. Perhaps we might try it. If all else fails." She shook her fair head. "We go quickly, then? Forthwith?"

"Aye. And secretly."

"How secretly?"

"Albany must learn, or suspect, nothing. And he has people everywhere. My father says even in Dalkeith, watching *him*. He, Albany, knows you hate him. So no doubt you are watched also. Why I came to you secretly. So you must not seem to be going to Turnberry. Some otherwhere. Do you ever visit your sister, the Lady Gelis?"

"I have not seen her this year past. She is . . . difficult. Her mind a little turned, I fear."

"Yes. But it would serve as pretext. You travel to Nithsdale. I, in your company, as your domestic chaplain. None will seek stop the King's sisters from visiting each other. Make for Nithsdale, and at Sanquhar or Durrisdeer turn west for Turnberry."

"It might serve, yes . . ."

The Lady Isabel was very much her own mistress at Edmonstone, and two mornings later they were on their way. Jamie had thought of borrowing a company of Douglas men-at-arms from Dalkeith, as escort — but decided against it as only liable to draw attention to them. The smaller the party the better, consistent with the princess's position. So, with only four of Edmonstone's men, they rode off south-westwards.

Isabel was a good horsewoman and fit enough for long days in the saddle — which was as well, for putting up overnight was bound to be a major problem, and therefore the largest daily mileage possible called for. Such as she could not sleep at lowly inns and wayside change-houses; and suitable lairdly houses or religious establishments and hospices, where they could rest secure from too much enquiry and subsequent report to the Governor's minions, were not of frequent occurrence. Fortunately most of the land to be covered was Douglas country, or that of their vassals, where Albany's influence would not be strong. Jamie had put much thought into this, reckoning the entire journey to be about one hundred miles. At this time of year it would be impracticable and unfair to seek to cover more than forty to fifty miles a day, even if Isabel was able for more — and without changing horses. Which meant two overnight halts at, say, forty and eighty mile stages. The first stage would bring them, by Kirkurd and Biggar, to the upper Clyde valley, in the Symington-Abington area. This was Lindsay of Crawford territory; and since the Earl of Crawford's wife was Isabel's sister Katherine, that should be a help. Not that the Crawfords themselves would be thereabouts — they lived mostly at their favourite castle of Edzell in Angus; but their vassals and servants would not be apt to fail or betray their master's sister-in-law. Also, Crawford was no friend of Albany's. Tower Lindsay, one of their original strongholds, was near the little burgh of Crawford itself, three miles beyond Abington. They would make that their first night's objective.

In the event, they could have gone further, for the weather improved, the land had dried considerably in a fresh breeze, the rivers were not running so high as to be difficult, and the horses were still fresh. After an early start they reached Crawford with still a couple of hours till sunset. But after this Clyde valley, their journey lay through the high and lonely Lowther Hills, and there would be little shelter for many a mile. They made for Tower Lindsay therefore, which guarded a ford of Clyde.

It could not be claimed that they did very well there. The place was little more than a stark, draughty and gloomy shell, in the keeping of a rough and oafish steward. They were received willingly enough, and the keeper probably did his best at short notice for their comfort, impressed by having a princess as guest; but clearly nobody of any quality or even modest refinement had occupied the hold for long, and its furnishings, like its provender, were of the plainest and most elementary. Fires were lit for them in chilly dank rooms which had not seen the like for years — and the resultant clouds of smoke indicated that jackdaws had taken over the chimneys. Isabel showed her spirit by making the best of it and even affecting a gay and holiday attitude. But running eyes from the wood-smoke, swirling draughts, pervading damp so that everything near the fires actually steamed, and only narrow wooden benches to sit upon, had their cumulative effect, and prevailed on her to retire early to an equally smoke-filled bedchamber where she announced that she would wrap herself in her travelling-cloak and horse-blanket rather than risk the mildewed sheepskins and soggy bed-coverings. She clung to Jamie tightly for a little at the door, and he kissed her hair before gently pushing her within.

At least they were secure from any hostile attentions.

A far from restful night saw them up with the dawn, anxious only to be on the move again. Isabel demanded to know just how far was the shortest route to Turnberry now, and when told over fifty miles, and hilly miles at that, declared that she would ride that distance and more, until she fell out of her saddle, rather than pass another night like that. Although sympathetic, Jamie was doubtful, but agreed that they should press ahead now by the most direct route and at best speed. He had intended that they took the Mennock Pass road through the Lowther Hills, as giving the impression that they were heading for Nithsdale and Dumfriess-shire, not Ayrshire and Carrick. But from discreet enquiries, and the conclusion that the Governor's grip was singularly loose in these upper Clydesdale hills, he felt that they could risk a direct westerly journey without much fear of alerting their enemies. Down-river some way there was a drove-road for the upland cattle to be taken across the Lowthers to the Cumnock fairs, partly on the line of an old Roman road. This should shorten their journey considerably.

It was a dull day with a cold wind, the clouds low on the hills; but it was dry and they made good time. Once they left the actual valley of the Clyde they saw no-one but the occasional shepherd or hillman. Hardy cattle grazed the hill-slopes, but apart from the infrequent herd's shack, there were no houses, much less communities. For some of the time they rode in the chill skirts of the clouds, which slowed them somewhat. But by soon after noon they were out of the major hills and following the Guelt Water down toward the foothill town of Cumnock, which they made shift to pass well to the south, and so down into the Ayrshire plain and populous lands again.

This was the danger area, the royal earldom of Carrick, and they certainly did not linger, chewing cold ribs of beef as they rode. They both knew the district well now, for Isabel had been reared partly at Turnberry and Dundonald, her father's favourite houses; and Jamie had quartered the vicinity in the late Prince David's spirited company years before. So they were able to avoid towns and villages as far as possible, and the houses of those who might be suspicious or inimical.

In the late afternoon, however, and only some few miles from Turnberry, their precautions proved to be inadequate. They were circling Crossraguel Abbey, wondering whether to risk a call there — for it was one of the King's favourite haunts — having already given Maybole town, the capital of Carrick, a wide berth, when one of their men announced that they were being followed. Looking round, they saw a mounted party of about a score, riding up at speed.

Jamie snorted. "We have been here before, I think!" he observed grimly. Years before, in the old King's reign, he had been escorting Isabel to visit her brother at Turnberry when they had been rudely intercepted and assailed by a party under her nephew, the Lord David Stewart — the start indeed of Jamie's love-hate relationship with that spirited and now dead prince. The memory of their alarming experience on that occasion made them draw up now in tight protective formation around the princess, swords loosened in sheaths, even the friar's.

The newcomers rode pounding up, to encircle them, amidst shouts and clanking steel. Their leader, a swarthy youngish man, handsomely dressed, spoke shortly.

"Where go you? And on what business?"

"To Turnberry. And on the *King's* business," Jamie returned, no less sharply. "Who are you to ask it?"

"Watch your tongue, sir priest! I represent the Governor of the realm."

"Then you do so but ill. Like any churl! Uncover your head, man — in the presence of the King's own sister, the Princess Isabel."

The other blinked, opened his mouth, and then shut it again. But doubtfully he removed his bonnet. "My lady," he jerked, then, "I . . . ah . . . greet you. I did not know." He turned back to Jamie. "Have you the Governor's authority to visit His Grace?" he demanded.

"I do not need my brother's authority to visit my brother, sir." Isabel schooled her voice haughtily.

The other coughed. "Your pardon, Princess, but my lord Duke's orders are definite. None may visit the King save by his written and signed permission."

"Fool! Insolent!" That woman could play the princess adequately, when necessary. "I could have you horsewhipped for this! Think you such instructions apply to His Grace's own family?"

At her demeanour the man looked both uncertain and unhappy. "My orders," he said. "His Grace is sick. I, I . . ."

"A plague on your orders, man! I shall speak with my brother anent this scurvy order, and *your* behaviour. Both my brothers. To be sure His Grace is sick — hence my visit. But he is still King of Scots, and can suitably punish any who insult his royal dignity. Mind it, sir! Who are you, who makes so bold as to insult the King's sister?"

"Kennedy of Ballure, Lady. The steward of Maybole . . ."

"Then, if you wish to retain your stewardship, Kennedy, escort us to Turnberry Castle, forthwith," Isabel commanded, and reined round her horse to kick it into a trot, Jamie and their four men only a little less prompt.

Their interceptor bit his lip, hesitating, and then scowling, waved his party on after them.

So they rode the four miles to the great sprawling castle on the low cliff-edge, which looked out across the Firth of Clyde to Arran, scarcely a word exchanged between any of the principals the while. As they neared the gatehouse, from the tower of which the royal Lion Rampant banner of Scotland streamed in the breeze, the drawbridge lowered, the man Kennedy spurred up.

"I will ride forward, Princess, to ensure your suitable reception," he said.

"You will not. I require no introduction to my brother's house, sir. Keep back where you belong."

Without pause she led the way, thudding over the drawbridge. Men-at-arms poured out of the guard-room and porter's lodge to bar their way; but the seeming confidence of the lady, aided no doubt by the presence of the Maybole steward at her back, gave them pause. She waved them aside imperiously and clattered through the gatehouse-pend into the great open courtyard beyond, to rein up. Then she beckoned to one of the soldiers.

"The captain of the guard, fellow," she commanded.

"Aye, Lady — oh, aye. But he's no' here the noo," the man said.

"Then he ought to be! See you, then — have the King's Grace informed that his sister, the Lady Isabel, Countess of Douglas, is here. Off with you. And you, man — do not stand gawping there! Aid me down from this horse."

In such fashion they arrived at Turnberry.

With their escort dismounting behind them, and the man Kennedy looking awkward, Jamie came close to Isabel.

"You do this passing well," he murmured. "But now for the test. They will watch the King closely, you may be sure."

"Yes. But . . . we must not stand here, as though humbly seeking admittance." And she set off across the cobbled yard, not for the main keep doorway but for that of the long low hallhouse, within the perimeter walling, which had always contained her brother John's personal apartments, with its chapel, library, minstrels' room and bedchambers, befitting a man who had never been any sort of warrior.

There was a guard with a halberd at the door, but he was one of the old members of the castle staff, knew the princess and hastened to let her pass, jerking a bow. But he looked strangely at Jamie, whom he knew also. Jamie gestured to their four men to wait outside.

They were making for an inner door when hurried footsteps behind them turned them. A big and burly red-faced and red-bearded man came, puffing somewhat. At sight of him, Jamie drew a quick breath.

"Ah, Isabel — God, here's a surprise!" this character gasped. "They've just told me. What do you here . . . ?"

"What think you, John — but to see my brother? My *lawful* brother John! I did not know that I was to see my unlawful one also!"

The big man coughed, but managed to grin at the same time, for he was a cheerful customer, if unpredictable. "I take it in turn with John of Bute and John of Cardney to . . . to see to our brother, lass. His Grace prefers his own kin."

"You mean that *Robert* prefers it — for no doubt sufficient reasons! For why he has made you, I hear, Clerk of the Audit and Lord of Burleigh!"

"No harm in that is there, Isabel woman?" the other protested. "A king's bastards can have their uses. Like a lord's — eh, Sir Jamie Douglas? And I, at least, am not one of the King's outlaws, however unlawfully begotten!" He hooted loud laughter.

Jamie threw back his cowl at last. This was Red John Stewart, Captain of Dundonald Castle, often called the Red Captain, one of the late monarch's many bastard sons — just as Mary was one of his many bastard daughters — and therefore one more of Jamie's brothers-in-law. He was a notable if wild and boisterous individual, and hitherto Jamie had got on well enough with him, although they had never been close. But now, if Albany had appointed him as one of those to guard the King, and from what Isabel had said, got him made Lord of Burleigh, and one of the officers of the Crown, it might mean a very different relationship.

"I gather that I have to congratulate your lordship?" he said carefully.

"Na, na, Jamie — no need. Any more than I have need to congratulate *you*, by all I'm told! Nor yet you, Isabel, by the Mass — for consorting with one prescribed and forfeit by law!"

"Sir James is outlawed solely by Robert's ill-will — as you well know," his half-sister said. "Partly, that is what we have to see the King about."

"Indeed. Ah . . . h'm. See you, Isabel — it is less easy than that. My instructions . . ."

"John Stewart — do not you *dare* to start quoting Robert's wicked and unnatural orders to me!" he was interrupted. "I will not have it — from you or from anyone else. I will speak with my brother the King if I so desire, in this house that was once my home, or otherwhere. I am a Princess of Scotland, and do not forget it, bastard half-brother! Now — take us to His Grace."

The other grinned uncomfortably. "Och, Isabel — the Governor is the Governor, mind. The King has resigned his powers of rule to Robert. It isna just a matter of ill-will and a high hand. Robert's word is the law."

"But not over the King! John is still the crowned and anointed King of Scots, and Robert is his subject. Nothing can alter that. John is absolute ruler, the Lord's Anointed, even if he chooses seldom to exercise that rule. He can countermand anything that Robert says or does. He can dismiss Robert from the governorship this very day! Do not doubt it. He can likewise forfeit your

101

lordship of Burleigh and dismiss you from your precious clerk-ship of Audit, if so he wills! Now — where is he? In his library?"

John Stewart shrugged wide shoulders. "You have become a right fierce dame, Isabel! Aye, he is in the library, at his poems and parchments. He does little else. But, see you — I canna permit Sir Jamie Douglas into his presence. No outlaw can ever have audience of the King. It isna possible."

"Sir James comes with me, in *my* company. He has word for the King's private ear. Come far to deliver it. He has long been my own knight and adviser. If you seek to stop him, I will have the King send you back to Dundonald and revoke your offices! He will heed me, I think. For John owes me much."

Doubtfully the Red Captain eyed her, tugging at his fiery beard. She did not wait further, but turned and marched to an inner door, Jamie close at her heels. Her half-brother followed on, protesting, but mutedly for so noisy a man.

The door led into the castle chapel, where candles glowed softly before a richly-hung altar and the scent of incense was strong. After an initial brief curtsy, Isabel strode to another door at the far side. This opened on to a corridor, at the far end of which was a fine large room where a great fire of logs burned on a hooded hearth, the walls lined with books, parchment rolls, missives, and where no fewer than five tables were littered with papers, charters, seals, ink-horns and quills. Over one such a man crouched short-sightedly, pen scratching. In a chair by the fire another and somewhat younger man, slept, mouth open.

They were in the presence of monarchy.

John Stewart, by the Grace of God Robert the Third, High King of Scots, *Ard Righ* and great-grandson of the hero Bruce, looked up, peering uncertainly, prepared to be alarmed. Un-kempt in careless clothing, white-bearded, sunken-eyed, frail, he was sixty-six but looked ten years more — indeed Jamie was shocked to see the change in him. He had a noble brow and good features, like most of the Stewarts, but there was a slackness about the mouth and chin. He raised his pen now, to point it waveringly.

"Isa!" he exclaimed, with something like a groan behind it. "It's Isa."

She curtsied again, and behind her Jamie bowed low.

"Your Grace," Isabel said. "I hope that I see you well, brother? Or . . . none so ill." She moved forward, to bend and kiss his drawn cheek. "It is long since I have seen you, John."

He eyed her less than welcomingly. "Aye, I am abroad but little, Isa. I am but poorly. Yet God keeps me in this vile body, when I'd fain have my sorry soul elsewhere, lass. Why, Isa — why?"

"No doubt because He has work for you to do yet awhile, John — as His anointed King of this realm," she suggested briskly. "You are not finished your work yet, brother, I think."

"No, no — that is done with. I am no monarch any more. Just an old done man, left with his sorrows. I'd be gone, Isa — gone. And the only epitaph I'd have you put above me is — Here lies the worst of kings and the saddest of men!"

"Tush, John — what way is that to talk? You *are* still the monarch. Nothing can alter that . . ."

But he was looking past her, eyes widening with their ready fears. "Who . . . who is this I see? This man, Isa . . .?"

"It is Sir James Douglas of Aberdour, Sire. You will remember Jamie Douglas, Mary's husband, your good and leal servant, who has ever served you well, and David likewise."

"Puir Davie . . .!" That was quavered.

Jamie sank on one knee and reached out to take the trembling, veined hand and raise it to his lips.

Behind them Red John spoke. "I regret, Sire, that this man has pushed past me into your royal presence — an outlaw. I told him that he must not appear before you. I shall send him away . . ."

"That you shall not!" Isabel said.

"What, what is this? Outlaw . . .?" the King faltered.

"Sir James was declared outlaw by Robert, in his spleen. Because of his support of your son David. And because he could not rescue Robert's oafish son Murdoch from Homildon field," his sister said strongly. "Did you not know?"

"No. I know naught of this. But, but . . . I do not meddle in Robert's affairs, mind, Isa."

"This is not Robert's affair but *yours*, John. The justice of your realm. And Sir Jamie has come a long way to speak with you, on an important matter. Important to *you*. Concerning your young son James."

"Eh? *James?*" As she had anticipated, that penetrated the armour of his fear and alarm. "What of James, the laddie? He's not sick? There is naught wrong with James, Isa? He's at St. Andrews, with good Bishop Wardlaw . . ." The young Prince James was the unhappy monarch's almost only link with responsibility and affection, for although he had three married daughters, all wed to Douglases, with none of them was he close, as with this belated second son.

"No doubt, Sire. It is not his present health we are concerned with. But . . ." She turned. "What Sir Jamie has to say is for your royal ear alone. Have Johnnie leave us, if you please."

"Aye, Johnnie. Do as Isa says."

"Sire — I cannot leave you in an outlaw's company! The Duke Robert would be most wrath! I will take him . . ."

"Sirrah — be off!" his half-sister exclaimed. "Do you dare to dispute the King's royal command? Who is master — Robert, or the King's Grace?"

"Aye, go, man," the monarch almost pleaded. "I mislike any dispute, see you. Best away, Johnnie — for a space."

The Captain grimaced, shrugged, and with the briefest bow, retired.

The sleeper in the chair had now awakened, and rose to his feet. Isabel bobbed one more curtsy, but a slight one, and Jamie made obeisance of a sort likewise.

"Shall I leave you also, Sire?" this younger man said heavily.

"No, no — bide you. His Grace of England can hear anything that I am to hear, Isa." Fairly clearly the King did not want to be left entirely alone with his sister and Jamie.

"Very well." The other sat down again. This was the man known in Scotland as the Mammet, allegedly King Richard the Second of England, deposed by the usurper Henry the Fourth and supposedly foully murdered at Pontefract four years before. Whether he was an imposter or not none knew for sure — although most suspected it. But King Robert accepted the strange and silent man as genuine, treated him as fellow-monarch and even made a friend of him. Indeed this strange pair were each the other's *only* friend. Albany did not object, seeing the Mammet as a possibly useful card to play against Henry in the unending tug-of-war between the two kingdoms. At least the man seemed to be harmless, and content to live thus in quiet retirement, putting on no airs.

Isabel nodded. "It is all a family matter," she said. "If His Grace of England will bear with us . . .?"

"What of James?" the King said, almost urgently for him.

It had been intended that the subject of the young prince's safety should only be brought up later, if necessary, very secondary to the Mar earldom question; but perhaps it could be handled at the same time. When Isabel glanced at Jamie, he inclined his head.

"Yes, Sire," he said. "I speak not for myself but on behalf of your nephew, Sir Alexander Stewart of Badenoch. The eldest son of your royal brother the late Earl of Buchan, until recently acting Justiciar of the North."

The monarch looked more wary than ever. "Alex," he muttered. "Alex's boy. Alex was aye difficult. Headstrong. A trouble-maker . . ."

"Yes, Sire. But his son, *this* son, is very different. A man of great worth, noble, responsible . . ."

"Yes, yes, no doubt. But this of my laddie James? What of that, man?"

Jamie recognised that this matter would have to come first. But he was relieved also that the King had not immediately denounced Alex for the murder of his beloved Queen Annabella's brother Drummond of Mar. Could it be possible that he had not heard of this either, any more than of his own outlawry? He appeared to live in a small, restricted world of his own, here at Turnberry, and would be apt to hear only what Albany and his guards wanted him to hear. Their policy might well be to keep him ignorant of much that went on, to minimise possible interference in the Governor's rule.

"Sire," Jamie said, "Sir Alexander is much concerned for the safety of the Prince James. You have sent him to the Bishop's care at St. Andrews, so it is clear that Your Grace is also concerned. But if he is so endangered, St. Andrews may be insufficiently secure a refuge. The Duke David, his brother, did not find it so!"

At mention of his elder son, the monarch's lips trembled, and his tired eyes filled with tears. He shook his head unspeaking.

Isabel added her voice. "All who wish the realm well, John, are anxious for young James. Robert was behind David's shameful death. Now only James stands between him and your throne. A bishop's palace is scarce the surest refuge. If Robert so desired, he could pluck the boy out of there with little trouble."

The King tugged at his beard. "Robert is none so ill, Isa. He is hard, strong — as I am not. But . . . none so ill." That was beseeching rather than convincing.

"Yet you sent James away from you, Sire. To St. Andrews!"

The unhappy man looked down at his twisting hands.

"Aye. After Davie, I . . . See you, James is all I have, Isa."

"Precisely, John. Therefore, heed you what Sir Jamie Douglas has to say, I'd counsel you."

"Your Grace — Sir Alexander Stewart suggests that there is only one place in this kingdom where the prince could be entirely safe — and that is north of the Highland Line. The Duke of Albany, or others in the South, have no hold there. The Governor's rule does not run north of Atholl. Nor is likely to do, unless . . ." He paused. "Unless the new Justiciar of his appointment is accepted, by the clans, the Highlanders. Sir Alex suggests that Your Grace should send the prince into *his* keeping. He will be safe at Lochindorb."

The monarch stared, slack jaw dropping. "Lochindorb? Alex's ill hold? Yon wolf's den! In the Hielands? My James, in the barbarous Hielands, man?"

"They are not so barbarous, Sire. I have lived there these many months. I have received nothing but kindness. In the Wolf's — in the Earl of Buchan's time, it was . . . different. Your nephew Sir Alex is a true man, and Lochindorb a fine house for a lad. My own son and daughter like it well. All that a boy could wish for. Better for a lad than any bishop's house. And secure, Sire — secure."

"But, but . . . the *Hielands*!"

"Part of Your Grace's realm, peopled by your subjects. Lealer subjects than many nearer here."

"I'd never see James again! If, if they took him away to the Hielands."

"Do you see him *now*, John?" Isabel demanded. "At St. Andrews? When last did you see him there?"

Her brother shook his head, wordless.

"They are not so far, these Hielands, Sire," Jamie said. "I come and go from them without overmuch trouble. Your Grace could visit the prince, if so you desired."

"No, no. Traipse the Hielands? I couldna do that, man. I am a sick man. Done. My days for traipsing the land are long by with . . ."

"And you would condemn James to remain in danger because you would not visit him, John?" the woman charged.

"No. But . . . he's maybe in no danger at all, the lad."

"Then why did you send him away?"

The King drew a deep breath. "I will think on it," he said. "Aye, I will think on it, Isa."

106

She glanced at Jamie. "More than thinking is required, Sire. And time may be short. Tell him, Jamie."

"I said, Your Grace, that the Highlands would be less secure a haven if the Governor appoints a new Justiciar, replacing Sir Alex, whom the Highlanders can accept. As they did not accept the Lord Murdoch. Then the Duke's rule might begin to run in the North, and Lochindorb be no longer so sure a refuge."

"Well, man — well?"

"Sir Alex has resigned the Justiciarship. Because of Sir Malcolm Drummond's death. The Governor proposes . . ."

"Death? Callum Drummond dead?" The King actually gripped Jamie's arm. "What is this . . .?"

"You did not know, Sire? None told you? Sir Malcolm was slain, in May month, shamefully. A bad business."

"He, he was my good-brother — my Anna's brother!"

"Yes, Sire. It was ill done. And some would seek to blame Sir Alex — although he had naught to do with it. Indeed was saving your realm from invasion by the Lord of the Isles at the time, in the West. While most of us were at Homildon . . ."

"You say so? Yon Donald is another trouble-maker. God save us — when will my troubles cease?"

The visitors exchanged glances.

"So Sir Alex resigned the Justiciarship, Sire, feeling that Your Grace's justice should be administered by other than he until this calumny was cleared — for he is a man of much resolve."

"No doubt. But that is no concern of mine, man. Appointments are Robert's business now — the Governor's, no' mine."

"Your pardon, Sire — but earldoms are the King's business, and only the King's."

"Earldoms . . .?"

"Yes, Your Grace. The Countess of Mar has granted to Sir Alexander, by her signed charter, control of the castles, properties and privileges of her earldom, With a view to future marriage. To wed at some decent interval after her late husband's death."

"Isobel Douglas! That woman! She would do that, at her age? She must be a deal older than he, is she not?"

"Thirteen or fourteen years, I think, Sire. But they are fond. She desires him to be her protector, meantime, and her husband later. And he is well agreed." Jamie reached into his robe and brought out the papers. "Here are the charter and a copy, Sire, duly signed and sealed. But because an earldom is concerned,

Your Grace's assent is required. Your royal counter-signature."

"She would make this young man earl? Earl of Mar? As she never would Callum Drummond?"

"Yes, Sire. That is her wish."

"And what does Robert say, my brother, the Governor?"

Jamie drew a breath. "It is no concern of the Governor's, Sire. The earls of Scotland are the *righ*, in the Erse tongue, the lesser kings. Only the *Ard Righ*, the High King, can say them nay. The Countess of Mar has every right to do this, without reference to the Governor of the realm. But to be complete in law the *Ard Righ*'s concurrence is necessary. His only. Your Grace's signature."

"I . . . I'll have to think on this, Sir James."

A quick exchange of glances.

"John — need you debate it?" Isabel asked. "There is no reason to say the Countess nay."

"What is the haste, Isa?"

She bit her lip, so Jamie answered for her.

"The haste, Sire, is this. Many men will seek to wed the Countess, to gain the power of her earldom — that is certain. Adventurers. Already there have been approaches, suggestions. The Countess fears for her safety even. She could be in danger of being forced. That is why she has moved thus, well before marriage. To halt all such attempts on her."

"And this Alex hasna forced her? As his father would have done, I swear!"

"No, Sire. He is her choice. Here is her own signature and seal, to prove it, myself and other as witness."

The King shook his head. "I mislike this," he muttered. "Robert would name it meddling . . ."

His sister's gasp was explosive. "John — were *you* crowned and anointed at Scone, or was Robert? Who took those vows before God, to judge and uphold your people? You, or Robert? What has Scotland got for a king? A man — or a frightened bairn!"

He recoiled physically before her outburst and scorn, and went limping about the room, with his damaged knee, kicked by a Douglas horse so many years before, which had turned this man into a cripple when Scotland needed a warrior to lead her.

"You do not understand, Isa," he said brokenly. "I am sick, weary. The rule is beyond me, has aye been beyond me. I have handed over the rule to Robert. He acts the king, now . . ."

108

"No, John — no! He acts the *Governor*. Only you can act King, the Lord's Anointed, whilst the breath of life is in you. Only you are the King of Scots. You cannot hide behind Robert in that."

Jamie, fearing a complete breakdown, greatly daring sought to intervene. "Sire — the Prince James is to be considered, in this. If Sir Alexander is Earl of Mar, he is in greatly better position to protect the prince — should Your Grace send him north. An earl of Scotland, controlling Mar and Garioch as well as Badenoch and Braemoray, he would be well placed to offer your son the security he requires. Also to help keep the King's peace in the North, Your Grace might well be very glad of his aid." That was as near to *lèse majesté* as that man was ever likely to get.

Strangely enough, the monarch did not seem to recognise it as such; or if he did, he was suddenly prepared to accept it as valid, the balance no longer to be contested. Or it may have been merely that his weariness took over. At any rate, abruptly the struggle was over. The King limped back to his table and took up his quill. Hastily Jamie spread the papers open while Isabel held out an ink-horn. Where the younger man's finger pointed, the older signed ROBERT R, in a shaking hand, without even glancing at the charter's wording.

"And here, Sire. This is a copy. For the Governor," Jamie added.

So the thing was done. Isabel took the pen, to witness the royal signature, and then bore the papers over to the Mammet, who made no bones about adding RICHARD R as witness below her own name. Alex could hardly have looked for two kings and a princess to underwrite his unconventional charter.

Jamie's impulse now was to get away without delay; but he recognised that this would scarcely do. Isabel went on to make polite converse, but obtained little encouragement from her brother. An uncomfortable pause followed, until the princess could decently request the royal permission to withdraw. It was granted almost eagerly. Her brother's eyes already were reverting longingly to his own interrupted writings. The visitors bowed themselves out.

Beyond the door, Isabel grasped her companion's arm. "Jamie, Jamie — that was a sore business!" she exclaimed emotionally. "I feared that we were never going to convince him. Poor John — he is a sorry creature! To harry him so was,

was unsisterly. And for folk I care naught for. Only for you . . . !"

"Yes. And I am grateful, my dear. You did nobly. None other could have achieved it. Alex has reason to bless you. But now, we must move fast."

"Move? How mean you? We have gained what you required. What now?"

"See you — John of Dundonald and the man Kennedy will have put their heads together. They will not like this, and will fear Albany's wrath. They will seek to undo what has been done, if they can, for sure."

"How can they? They cannot take back the King's signature. Nor interfere with the King's sister in the King's house — or elsewhere."

"Not *you*, no. But I am another matter. They will pull me down if they can. I am only safe so long as I am with you. And yet, I must leave, and quickly."

"Why that? So long as I am here?"

"They will assuredly have sent word of this to others. Albany himself is like to be too far away, at Doune or Falkland, to be reached quickly. But he will have important men nearer — the Sheriff of Ayr, your other half-brother of Bute, Sir James Sandilands of Calder. Red John will seek such aid and authority. My arrest will be ordered, as outlaw — nothing surer. So I must be gone, with this charter, before they can gain such authority. Meantime, they will probably seek to hold me here."

"Jamie — what can we do, then?"

"Get out of this castle. Somewhere. Say that you must see the Abbot of Crossraguel, on the King's business."

"Now? But it will soon be dark."

"That matters not. Say that you will be back. It is only three or four miles. I do not see how they may stop you. I go with you — but I do not come back with you. Abbot Mark is a friend of the King. He will help."

"And you? Where will you go, Jamie?"

"Never fear. I will make my own way. I got here, from the Highlands, secretly. I will get back. I have siller — and much may be done with siller!"

She was very doubtful, and clearly unhappy at the thought of losing his company so soon. But she could think of no better plan. They moved on.

Red John and Kennedy were waiting in the chapel, and eyed them warily.

"John," Isabel said, at once. "You have been unhelpful. You had best improve upon it! Have suitable repast prepared for us. And bed-chambers readied. But first, a guide to take us to Crossraguel. I have to see the Lord Abbot, on the King's business at once."

"*Now*, Isabel? At this hour?"

"Now, yes, before they close the Abbey up for the night. This cannot wait."

"But . . ."

"No buts, sirrah! Or must we find our own way, in the dusk, man?"

She swept on towards the outer door and the courtyard, where their four-man escort waited.

"Horses!" she called.

With ill grace John Stewart told off one of the Maybole men to accompany them as guide, and watched them mount. Jamie half-expected any moment to be summoned to remain. But Isabel's imperious-seeming confidence won the day. They trotted out over the drawbridge, followed only by hostile stares.

Crossraguel Abbey was a medium-sized monastery of the Cluniac Order, very different in character from the last abbey Jamie had visited, at Ardchattan. It was indeed more like a fortified strength, with gatehouse, curtain-walling and towers — as was perhaps necessary amongst the quarrelsome Kennedys. The mitred Abbot Mark was himself a Kennedy, but owed much to the King, who was apt to use this Abbey almost as a personal sanctuary. An elderly man, he had known Isabel almost from childhood — knew Jamie also, from his stays at Turnberry in the past. Secure in the King's favour, and in Holy Church's own strength, he was prepared to be helpful.

Presently, then, Jamie was saying his farewells and thanks to the princess, in an emotional scene, promising that he would be careful, that he would make every endeavour to return to see her again before too long, and assuring her of his faithful regard and undying gratitude. He was indeed very fond of her, and greatly admired the part she had played in this project. He left the copy of the Mar charter with her, to hand over to Red John when she left Turnberry, for onward transmission to Albany; and with a lay brother of the monastery as guide, slipped out of a postern gate in the rear curtain-wall, into the November late gloaming, a travelling friar once more.

His companion led him seawards again, north by west, over

an hour's walking by round-about ways, to the bay of Culzean, well north of the Turnberry area. Here, between the two Kennedy castles of Culzean and Dunure there was a little haven, where he was quietly installed in a barn and warehouse belonging to the Abbey. Groping about in the dark he made himself as comfortable as he could for the night, chewing at a cold leg of mutton and seeking to accustom his nostrils to the warring smells of oily wool bales, the tang of tanned hides and the sweet scent of innumerable barrels of cider apples, all awaiting shipment. His guide went to arrange with one of the boatmen who worked for the monastery for the fugitive to sail with him at first light up the Firth of Clyde to the island of Cumbrae, a score of miles. From there he ought to find no difficulty in taking further passage to Dumbarton.

So, in a few hours, clutching his robe around him against the chill of a grey November dawn, Jamie Douglas put to sea next morning in a heavy, slow, but seaworthy craft under a single great square sail and four long sweeps, on his way to what he was beginning to think of as home. It would be a long, weary and uncomfortable road, but with luck its dangers ought to be no more than those usually faced by any law-abiding traveller in winter. Without being in any way smug, he was satisfied. He had in his satchel what could give his friend what he wanted and at the same time outwit the Duke of Albany. He asked for no better than that — meantime.

VII

THE GREAT DAY was no more than a month later — for others besides Isobel of Mar had united to convince Alex Stewart that time was of the essence now and any further delay for the sake of appearances sheerest folly. Appearances were still important, admittedly, but delay formed no part in it all.

Considering that it was only two weeks since Jamie had arrived back in Badenoch, indeed, appearances were remarkably effective — especially as there had been problems. Bishop William of Moray had, most inconveniently, fallen ill; and since Alex felt that in the circumstances a bishop's attendance was imperative, he had had to go in person all the way to the Black Isle to convince Alexander of Ross to put in an appearance. Then Mariota de Athyn had been anything but helpful, and this had had an inhibiting effect on Mary — which in turn had unsettled Jamie. Mary was with him now, but it had all been rather difficult. Mariota, needless to say, was *not* present. Then the weather might well have been unkind. After all, December was scarcely the month for travel and outdoor festivity in the North; but in fact conditions remained dry, crisply cold and almost windless, with frosty nights.

Alex's party, large and colourful, the churchmen, Highland chiefs and Badenoch vassals at their picturesque finest, came to Kildrummy from the north-east, by Strathbogie and Rhynie, not risking the direct route through the Mounth passes and the Ladder Hills in mid-winter. Long before they reached the castle the crowds were to be seen, hundreds upon hundreds converging on the scene from all quarters. Outside the fortress great numbers were already assembled. Clearly the Countess Isobel had well carried out her share of the arrangements.

"There is to be no lack of witnesses, at least!" Mary observed. "A bishop, a choir, music, feasting also, no doubt. All it lacks is . . . decency!"

"You women are hard on each other," her husband said.

"Alex should know better, too. But men have little sense of fitness."

"It may be that our fitnesses differ, my dear."

Kildrummy Castle's grey walls were aglow with flags and banners, flapping from every tower and bastion. The blue and gold crosslets of Mar dominated, but the fess chequey on yellow of Stewart and the red heart of Douglas were well represented. The chapel bell was ringing out strongly. Heaps of wood and brush were piled up at intervals along the battlements, to be lit as beacons and bonfires. If one thing was evident, it was that there was no lack of enthusiasm for this day at the Mar end.

As the Stewart party drew near, Alex signed to his two trumpeters to sound. They blew a resounding fanfare — which they had been rehearsing for days, to Lochindorb's considerable affliction — and this echoed and re-echoed from the surrounding braesides. Cheering arose from the throng outside the castle, and continued as the newcomers rode up.

It was to be seen, now, that the castle drawbridge was up and the portcullis lowered, shutting off all entry.

They sat their horses amongst the crowd, waiting. Alex ordered the pipers with them to play, and these dismounted, to strut up and down before them, puffing lustily.

Then a clanking sounded from the castle gatehouse, and slowly the heavy iron grating of the portcullis was raised. When it was fully up, a different groaning and creaking succeeded, which was the drawbridge being lowered. Cheers rose from all around. Signing to the pipers to discontinue, Alex dismounted — followed by the Bishop of Ross, the Prior of Pluscarden, the chiefs of Mackintosh, Macpherson, MacGillivray and many another, including Jamie and Mary Douglas. The great banner of Badenoch was brought to flap above its lord.

When the drawbridge finally settled into its place with a thud, the great castle doors within the gatehouse pend were thrown open, and out paced a choir of singing boys chanting sweet music, high and clear. These divided to line both sides of the bridge, facing inwards. Then a single figure strode forth, the portly Chamberlain of Mar, holding his staff of office. This he raised high, and the singing stopped. There was silence save for the champing of horses' bits and the calling of curlews from the hillsides.

"My lords, chiefs, knights, gentles and all true men," the Chamberlain called. "Your duty and respect for the most noble and puissant Lady Isobel, Countess of Mar and of the Garioch, Lady of Mid-Mar, Cro-Mar, Brae-Mar, and March-Mar, Baroness of Strathdon, Strathdee, Strathhelvich and Crimond, whom God empower and support."

Alex, bonnet off, led the cheering.

As a single bugle-note shrilled, Isobel Douglas came walking slowly through the pend between the drum-towers, backed by a dense pack of Mar vassals. She was superbly gowned in black and silver, which well suited her mane of tawny hair, a-glitter with jewellery, her magnificent bosom notably bare for exposure to the December air. She had never looked more handsome, more vivid, or more sure of herself. Even Mary perforce admired. But she qualified her admiration.

"Does Alex know what he does, I wonder?" she murmured.

The Countess stepped out on to the drawbridge timbers, and there halted. Unspeaking, she held out her hand, open, towards the waiting throng.

Alex Stewart strode forward then, on to the bridge, seeming almost to have to restrain himself from running, flinging aside his tartan plaid. He was seen to be dressed in Lowland garb, at his finest, in velvet and cloth-of-gold. He carried in his hand a small velvet satchel.

Everywhere people watched in silence. Both supporting parties moved slowly up behind the principals, but not so close as to block the view for others.

Alex came up to the Countess, and bowed low. She inclined her head.

He cleared his throat. "Isobel, Countess of Mar," he said loudly, "I hereby hand back into your own keeping the keys of this your castle of Kildrummy." He withdrew the great iron keys from his satchel, and held them out. "I do so before all, of my free will and in good heart, for you to dispose of as you will. This in restitution for my taking them, and it, for what seemed to me good reason, and in token of full submission and goodwill."

Reaching out she took the keys from him. "I accept these keys and your goodwill, my lord of Badenoch," she said slowly, clearly. "I hold them again, as wholly mine, in token. And . . .

115

I hereby hand them back into your hand, also in token. That I hereby choose and select you, Alexander Stewart, to be my lord and wedded husband from this day forth, keeper of my body as of my castles and lands. In token also that when presently God has joined us together in holy wedlock, I freely and heartily bestow upon you, Alexander Stewart, the styles, title and dignity of Earl of Mar and the Garioch, as is my undoubted right."

Taking the keys again, he retained her hand and raised it to his lips.

It was the signal. Loud and long the cheers rang out — and if some of the Mar vassals ranked behind the Countess seemed slightly less enthusiastic than the crowd outside and the party which had come from Badenoch, it was barely enough to be noticeable. Alex moved to her side, and together they faced the company smiling and bowing, before turning and doing the same towards those behind.

"It was decently done, at least," Jamie said. "You will not deny that?"

"Those Mar-men are less impressed than you, I think!" his wife commented. "Alex may have his hands full — with them, *as* with her!"

"If he can master her, she will master *them*, I wager!"

The choristers had, at a sign from Isobel of Mar, struck up their chanting once more, and turning, began to pace back whence they had come, the crowd behind the Countess squeezing back on either side to allow them passage through the pend again. After them the two principals walked slowly, arm-in-arm, acknowledging the salutations of those they passed, whilst the Bishop of Ross led forward after them the company assembled outside. There was some jostling for position with the Mar people as they streamed into the courtyard.

The singers progressed across the wide cobbled triangular area, making for the chapel on the east side, next to the great circular Warden's Tower. At the narrow chapel doorway there was some hold-up, but eventually most of the company managed to get inside. Here, after more jockeying for precedence, the clerics pushed forward to the vestry, the principal guests and witnesses struggled and elbowed their way to the front, near to the chancel steps, where the Countess and Alex stood waiting, facing the altar, and the choir, at each side, continued to chant a little breathlessly.

116

Isobel of Mar looked around her in a sort of sardonic amusement, Alex appearing strained.

The Bishop of Ross, gorgeous robes over his travelling clothes, supported by the Abbot of Monymusk, a Mar foundation, and the Prior of Pluscarden, the castle chaplain and other clergy behind, came out, to process up to the altar. The stir and chatter died away, as did the singing.

There followed quite the briefest and simplest marriage ceremony Jamie for one had ever attended, despite its notable significance and the lofty rank of the participants. The Bishop gave the impression of scarcely approving of the entire proceedings, and being anxious to get his part over as quickly as possible. Undoubtedly Alex had had to bring strong pressure to bear to obtain his presence at all. There were no attendants on bride or groom, nothing other than the bare essentials of the exhortation, the vows, the ring, the pronunciation of man and wife and the benediction. Indeed, it seemed as though the main import of the proceedings was what happened after, when the woman turned away, stepped over to a bench, and picked up from it in both hands what was obviously a very heavy object. This, gleaming subduedly in the dim religious light from the candles and the three narrow lancet windows, proved to be a sword-belt of solid gold links, enhanced with coloured enamel heraldic medallions of Mar and its constituent lordships and baronies. This earl's belt she brought to raise, with some little effort, and placed over Alex's head and one shoulder.

"My lord Earl of Mar!" she announced firm-voiced.

At the stir, with this the signal, Jamie Douglas stepped forward to mount the chancel-steps, drawing from his doublet the folded paper which he had carried across half Scotland. With a bow he handed it to the Countess.

"This charter," she called, opening it up, "embodies the bestowal of my earldom on this my lawful wedded husband, to descend in due course to whatever child may be begotten between his body and mine. It is countersigned by His Grace, Robert, King of Scots, as required by the law of this realm, and duly witnessed. Let none seek to dispute it." She handed this to Alex also.

Folk could scarcely cheer before a bishop in church, but there was a continuing murmur. Jamie took the Countess's fingers to raise to his lips, then stepped over to shake Alex's hand.

"My lord Earl!" he said.

117

His friend threw an arm round his shoulder, wordless but eloquent.

At their backs the Bishop cleared his throat loudly, and the trio moved aside to allow the tall, stern-faced prelate to lead the clergy back to the vestry.

The congregation threw off its reserve and surged forward.

Later, in the great hall, after the feasting but before the entertainment began and whilst most of the guests were sufficiently sober to understand him, Alex made his speech.

"My lords, ladies and friends all — hear me for a little," he said. "As you know, there has not been an Earl of Mar for over twenty-five years, to the realm's loss. It is my wife's desire, as it is my own, to have her ancient heritage, the premier earldom of this kingdom, play once again its due and proper part in the affairs of Scotland, here in the North in especial. For too long there has been a lack of due authority here — save of course in matters spiritual. There is at present no Justiciar and Lieutenant. The reason for my own resignation is known to all, and I still believe it to have been the correct course. Who the Governor may appoint we know not — nor whether he will be accepted here, as others have not. John Dunbar, Earl of Moray, seldom shows his face north of the Highland Line. The Earl of Ross is dead, leaving only a child countess of whom the Governor has the wardship. The earldom of Buchan, since my father's death, is vacant and vested in the Crown. The earldom of Angus is in Lowland hands, and its lord a captive in England, as is Moray. There are Earls of Sutherland and Caithness. But Caithness is a Norseman, looking to that king as his liege; and Sutherland, although married to my own sister, never looks south of the Great Glen. The Lord of the Isles is a high-born brigand who raids and robs our land. There is none, then, not one, to bear the King's rule and governance in this great part of the realm, twice as large as all the Lowlands put together. Can any say otherwise?"

None spoke.

"As a consequence," he went on, "there is lawlessness, feuding, rapine, murder. It is widespread. Even amongst my own family, as you know, to my sorrow. This must not be allowed to continue. I speak now to tell you all, that this my wife's creation of myself as Earl of Mar, although an honour, is not only that. An earl of Scotland has many powers that other lords have not, and that a countess, although they belong to her position,

118

cannot wield. Those of Mar will now be wielded, to her satisfaction and mine, to the best of my ability. In the interests of order, justice and the weal of this land. This I swear to you all. Not all will trust me so far, but it is my aim to make them do so before I am finished. This I would have you to know."

He paused and looked round them all. It was serious talking for a wedding-feast speech. None of the guests commented; but neither was there any of the raillery common on such occasions. The Countess toyed with the silver loving-cup which she was sharing with him.

"If you will bear with me, in all this there is one duty which I wish to declare before I sit down," he went on. "It is to acknowledge the debt my wife and I owe to our good and valued friend Sir James Douglas of Aberdour, here present, most unjustly outlawed by the present Governor, but not with the knowledge of the King's Grace. Without Sir James's notable aid, the risks he has taken and his great trouble, this bestowal of the earldom could not have been ratified and so made fully lawful. He it was who went to the King, supposedly outlaw as he is, explained all to His Grace, and with the help of the Princess Isabel, former Countess of Douglas, my good lady's brother's widow, gained the royal endorsement and signature. For this great service it is my hope that one day not only myself but all Scotland will recognise its debt. To spare Sir James further embarrassment — for he is a most modest man — I will say no more. I thank you all for hearing me, for honouring our marriage with your presence, and for the good wishes all have showered upon us."

He sat down, to relieved applause.

"Isobel Douglas did not like that last," Mary murmured to her husband. "I was watching her. I swear that she did not know that he would say it. I am beginning to have hopes for Alex Stewart, after all!"

Jamie was scowling. "He should *not* have said it."

"He should indeed! He could do no less. But *she* does not think so. She does not love you, Jamie, I vow!"

"As to that, I care not. He it is I care about, not her."

"But you will have to care about her, my dear, if you are going to continue close to Alex now. Since God and this bishop have joined them as one! For she is a clever and determined woman — and I swear that her ambitions for the earldom of Mar are other than his. She seeks to use him for her purposes — and he

119

seeks to use her earldom. It will be interesting to see who wins."

"He much loves her, see you — and she him, surely. It need not work out so ill."

"You are a bairn yet, Jamie! As is Alex. What know you of strong and scheming women?"

"Plenty!" he declared, with apparent heartfelt conviction. "And learning more every day that I am married to one Mary Stewart!"

"Then I will have to take your education further in hand, husband! For Scotland's sake, if we are to believe Alexander, Earl of Mar!"

PART TWO

VIII

FOR THE REMAINDER of the winter Jamie Douglas led a quiet, peaceful and relatively normal life — and was glad indeed to do so. He was far from idle, by any means, for with Alex now most of the time at Kildrummy and elsewhere in Mar, he was acting almost as his deputy at Lochindorb — the other sons of the house being conspicuous by their absence. The Lady Mariota seemed well enough content with this arrangement. When Alex made visits to his home, she received him warmly, but never referred to his marriage, his wife or his new status, nor asked about his doings at Kildrummy. Mary was delighted to have Jamie living a normal husbandly life with her and the children, and prayed that it might long continue — without a great deal of conviction nevertheless. The man himself might not have gone quite so far as that.

Once or twice he went to Kildrummy himself; but in winter with the high passes and bridgeless rivers to cross, it was a three-day journey, detouring by the coastal plain. He never found himself really welcomed by the Countess, however happy Alex was to see him. Nevertheless, he could not honestly claim to sense anything wrong or strained in the atmosphere there, with Alex active in the role he had set himself, the Countess reasonably amenable in all matters, and no visible signs of Mary's feared clash of interests. The new Earl was in process of getting on good terms with the Mar vassals, seeking to dissolve any suspicions they might have of him as a mere adventurer — for although they now owed him full feudal duty, their goodwill and positive support could make all the difference to his proposed programme. And it was a vast undertaking, for the Mar territories and sphere of influence covered something not far short of sixteen hundred square miles, only half of that Highland country.

That programme became real and significant, for Jamie at least, in early April, with spring at last beginning to loosen winter's grip on the Highlands. On a day of sunshine and showers, with the snows left only on the mountain-tops and gleaming ice-cornices left as rims to every corrie, Alex arrived at Lochindorb, this time with a fine company of Mar lairds, suitable for an earl's 'tail'. He had news, relayed to him by his ever-well-informed churchmen friends.

"There is to be a Council called for the Feast of St. Mark, at Linlithgow," he announced, "not a Privy Council but a *General* Council. Not a parliament. Why my Uncle Robert has called such is not clear but he has. I have not been summoned, I need not say — but as Earl I am entitled to attend. I *shall* attend — and I want you to come with me."

"Me? Put my head into that noose, Alex? Have you mislaid your lordly wits?"

"Not so. For one of the matters I wish to raise at that Council is to have your outlawry lifted."

"But . . . what hope is there of that? The Council, whatever sort, will be packed with Albany's men, you may be sure. You will achieve nothing, but much endanger yourself. Albany could not conceive of anything better, I swear!"

"Be not so sure, man. You do not know, but there is more news. Your chief, the Earl of Douglas, is released and will be there, for sure. King Henry has allowed him to return to Scotland temporarily, in exchange for three other Douglases, whom he will hold hostage until the Earl returns — one, your friend Sir William of Drumlanrig. The Earl will speak for you."

"Why should he? I left him on Homildon Hill likewise, you will recollect!"

"He will know well enough whose fault was all that sorry business. And that you, in fact, came out of it with credit, Jamie — you alone. He is a strange, moody man, but honest, I think. He will bear you no grudge, I wager. And if he attends this Council, other Douglases will do so, you may be sure. Your father — have you heard how is his health?"

"Not for long. But his days for attending Council meetings are past, I fear!"

"Dalkeith must be represented on the Council, surely? The second house of the Douglas clan."

"My half-brother James is now on the Privy Council, I am told."

124

"Better still. He will speak for you. Other Douglases will be entitled to be there. Angus is still prisoner in England — sick, they say. But there are many others . . ."

"Not sufficient to out-vote the Governor's men."

"Not out-vote, perhaps. But sufficient to make my Uncle Robert change his mind, it may be. See you, I have thought well on this, Jamie. Apart from the Governor's minions, there are some entitled to sit on the Privy Council by right — earls, certain lords and officers of state, and, of course, the churchmen. This is not a Privy but a General Council, so it applies even more to that. Many have ceased to attend, out of disgust with Albany — David Lindsay, Earl of Crawford; Sir Thomas Hay, the Constable; the Lord Maxwell; Scrymgeour the Standard-Bearer; Montgomerie, Lord of Eaglesham, your old associate; Ramsay of Bamff — and others. Wardlaw, the Primate, in particular. I shall write to certain of these. Send secret and fast messengers. Urge their attendance, even though like myself, not summoned. Declaring the opportunity to strike a blow for the good of the realm. Prove to Robert Stewart that he has not yet *all* in his pocket! We might get your outlawry lifted, amongst other matters. Do you not see it?"

"I see that you might well achieve something, yes, Alex. I see that much might be possible. But . . . *I* need not be there, for that."

"I would wish you to be there, Jamie. To guide and advise me. You know these Lowland lords a deal better than do I. Moreover, the Douglases might well make a better showing with you present than with you absent. You must be there to refute any charges against you. I cannot swear that you will be safe from Albany's spleen, any more than I will be myself. But if *I* am safe — and I intend to safeguard myself — then you will be. That I *can* promise you. Will you come with me, Jamie?"

The other spread his hands. "I do not see how I can refuse," he said.

*　　*　　*

So, ten days later a gallant and sizeable party of about a hundred and fifty rode jingling southwards down through Atholl, a notably Lowland-seeming company for those surroundings, for Alex was concerned that no prejudice should attach to his entourage in the South on the grounds that they were nothing more than a set of wild Hielandmen, always a hazard. So no

125

clan chiefs were included, vassals of the low country of Mar, Badenoch and Braemoray were there in strength, and the armed escort likewise was drawn from such territories. Not a yard of tartan was to be seen in the entire contingent.

That is, until at Dunkeld in South Atholl they found another party awaiting them. And of these some did wear the tartan. Jamie was much surprised to discover the leader of this group to be none other than John Stewart, Lord of Coull and Onele — whom he had never thought would fit into Alex's plans, nor would wish to do so. But he was, of course, an important vassal of Mar, and entitled to be included in any of the earldom's corporate activities, as also to attend the General Council. Indeed it transpired that he had been *invited* to attend — which was more than his new Earl could say. He appeared to bear no least grudge over being outmanoeuvred concerning Isobel of Mar, and greeted Alex, and Jamie likewise, with cheerful good-will. It was difficult to remain suspicious of so amiable and friendly a character, although they could not but recognise that he was no fool — and that he was Albany's son, even though reputedly not on the best of terms with his father. Jamie, by nature more suspiciously-minded than his friend, determined to keep an eye on him. Jamie himself had been a little doubtful about appearing openly, in the South, with this fine company, foregoing the secrecy of his recent travels. But Alex convinced him that he was safe, meantime, from Albany's attentions, with the Douglases in a strong position and the Earl Archibald able to declare the truth about Homildon, moreover with Alex's own and Brave John's influence in his favour.

Brave John of Coull seemed in excellent spirits altogether, addressing Alex as 'my lord Earl' with no evident edge or tartness to his voice, as they trotted on their way. There was a distinct family likeness between these two, brothers' sons as they were, and both frequently reminding Jamie at least, in feature and gesture, of the son of still another brother, the murdered Prince David. The Stewarts were, in so many ways, an extraordinary family.

John was, in fact, able to tell them much more about this Convention or General Council of his father's than Alex had learned from the churchmen. Its primary object was to renew the Governor's mandate for another period, the present three-year term of office expiring within months. This should really have been done by a parliament, but that would entail the King's

126

calling and presence, and Albany much preferred to have an assembly of his own calling, the King's alleged agreement having been obtained beforehand. In announcing this, John Stewart did not attempt to make it sound like anything other than a mere device of his father's. There was other business to conduct, especially relations with England — where there appeared to be interesting developments; matters of taxation and finance, with the Treasury empty; and sundry new appointments to be made, notably that of Justiciar and Lieutenant of the North.

"Do you yourself expect to be so appointed, Cousin?" Alex asked calmly.

"I have no wish to be so, my lord. I would prefer to go soldiering."

"Soldiering . . .? Where, man?"

"There is talk that there will be work for sharp swords in England, before long. I would find that more to my taste than holding courts of law! So, if you seek reappointment to the position, Cousin, I will not oppose you. Indeed, I will support you."

Alex eyed him thoughtfully. "I have no such intention," he said. "But . . . I thank you."

At Perth they put up at the same Blackfriars monastery where eight years before Alex had come with the Clan Chattan contingent for the great contest on the North Inch. He had been afraid of apprehension then, by the Governor, and here he was now, an earl of Scotland, still on the alert for the same interference. They had no reason to believe that Albany would have learned of their coming, for though well served by spies, the Highland North was largely outwith his sphere of influence. But learn he must, sooner or later, and it behoved the Mar party to go warily.

Alex was in something of a quandary, however. They had made rather better time so far than he had allowed for, with the weather kind, and there were still two days to pass before the Council — and they could reach Linlithgow from Perth in one day's fairly hard riding. They could dawdle, of course — but the longer they took on the road, the more likely Albany was to hear of their coming, and possibly to make his own arrangements to counter any impact they might effect. The same applied to waiting for a day at Perth. Jamie made a suggestion. The keeper of the royal castle of Linlithgow was James Douglas of Strabrock, a distant kinsman of his father's. Strabrock lay in the Almond valley of West Lothian only some six miles from Linlithgow, but with a ridge of the low Riccarton Hills between, and little coming and going from one vale to the other. They might rest hidden and secure at Strabrock for two nights at least, for it was on no major route to Linlithgow; and from there descend upon the Council unannounced. This seemed good to all — although glances were turned in the direction of Brave John. That young man declared, however, that this programme would suit him very well, for he had no desire to meet his father before the public sessions in case he sought to persuade him to certain courses he had no liking for — in especial to agree to go to England as a hostage for the temporary return of his half-brother, Murdoch, Earl of Fife, as was being suggested. If the Earl of Douglas had been allowed to come home under these exchange conditions, Albany wanted his heir back also. And he, John, had no wish to act surety for a half-brother whom he cordially disliked.

So, next day, they rode on southwards, by Forteviot and the skirts of the Ochils and Sheriffmuir, to cross the Forth at Stirling. They began to see other groups and parties riding in the same direction now, but carefully kept to themselves, prudently eschewing all banners and displays of identity and heraldry, unrecognised they hoped. In late afternoon they emerged from the constrictions of the vast forested areas of the Tor Wood into the Falkirk brae country where the great Wallace had been defeated, with the low green hills of West Lothian ahead of them. Keeping well to the south of the direct route to Linlithgow, by the Roman Wall and the Avon valley, they crossed the skirts of the Slamannan moors and turned eastwards through quiet cattle-pastured hills, avoiding the Hospitallers' Preceptory of Torphichen heedfully, and the sleepy village of Ecclesmachan, to come down into the valley of the Brocks' Burn, tributary of Almond, with the sinking sun at their backs.

Strabrock Castle crowned a knoll in the midst of this quiet vale, no very large establishment to receive some two hundred men. The laird thereof was not at home, having gone to Linlithgow to prepare all for the great gathering; but the visitors were well received by his lady, who was another Douglas, from Long-niddry in East Lothian, and who had once been a maid-in-waiting to the Lady Isabel when she was Countess of Douglas, and in consequence was an old colleague of Jamie's. A comely, uncomplicated creature now inclining to stoutness, she was probably more pleased to see them than her husband would have been, and did not appear to find the unannounced entertainment of some two hundred men for a couple of nights any trial, especially when two of them were as personable and good-looking as the Earl of Mar and the Lord of Coull and Onele. The visitors were concerned to pay their way, of course, forage for hundreds of horses alone amounting to a major item.

The lady of Strabrock was able to give them quite a lot of useful information — in especial the news that the King himself was to attend this Council; indeed he was already present at Linlithgow Castle. This had been a wholly unexpected development, certainly not suggested by the Governor. The monarch had arrived unheralded two days before, from Turnberry, and her husband had had to hurry off to receive him. It was thought that he had been prevailed upon to do this by Bishop Wardlaw, the Primate, who was now with him, for purposes as yet not clear — but presumably not in the Governor's favour. Since almost the only thing which was known to stir the sovereign these days was the welfare of his son James, who was in the Bishop's care, it might be assumed that something concerning the prince was involved. Also there were rumours that the Mammet's future was to be under discussion, and the King was known to have an interest there also.

All this much intrigued the visitors, naturally, Jamie especially. He wondered whether his secret journey to Turnberry had had anything to do with it. The King's presence at the Council would undoubtedly make a major difference, whatever the reasons. It looked as though Alex was not the only one seeking to counter the Duke of Albany — which was hopeful.

The lady's further tidings revealed that the Earl of Douglas was already in the vicinity, with a large train, lodging at his house of Abercorn, east of Linlithgow a few miles, on the firth coast.

The following evening, wrapped in their cloaks, Alex and Jamie rode alone over the shadowy braes the four miles northwards by Niddry and Duntarvie to the wooded shore at Abercorn. Here was quite a large castle, beside an ancient monastery, actually the seat of Douglas's oafish brother, Sir James the Gross. The place, castle and friary, was astir with Douglas men-at-arms, encamped around; but Jamie was well known to many of these, and they had no difficulty in obtaining access to the castle itself — from which the sound of hearty, bellowed singing emanated.

129

Disclaiming the need for any escort or introduction, Jamie led Alex up the turnpike stair to the great hall on the first floor, whence came the noise. Squeezing through the pack of servitors watching at the doorway screens, the first person he saw was his own brother Sir James, pewter tankard in hand, standing on top of the dais-table, bawling out an explicit if anatomically unlikely version of a rousing drinking-song, beating time with the slopping tankard and with his other arm around a half-naked serving-wench giggling beside him, while the company roared encouragement and chorus. James had always fancied himself as a vocalist. The next Jamie perceived was his other legitimate half-brother, Will, supporting or being supported by Sir Archie Douglas of Cavers, making for this same doorway, no doubt intent on the relief of overtaxed bladders, but singing as they lurched.

"Think you we will appear spectres at the feast?" Alex murmured. "Your Douglases would seem to be warding off despondency!"

"Drowning the memory of Homildon, perhaps . . .!"

Will recognised Jamie, raised a pointing if unsteady hand, and then emitted a high-pitched yell and came plunging forward to throw his arms round and embrace his brother, all but upending Sir Archie in the process. Words were unhearable but not really necessary.

Archie of Cavers thought otherwise. He turned to shout at the carolling Sir James — who continued to bellow lustily. Further cries proving equally unavailing, he gained his ends by the simple expedient of grabbing a beaker of ale from the nearest drinker and, stepping across, tossed the contents over singer and lady both. Douglas Younger of Dalkeith spluttered to an abrupt close, his partner screamed, and quiet of a sort was achieved.

"Look who is here!" Cavers cried into the momentary lull. "Jamie! Jamie of Aberdour! Outlaw Jamie!"

The roar from the company at that shook the building, frightening had it not been for the grinning expressions of what was presumably goodwill and welcome on all faces. Jamie had been more than a little doubtful as to what the majority of the Douglases thought of him, after Homildon; but as the noise and acclaim went on and on, and men surged forward to thump his back and shoulders, to pat and paw him, there could be no further question. He was no pariah amongst his own clan. Alex Stewart, Earl of Mar, held back, scarcely noticed.

At length, as the racket continued, Jamie himself made a move. Taking Alex's arm, he pushed bodily forward through the pressing throng, to the dais-table, where his brother James, dripping ale, jumped down to enfold him with a wet hug, leaving the forlorn female neglected on the table-top to gather her clothing around her and clamber down as best she could, forgotten by all. But Jamie, grinning at his brother, pushed him aside and struggled on, to the front of the table, still drawing his friend after him. There, in the centre, was the Earl of Douglas and Lord of Galloway, on his feet now, with his brother James the Gross and sundry other Douglas lords. Both Jamie and the Earl held up their hands for quiet, and so stood, looking at each other, while slowly the shouting died away.

It was a dramatic moment. Last time these two had seen each other it had been on a blood-soaked Northumbrian hillside, with dead and dying all around, and the Earl ordering Jamie scornfully to remain behind and look after the horses and baggage since he disapproved so strongly of the attack to be made against the massed English archers, when the flower of Scotland had gone down in useless bloody ruin and complete disaster, never winning near enough to the enemy for a blow to be struck. The fact that the Earl had been wrong and Jamie right, and that since then his chief had gathered the soubriquet of The Tyneman, the Loser, was by no means calculated to ensure harmonious relations now, especially as the Earl was a notably moody and awkward man at the best of times.

As he looked, Jamie was shocked at the change in the appearance of his chief. He had fallen with five English arrows projecting from his person at Homildon, one from his left eye-socket; and then had been wounded again at the Battle of Shrewsbury ten months later. Not only did he now lack an eye, but his face was twisted to that side, his right shoulder drooped and he held himself with a curious stiff forward stance. Never a good-looking man, stocky and somewhat hulking, now he was unprepossessing indeed, almost deformed.

He leaned across the littered table at length, however, as the noise died away, and held out his hand.

"Jamie!" he said — the one word, but sufficient.

With a gulp of relief and emotion, the other gripped that hand strongly. "My lord," he said thickly. "This is . . . good."

"Yes. It has been long. A bad business."

"Bad, yes." Neither of them effusive men, they nodded at each

131

other. Then Jamie recollected his duty. "Here, my lord — here is my lord Earl of Mar and the Garioch, whom it is my honour to present to you." He turned. "My lord — the Earl of Douglas and Lord of Galloway."

The two earls eyed each other, the one so darkly ugly, the other so fairly handsome.

"Alex Stewart!" the Douglas said. "I have heard tell of you."

"No doubt, my lord. But it may not all have been true!" That was said with a smile which only the sternest could have resisted.

The other said nothing, however.

"My lord of Mar is my very good friend," Jamie observed, significantly.

"Ah. Then he must be my friend also."

Alex bowed.

There was a pause as all men watched and listened — a pause on which so much depended. Then Douglas lifted one shoulder in an awkward movement, and gestured with his hand.

"Come you round here, my lord. And you, Jamie. Sit one on either side of me, and let us have your crack. We have much to hear, and tell, I wager. Come, you."

The crowded hall breathed freely again, and men went back to their seats.

There was an uneasy pause at the dais-table — at least between the Earl of Douglas and James the Gross and the new arrivals, although James and Will Douglas of Dalkeith kept up a cheerful chatter. At length Jamie himself said what had to be said.

"My lord — we disagreed when last we were together. I am sorry for that. It was a bad business, in every way. Unhappy."

"The unhappier for my folly," the other jerked. "Many good men died for it, many suffered."

Jamie said nothing — for it was no less than the truth.

"I have had much opportunity to regret my folly," the Earl went on, heavily. "Had I heeded you, Jamie, all might have been otherwise. I listened to other men, who lacked your wits and experience. And all paid the price. You also, it seems."

"The price I paid, am still paying, was scarce your fault, my lord. It was spleen, engendered long before. Homildon but provided the opportunity to display it. The Earl Murdoch was a prisoner and *I* was not! I bolted, where he fell fighting. As simple as that. So I am outlaw, a traitor . . ."

"Worse folly than even my own, by God!"

"Not folly, my lord — but worse, yes," Alex interposed, quietly. "Malice, hatred, and ill governance. Which is in part why I am here."

Warily the Douglas turned to look at him.

"At tomorrow's Council, I shall seek to have this shameful outlawry lifted. Can I rely on your lordship's support?"

The other stared ahead of him for a long moment. "Yes," he said, at last.

Jamie cleared his throat. "I thank you, my lord."

"Do not thank me. I could scarce do other. But . . . there is little hope, I think, that we shall prevail. Robert Stewart is too strong."

"Less strong than he seems," Alex contended. "Like lesser men, he has to pay for his misdeeds, in unpopularity. Few men love the Governor. Many *fear* him, yes. You call him strong. But is he so? Determined, yes. Cunning, yes. Without scruple, yes. But strength, now, is something different."

"Strength in a ruler, sir, depends on how many swords and lances he can deploy. And on how many votes he can command in council and parliament."

"Agreed. But by those very tokens my Uncle Robert lacks strength, in fact. He relies for both on the goodwill or fear of others. That goodwill he lacks. The fear depends on his ability to wield armed strength. Armed strength of his own he lacks. He needs others' strength. Notably that of the house of Douglas!"

There was no visible reaction to that. Jamie shifted on his seat uneasily. Along the dais-table men listened, all ears.

"The Douglas power Albany requires," Alex went on, almost conversationally. "Lacking it, he is hamstrung in much that he would do — for it is the greatest power in this realm. With it *against* him, he is finished."

Douglas drew a deep breath. "Are you, sir, suggesting that I throw the power of my house against the realm's lawful Governor?"

"I am suggesting, my lord, that you consider well where that Governor is leading the realm, and use your power to control and better it — as is surely the simple duty of any leal subject of the King, with any power. Especially the earls of Scotland. That is the other reason why I am here tonight. Being bastard, I could not inherit my father's earldom of Buchan. It is now in Albany's hands. As are the earldoms of Menteith, Fife, Carrick,

Strathearn and Ross. Moray is a prisoner in England. Angus also."

"Angus is dead," Douglas said. "He died of the plague, a captive, some six weeks past."

"Dear God! George Douglas dead!"

"Aye — more of the price of my folly. And leaving only an infant son, a bairn of four."

"Worse and worse, then. For, I swear, Albany will not be long in seeking the wardship of that bairn also — and so controlling yet another of the earldoms. After all, Angus's countess is the King's daughter, as is yours, Albany's niece. You are still prisoner on parole — to return to England in due course, I understand? He will claim wardship for the Crown — which means himself."

"M'mm."

"Which leaves how many independent earldoms? Lennox's daughter is married to the Earl Murdoch, and he will do what Albany says. Dunbar and March are gone over to the English. Sutherland and Caithness do not count, as Norsemen. What are we left with? Crawford, the new earldom — Albany's goodbrother. And Mar and Douglas! That is all. You will perceive, then, why I have made it my business to become Earl of Mar — with my lady's kind goodwill? For Mar was intended for John Stewart of Coull, Albany's other son."

"Lord — young John? He is scarce of age . . .?"

"He reached majority less than a year past. Which makes the death, then, of Malcolm Drummond . . . interesting!"

"By the Powers!" Douglas turned to stare at the other with his one eye. "You are saying . . .?"

"I am saying that *I* had naught to do with Drummond's death. And that the Governor is in process of gathering all the realm's earldoms into his own grasp and control. So that, in turn, he can control the Privy Council, by the earls' votes, and parliament or convention by the earls' vassals' votes. Do you not see it? The strategy? And see where stands Douglas!"

There was a long pause.

Jamie took a hand. "My lord — after the Cocklaws ploy, you and Hotspur Percy expected Albany to join you against Henry, did you not? Before Shrewsbury?"

"Aye. But he was delayed. Hotspur could not wait longer. I sought to hold him back awhile, to wait longer. But Henry struck . . ."

"Albany was not delayed — or not save by his own will. He took three weeks to march the fifty miles to Cocklaws! Roundabout. And on the way — if you could call it on the way — he sat down and besieged Innerwick Castle, near to Dunbar. *Your* Dunbar — since you were controlling that earldom. Your Innerwick. Why, I have not discovered. But be sure that there was gain for Albany in it. But not for you. Or Hotspur! Can you still trust and support the Governor, my lord?"

The Earl of Douglas's fists were clenched, knuckles white.

"I am assured that my Uncle Robert has been seeking to move heaven and hell both to gain his son Murdoch's release from England," Alex mentioned. "I have not heard of any such move on your behalf, my lord — although you are Chief Warden of the Marches, commander of the realm's forces and greatest noble of the kingdom. This parole and exchange of hostages was not his doing, I think?"

"No." Abruptly, Douglas thrust back his chair and rose, a little unsteadily, a hand up to his brow. "Enough!" he jerked. "I must think. I, I seek your pardon. I fear I have drunk overmuch wine. I am not . . . the man I was. I need to think on these matters, when my head is clearer. Before tomorrow's Council. That arrow in my head . . . I, I bid you a good night my lords . . ."

In some discomfort the company watched him leave the hall.

"You think that we went too hard at it?" Alex murmured to his friend. "Overplayed our hand?"

Jamie shrugged. "Who knows? He was ever a strange man . . ."

They left soon afterwards, despite Jamie's brothers' pleas to stay, and picked their way back through the April gloaming to Strabrock.

IX

THE GREAT CHURCH of St. Michaels, Linlithgow, which
shared the hillock above the loch with the royal castle, was
full to overflowing, at least, as it were, at its perimeters,
although the central parts were less so, and the chancel all but
empty. The nave was reserved for the commissioners, that is
those attending the Council with right to vote, and there was a
decent sufficiency of space for these. But the transepts and side-
chapels, the aisles, the embrasures of the tall windows and the
clerestory galleries were packed with onlookers, churchmen,
townsfolk of the royal burgh, representatives of other burghs
and communities, knights, officers and lairds not entitled to be
commissioners, sons, kinsmen and senior supporters of the lords
and magnates present. Jamie Douglas was skied up in the last
clerestory window-embrasure on the south side before the crossing, which afforded him an excellent view of the proceedings,
but, with his back to the noonday light, did not make his
identity too obvious. His brother Will was at his side, James
being down amongst the lords.

All now awaited the arrival of the principals, amidst much
noise and stir, with the clergy in St. Katherine's Chapel, the
south transept, frowning disapproval. Already in the choir were
the bishops, five of them, on one side, and the earls on the other,
only three with Lennox sick — Douglas, Crawford and Mar.
Behind the bishops were eight mitred abbots, entitled to vote in
parliament, and behind the earls sundry officers of state. Below
the chancel steps forms had been brought to seat the lords, at
the front, twenty-one of them, of whom no fewer than seven
were Douglases. The rest of the commissioners could stand
behind, numbering perhaps fifty. Men-at-arms of the royal
guard stood likewise, in strength.

As they waited, Jamie weighed up chances and probabilities. Without being actually optimistic — something he tried always to suppress — they were better considerably than he had feared when he left Badenoch. As it transpired, Albany almost certainly would be handicapped by the King's presence, whatever the reasons for his coming. He would be *there*, representing higher authority than the Governor's. It might as well have been a proper parliament, after all — although that would have entailed a larger attendance, all who had the right to attend being sent summonses and given the stipulated forty days notice. As it was, unsummoned folk were here, including Alex and his Mar vassals; but the Governor would be in a quandary regarding challenging every voter, when such could claim that they *should* have been summoned, by right, and had been deliberately excluded. Permitting an audience of non-voters could also be deleterious to the Governor's interests; yet the public were entitled to watch at a parliament, and presumably at a Council General — although not at a Privy Council, of course. Albany must have considered this, to be sure. He could have tried to squeeze all the commissioners into the great hall of the royal castle, and so left no room for onlookers, but it would have been a tight fit. It was all very much in the balance — which at least was an advance on what had seemed probable. So much might depend on the attitude of the Earl of Douglas. So many would take a lead from him . . .

His assessings were interrupted by a herald of the Lyon Court coming out, with two royal trumpeters, who sounded a short fanfare. Two splendidly robed prelates paced in from the vestry, Bishop Wardlaw of St. Andrews, the Primate, a stocky, grey-haired, quietly authoritative man, nephew of the late Cardinal; and Gilbert Greenlaw, Bishop of Aberdeen, the Chancellor, tall, pale, brisk and competent, but coldly so, a creature of Albany's. He went to his place at the end of the table placed between the high altar and the choir-steps, already spread with papers. Wardlaw moved over to a stall set in front of the row of bishops.

There was another and longer fanfare, which set the hammer-beam roof quivering, and all who sat rose to their feet. The Lyon King of Arms and the Albany Herald strode in. Then Sir James Scrymgeour, the Standard-Bearer, now bearing the Mace, which he laid on the table. Then there was something of a wait, before two very much less resplendent figures emerged from the vestry, the hobbling, limping, stooping monarch leaning on the stiff arm of his brother the Governor.

"God save the King!" Lyon declared loudly. "God save the King's Grace!"

The cry was taken up with vigour throughout the church.

The monarch never dressed regally, and looked today like a distinctly seedy brother of a mendicant order. Albany, only a year younger but looking more so by a dozen years, did not go in for sartorial display either; but he was richly clad in black velvet with white lace, a spare, lean, upright man of a rigid dignity, good-looking in a tight-lipped way unusual amongst the Stewarts, with a self-contained, ageless quality to him, that belied his sixty-six years. He kept his head high, where the King's was sunk, and stalked just sufficiently far away from his brother to indicate how distasteful he found such contact with debility and weakness. Neither acknowledged the dutiful acclaim of the assembled company.

Leading the monarch to his throne-like seat in front of the earls, the Duke of Albany inclined his head briefly, stared blankly from almost colourless eyes at Alex Stewart behind the King, moved over to his own chair behind the central table, and sat down. Without pause, or even looking at the Chancellor, he raised a hand and flicked a finger. He was a man to waste neither time nor words.

As Bishop Greenlaw bowed, all others who had seats sat down.

"Your Grace," he intoned, towards the King, "my lord Governor," he bowed again, "my lords spiritual and temporal, and all fellow-subjects of his royal Grace, as Chancellor of this realm I declare that this Council General of the Estates of Parliament is now in due and proper session. My lord Bishop of St. Andrews will now pray for God's good guidance and blessing on our deliberations." His tones were a nice admixture of the authoritative, the respectful and the businesslike.

The Primate offered up a short and simple prayer in a much plainer voice.

The Chancellor remained standing. "Your Grace, my lord Governor and my lords — to proceed, I . . ." He paused at another flick of Albany's hand.

"Have you ascertained well, my lord Chancellor, that all who are here are entitled to be here?" That was thinly said, as the speaker looked directly at Alex Stewart.

138

The Bishop coughed. "Such is my belief, my lord Governor. The Lord Lyon King of Arms has checked all credentials, I am assured."

"Then proceed."

It was a warning, that was all. Albany would have received his copy of the Mar charter and would know well that Alex's assumption of the earldom had the King's confirmation. He was but indicating displeasure, and demonstrating who controlled this assembly.

"Yes, my lord. The first business is the appointment of Lord High Admiral of this kingdom, for some time vacant. My lord Governor, with His Grace's agreement, recommends that the office and all dues, privileges and emoluments pertaining thereto should be held by the King's good-brother, and his own, the Lord David, Earl of Crawford. It is not within the power of this Council to withhold agreement, but objections may be heard."

There were, of course, no objections raised. David Lindsay of Crawford, although now elderly, was popular enough, and reliable. Jamie looked at Will.

"Clever," he murmured. "The said emoluments include customs dues at every port of the kingdom. So Albany seeks to stop Crawford's mouth, and to buy his vote, before ever a start is made — and none can say him nay."

The Lindsay stood, bowed, and sat down again.

"The next business concerns the King's peace. And relations with the realm of England," the Chancellor went on. "And in such case it would be meet, and His Grace's wish, that we should express here the pleasure and satisfaction of all at the presence with us of my lord Earl of Douglas, who has led valiantly in the defence of the realm. He is here but on parole and must return to captivity. But we salute him."

Men could cheer that, at least — although Douglas himself looked grim.

"As is well known, the Earls of Fife and Moray are still prisoners in England, with many lords and knights, captured at Homildon," Greenlaw went on. "And the Earl of Angus has died a prisoner, to our sorrow. The Governor has been seeking the release of these, but without success. It may now be revealed that there was an attempt made against the usurper Henry of Bolingbroke some months past, after Shrewsbury fight, a compact between the Earl of Northumberland, the late Lord Henry

Percy's father, Scrope, Archbishop of York, and sundry North of England lords, to go to the aid of the Welsh under Glendower, the King of France to send an expedition likewise. My lord Governor was privy to this endeavour, and sent envoys to York to assist. By misfortune, this good attempt was betrayed to Henry by Neville, Earl of Westmoreland. The Archbishop and the Lord Mowbray were beheaded, and the other leaders now fugitive. Some escaped to France, but others, including the Earl of Northumberland, the Lord Bardolph and the Bishops of St. Asaph and Bangor, are believed to be making their way to Scotland and His Grace's protection, to join His Grace King Richard, already here."

There was a murmur at this depressing catalogue — and some wondered why it was being announced. Crawford spoke.

"My lord Chancellor — Henry may be usurper, but he is now firmly on the throne of England. He may well construe protection given by the Scots Crown to his rebels as an act of war. Are His Grace and the Governor prepared for the possible consequences?"

Greenlaw glanced at Albany, who remained silent, expressionless.

"It is believed that Henry will not take action on such account, with insurrection at home and the Welsh still undefeated, my lord. He has not done so against King Richard's presence here, to be sure. Whereas the holding of the Earl of Northumberland, Lord Bardolph and others in Scotland would be a distinct advantage in any bargaining with Henry, would it not?"

"Holding? Advantage? Bargaining?" That was the Primate, Wardlaw, in his quiet but firm voice. "My lord Chancellor — do we take it that these Englishmen are to find refuge here? Or to be held and used as pawns in a game of statecraft? I cannot think that His Grace's honour would be enhanced, if this is so."

Bishop Greenlaw looked again at the Governor. He was in a difficult position in any debate with his own Primate and superior.

With obvious displeasure Albany spoke. "His Grace's honour is at no risk," he said. He had the slightest hesitation in his speech, and always spoke slowly, deliberately, coldly. "I mislike the term pawns. Offering shelter to Northumberland and others is no less than a duty, since they are allies against the common enemy. But none will deny the advantage of having the chief nobleman of Northern England in our midst. Will *you*, my lord of Douglas, Chief Warden of the Marches?" That was quite a speech for Robert Stewart, who preferred others to do the talking, whilst he manipulated.

The Douglas frowned his twisted brows. He could by no means controvert that, whether he would or not. Douglas lands lined the Border, east, mid and west, that Border kept in a state of perpetual turmoil and trouble largely the age-old feud between the Douglas and Percy families, excuse for any barbarity on either side. With Douglas himself a captive and unable to lead in the protection of his lands, nothing could be more suitable than for the Percy earl to be in Scots hands.

"Damn him — he knows what he is at, that one!" Jamie whispered. "He has our earl gripped tight! And . . . he has not said so, but by naming Douglas like that, he as good as hints that an exchange might well be suggested."

"Why not?" Will demanded — to his half-brother's look of pitying scorn.

"Because, if there is any such exchange, dolt, it is his *son*, the Earl Murdoch, who will benefit, not Earl Archie. Of that you may be sure."

The Earl of Douglas, who was no fool, whatever else, contented himself with a shake of the head.

Albany waved his hand to the Chancellor.

"Is it agreed then, my lords, that this matter is best left in the Governor's capable hands?" Greenlaw asked. "Since no other is in a position to effect the issue." He turned. "With, of course, my lord of St. Andrews, fullest concern for the King's honour, as always."

"Aye — but why raise it in the first place?" Jamie muttered. "I say it was only done to show the Earl Archie where his advantage lay. Albany controls all, like any puppet-master. There is none here clever enough to upset him."

"Not your friend the new Mar, I warrant!" Will said.

"Further to this of England," the Chancellor resumed, confidently now, "His Grace is concerned for the welfare, good guidance and upbringing of his grandson, the new Earl of Angus, in consequence of the sad death of his father, captive. His Grace deems it proper that the child, of but four years, should be taken into the care and wardship of the Crown, his widowed mother being the King's daughter."

Alex Stewart looked at the Earl of Douglas beside him — who sat still. Just as the Bishop began to speak again, he himself rose.

"My lord Chancellor," he said in his clear and musical Highland voice, softly sibilant but carrying, "guide the Council, if you will. Does the care and wardship of the Crown refer to His Grace the King's own keeping? Or that of my lord Governor? Or of another? For instance, the Bishop of St. Andrews — who indeed presently has the care and keeping of His Grace's own surviving son, the Prince James, Earl of Carrick?"

That mildy-spoken enquiry might have been the harshest of challenges by its impact upon the crowded church. Men stared at the speaker, the Governor, the King and each other. Here was a bold man, with a vengeance! Seeming to question even the royal prerogative, and in the King's own presence — although none could fail to grasp the significance of the point implied, that if the monarch could not ensure the keeping of his own son and heir, he was unlikely to do better for his four-year-old grandson.

"My lord, I . . ." the Chancellor began, when he was halted by a peremptory snap of the fingers from the Governor.

"Who speaks?" that man said.

Greenlaw looked uncomfortable. "The Lord Alexander, Earl of Mar, formerly Lord of Badenoch and acting Justiciar of the North, my lord Duke," he replied, in almost a gabble. "Earl by charter of the Countess Isobel of Mar, confirmed by the King's Grace." The Bishop's diocese of Aberdeen was near enough to Mar, and with rich endowments therefrom, to ensure that he wished for no trouble in that direction.

"Vacated the Justiciarship on possible implication in the vile murder of Sir Malcolm Drummond, the lady's husband and good-brother of His Grace," Albany said tonelessly. "Then married the widow."

"Precisely, my lord Duke," Alex agreed genially. "If . . . abbreviated."

"Found to be innocent of any such implication by the highest Court in the North, on which sat the Bishop of Moray and the Lord John Stewart of Coull, both here present. Which Court also learned that the said vile murder had been carefully arranged from south of the Highland Line!"

Moments passed in tense silence, before the Governor inclined his head.

"Proceed," he said.

It had been an exchange of warnings.

A sigh of relief escaped from many, not least from the

Chancellor. But he still had a difficult question to handle, since Alex remained on his feet.

"Royal wardship, my lord, means that the minor is placed within the protection of the Crown. In whose care the child resides is not the vital matter, and is at the Crown's best judgement."

"Ah. I thank you. Then, my lord, I suggest that this Council advises the Crown to place the child George Douglas in the care and wardship of his own chief and uncle, the Earl of Douglas, whose wife is sister to the Countess of Angus, and likewise the King's daughter. Thus putting no unnecessary further burden on the already much burdened shoulders of His Grace and the Governor." He sat down.

"If that is a motion for decision, I second it," the Bishop of St. Andrews said.

It was hard for Jamie, who could not hide a foolish grin, to decide who was most put out, the Governor, the Chancellor, or the Earl of Douglas — although undoubtedly Albany hid it best. All were placed in an obvious quandary. Albany needed Douglas's aid and power, therefore would be loth to offend him; the Chancellor did not know how he should proceed; and Douglas was having his hand forced cleverly — for he could scarcely refuse wardship of the third most important Douglas before all his own lords and vassals without jettisoning respect.

Slowly that twisted man got to his feet. "I will accept the wardship, if Your Grace permits," he said thickly, looking at the King.

Almost imperceptibly the monarch nodded, biting his lip.

Greenlaw looked at the Governor anxiously. "Is the motion contested? Or any other motion?"

Albany eyed his finger-nails, and said nothing.

"Then, then with His Grace's approval, I declare the matter settled. The young Earl of Angus, his earldom and lands, are placed in the care of the Earl of Douglas until such time as the Crown declares him fit and of age to manage all for himself. With, to be sure, good and proper provision made for his lady mother, the Countess Mary. Is it agreed?"

Jamie was not the only one who could scarce forbear to cheer. The Duke of Albany had suffered his first open defeat in years. It was no large matter; but the significance was there — not least in that the gently-spoken stranger had contrived it, and in his support by the primate.

The Chancellor was rather evidently hurrying on to the next business when he was interrupted by the said Primate.

"Your forbearance, my lord," Wardlaw said, standing. "But on the matter of wardship and the safety of minors, there is more to debate. I have the honour to speak for the King's Grace in this. As all know, owing to ill health and infirmity, His Grace has been pleased to place his heir, the Prince James, Earl of Carrick and High Steward of Scotland in my care and keeping, at St. Andrews Castle — to my great satisfaction. It has come to the ears of His Grace and myself, however, that possible attempts might be made upon the prince's safety by ill-designing persons. My bishop's palace, and resources in armed men, could well be inadequate in such evil attempt, we fear. Other houses likewise. Therefore it is His Grace's design that the prince be sent into the care either of His Holiness the Pope, or of His Most Christian Majesty, the King of France, for true security. This is His Grace's considered desire, and my own advice. But before sending the heir to his throne outwith the realm's borders, he would seek the agreement and understanding of this parliament or council."

As though thunder-struck, the great company sought to gather its wits. This was why the King had come here in person, obviously. Whatever else was behind it, none could fail to see it as the direst commentary on the state of the realm, when its monarch felt his own son would be safer elsewhere. Therefore, at the very least, it was an open indictment of the Governor's rule and inability to protect his nephew — although few there of any knowledge of affairs doubted that it was the Governor himself who was believed to pose the threat. Nothing could more strongly underline the gap and enmity between the royal brothers, he who reigned and he who ruled. Men would be forced to take sides — loyalty to the weak King, or adherence to where the power lay.

The quivering hush was broken by Albany's dull, factual voice.

"Who, my lord Bishop, are the ill-designing persons whose evil intents have come to your clerkly ears, and His Grace's? Sharper ears than mine and the realm's government, it seems!"

"My lord Duke, you would not have me to name names, I think, here in open assembly, for a crime not yet committed?" the Primate answered. "But that must not prevent us taking due precautions. I may say, however, that one who might consider laying violent hands on the prince, not necessarily the most

144

dangerous, is your own nephew the Lord of the Isles, who has already made attempted invasion, twice, and failed, thanks only to the strong and bold efforts of my lord Earl of Mar."

A buzz of comment and approval swept the church. It was a shrewd tactic. Donald of the Isles was an ominous figure in Lowland Scotland, something of a bogeyman. Albany could not pooh-pooh the constant threat he posed, nor publically dismiss Alex's service in thwarting him. Whether or not Donald had ever had any intention of abducting the prince his cousin, none could doubt that such an attempt would be in character.

"The Islesman is a long way off," the Duke observed. "If ever he made any such attempt, there would be ample time to move my nephew to a more secure hold than St. Andrews — Stirling Castle, or Edinburgh. Would any claim that the boy could be lifted out of these? Why send him to France?"

Wardlaw hesitated, but only for a moment. He could not say baldly that Albany himself was the danger, and could lift the prince out of Stirling or Edinburgh even more easily than out of St. Andrews Castle.

"His Grace considered that," the Primate said slowly. "But these are fortresses, military strengths. He could have sent the prince there in the first place. But great fortresses are no places to confine a growing lad. He would become all but a prisoner. The prince needs space, freedom, the company and influence of cultured minds, my lord. The Papal or French Courts would be excellently to the advantage of our future King. This is His Grace's decision." He emphasised that last word slightly.

Albany was a determined man, but not obstinate. He knew well when to abandon an untenable position. He shrugged. "His Grace's wish, of course, is our command. Proceed, Chancellor."

The Bishop of Aberdeen swallowed. Evidently there was not to be any further discussion on the subject by the company.

"Yes, my lord. The next business concerns the good governance of the realm. My lord Duke's term of office as Governor expires within a month or so. It was for three years. It is necessary that further arrangements be made. I have a letter here from my lord Earl of Lennox, absent through sickness, thanking my lord Governor for his valuable and unremitting services in the past, and praying that he favours the realm by accepting office for a further term of three years. He authorises Sir Malcolm Fleming, Lord of Cumbernauld, to so move, in his name."

145

"I so do," Fleming declared briefly.

"And I make it my privilege to second," the Bishop of Dunblane added. Doune Castle, Albany's favourite seat, in Menteith, was near Dunblane.

"I thank you, my lords. Is there any contrary motion?" Greenlaw actually smiled as he said that.

There was silence. It would have been a rash man indeed who would have proposed any other name — and a rasher who would have accepted nomination. In fact, there was nobody else of sufficient seniority and experience for the role, unless perhaps the Earl of Crawford, who almost certainly would refuse, and was indeed older than the Duke, and with no fondness for the business of statecraft. The only other brother of the King was Walter, Lord of Brechin, not present, never present, a drunken irresponsible who could not manage himself much less a kingdom. Douglas conceivably could have been appointed — but he had to return to his captivity in England. It was all part of Scotland's tragedy.

"Very well . . ." the Chancellor was saying when Alex Stewart rose to his feet.

"My lord — one moment," he said pleasantly. "We are all very much aware of the Duke of Albany's prolonged activities in the realm's name. But too much can be laid on one man's shoulders, however willingly he bears the burden. I cannot, for the life of me, think of any name adequate or fit to take his place — as yet. But, in view of his advanced years — sixty-six, if I mistake not, my lord Duke? In view of this, I propose that his appointment be renewed for only *two* years, not three. Perhaps the Earl of Douglas, or other, will be available to take on the task by then." Smilingly bowing to the Governor, he sat.

Albany had half-risen from his chair. Sternly impassive of appearance always, he could not wholly control his features now, his cold fury the more frightening for being under such evident restraint. He raised a trembling finger, to point.

Before he could speak, another bold voice broke the tense silence, from the lord's seats at the front of the nave this time.

"It is my filial duty, and my pleasure, to second such motion," John Stewart of Coull declared.

As men caught their breaths, Robert Stewart sank back in his chair, his eyes closed.

In agitation the Chancellor looked at him, as men stirred and whispered. "This is . . . this is . . ." He bit his lip. "I, I have no option, my lord Duke, and Your Grace. I have two motions before the Council. Both duly seconded. Is it your wish that I proceed to the vote, my lord?"

Clear, precise, definite, so much in contrast with Greenlaw's, the words came from behind the table. "No vote. I accept the two years' term. Proceed, man." Those colourless eyes remained closed.

The Chancellor looked unhappy and relieved at the same time, shuffled his papers as though in doubt as to what to do next in an assembly all too evidently not going as planned. "Er . . . there is the matter of moneys," he said, almost tentatively. "Moneys for the costs of government. Further moneys to reimburse my lord Duke for much expense. He is sorely at loss."

"Provision was made for this," Crawford said shortly.

"It has proved . . . inadequate, my lord."

"It is unsuitable that the Governor should be put to expense as well as trouble in the realm's service," the Bishop of Dunblane said. "My lord of St. Andrews — cannot Holy Church help in this matter?"

"The Church is already helping, my friend. More than is her due, I may say," the Primate observed. "Save, perhaps, for the See of Aberdeen, where I am informed, dues and contributions, not only to the Exchequer but to Holy Church's own Treasury, are unaccountably held up."

Mirth, for the first time that day, broke through, especially amongst the laity.

"Not so!" Greenlaw expostulated, flushing. "My diocese is most concerned to make full and generous contribution. But it must be understood that much of the see's revenues come through the port and haven of Aberdeen and its merchants and shipmen, its fishers also. For lack of a Lord Admiral of the realm, these past years, such duties and customs have not been properly farmed, and we, the Church, have suffered grave loss. . ."

"My lord of Crawford will attend to it," Albany intervened levelly, his eyes open again. "Observing therein the requirements of the Exchequer and of the Church, both. My lord Chancellor — the matter of Atholl."

Some grins were turned in the direction of Crawford, but that was the end of the mirth. Such seldom survived long in the Governor's presence.

"Ah, yes — Atholl. Further to this of moneys, my lords — and Your Grace — it is considered that the revenues of the earldom of Atholl could well be used for the realm's weal. As all know, the earldom of Atholl has been merged in the Crown for many years — since 1342 indeed. It seems now good and proper that its revenues should be made available to the Governor for defraying the costs of government with His Grace's agreement."

"My lord — is that a statement or a question?" That was Wardlaw the Primate.

"Is what . . .?"

"Is His Grace's agreement obtained, or to *be* obtained?"

Greenlaw looked, as always, at the Governor — who looked at his brother. The King's head sank lower, but shook. Whether it was a shake or a wag, in denial, helplessness or agitation, was for individual assessment.

Wardlaw chose to interpret it as a denial. "I would point out, my lord Chancellor, a slight error in your pronouncement," he went on. "You say that the earldom of Atholl has been merged in the Crown since 1342. But this is not so. In 1342 King David Bruce was on the throne. This earldom was conveyed to Robert, the High Steward — who did not become King, as Robert the Second, until 1370. The earldom, then, is merged in the Steward-ship, not the Crown. I feel it to be my simple duty, in whose care the present High Steward has been placed, the Prince James, to here assert his undoubted claim and title to this earldom and its revenues."

Once again there was all but consternation.

"A minor," Albany said briefly, apparently to no-one in particular.

"Yes. To be sure. My lord Bishop — the High Steward being a minor, and so unable to manage the affairs and revenues of an earldom, they therefore must be in the hands of his guardians and elders," Greenlaw said.

"In this case, the King's Grace, the minor's father — not the Governor, his uncle. May I ask how the Atholl revenues have been disposed, hitherto?"

"M'mm. Into His Grace's privy purse, I believe."

"For the benefit of the prince. Then, I say, that they must remain so. That when the High Steward comes of due age to require and use such moneys, they are awaiting him — not drained off otherwise. If it pleases the King's Grace?"

The monarch raised his head, moistening slack lips. "It does," he said — although only those nearby could hear him.

"Albany's fourth defeat!" Jamie declared elatedly, to his

brother. "And in none of them did he dare put it to the vote. Alex and the Bishop Wardlaw between them have him hobbled!"

"Here, perhaps, Jamie. But, wait you! Wait until we are all gone home, and the Duke is ruling the land again. Then see who wins!"

Grimly, unwillingly, the other nodded.

"Next business," the Governer said, apparently unmoved.

The next business was controversial also — but one in which at least Alex's hands were tied. It was the appointment of an acting Justiciar of the North. The Chancellor explained that the new Earl of Mar had resigned the office for good and sufficient reasons, and must be replaced. The office was only an acting one, because of course the true Justiciar was the Lord Murdoch, Earl of Fife, presently unfortunately captive in England. In the circumstances, and since it was advisable that the Justiciar should be a man known and accepted by the people of those parts and acquaint with their curious language, it was appropriate that the brother of the said Earl of Fife, the Lord John Stewart of Coull, Onele and Oboyne, who was now of age to play his due part in the governance of the realm, should be appointed . . .

"No!" the Governor rapped. "I have decided otherwise."

Greenlaw, put out of his stride again, spread plump hands, looked pained, but said nothing.

Albany allowed moments to pass before again raising that strange voice. "On due thought, it may be that my son John is still young enough to lack mature judgement for such office — where judgement is important. I shall retain the Justiciarship in my own hands meantime. Appoint deputies when and as required. It may be, test the Lord John as to improved judgement in due course. You may proceed, Chancellor."

John Stewart rose, and bowed, half-smiling, to his father, and sat again, whilst the hum of talk and comment arose.

Greenlaw had to beat the table for quiet. "Your attention, my lords. There is the matter of the fortress and castle of Roxburgh. The people and vassals of Teviotdale, through the Sheriff thereof, Sir Archibald Douglas of Cavers, have petitioned the Governor to assail and eject the English garrison therefrom, long established. My lord Duke declares this to be the business of the Wardens of the Marches, in especial the Chief Warden, the Earl of Douglas. Do you wish to speak further on this, my lord of Cavers?"

"I do," Sir Archie said vigorously. "The English have shamefully held this Scots castle for sixty years, despite all truces and treaties. They frequently raid out from it, to assail and ravish in Teviotdale and the Merse, in especial my town of Jedburgh. It is a very strong hold, and cannot be taken but my major assault and siege, with engines. My lord Earl of Douglas, being captive on parole, may not lead any such warlike attempt against his captors. His brother, Sir James Douglas of Abercorn, who acts deputy Chief Warden, is in no position to mount any such major siege. We say that this is a matter for the Crown."

"If the Earl of Douglas, or his deputies in the house of Douglas, are unable to control the Marches of the Borders, then his right course is to resign the Wardenship to others who can," the Governor said, almost primly. "Do you so, my lord of Douglas?"

"No," that uncommunicative man said shortly.

"Then I suggest, Sir Archibald, that you confer with your own lord on this matter, instead of taking up the time of this Council."

"But — surely it is the realm's business? A great castle within the Scots Border, held by an enemy garrison. *You*, my lord Duke, led a large army of fifty thousand not so long since, to relieve the small tower of Cocklaws, in my lordship and sheriffdom. It was a strange business — but no doubt you had your reasons! Why cannot you do the same for Roxburgh?"

"I went to Cocklaws, young man, on the invitation and with the agreement of the Earl of Douglas, then in the care of the Lord Henry Percy. This of Roxburgh is quite otherwise."

"Then I urge the Earl of Douglas again to seek your aid, my lord Duke!"

"That he cannot do, while on parole. It would be construed an act of war. We are at truce with England. The Crown will not break that truce until it is fully prepared to do so. You may sit down, Sir Archibald. The matter is not for discussion here. Chancellor — is there aught else?"

"Other than confirming in office sundry sheriffs and officers appointed since the last parliament, I think not, my lord Duke..."

"I have a matter to raise," Alex announced, rising. "It concerns the outlawry wrongfully pronounced upon Sir James Douglas of Aberdour — pronounced in the King's name but without the royal knowledge. I move now that this be revoked, as mistaken and unsuitable."

"This surely is a matter entirely within the prerogative of the Governor," Greenlaw said, looking grieved.

"As I understand it, nothing that the Governor, or any other subject of the King may do, cannot be overturned by the King in parliament. Am I misinformed, my lord?"

"I . . . ah . . . mmm."

"This man is a trouble-maker," Albany observed.

"I presume that my lord Duke refers, not to myself, but to Sir James Douglas?" Alex said, genially. "In which case, I would agree — but point out that the trouble he makes is invariably for the King's and the realm's enemies, the English, the Islesmen and others nearer home who endanger the peace and well-being of the kingdom. His valour on the fields of Otterburn, Glenarkaig in Lochaber, and Preston in Lothian, as elsewhere, is well known. His sound judgement — which my lord Duke recognises as so important — both in the field and in council, is known by many here, in especial by such as are soldiers themselves. His services to the King and to the *late* Governor, the Duke of Rothesay, are without question. I ask, as I think is my right, for the reasons for his outlawry to be stated."

There was actually a sort of cheer at that.

"I am not obliged, sir, to give account to you, or any other, for the actions I require to take in the day-to-day rule of this realm," the Governor said.

"Not even to the King in parliament? This may not be a true parliament, but it is a convention of parliament. And the decisions already taken here have the force of a parliament, do they not? Else the King, you my lord Duke, and all others, but waste their time. I appeal to His Grace for a ruling, as one of the earls of his realm."

The King of Scots wrung his hands, but nodded. "Yes," he said.

His brother shrugged. "As His Grace wishes. Douglas, formerly of Aberdour, now forfeit, fled from the affray at Homildon Hill, with a thousand men, without a blow struck. Leaving his commanders, like all his comrades, on the field, their rear and flanks open to attack. So I am informed."

Various cries of denial rose from Douglases throughout the church. But these stilled as, at last, the Earl of Douglas rose to his feet.

"You have been misinformed," he said, heavily. "I commanded there. I ordered Sir James Douglas to remain behind after rejecting his advice earlier. When all was lost, by the failure

151

of his commanders, he contrived to save what he could of the Scots force. I say that his conduct on that field was more to be admired than that of any other present. I second my lord of Mar's motion that his outlawry be revoked herewith."

Now there were cheers indeed, every Douglas, and many another, rising in acclaim.

Albany pointed at the Chancellor. "My lord — have this unseemly uproar stopped! Forthwith. This is a Council General, not a bear-baiting!" And as the noise died away before his cold but frightening anger, he added, "Since it is the wish of my lord of Douglas, the outlawry is withdrawn. Chancellor — this of the confirmation of sheriffs' and officers' appointments. And let us have done!"

Although the dull task of listing and agreeing, or otherwise, many minor appointments took some time thereafter, the Linlithgow Council General was in fact over with that last statement by the Governor — for he did not again open his thin lips. Many of the onlookers undoubtedly would have streamed out had not the monarch's presence forbidden it. But at last it was done, the Chancellor thanked the Commissioners for attending, hurriedly, the trumpeters sounded, and the King, Governor and principals filed out.

Outside the church, Jamie was surrounded by a back-slapping, vociferous and congratulatory crowd, to his embarrassment. But when, presently, he was joined by Alex Stewart, and it was his turn to congratulate and thank, he found his friend not embarrassed but preoccupied.

"See you, Jamie," Alex said, when they could be private, "we gained what we wanted there, and more than we could have hoped for. Thanks to Wardlaw, and, of course, your Earl. Aye, and the King himself. But let us not lose our heads, in one fashion or another! My Uncle Robert is still Governor — and will love us even less than heretofore. He never forgets nor forgives, as you well know. If he cannot win one way, he will, I fear, try to gain his ends in another — less openly."

"You mean, my safety is still at risk, you think?"

"Yes. My own too, perhaps. After all, he murdered his other nephew, David, who challenged him! But you are in more immediate danger, I would judge. Your outlawry may be over — but you are still a stone for stumbling in his path. I say, the sooner we are back over the Highland Line the better, my friend. Before there is any possible . . . mischance!"

"Is all that we have achieved today of little value, then?"

"Far from it. That was just the beginning, I hope. But we can continue to assail our foe from *our* hold, not from inside his! Do you not agree?"

"Aye, you are right. Back to Strabrock, then. And ride north tomorrow? Banquet tonight or none."

"I saw my uncle in close converse with Lindsay of Rossie, before I came out to you. I think that we might with profit ride *tonight*, Jamie . . ."

X

STRANGELY ENOUGH, THE first overt move by Albany *vis-à-vis* the new Earl of Mar and his ex-outlaw friend was not made until well into the following summer; and when it was, it seemed to negate their apprehensions. It came in the form of an olive-branch, indeed, unexpected as this was.

Jamie was comfortably settled and well enough content, acting more or less as steward for Alex at Lochindorb. Albany might not take active steps against him; but he was far from assured that he and his family would remain secure and unmolested if he returned to live in the South. Besides, he had come much to enjoy the Highland way of life, the folk and the country. Alex strongly urged him to remain. The fact was, he trusted Jamie to look to his interests there adequately, where he did not similarly trust his brothers. Where Duncan might be, none knew; but he might possibly seek to bring some dangerous pressure on Andrew and Walter Stewart. James, the youngest of the family, had married and gone to manage a detached portion of their father's lands, at Garth in Atholl. Andrew now managed the Strathaven and Lower Spey lands to the east, and Walter those of Upper Donside; but for the central Badenoch and Strathspey territories, his main inheritance, Alex was happier with Jamie as his representative.

One day, early in July, Jamie was interrupted, at the business of building a new timber jetty to serve the castle-island, by the arrival of Alex from Kildrummy, in company with John Stewart of Coull — the first they had seen of that young man since Linlithgow. The cousins seemed to be on excellent terms.

As they were rowed over to the castle, Alex explained. "Cousin John brings interesting tidings, Jamie. He is but recently from the South. He tells of some change of attitude by the Governor. Or so it would seem."

The Douglas eyed the other without comment but in entire disbelief.

"My esteemed sire has qualities which even you must grant him, Sir James," John Stewart said, smiling. "He has a notably clear and discerning eye, however chilly! He sees things as they are and wastes no time and concern in wishing them otherwise. He may be devious, but none is more practical than my lord Duke. What he cannot beat down or bring low by guile he will work with — and seek to use to his own ends. If one path is blocked he will take another, and care naught for what men say. He is a proud man — but does not allow pride to injure ultimate advantage."

"So?"

"Jamie, I think, is almost as practical a man as your father, Cousin! He will be hard to convince that the Governor loves us."

"That he does not. But he has decided that you can be of use. And are better working if not for him, at least not against him. He was quick to learn the lesson of Linlithgow. You, and perhaps myself, offer a threat to his rule. He does not like that. He cannot remove you, here behind the Highland Line, and so takes other steps. To use you and me."

"We should rejoice at that?" Jamie asked bluntly.

"Why not? If you can use it to your advantage. Learn from him." They had reached the castle landing-stage, but John of Coull sat still, intent on what he had to say. "He sent for me, from Coull — for, like you, I did not linger after the Council General. He is never affable, even with his own family, and he did not fall on my neck! But nor did he assail me for countering him that day as he might have done. He has never concerned himself with me hitherto, as a father might, and I have kept out of his way. Now, it seems he would have me for him, not against him."

"I can understand that," Alex said. "I would wish the same."

"Thank you! So I am sent up to Elgin and Inverness, to take the justiciary courts, after all. To try me out, he says. I am not Acting Justiciar yet. He keeps that for himself — and all the revenues pertaining. He has a great stomach for siller, has the Duke! I am but to be his deputy, this time. And if I do well, or at least please him, he will consider giving me the acting office. Also the earldom of Buchan — which my lord of Mar's father held and is now reverted to the Crown. Moreover, he threatens to find me a suitable heiress to wed!"

"Another one!" Jamie said, unkindly.

"Ah, the first was *my* choice. My father only thought to make use of it. Woe is me, I lost to a better man!"

Neither of his hearers commented on that. But Jamie went on, "Where do we come into this? Or, leastways, the Earl of Mar?"

"My father, if you will believe it, advised me to seek my lord's advice and help, saying that his aid and guidance would not be forgotten. Also that all question as to the death of Sir Malcolm Drummond was now closed."

"Which might have its own convenience for himself!"

"There is something for you also, Jamie."

"Yes. He says that forfeiture on properties, consequent upon your outlawry, is now revoked, that you may come and go freely, within the realm."

"Was that not understood when the outlawry itself was lifted?"

"A mere understanding and the Governor's stated assurance are different!"

"The Governor's stated assurance could mean anything or nothing." That was flat. "His words and deeds are apt to differ! With all respect, I have had to deal with him longer than you, my lord. I think I will continue to bide in the North yet awhile."

"Good — in that at least I rejoice," Alex said. "Since Cousin John brought these tidings, I have been concerned that I might lose you. And I need you here. But . . . it will be to your much advantage, Jamie, to have your property restored, and to move freely in the South, without fear of apprehension."

"I shall go warily, nevertheless . . . !"

At this stage Mary arrived at the landing-jetty to greet them, wondering why they sat there in the boat. She welcomed the new arrivals warmly, both her nephews, declaring that she liked personable young men so long as they had not come to take away her husband from her, as seemed to be their custom — and his delight. Alex reassured her. There was no suggestion of taking Jamie away — although if he would come with them to Elgin next day, it might be advantageous and pleasant. She could come herself, if she cared. It seemed that John of Coull intended to adopt the widest interpretation of his father's suggestion, and would have Alex actually to sit with him on the judicial bench at this assize, possibly with some churchman or other of his choice — Bishop Spynie of Moray being a dying man. This procedure, of course, would fairly well ensure his own acceptance as Justiciar; but it would also be of advantage to the new Earl of Mar, in building up his image as a power in the North irrespective of authority in the South. There might well come a time when these two Stewarts' interests would clash, and then sparks would fly indeed; but meantime their mutual co-operation could achieve much.

John Stewart told them, that night, much more of events in the South than had emerged in the boat. He informed them that the Earl of Douglas had returned to captivity in England, and the first three hostages were on their way home, with another three to be ready to stand in for him next year — these to include Jamie's brother James of Dalkeith, the Earl's own son the young Master of Douglas, and Sir Simon Glendinning, Jamie's old colleague at Otterburn. Just why King Henry was allowing this especial privilege to the Douglas, while still refusing to ransom him outright, was not clear; possibly he believed that the power of Douglas, much the greatest in Scotland, could thus be kept restrained. But it much offended the Governor, for whose son Murdoch of Fife no similar concessions were being offered, despite many pleas and letters.

The old Earl of Northumberland, with his grandson young Harry Percy, son of the late Hotspur, the Lord Bardolph and the Bishops of Bangor and St. Asaph, had duly arrived in Scotland; the boy was now sent to study with Prince James at St. Andrews, while his grandfather and the others were domiciled at the Blackfriars in Perth, ostensibly guests of the Governor but in fact little better than hostages. The King had sent an envoy to King Charles of France asking him if he would accept the prince at his Court for a few years, in theory to learn chivalry and kingcraft, such as he could not learn from Bishop Wardlaw — renewed squabbling between the rival Popes at Avignon and Genoa had ruled out a papal destination for the boy.

John Stewart was very good company, and Alex and he made a notable pair, amusing, quick-silver, tossing the ball of repartee, allusion and challenge between them in lively fashion, with Mary joining in not infrequently, another Stewart with her own shrewd contributions to make. Jamie, on the other hand, was content to listen and watch. Not for him this conversational sparring and gymnastics. He could appreciate and admire but not take part. Also he had a fairly pronounced critical faculty, and he was by no means certain that he was as happy with John of Coull as was Alex most obviously. Perhaps it was merely that this was Albany's son, and he could not forget it. There might even have been a kind of jealousy. Jamie Douglas did not make friends easily, and Alex he had grown to be very fond of, without putting it into so many words. This comparative newcomer, although a kinsman to be sure, seemed to have jumped into an association and understanding with his cousin almost overnight. Moreover, clearly one day he would be an earl likewise, a major figure in the land, on an equal footing with Alex — which the Douglas could never be. So he reserved his acceptance somewhat, like his judgement — in which he was abetted by Mariota de Athyn, who remained cool towards the visitor.

The Countess Isobel was not once mentioned throughout the evening, but her shadow was very much present.

* * *

As they rode to Elgin the next day, Mary gladly accepting the invitation to accompany them, it became clear that John Stewart's desire to have Alex sit in judgement with him was not entirely disinterested and out of friendly good-fellowship. It transpired in fact that, in addition to the many straightforward and lesser cases and disputes remitted to the Justiciar's assize from barony and sheriffs' courts, there was a major dispute to be pronounced upon concerning two of the principal vassals of the earldom of Mar, Sir Andrew Leslie of Balquhain and Sir Alexander Forbes of that Ilk. Alex, Hereditary Sheriff of Aberdeen as well as Earl of Mar, could have sat in judgement on these two himself; but had avoided doing so for fear of alienating the support of one or the other, which in his present stage of building up goodwill and a solid base in his new feudal situation, he could not afford — for these were both very powerful men, heads of their respective houses. So, since the dispute concerned alleged murder and mayhem, as well as other mutual irritations — the two houses had been at feud for generations — the thing was referred to the Justiciar for decision, the hearing to be held at Elgin rather than at Aberdeen, where rival influences might well be brought to bear. John of Coull, himself a Mar vassal, and much younger and junior save in royal descent to either of the litigants, had not failed to recognise that he was going to require support and guidance in this matter, and the Earl of Mar was the obvious choice. Alex saw it as a means of influencing the decision without having to accept the responsibility of judging against one or the other, which must remain the Justiciar's duty. They decided to ask the Prior of Pluscarden as third and independent member, he having no links with Mar, and Pluscarden being on their way to Elgin.

So once again Jamie and Mary sat in the great hall of the royal castle of Elgin, next morning, as the Justiciar and his two co-adjutors were ceremoniously ushered in to take their seats on the dais, with due pomp and dignity. John Stewart played his part well, easy, confident but not arrogant, and deferring pleasantly to his colleagues. When truly Highland questions arose, he put them all in the first instance to Alex, whose knowledge of clan justice, traditions and attitudes he could not hope to rival — thereby gaining a vital acceptance which could so easily have been withheld, a problem which was always inherent in the Crown-appointed Justiciar of the North's office. The dichotomy between the true Highlanders and the clans and communities east of the various Mounths, in Angus, the Mearns, Aberdeenshire and the Moray plain, although nothing like so sharp as between Highland and Lowland, North and South, was very much a reality. Alex's strength of position was that he had been brought up as a true Highlander, with a Mackay Highland mother, and yet was of Lowland and royal descent — illegitimacy meaning nothing here. Now that he was also Earl of Mar, he was enabled to straddle the divide the more effectively. Undoubtedly Albany had not failed to recognise this unpalatable fact in his instructions to his son.

There was a succession of cases remitted by sheriffs, barony courts and clan chiefs, which for one reason or another required the Justiciar's decision — not because these authorities lacked judicial powers, for every baron had the ultimate sanction of pit and gallows — but for reasons as to side-effects, conflicting interests of the involved authorities themselves, prestige and seniority; and where the Crown's own interests were concerned, as in unlawful customs dues collection, offences on royal lands and forests and complaints against Crown officers. Claims against raiding Islesmen and other mainland MacDonalds and clans allied to the Lord of the Isles, constituted the most troublesome sector of the day's proceedings, since there was really little that could be done about these, short of major armed intervention which the Governor certainly was not prepared to consider. In all this, decisions were in the main expeditiously reached, crisp, clear and generally acceptable, whilst in line with

159

realities. John Stewart proved an apt pupil, and the Prior Moray of Pluscarden a wise and succinct diviner of the truth and heart of the matter.

It was, consequently, late in the day before the testing issue of the two Mar vassals came before the Justiciar — deliberately withheld until now so that the doughty protagonists might have ample time to partake of their earl's hospitality in food and especially wine — kept well apart, of course — and so, hopefully, be in a state of mind not to insist too much on finicky details and hierarchal precedences and the like. Their dispute, although somewhat ridiculous, was important for the peace of a large area, for the well-being of the earldom and to some extent that of the entire North-East. All recognised that this was likely to be an exercise not so much in justice as in tact and ingenuity.

On Alex's advice the thing was suitably stage-managed. A single trumpet-blast introduced a pursuivant, who announced in ringing tones that the King's Justiciar, aided by the most noble Earl of Mar and the Garioch, and an illustrous representative of Holy Church, would now hear and consider the notable cause and arbitrament between the puissant and high-born lords, Sir Andrew Leslie of Balquhain, Lord of Urie, Conglas and Harlaw, on the one part and Sir Alexander Forbes of that Ilk, Lord of Forbes, Putachie and Kinnernie; in which the said Sir Andrew made accusation against the said Sir Alexander of injury and offence; and the said Sir Alexander counter-charged the said Sir Andrew with grave intrusions against his rights and privileges, to his hurt and undoubted loss. There had been some doubt, even at this stage, as to which name should be enunciated first; but Leslie was the original complainer and considerably the elder. So a risk was taken.

"Sir Andrew and Sir Alexander!" the Mackintosh pursuivant concluded, loudly, as though at a tournament.

Out from the opposite corner-doors of the dais-area, precisely at the same moment, strode the distinguished litigants, heads high. Their progress towards the front of the table was a little less exact, for Leslie was undoubtedly a little drunk and lurched rather, and Forbes was slightly lame in one leg. They did not so much as glance at each other, nor yet at the company, but somehow managed to reach their indicated places before the table, well apart but simultaneously, bowed stiffly to the judges and so stood, glaring.

Leslie, known as Red Andrish, was a man in his mid-fifties, bulky, florid, hot-eyed, with a shock of wiry red hair so far not in the least diluted with grey, bull-like of shoulder, carelessly clad. Forbes was a dozen years younger, tall, good-looking in a hatchet-faced way, dark-eyed, beak-nosed and notably well dressed. He was a Crowner or Coroner of Aberdeenshire, chief of his name. Unfortunately, although their principal seats of Balquhain and Forbes Castles were over a dozen miles apart, in mid Strathdon, downstream of Kildrummy, their baronies touched at various points, with evident friction.

John Stewart, wisely, was notably careful about how he handled these two, from the start. "A good day to you, my lords," he said. "I greet you well, in the name of the King's Grace, and regret if you have been kept waiting. I am informed that you have certain matters between you on which you desire the ruling of this court of High Justiciary, and I am happy to oblige you by all means within my power. But before doing so, I must remind you, and all others, that we have here present the person of your feudal superior, the most noble Earl of Mar, whose undoubted privilege it is to hear and pronounce upon all such controversies within his earldom, if so he chooses, by the powers vested in him as one of the great earls of Scotland."

"I do not so choose," Alex said easily. "Both these lords are my very good friends, and long-time supporters of my lady-wife. I have eaten the salt of both. I therefore find myself in no position to pass judgement on one cause or the other. But, if I may, I will assist you, my lord Justiciar, in the honest assessment of each or either."

"Very well. Do your lordships wish to speak to your own causes, or be represented by others?"

"Only Forbes speaks for Forbes!" the dark man barked, deep-voiced.

"None other *would*!" Leslie declared.

"H'mm. Then, my lords, may we proceed with the hearing? In all order and due respect for this High Court of the King's Grace. Sir Andrew, as the elder and with whom complaint to this Court originated, will you commence? Sir Alexander agreeing?"

"By God, I will!" Red Andrish cried. "I demand justice on this, this upjumped cattle-thief and all his misbegotten tribe! He insults me. *Me*, Leslie! He injures . . ."

"I say that it is impossible to insult a Leslie!" Forbes interjected. "All men know that."

161

"Fiend seize you — Leslies were noble before ever your fore-bear issued from the arse of the bear or the pig or whatever brute you claim to descend from, Forbes!"

"Noble? Leslie! You come of a line of Low Country huck-sters, Hungarians or Flemings, or such, Bartolph by name . . ."

"My lords!" Brave John interrupted strongly. "These may be matters of opinion, sincerely held. But this Court is only con-cerned to hear *facts*. I ask you to confine yourselves to such. Sir Andrew — what are the facts you wish to bring before us?"

Leslie swallowed audibly, almost as though in reluctant alter-native to spitting. "This man's bastard brother, Out-with-the-Sword John Forbes of Callievar, has stolen the bell I gave to God and the church of Forbes in blessed memory of my mother, from that parish. He has removed it and taken it up the Hill of Callievar above the said church, and hung it from a tree. The godless ruffian rings it there. To the hurt and distress of the lieges. *My* bell!"

"How can it be your bell, Red Andrish?" Forbes demanded. "Given to my church of Forbes years back. What we do with our bell is no concern of yours."

John Stewart drew a hand across his mouth. "My lords, bear with me. But I scarce perceive, as yet, what the present location of the church-bell of Forbes parish has to do with the King's Justiciar? Nor how His Grace's lieges are so grievously hurt?"

"Hear this, then," Leslie cried. "This man's ill brother mis-rings it. He jangles and clangles it. At the wrong times, whatever. Turning decent folk out to the kirk when there's naught to go for, when no priest is present. Whanging it during sermons so none can hear . . ."

"When were *you* at sermon in the kirk o' Forbes, man Leslie?" the other demanded. "If you ever attend the kirk at all, which I misdoubt, it is not *my* kirk . . ."

"I am a god-fearing Christian, Sandy Forbes — not a heathen barbarian worshipping idols like your own self, fiend seize you!"

"That's a lie, by the Mass! I am as good a Christian as any man in Mar — and a deal better than you, you adulterous old goat! We all ken fine what you do of a Lord's Day — aye, and every other day, and night too!"

"I say you are an idolator. An open worshipper of false gods, Forbes! You'll no' deny that you keep yon shameful and heathenish image in your own hall. And bow down before it

162

when you eat. The stinking, shrunken head of a bear — forby it looks more like a pig, to me! The bear out of whose filthy arse you and your line issued . . .!"

"Fool! That is the mighty bear my great ancestor Ochonachar slew, in the days of the Cruithnie. And was given the lands of Forbes in consequence, and the name *Fear-boisceal*, Brave Warrior, by the Cruithnie king. In the days when you Fleming Leslies were still painted Goths scratching for acorns!"

"Liar again! *Boisceal* means savage, unlettered savage, not warrior. All know that . . ."

The Justiciar banged on the table, to make himself heard. "My lords — I must rule that all this controversy is out of my jurisdiction. Church-bells, interrupting sermons, worshipping bears — these are not matters for this Court. If aught, they appear to be subjects for Holy Church's consideration. But . . . not here! Unless, to be sure, my Lord Prior wishes to make observation?"

The Valliscaulian, a stern-faced, muscular prelate, shook his fair but tonsured head. "I recommend remitment to the Diocesan, my lord Bishop of Aberdeen," he said, in pained fashion.

"Now you see why Alex did not want these two beauties before his earldom court!" Jamie said to his wife — who for some time had been sitting with one hand pressed tightly over her mouth and the other held against her stomach, in an effort to contain her emotions.

"Yes. Excellent," John Stewart was acceding. "The Bishop of Aberdeen it must be. You agree, my lord of Mar?"

"Not so!" Leslie objected. "I demand my rights. From the King's Justiciar, not any snivelling churchman! This man Forbes is Crowner of Aberdeen, a bishop's man. Think you I will win my rights from Greenlaw?"

"H'mm. My lord of Mar?"

"I would agree, my lord Justiciar, that these matters complained of are not such as we can pronounce upon here. Reference to an ecclesiastical court would appear to be proper. If not the complainant's own Diocesan, then to another. The Bishop of Ross, perhaps? Since I cannot see the Justiciar's jurisdiction extending to church matters. Unless, to be sure, there is further complaint of a more secular nature?"

"There is indeed!" Forbes put in. "I demand to be protected from the calumnies and assaults of this madman. And that the

King's Grace punishes him suitably. He is naught but a thorn in the flesh to all decent men — and women. Forby, it is not so much a thorn as a *rod* in the flesh he is to them!"

"*You* say it? Whose whorings are known from Dee to the Spey!"

"*I* cannot claim seventy bastard sons — to say nothing of the queans! He cannot deny that, my lords, I warrant!"

For the first time Leslie had no ready answer. It might be that he could not indeed deny the charge; more probably that he did not wish to do so, as a man of some spirit.

"I have heard no complaints!" he said, shortly.

"No — not from your wife, by the Mass!" the other charged. "Who is rejoiced to have you out of her bed, I am assured, whosoever else's you are in!"

"Do not soil my wife's fair name with your foul lips, bear-worshipper! I have been a good husband to her — which is more than you have been to yours. I have given her seven good sons and seven daughters living. *She* has no cause to complain!"

"My lords . . ." Brave John attempted, but hardly hopefully. He was, of course, overborne. "Deny that your wife, Isabella Mortimer, so rejoiced to be quit of you, even for one night, that she sent seven of your doxies a thank-offering of meal and meat!" Forbes exclaimed.

"You do not have even that right, man. It was an especial occasion, my lords. Those seven women I bairned all in the same night and in four parishes. By God's mercy they were all brought to bed the same day, and delivered with fine sons. My lady was pleased to send each a half-boll of meal, a half-boll of malt, a wedder-lamb and five shillings siller. I say that shows a good and satisfied wife."

Mary Stewart emitted an unusually inelegant squeak and squawk from behind her hand. "Sakes, Jamie!" she gasped. "Is he not a joy? Seven! *You* could not rise to that, I swear! Lord — my belly aches!"

"So it should — and more than your belly, woman!" he asserted severely. "For so great a Christian, this Leslie sounds to be a menace to all decent husbands — and wives abetting him, to their shame. The man's no more than a stallion! I would find for Forbes, whatever, bear or not, if I was John Stewart."

"For why? What is the charge? We have not heard it yet. Or have I missed it?"

Clearly something of the same sort was preoccupying the judges, who were conferring together, whilst Sir Alexander proclaimed his disgust.

John of Coull waved a hand. "No doubt these, h'm, informations are interesting and instructive, my lords," he said, "but still they do not concern this Court. We are not here to try matters of adultery or illegitimacy, any more than offences against the Church. Either we hear of injury to the King's peace and lieges, or we must refer all to an ecclesiastical court." He pointed at Leslie. "*Have* you a personal injury to complain of, Sir Andrew? Other than to your name and pride? Which are not our present concern."

"I have, Christ God! I was assailed by this man's bastard brother, John Out-with-the-Sword, of Callievar, at the funeral of a kinswoman of my own, at the kirk of Forbes on the feast of the Assumption of the Blessed Virgin, I tell you."

"Assailed? How assailed, my lord?"

"He lies," Forbes observed, but almost dutifully, wearily, now.

"By that damnable bell! He rang it at me, shouted. Mocked the dead, and me, from his hill — all through the interment."

"Unseemly, yes," the Justiciar sympathised. "Lacking due respect. But . . . a matter for private adjustment, surely? For you and your seven good sons?"

"When I sought to do the same, and sent my son Davie and my servants up the hill at him, this damnable John assailed them, first with arrows then with the sword. He struck Davie to the effusion of blood."

"Ah. So there *was* an attack upon the person? Of your son."

"In self-defence," Sir Alexander pointed out.

"The creature assailed us."

"In self-defence. You sent your people up at him, from the kirk. If your miserable son Davie sustained some small hurt, he had but himself to blame. Or you, for sending so poor a sworder against Johnnie!"

"He shot arrows whilst yet distant. Was that self-defence?"

"Was your son injured by an arrow?"

"No, by the sword. But three of my servants were slain by the arrows on the way up, I'd mind you, Forbes."

"Johnnie is a fair archer, yes. Good with the axe and quarter-staff, likewise. Though best of all with the sword . . ."

"Wait you — wait!" John Stewart exclaimed. "Sir Andrew —

you say *slain*? Three servants killed? By this John Forbes?"

"Aye, as they climbed the hill."

"But . . . this is altogether different! Why did you not say so, long since? Here was slaughter, of the King's lieges. Why all this talk of bells and idolatry and the like, when you had this slaying?"

"They were but servants," Leslie pointed out.

"Servants," Forbes agreed — the first agreement between them that day.

The judges exchanged glances.

"Nevertheless, subjects of the King's Grace and entitled to the King's protection," Alex said, sternly for him. "Why were we not told?"

Silence — this too for the first time.

"Do I take it, Sir Andrew, that you in fact are not petitioning about these deaths, but only of the injury to your son? And the offence to yourself?" John of Coull enquired slowly.

"That is so."

"And you, Sir Alexander, are not concerned with the fact that your brother slew these men?"

"It was unfortunate. But the responsibility was Leslie's. They were armed. He should not have sent them up the hill to attack Johnnie. He shot no arrows until they climbed the hill."

"Then, my lords, since you both hold barons' courts, with power of pit and gallows, you could have settled this between you. Or you could have appealed to the Sheriff of Aberdeen. I am at a loss to know on what this Court is expected to adjudicate."

"The Sheriff of Aberdeen is Forbes's good-brother," Leslie reminded.

"I understood it was my lord Earl of Mar, himself."

"Now. Not then."

"When, then, did this offence take place? The Feast of the Assumption did you not say?"

"Aye. But two years back."

"Two years? Why, then, wait until now, to bring it before this Justiciary?"

"Because . . . I wasna like to win justice before."

"I do not understand you, my lord. If your barony courts were of no avail, and you could not rely on the Sheriff, there was still the Mar earldom court, and finally this royal court of appeal. Why wait two years?"

Red Andrish looked almost uncomfortable — as, oddly enough, did Forbes. "It was difficult, see you," he said.

"I do *not* see it, I fear."

The litigants actually exchanged glances.

"Come, my lord — answer me."

"There was no earl, mind. And, and my lord of Badenoch was Justiciar."

"So?"

"Sir Malcolm Drummond was no superior of mine."

"Nor mine," added Forbes.

"But the Countess was, and is. And she controlled her own earldom."

"She did, aye."

"And you did not appeal to her, to Lady Isobel?"

"No."

"Why?"

Leslie's florid features were purple now. After a pause, he burst out. "Because this Forbes knew her bed ower well, that's why!" He glanced at Alex, half-apologetically, and then away again.

There was a profound hush in Elgin Castle's hall.

John Stewart was at a loss as to what to say. He did not look at his fellow-judges, but considered his finger-nails and cleared his throat.

It was Alex Stewart who spoke, eventually. "We need not here consider such hearsay," he said evenly. "It is not evidence. By the nature of matters Sir Andrew Leslie can have no proofs to support his unfortunate statement. I request that it be removed from any record of these proceedings."

"Most certainly, my lord Earl," Brave John acceded, almost eagerly. "This Court regrets that it was said, Sir Andrew. We can consider only testimony which can be substantiated."

"I . . . ah . . . mmm." Red Andrish said.

"I, my lords, wish to repudiate what this man has said," Forbes declared strongly. "It is a calumny on our feudal lady. And false, like all else he has said this day. All lies."

"Damn you, Forbes — it is no lie, as well you know!" his enemy cried. "As I could prove, if I wished."

"How prove? You but disclaim our lady's honour."

"It is not *her* honour I disclaim but yours, man! You made but a poor showing in her bed, compared with my own self. She told me so, herself!"

There was uproar in court.

It took some time to achieve silence, even the Justiciar seeming to be in no great hurry to make himself heard. Mary, gleaming-eyed, shook her husband's arm.

"Now you see what your Alex has taken on," she said. "I told you he would not have his troubles to seek, with that one."

Jamie shook his head unhappily. "Damn the man!" he muttered. "This is beyond all."

John Stewart had found his voice. "Sir Andrew — I forbid any further such ill-considered and unmannerly statements in this Court. Your spleen has deprived you of your wits, it is clear. You will no more traduce the fair name of this great lady, or any other. Mind it." He turned to his colleague, doubtfully. "My lord of Mar — do you wish to make any comment?"

Alex drew a deep breath. "Little," he said. "Save to assert my lady's good name and honour before all, and to declare its safety from the slanders of so great and self-confessed a lecher and defiler of women. All that has been spoken of took place before my marriage to the Countess, but I personally vouch for their untruth." He paused. "And now, my lord Justiciar, I suggest that overmuch time has been taken up by this unsuitable and unnecessary cause. I say that we should come to swift decision and have done."

"So say I, my lord, and most heartily." Brave John frowned. "Only . . . I confess to being uncertain as to what it is we are to decide upon. We have heard so much that is irrelevant to this Court — and what *is* relevant, the slaying of these three servants of Sir Andrew's, does not appear to be before us. I fail to see what pronouncement we can make."

"I, likewise," Prior Moray said. "May we not dismiss the entire matter as irrelevant and beyond the jurisdiction of this Court? Or remit it to a court of Holy Church?"

"Perhaps. As former Justiciar, my lord of Mar, how would you have dealt with this?"

Thus appealed to, Alex spoke carefully. "I would say that, despite Sir Andrew's intemperate and ill-judged statements, he has shown himself to have suffered wrong, which we cannot dismiss. On the other hand, nothing has been proved against Sir Alexander's good repute. We are not concerned with matters under the jurisdiction of the Church. But we are concerned with the keeping of the King's peace. And it has been established, I think, that this John Forbes of Callievar has indeed offended against and broken that peace, to the distress of the lieges and the effusion of blood. We can, and I believe we should, therefore, require Sir Alexander Forbes, in whose baronial jurisdiction his half-brother undoubtedly is, to take full and due steps to remedy this situation, and to ensure that the said John Forbes no longer breaks the King's peace. Less than this we cannot do. More is not within our competence."

"Exactly. Excellently said," his cousin agreed thankfully. "You accept, my lord Prior? Very well. I so pronounce, in the name of the King's Grace. You, Sir Andrew, accept this judgement?" That was not so much a question as a challenge.

Leslie pursed thick lips, frowned, and then shrugged. "I do."

"And you, Sir Alexander — you will take due action to control and punish John Forbes of Callievar?"

"I will."

"So be it. This cause is closed. As, also, is this present assize of Moray." Relievedly, John Stewart rose to his feet — as must all others. "God save the King's Grace!"

The trumpets blared.

"What are you going to say to Alex now?" Mary asked, as they filed out after the judges.

"I do not know. That was an ill mouthful for any man to stomach," Jamie said, "regarding his wife. But . . . if any man can face it with dignity, he can."

"Yes. But it is the effect on *other* men, and on his control of her earldom, that is important."

"I think that will be none so great. Isobel of Mar's reputation has been well known for many a year. In her own Mar in especial, no doubt. I mind Duke David told me of it, long ago. But she was strong enough, as woman as well as countess, to carry it off. This, today, must have been a sore offence for Alex — but I do not think that it will injure him."

"Perhaps. So long as she does not continue on her course, now she is wed to him!"

"I think not. She is older now. And she loves him — that I swear. She says openly that she has never loved another. She will wish to hold Alex now — a younger man. And that would not be the way to do it. No — Alex knew her reputation when he wed her. Part of the price he had to pay."

"For . . . what?"

"For power, no less. Power for good, yes. But power, nevertheless. Alex is as much a Stewart as the rest of you! Though better than most . . ."

XI

JAMIE DOUGLAS'S PROGNOSTICATION was proved fairly accurate. Alex Stewart went quietly ahead with the consolidation of his hold over the earldom of Mar in the months that followed, apparently unaffected by the unfortunate revelations of Sir Andrew Leslie. Whatever he may have felt personally in the matter, he revealed no sign of it. As for the Countess Isobel, she only laughed when she heard of the allegations, called Red Andrish an old goat and Sandy Forbes too touchy by half — a verdict which was reinforced when it was learned that Forbes had gone home to Strathdon from Elgin, straightway summoned John Out-with-the-Sword into his presence, and without further ado took the said sword and struck off his half-brother's head with a single stroke, by way of interpretation of the Justiciar's order to remedy the situation. Thereafter he had had the body buried without ceremony at the back of the kirkyard — which was considered by most of Mar to be almost a more drastic punishment than the beheading itself, for only the least respected outcasts and the nameless were interred in such a position — indication, it was realised, of the Laird of Forbes's resentment at being caused inconvenience and public affront by any, kin or otherwise, rather than any kind of acknowledgement of injury done to the Laird of Balquhain. Alex, after a due interval, made a point of calling upon each protagonist, avoiding all reference to the dispute, and being well received by both. Which was the most satisfactory outcome, in the circumstances — for between them these two could field five hundred armed men at least, more at a pinch. The feudal system was much concerned with realities.

Jamie Douglas did not venture south during the months that followed, despite his officially-proclaimed immunity from arrest, being, as has been indicated, of a somewhat suspicious nature. He did send letters, however, mainly by travelling churchmen, to his father and brothers, requesting the payment to himself of the dues and rents from his restored estates of Stoneypath and Baldwinsgill. But, after due consideration, and discussion with Mary, he did not ask that his brother Johnnie vacate Aberdour Castle. For two reasons; one that it was set in Albany's county and earldom of Fife, and was just too close to Falkland and Rossie and other seats of his enemies for comfortable living; the other that he had a fondness for Johnnie and did not want to deprive him of his new style and status — or of his young woman there, Jeannie Boswell, which might well have resulted from any dispossession and return to Dalkeith. Unexpectedly this gesture produced an appreciative reaction from their father — who appeared once again to have regained a new lease on life — in the announcement that he was settling the barony and lands of Roberton, in Borthwick Water at the head of Teviotdale, on Jamie in compensation, a more valuable and extensive property than Aberdour. Mary, when she had heard of Jean Boswell's occupancy of her former house and home, had announced, in possibly typical feminine fashion, that she wanted nothing more to do with it, and was quite content to remain living at Lochindorb, where she and the young people were now firmly installed and beloved of Mariota de Athyn. She did not trust her half-brother Robert any more than did her husband. So, with Alex in Mar much of the time and Jamie a useful steward of his interests in Braemoray, enabling him to avoid having one of other of his awkward brothers in control at Lochindorb, the new Earl was well pleased to leave the situation as it was. The fact that the Douglases no longer felt themselves to be paupers, and dependent on Alex's charity, helped. Jamie, in fact, led a more normal, congenial and satisfying life than he had ever done.

But in the Scotland of this new fifteenth century, normality, congenial living and peace were conditions which not many were permitted to enjoy for long. That winter was punctuated by reports coming north that the Duke of Albany, far from taking his defeats at Linlithgow to heart, or at least amending his gubernatorial ways thereafter, was wielding an increasingly heavy hand. He was not a tyrant in any sense of oppressing the ordinary people; but no more did he seek to protect them from the ravages and savageries of others — especially some of his own minions. It seemed that he could not have been less interested in the state of the common folk, whom he was so determined to rule. He made a great proclamation of his resolve not to impose general taxation on the realm — which, of course, applied only to the land-owning interests and nobles, the burghs and the larger merchants and guilds, for the commonality had no wherewithal to pay tax anyway. Yet he increased customs dues, both greater and lesser, import licences, immunities and fines; but instead of applying the increased revenues towards the necessary maintenance of public works, roads, bridges, city walls, ports and harbours and so on, and the building up of a nucleus of a standing army which could bind together and service the feudal levies of the lords — as various parliaments and councils had decreed — he farmed out the customs collection lavishly to new men of his own raising, many of whom were blatant and harsh extortioners avid to grow rich quickly. Clearly the Governor was buying support in a big way. But support for what? He was already, and had long been, the power behind the throne. The King was unlikely to live long, and the new monarch would be only a boy, whom Albany could dominate as he did the father. Why then this suddenly much increased purchase of supporters, not only with Treasury and Exchequer revenues but with those of the earldoms and lordships Albany controlled personally? He himself was a man of fairly frugal tastes and habit — unusual in a Stewart. Another ominous theme was his new wooing of Holy Church, something he had little troubled with hitherto, never previously attempting to hide his contempt for upjumped prelates, clerics and clerks. Jamie wondered if he, the Governor, feared a link-up between the North, as represented by Alex, and the Church as represented by Bishop Wardlaw, with the young prince as pawn, and was taking countermeasures? Suspicious as ever, the Douglas considered that in such circumstances a very watchful eye should be kept on John of Coull, excellent company as he might be. Nothing altered the fact that he was Albany's son, legitimate and therefore in line, at two removes, for the throne.

Alex did not commit himself to more than general comment.

Then, with the winter well advanced, in late February they learned that young James, Earl of Carrick — he had not been advanced to his late brother's dukedom of Rothesay although some called him that — had started on his journey to France. The French King had sent the necessary invitation to his Court, and was indeed despatching a special ship to collect the boy. Until the vessel arrived James had been moved secretly from St. Andrews and in the care of the Earl of Orkney to — of all places — the Bass Rock, the towering isolated stack in the mouth of the Firth of Forth, with its small fortalice perched high thereon. Nothing could illustrate more significantly the fears felt by the King and Bishop Wardlaw for the safety of the prince. The Bass Rock was an utterly impregnable if extremely uncomfortable roosting-place, from which none could snatch him; the Earl of Orkney, Henry St. Clair, although a Scot was a subject of the King of Norway for his earldom, and so could not be attacked in any way without international complications; and the same applied, of course, to the ship being sent by the King of France, to interfere with which would breach the cornerstone of Scots foreign policy, the Auld Alliance. No chances were being taken.

This news was welcomed with great relief by Alex and Jamie, as by innumerable other loyal lieges of the Crown. The prince seemingly now was safe, the succession assured. Whatever else, Albany could not now gain the throne for himself, or at least not by any obvious means.

However, the tidings which reached Lochindorb, via the Church, a few days later, perturbed Jamie. Sir David Fleming of Cumbernauld, a friend of the King, who had been responsible for conveying the young prince to the Bass Rock, by sea, had been set upon and foully slain on his way home, at Herdmanston in East Lothian, not much more than a dozen miles from the Bass. And his slayer had been Sir James the Gross, next brother to the Earl of Douglas, who was making no secret of the fact, indeed boasting of the deed, clearly in no danger of retribution from the Governor. Which implied Albany's anger at the prince's escape, and at the same time, unhappily, the house of Douglas's involvement on the Governor's side, at least under its present direction. Jamie decided that he had been wise to remain in the North.

It was almost a month after this last news reached Braemoray, and the first promises of spring were beginning to stir in that world of the mountains and glens, when, on a windy fresh day of late March, Alex Stewart came in haste to his former home, and was rowed out over the slap-slapping wavelets of the loch, with a dark young man at his side, a stranger to Jamie. Alex was in Highland garb — he had been away in upper Strathspey in his capacity as Lord of Badenoch, seeking to settle a dispute between the Cattanachs and the Macphersons which his brother Sir Andrew had signally failed to do. The stranger wore Lowland dress.

"Jamie — this is Patrick Leslie, Younger of Balquhain. He came seeking me, with tidings. Sir James Douglas, my good friend." Alex looked preoccupied, less at ease than his usual.

"I had not thought to see you so soon. When you left here three days back, you thought to be away as much as two weeks," Jamie commented, nodding to young Leslie.

"Yes. I have had to make change of plan." He frowned. "I will tell you presently. Come, Patrick man — you will be hungry. I know that I am . . ."

When Alex decently could, he got Jamie alone.

"I am in a sorry pickle," he declared. "I am at a loss just what to do. I would value your good counsel, Jamie — as often ere this. It is about Isobel, my wife."

"Ah! I'd be something loth to advise between man and wife, Alex."

"No doubt. But I know no other I can turn to. And I need to talk this out with someone. You have a notably level head."

"Where women are concerned, Mary says that I am but a bairn!"

"They say that of us all. Perhaps it is true. But — bairn or not, I need guidance. Red Andrish Leslie sent his son seeking me, followed me to Ruthven — to tell me that Isobel, after I left Kildrummy five days back, went secretly to the old castle of Piell, in Kennethmont, to meet Sir Alexander Forbes. It is a remote hold in the northern tip of the Lordship of the Garioch, bordering on Strathbogie, a hunting-house. She said nothing of this to me. And it is scarce the time of year for hunting!"

Jamie made no comment.

"See you — I do not wish to play the jealous husband, spying on my wife. If I am insufficient for her needs, I must bear it with such patience as I may, Jamie, I recognise. At least, before others. She is a, a lusty woman. No doubt but you are aware of that. And I have been leaving her much alone these months, as I sought to bring her earldom into shape. But . . . that is what divides my mind — the earldom. Red Andrish, you see, is concerned with more than proving to me that he was telling the truth that day at Elgin. He claims that Forbes has been boasting that he has my Countess in his breeches pocket, or thereby!

174

That he is going to get her to transfer the keepership of the Forest of Kennethmont to himself, from Leslie. And this Piell Castle is the main house for that Forest."

"Is this so great a matter?"

"It is, yes. Not the keepership itself, perhaps, but this of transfer. Whether it is true, or not, I do not know. But it could do the earldom the greatest hurt. Do you not see? Here I am trying to hammer this Mar into a strong and united whole, a force to wield in the North, a rallying point for other forces, a link between the Highland clans and the low-country lairds. And here are two of the most powerful vassals of the earldom like to be thrown at each other's throats. They have always been at feud, yes — but this is different. This transfer of the keepership could be like throwing a meaty bone between two savage hounds. They have been content to growl at each other for long; this could set them tearing and rending. And with it, my earldom."

"Scarce so bad as that, Alex?"

"I say that it could be. Kennethmont abuts the Leslie lands — and it is far from the Forbes properties. Moreover, it lies next to the great Gordon lordship of Strathbogie — delicate folk to handle. There is an heiress at Strathbogie now, as you know, since her father Sir Adam Gordon was slain at Homildon. Leslie hints that Forbes would like her for one of his sons! I have been trying to bring the Gordons into my fold. This is no time to play such games. Do you realise how many Leslie lairdships there are in Mar? Red Andrish is not the head of the family; but any such open affront to him would bring in the rest. Forbes is less strong — but he is linked in marriage with other great houses of power. So, indeed, is Leslie. I would not have Mar divided into warring halves, and all my labours spoiled."

"The Lady Isobel must herself know this."

"No doubt she does — since she has managed Mar herself for long. But it is folly, nevertheless. Perhaps she recognises the danger, perhaps not. Perhaps she cares not? That is why I am at a loss. She does not see my use of the earldom with quite the same eye as I do! She is not greatly concerned with uniting the North against my uncle Albany. She may even be seeking, in her own way, to halt me somewhat. You see my difficulty?"

"To be sure. But it may not be so ill as you fear. This Leslie may be making overmuch of it, for his own purposes. He is a wild man . . ."

"There you have it. He *is* a wild man, and would not hesitate to sound to arms from what his son tells me. Much of any earl's, or other great lord's, time and effort is taken up with keeping his vassals from quarrelling and so weakening his power. That is what I have been doing at Ruthven, between the Macphersons and Cattanachs, for my lordship of Badenoch. Leslie asks me to intervene now, in Mar — and uses this of my wife's dalliance with Forbes to force my hand. I do not wish to seem to go rushing after my wife like any jealous husband. You know how she would deal with that! Yet I must do something."

"To me, it seems that you have to choose, Alex. Which means most to you? Your wife or your earldom?"

"I am fond of her, Jamie. We match each other well, for the most part. But . . ."

"Aye — *but*, my friend?"

"You must know how much the power of Mar means to me, man. For what I can do with it. Have already begun to do. With it I can build up the North into a force to halt Albany. Young James Stewart may well need that force, one day. The realm will need it, I say. Only I can provide it, I think."

"You have sufficiently answered my question, my lord of Mar! You go to this Kennethmont."

The other stared at him, nibbling his lip.

"You will require some excuse, to be sure. Could you not say that the Ruthven business was settled speedily, and coming back, you were given word that she, the Lady Isobel, was at Kennethmont? You could say that coming by Lochindorb, the place, this Piell Castle, was on your way home to Kildrummy, could you not? So, like any loving husband, you thought to join her."

"It might serve, yes. But . . . it is damnable to be thus held. To have to choose . . ."

"You chose before ever you came here, Alex, I think. When you cut short your time at Ruthven and rode here in haste, you had already chosen. Else why come?"

"On my soul, you are devilish blunt, stark, Jamie Douglas!"

"What would you prefer that I told you, then . . . ?"

* * *

Nothing would do but that Jamie must accompany the Earl on his uncomfortable errand. It seemed that the latter still found

176

him an aid and comfort in certain dealings with his wife — little as that man relished the role. The high passes were still blocked with the winter snows, and many rivers running too high to ford, so that a roundabout route had to be followed — and one which would make a passing near to the Forest of Kennethmont seem realistic. This involved going down Spey to Craigellachie, and up Glen Fiddich to Auchindoun, and then crossing the low pass of Glass to the Raws of Strathbogie and up that Gordon valley by the narrows of Gartly and Noth, a journey of nearly sixty rough miles. In the present state of the terrain and the hours of daylight, they would take two days to do it, halting for the night at the castle of Bucharin near Craigellachie.

They sent off Patrick Leslie homewards on his own, advisedly.

Two days later, then, after paying due respects to sundry Gordon lairds — that proud clan, half-Highland, half-Lowland, being in a touchy state following the death of their chief at Homildon, with only a child heiress and two powerful and assertive but illegitimate uncles, to steer it meantime — they rode up the Water of Bogie, the sun already dipping behind the steep ramparts of the Tap o' Noth rearing on their right, notable country for ambushes, as well the Gordons appreciated.

The Forest of Kennethmont lay just outwith mid-Strathbogie to the east, covering a vast area of the low Foudland Hills around the vale of the Shevock Water. It was a forest in the hunting sense, by no means all woodland, with braes and valleys, moorland plateau, peat-bog and empty wilderness, dotted with Caledonian pines, oak and ash and endless silvery scrub birch, a place alive with deer and boar, wildcat and foxes, a great haunt of wildfowl. Wolves too, infested its fastnesses — and one of the principal tasks of the keepership was to keep these down, or at least to prevent too many complaints from neighbouring landholders as to depredations amongst their flocks and herds. The Gordons, of course, poached the forest shamelessly, always with the excuse that they were really only putting down the wolves for their own protection. Nothing could be done about this; but Sir Andrew Leslie, as Keeper, had a working agreement with them whereby they were reasonably discreet in their activities and helpful in keeping lesser offenders away. Matters such as these were of quite major importance in the smooth running of a widespread lordship in the North.

Piell was a commodious but fairly elementary establishment, a hall-house capable of a moderate defence rather than any forti-

177

fied strength. It lay in a hollow re-entrant of the wooded hills on the north side of the main valley, under Knockandy Hill, a pleasant place surrounded by the cabins of the foresters, its kennels and stabling. Almost the first person the newcomers saw about the place, other than the servitors and woodmen, was the Lord John Stewart of Coull, handing his horse over to a groom.

It would be hard to declare who was most surprised by this cousinly encounter. Being the men they were, both Stewarts recovered quickly, and greeted each other with some appearance of pleasure and normalcy. But there was no doubt that each was concerned at the possible implications of the other's presence. Jamie made little attempt at a like cordiality.

In the hall, cheerful with chatter and clatter and the roaring of two great log fires, they found quite a sizeable company about to sit down to a meal, servitors bustling. Gradually, however, a profound hush developed as the newcomers' appearance and identity was perceived.

Isobel of Mar's ringing laughter ended that silence. "Alex!" she cried, rising. "My devoted lord and master!" And she moved from her place at the centre of the dais-table to come round to meet and greet him, neither hurrying nor with any evident hesitation. They embraced with every sign of affection.

John of Coull watched them, and smiled with what need not necessarily have been relief. Jamie Douglas watched them, and John Stewart, and did not smile.

"How great and unlooked for a pleasure, Alex," his wife declared, standing back a little. "I thought you deep amongst your wild Highlandmen in Badenoch."

"No doubt you did," he agreed. "But I finished there more speedily than I had thought to. And coming home by Lochindorb, by chance learned that you, my dear, were here at Kennethmont, for some reason. And so came by Strathbogie, as none so far out of my road to Kildrummy. For the pleasure of seeing you the sooner!"

"How considerate of you, my love! And how . . . well-informed!"

"Aye. News travels apace in my Highlands. Is it not fortunate?" He turned. "Cousin John, too — you seem to have been equally fortunate! Or were you at Kennethmont purely by chance? It seems a long way from Coull."

"John came, quite in haste, at my request," the Countess said easily. "He is, as ever, kind."

"Ah, yes. And what for was the haste? Which brought you all here?"

"Sufficient — as you shall hear. But come, sit you. And you, Sir James. When *you* appear, with Alex, I am apt to fear the worst! Were you also on your way to Kildrummy?"

"I am, as ever, at my lord's command, Countess," Jamie said briefly.

"I see. One day, you and I must come to some conclusion, Sir James! Alex — here is Sir Alexander Forbes, and his sons."

"So I see. Greetings, Sir Alexander. How fortunate that you too found yourself at Kennethmont!"

"Sir Alexander it was who brought us here, Alex. To our much advantage." Isobel of Mar was very much in command of herself and of the situation. "Sit by me here, husband. John, you at my other side. Sir James — find yourself a place. How far have you ridden today, Alex . . . ?"

Determined small talk was maintained whilst the meal was being served, Alex clearly awkwardly placed to force the pace, or to seem to cross-question his wife in front of others. Jamie, between two of the Forbes sons, ate stolidly.

It was the Countess herself who presently returned to the subject of their presence there. "We owe a debt to Sir Alexander," she announced, pushing back her platter. "He sent me timely word, suggesting that I should come here to Kennethmont, secretly. Or *we* should come — but you were already gone to Badenoch. Come, for the well-being of the earldom. Yourself absent, I came at once."

"It must have been a grave matter?" Alex said carefully.

"Yes. He believed so. As do I. Sir Alexander has discovered that Sir Andrew Leslie desires to gain control of the great lordship of Strathbogie, by seeking to wed his second son, Norman, to the heiress, Elizabeth Gordon. He has made offer of this Forest of Kennethmont to the Gordons as inducement to the match. It is not his, to be sure, but mine. Or ours. But his family have been the keepers of it for so long that he appears to deem it his own, in fact if not name. And the Gordons have long wanted it, reaching into their own lands as it does."

Forbes nodded strongly. "That is so, my lord."

Alex caught Jamie's eye, down the table, and then went back to considering his rib of beef. "I do not see Sir Andrew Leslie here, to answer such charge," he said, slowly.

"He would but deny it," Forbes declared.

179

"Perhaps. But he might possibly have a different tale to tell, some other side to the story."

"What do you mean?" the Countess asked sharply.

"I but mean that before we make any judgement on this, we should at least hear the other side. As we did at, h'm, Elgin! Moreover, there may well be others than Leslie wishful to marry this heiress of Gordon. And bidding other offers for the privilege."

"What has that to do with it?"

"I but wondered, my love. Wondered why Sir Andrew was not here. Indeed why any of us are here. Sir Alexander lives but six miles away from Kildrummy, at Forbes. Why come sixteen, to Kennethmont, to discuss this? Why indeed *you* required to come here at all, my dear? As Countess, should not Sir Alexander have come to you, at Kildrummy? By the same token, much as I rejoice to see him, how comes my good Cousin John here, likewise? From Coull — all of forty miles, I'd say."

Isobel of Mar was tapping finger-nails on the table. "As to the last, I *sent* to ask John to come — to aid me with advice. *You* were far away, and like to be gone many days. John acts Justiciar, does he not? And ought to be able to give a mere woman good counsel. I did not summon Sir Alexander to Kildrummy, but came here, because he besought me to. *He* was here, and this is where any decision should be made. It was expedient that I, as Countess of Mar, should be known to be here, by the Gordons. That they should recognise that Kennethmont is *mine*, not Leslie's. Perhaps they, like Red Andrish, have forgotten it! I have not summoned Leslie yet, until I learned fully on the matter. An' it please your lordship!" That last was less than sweetly added.

"I see," Alex said. "And what have you decided? Or been advised?"

"That it may be necessary to have a new Keeper of Kennethmont Forest."

"Not, by chance, Sir Alexander Forbes?"

"That is possible. Have you better counsel?" That last word was stressed.

Her husband drew a long breath. "I have not yet had opportunity fully to consider the matter. Any decision demands considerable thought, you will admit? For its divisive effect on the earldom, if for naught else. Have you considered what the Leslies, the whole house of Leslie, would have to say to any such

180

transfer of the keepership? A dozen lairdships, at least."

"I do not require to be advised as to the number of my vassals! Sir Andrew might be otherwise . . . compensated."

"It would have to be large compensation, to appease that one's pride."

"I am not greatly concerned for Red Andrish's pride."

"But I *am*, my dear. Or, more truly, the pride of the house of Leslie. As Earl of Mar, I will not see the earldom divided, if I can help it."

"Earl of Mar by *my* gift!"

"To be sure, Isobel. But Earl of Mar, nevertheless — by the King's edict and confirmation."

She started to speak, and then restrained herself.

It was John Stewart who spoke, conversationally. "The Gordons are uppity — whoever weds their heiress. Jock of Scurdargue and Tam of Ruthven make a rough pair of uncles. They will require watching, I think. The presence of the Countess here today, and of your lordship, may serve to make them more careful."

"I am glad that you, Cousin, and all others, recognise that they are dangerous," Alex acknowledged steadily. "I have done so, for long. They have represented one of my principal problems in this earldom. They are not of it, yet they much affect it, encircling it to the north, and, moreover, coming between it and my lordship of Badenoch. They can muster two thousand men. And these two half-brothers of the late Sir Adam are strong and violent men. Let none here think to handle them lightly — or you may bite off more than you can chew!" It was not often that Alex Stewart sounded almost grim.

"Exactly my own estimate, Cousin. Else I might have thought to marry this Elizabeth Gordon my own self!" John of Coull exclaimed, laughing. "After all, she is also my cousin. Her mother, Sir Adam's wife, was sister to *my* mother, both daughters of the late Keith, the Marischal. But . . . I would wed none with two uncles such as those!"

This jocular note served to release the tension in the hall. Both the Earl and Countess of Mar accepted the relief.

"Traitor, Johnnie!" Isobel said.

"A Justiciar's judgement, indeed!" Alex commended.

The talk at the dais-table became general and at least superficially easy.

It was some time thereafter before Alex could have a word

with Jamie Douglas apart. On the excuse of having to see to their men's comfort and lodging in the overcrowded purlieus of Piell, they later strolled to and fro in the courtyard, in the April dusk.

"What think you of it all, Jamie?" his friend asked. "This tangled web?"

"I think that you were wise to come."

"Aye. That at least is sure. But the rest? How think you? What is Isobel at? Did she come here in lust, in concern for the earldom, or to counter *my* efforts?"

"Who am I to tell you that, Alex? It could be any — or all!"

The other pursed his lips. "Perhaps. That is the curse of it. I still do not see why she had to come here, to Kennethmont, at all. This declared warning-off of Gordon, or indeed of Leslie, could have been done equally well by letter."

"But that would not have allowed her the company of Alexander Forbes."

"If she wanted that, why send for John of Coull?"

"He did not arrive until a deal later. She has been here for four days, it seems. The Lord John came only yesterday."

"So?"

"Perhaps your lady planned it that way? Reckoned that she would have had enough of Forbes by then. And would be glad of alternative company!"

"God's Eyes, man — you are suggesting that my wife is so hot for other men than her own husband that she planned this meeting, in a remote house, when I was gone for sufficient time — and arranged to have not one but two paramours, in succession?"

"I suggest nothing that you have not considered yourself, Alex, when you asked your question. But — it may be that we greatly wrong her, in this. It could be that Forbes indeed planned it, and that the Countess came, judging it necessary for the earldom's sake. But sent for the Lord John to join them, to safeguard her name and repute. As well as to advise."

"You think that is the likelier explanation?"

"No," the other answered simply.

"Damnation — you are as bad as my mother! You have never liked Isobel."

"I admire much in the Countess." That was stiff. "But I see her as other than most men's wives — of an independent mind and lusty body. She has been as a queen up here in Mar, for

182

long. Her former husband did not interfere, it seems. If you do not like that, you should perhaps have heeded your lady-mother — who has known the Countess Isobel much longer than have you!"

Angrily the other increased his pace, and Jamie dropped heedfully behind. But presently Alex paused for his friend to catch up again.

"You are right, to be sure," he said, shaking his head. "I knew Isobel's repute before I married her. Foolishly, I believed that I could change her. And, and . . ."

"And you wanted her earldom."

"I did, yes. It was the answer to so much. But . . . I am fond of her, Jamie. Still. That is the devil of it . . ."

He was interrupted by the clatter of hooves, as three horsemen came riding into the courtyard on steaming, mud-spattered beasts. Drawing up, one, travel-stained and weary-seeming in his saddle, pointed at the two strollers.

"You, there. I seek the Lord John Stewart of Coull. Is he here?"

Alex was not the man to stand on his dignity. "Yes. He is within," he called back.

The trio dismounted stiffly, and the man who had spoken tossed his reins to one of his escort and stamped heavily in at the hall-house doorway.

"You saw?" Alex asked quietly.

"Aye." It was not so dark that Jamie had failed to distinguish the royal livery. "From his father. Ridden far and fast. No doubt from Coull."

"It could be Justiciary business . . ."

When, presently, they went inside again, one of the Forbes sons came to Alex.

"My lord Earl — the Lord John Stewart asks that you will be pleased to go to him — in yonder small chamber, with the Countess and my father."

Alex nodded. "Come, Jamie."

In a withdrawing-room off the hall the three men rose as the newcomers entered. The Countess herself was placing food and drink before the latest visitors, no servants being present. The indications of fatigue in face and posture were most evident in the candlelight.

"My lord Earl of Mar — a courier from the Governor," John Stewart said.

"I regret, my lord, any offence given," the man said, words slurred somewhat, "I did not know your lordship."

"No offence taken, sir. Sit you to your refreshment. You look tired."

"A bearer of ill tidings, Cousin," John said. "My father sends word that the Prince James's ship, sent by the French king, and sailing from the Forth, has been attacked and captured by English pirates off Flamborough Head. James is now a prisoner of King Henry, at London."

Appalled, the others stared at him.

"The boy is unharmed, but a captive. The Earl of Orkney with him. They are held in the royal palace at Westminster."

"But, but . . . the realm is at truce with England!" Alex exclaimed. "Henry has no right to hold our prince."

"Does Henry Bolingbroke require a *right* for what he does?"

"Fall foul of him — this is as good as a declaration of war! The heir to the throne, aye, and a ship chartered by King Charles of France. So he challenges France also. As well as the King of Norway, whose subject Orkney is. Has this king lost his wits?"

"I know not. But it seems that *our* King has! On being given the tidings of his son's capture, old King Robert, our uncle, fell under a stroke. Now he lies between life and death."

"Dear God!"

There was silence in that room for long moments, as all that was implied sank in.

It was Jamie who spoke. "His Grace will die," he said, flatly. "He has wanted death, for long. This will end all for him. So now the Governor will both rule and reign in this realm."

None challenged that realistic summary.

"My father has called a parliament, in the King's name, at Perth. For Saint Columba's Day, at the beginning of June."

"Is Henry saying that he will continue to hold the prince?" Alex demanded of the courier.

"We do not know, my lord. The Governor has had only the bare word, a short letter, from King Henry. Saying that the Earl of Carrick is safely in his custody, after his adventure with the pirates. Saying indeed that he is in safer hands than those of the French! Saying also that he will take it upon himself to instruct the prince in manners and chivalry, better than would any Frenchmen!"

"The insolence of him! That means, then, that he does intend to hold him as hostage, for long. This is intolerable!"

"Intolerable or not, my dear, we must need accept it, tolerate it — since we can do no other," the practical Countess said. "Or would you suggest outright war? Thousands to die? And Donald of the Isles awaiting his chance!"

They eyed each other.

"We shall see," Alex said heavily. "This parliament will decide. But . . . till June is a damnable time to wait."

"A true parliament requires forty days of notice to be lawful," John of Coull reminded. "And nothing less than a full parliament will be required in this pass. No mere council will suffice."

"A Privy Council should be held at once, at least . . ."

By unspoken consent their immediate controversies and the reasons for them all being at Kennethmont were, if not dismissed or forgotten, at least laid aside meantime in the face of this national crisis. John Stewart had been summoned south forthwith by his father; and Alex wanted to get back to Kildrummy without delay. The Countess recognised that changed circumstances made the Forbes-Leslie-Gordon controversy presently untimely and, possibly, romantic adventures scarcely convenient. She agreed to a return to Kildrummy.

Jamie went back alone to Lochindorb, with Alex's instructions to warn the Badenoch clans into readiness for possibly swift mobilisation.

Confrontations fell to be postponed, in public at least.

XII

THE SCOTS PARLIAMENT of 1406, held in the Blackfriars monastery, Perth, was a very different affair from the Council General at Linlithgow of the year before. This time the Duke of Albany was in undisputed control — for King Robert the Third had died some weeks before, and his brother had immediately proclaimed himself Regent as well as Governor, as indeed was his almost incontestable right and duty. Now he was both actually and lawfully supreme in Scotland — or would be, once parliament had confirmed his regency — wielding more power than anyone had done since Robert the Bruce. The King's authority could no longer be used against him, either as rallying-cry or modifying influence. None were left in any doubt of the fact.

It was a much larger assembly than that at Linlithgow for, in the national emergency, all who had the right to be present had flocked to Perth — earls, officers of state, lords of parliament, representatives of the sheriffdoms, shires and burghs, and, of course, the churchmen. The Highlands were, however, as usual, grievously under-represented, and Donald of the Isles a notable absentee. Oddly enough Jamie Douglas, who had again gone south in Alex's train, found on arrival at Perth that he was now entitled to attend as a commissioner, no longer a mere spectator, on account of his new barony of Roberton, gifted by his father to replace Aberdour. It was a freeholding, held direct of the Crown, and as such carried this privilege — like many another, not always utilised. So now he sat amongst the barons and freeholders.

Albany made it clear from the start that all was changed. For one thing, the Chancellor referred to him as Your Grace, and was not corrected. Instead of his accustomed chair behind the central table, the Duke now sat on a splendid throne, brought from Scone, well apart, flanked by two magnificently tabarded heralds who bore above him between their staffs the Lion Rampant banner of Scotland. The Lord Lyon King of Arms stood directly behind.

After Bishop Greenlaw had said a brief prayer and declared that this duly called and lawful parliament of the Three Estates of Scotland was now in session, he announced that His Grace the Prince-Duke of Albany, Regent and Governor, would address the commissioners.

At least Robert Stewart's flat, factual voice, with its strange slight hesitation of speech, had not altered; nor his preference for brevity.

"My lords," he said, "owing to the capture of my nephew James, Earl of Carrick, by English pirates, and his subsequent holding by Henry Bolingbroke, calling himself King of England, and the consequent death of my brother, the King's Grace, it became my duty, both as heir presumptive to the throne and Governor of the realm, to assume forthwith the position, style, title and authority of Regent of the Kingdom of Scotland. Which appointment it is the first business of this parliament to confirm. My lord Earl of Crawford will now so move."

As Crawford began to rise, another voice intervened. "One moment, my lord Earl." It was Henry Wardlaw, the Primate. "Is this indeed the first business of this parliament, my lord Chancellor? Is it not our first and most important duty to proclaim and declare the accession to the throne, consequent on the sad death of our late monarch, of his only remaining son and undoubted heir, captive though he may be — James, by the Grace of God, King of Scots?"

A muted cheer rose from the body of the refectory.

The Chancellor looked at Albany.

"The Bishop of St. Andrews is mistaken," that man said coldly. "Until my position of Regent is confirmed, this parliament lacks its full authority, and is merely another Council General, unable to proclaim the succession. Only by the Crown's express pronouncement does it become a parliament. Proceed, my lord of Crawford."

"I so move," the Lindsay said, with notable lack of apparent enthusiasm, "that this Council declares Robert Stewart, Duke of Albany, to be Regent, with all the powers of the Crown — until such time as our lawful monarch returns to his realm.

187

There is no other who may so act. He is the heir presumptive."

"I second," the Bishop of Dunblane added. "Any other nomination is inconceivable."

There was silence in the great chamber.

"Very well," Albany said, at length. "I, the Crown, declare this a parliament of the Three Estates. The Chancellor will further pronounce."

"Yes, Your Grace." Chancellor Greenlaw nodded eagerly. "I hereby declare that this parliament assembled duly confirms the appointment of His Grace the Duke of Albany as Regent as well as Governor of the realm, with all the powers of the Crown duly vested in his person. God save His Grace!"

Men looked at each other doubtfully. Some rose to their feet with alacrity, others did not. By no means all there — including of course the Earl of Mar and Sir James Douglas of Roberton — were prepared to stand and urge the Creator to look upon and save Robert Stewart as His Grace, whatever his new powers. On the other hand, it was just possible that the Chancellor's last four words referred to young James in London. Some were prepared to rise, on that assumption.

Bishop Wardlaw called out, "God save the *King's* Grace!" and so stood, putting the matter to rights.

All now rose, save Albany himself.

There was a pause, as men muttered to each other. Some sat, some remained on their feet.

The Duke pointed a finger at Greenlaw, who banged on the table with his gavel and motioned all to sit.

"His Grace will speak," he announced.

Albany waited impassively for silence. "It is my duty now to proclaim that, the throne being left vacant by the decease of my royal brother, my nephew James, Earl of Carrick and High Steward of Scotland, although a captive in England, succeeds to the style and title of nominal King of Scots. Being a minor as well as a captive and outwith the realm, no powers as King may be exercised by him, but fall to be exercised by myself as Regent. This for the well-being and good governance of the realm." As an afterthought, he added levelly, "God save the King."

Seldom can a new monarch have been less heartily proclaimed.

Those who did not mind risking the Regent's displeasure did their best, led by the Primate and the Earl of Mar, getting once again to their feet, chanting 'God save the King' again and again, and cheering. But it was only a moderately successful demonstration, realities being altogether too evident. Gradually quiet was restored.

"To business," the Chancellor said. "On His Grace's instruction, a new Great Seal of the realm has been cast, to establish the new rule and reign, and the former Great Seal duly broken. From now onwards this Seal's impression will represent the Crown's authority . . ."

"May we see this new Seal, my lord Chancellor?" the Primate requested. "I have heard tell that it is . . . unusual, in wording and design."

Greenlaw looked at the Regent, who nodded. He leant over to open the handsome silver casket on the table, and took out the large and heavy disc of shining bronze. He carried it across to his senior bishop, lips compressed.

Wardlaw took the thing, turning it up this way and that to gain the best light from the not over-generous windows. "This shows a man sitting on a throne, flanked by the arms of Albany and the kingdom," he reported, for all to hear. "The man bears in his right hand the Sword of State. And around are the words SIGILLUM ROBERTI DEI GRACIA INTERREX SCOTTORUM. That is the Seal of Robert, by the Grace of God . . .!" He paused. "My lord Chancellor, is this not the seal of a monarch, rather than a regent? Robert, by the Grace of God!"

There was a hush. No word came from Chancellor or Duke.

"My lords," the Primate went on, "this seal appears to me to be neither one thing nor another. The Great Seal of the realm should surely bear the monarch's image and superscription — James, by the Grace of God. If this is but the *Regent's* seal, as the name Robert implies, then surely he should not be sitting on the throne, nor should he be described 'by the Grace of God'. It appears to me that a mistake has been made."

Albany spoke, without turning his head to glance at the Bishop. "No mistake, Sir Clerk. That is the Great Seal of this realm. Until James my nephew has received his coronation, he is but presumptive and postulate monarch, not true King. In present circumstances it may be long before such coronation. And since he is a child and his authority vested in myself, it is proper that meantime my name appears on the Great Seal."

There were murmurs from various parts of the chamber.

"I would wish to enquire further into this, my lord Duke,"

189

Wardlaw said, "into the correctness of it. Proper you may consider it. But is it lawful?"

"Enquire then, sirrah. But — have you, and others, considered who now *makes* the laws of this realm?" That question was none the less ominous for being tonelessly said.

"The Crown in *parliament* makes the laws. Only so, my lord."

"As it will do. Proceed, my lord Chancellor." The flick of Albany's hand indicated that the subject was closed.

Greenlaw retrieved the seal and put it back into its casket, making something of a ploy of it. Then he banged with his gavel to gain quiet.

"There is the matter of the succession," he announced, consulting his papers. "With the King in enemy hands, and a child, unwed, this becomes of vital import. His Grace the Regent is, to be sure, the heir presumptive and in the event of the demise of the Crown would forthwith become King in name as well as in fact. But since His Grace is in his sixty-eighth year, and although we pray God that he may be preserved to reign over us for many more years, yet he esteems it right that parliament should recognise and confirm the further succession. His Grace's eldest son, of course, Murdoch, Earl of Fife, is next in succession. But he is prisoner likewise. He has infant sons who would be in line for the succession. But . . ."

"My lord Chancellor — I do protest!" That was Alex Stewart, on his feet. "I say that this of the possible succession, in the Duke of Albany's family, may be important, in some measure. But it is scarcely so vital as the recovery and saving of our young sovereign lord James from enemy hands! Surely the first and foremost matter this parliament should be discussing is what steps are to be taken to show our anger at the outrage done to our prince, in time of truce; and how best we can ensure his speedy return to his realm and throne . . ."

Shouts of approval from all over the refectory drowned his voice. There was no question but that he had the vast majority with him in his protest.

"Yes, yes," the Chancellor began, when he could make himself heard. "All in due course . . ."

He was interrupted by Albany. "My lord of Mar is impatient. A youthful failing, which may perhaps be forgiven, but unsuitable in those who seek to bear rule and governance. All is to be done in proper order. Measures will be taken regarding my nephew's unfortunate position. But before we consider what we may do to that end, we must set our house in order, here at home. The change in rule, kingship and authority here must be firmly established, consequent upon the King's death and his son's capture, that duly authorised steps may be taken in our relations with England. And that includes the due succession. Proceed, my lord Chancellor."

Alex frowned, but resumed his seat.

"To resume," Greenlaw said, looking about him warily. "Since His Grace's eldest son, the Earl Murdoch, is also in enemy hands, and his children as yet but bairns, the Regent, aware of the transience of this life and man's impermanence, sees himself as in duty bound to make due provision for the carrying on of the regency and governance should he himself — which God forbid — suffer removal from our midst. He therefore would make provision for his second son, the Lord John of Coull and Onele, next in succession to the throne, to be able to step into the regency, with the consent of parliament, in the event of his own demise. The Lord John is now a man of full age and ability, and an increasing experience in affairs of state. In pursuance of this aim, His Grace has decided now to advance the said John Stewart of Coull and Onele to the position, style and dignity of Earl of Buchan. Which earldom, since the death of His Grace's brother, the late Lord Alexander of Badenoch, has been vested in the Crown. Moreover, since it is no longer suitable that the Regent should fill the office of Great Chamberlain — which His Grace has supported for many years — with the agreement of this parliament he now confers it upon the said Lord John."

The stir in the chamber was pronounced, but not in the main hostile, for the personable John Stewart was gaining in popularity and much to be preferred to his arrogant, yet moody half-brother Murdoch. None failed to perceive, of course, the principal implications of this promotion; for so long as his brother remained a prisoner in the South, it made Brave John of Coull second most important man in the kingdom — an extraordinary advancement for one who had been almost unknown a year or two before.

Jamie Douglas looked from John to Alex Stewart, anxiously, his mind busy. This move, shrewd in more ways than one, he well perceived would reverse their respective positions in the North. No longer would the new Earl of Mar be the most important figure above the Highland Line; the new Earl of Buchan, Great Chamberlain and in line for the throne, would outrank him. The fact that the earldom of Buchan would have been Alex's own had he been legitimate, must be the more galling. Had Brave John known of all this when he came south? The new appointment would not do away with Alex's great influence with the Highland clans, of course, which his cousin did not possess. But it must have a major effect on the former's plans, and tend to set these two on a collision course — which no doubt was partly the objective.

Almost as though he himself had been following Jamie's line of thought, Albany intervened.

"The earldom of Buchan marches with the earldom of Ross, to north and west, formerly held by my daughter's husband, the late Alexander Leslie, and now in the name of their only child, my grand-daughter and ward, the Lady Euphemia. The said Lady Euphemia has declared her desire to wed only Holy Church and to retire to the life of sanctity in a nunnery, to her exceeding renown. Therefore the earldom of Ross also falls to the Crown. It is suitable that, situate so importantly for the Highland polity, it should be held in strong and capable hands. I therefore place the earldom of Ross also in the hands of my son John, for the North's security. It will also aid him in his position as Justiciar of the North, the revenues thereof to help in defraying the costs of the chamberlainship. The Lord John now to step forward."

As everywhere men craned their necks to see this newly exalted star in the Scots firmament, Will Douglas spoke in Jamie's ear.

"There is no doubt as to who is to be King of the North! Your friend Mar's days are numbered, I think!" Will was sitting beside his half-brother once more, now also a baron commissioner; their uncle, Sir Will of Mordington, had died suddenly, leaving no heir, and their father had conferred his Merse barony on his second legitimate son.

"Alex will not be so easily brought down," Jamie was saying, but through tight lips, when there was a dramatic development. Brave John was on his way from the barons' benches to the dais, when Alex stood up again amongst the tiny group of earls.

"My lord Chancellor," he called strongly, "may I be the first to congratulate my cousin and friend the Lord of Coull on his advancement to the earldom of Buchan — particularly as it was long held by my own father and I was, as it were, partly suckled on its revenues! The Great Chamberlain's office, also, I am sure that he will adorn. But this last of the earldom of Ross is a very different matter. I say that we must consider well before handing over Ross to any soever — unless we are prepared for major warfare."

John Stewart had halted, looking from Alex to his father doubtfully.

"The Earl of Mar is over-fearful," Albany said.

"I think not, my lord Duke. I have three times had to fight the Lord of the Isles or his brother. I have no wish to have to do so again. Especially if Donald has a fair cause. I would remind this parliament that the late Earl of Ross, Alexander Leslie, left a child heiress, yes, the Countess Euphemia — who would appear, at ten years, to have chosen a life of religion at a notably early age! But he also left a sister, the Lady Margaret, who is wed to the Lord of the Isles. Therefore, if the Lady Euphemia indeed resigns the earldom, her aunt, the Lady Margaret, is surely entitled to claim it as heir of entail. And nothing is more certain, I do swear, than that Donald of the Isles will ensure that she does!"

"The Earl of Mar, I think, forgets," the Regent commented, apparently unmoved. "He ought not to do so, since he was at some pains to ensure the matter for himself, not so long ago! The disposition of earldoms is subject to the Crown's agreement. The natural heirs are always given first consideration. But the safety and well-being of the realm is the Crown's prime concern. Donald of the Isles is a man guilty of ravagement and rapine, but also of armed invasion and insurrection — treason. The earldom of Ross is so placed that, if he had his hands on it, in the right of his wife, he could do enormous hurt to the North, to the entire kingdom. He would be no longer confined to his heathenish Hebrides, but would have a base reaching across the breadth of Scotland. It must not be. The earldom must be in sound and strong hands. Therefore I have so ordained."

"Your ordaining, my lord Duke, will, I fear, not prevent the Lord of the Isles seeking to take what he believes should be his by right. Safer to leave the earldom vacant meantime. Better still, that the child Countess should be, h'm, dissuaded from her sudden and youthful desire to embrace Holy Church! Then no new destination need be made."

"I support the Earl of Mar in this," the Earl of Crawford said,

193

at Alex's side. "We have trouble with England before us. We want no trouble with the Islesmen, meantime."

"I agree, my lord Chancellor," the Primate added. "This child's vocation will be the more acceptable to Holy Church at a more mature age!"

"May I speak, my lord Chancellor?" John of Coull requested, from his midway stance. "It seems to me that there need be no dispute. The earldom of Buchan marches with that of Ross for long distances. As Earl of Buchan and acting Justiciar of the North, I should, with the Earl of Mar's aid, be able to maintain good and sufficient watch over it, and ensure its peace and the security of the realm, without myself being appointed Earl of Ross at this time."

There was a pause. Then his father nodded briefly.

"Step forward," he commanded. Undoubtedly one of Robert Stewart's greatest strengths lay in his ability to judge shrewdly when to change his stance in any controversy, and to do so swiftly and without evident animus, whatever his private feelings; not, of course, allowing such minor deflections to alter his major intentions.

None making further objection, John Stewart paced up to the dais. With the minimum of ceremony Albany rose, moved over to the Chancellor's table, picked up a golden earl's belt where it had lain hidden amongst the papers, and placed it over his son's head and one shoulder.

"Earl of Buchan," he said.

John bowed, kissed his father's hand, bowed again, and walked over to the earls' seats.

A somewhat ragged cheer arose.

"Proceed, my lord Chancellor," the Regent ordered.

Some shuffling of papers followed. "The matter of steps to be taken regarding the unhappy situation of our young liege lord, the King," Greenlaw intoned. "Protest has been made to the so-called King Henry, but this has been spurned. His Grace the Regent therefore purposes that a strong and important embassage should be sent forthwith to the English Court, under safe conduct, in terms of the signed truce still pertaining, to make representations, to ascertain Henry of Bolingbroke's intentions and to seek negotiate the King's release . . ."

Strong applause resounded from all quarters.

"His Grace declares that this embassage must be of the most illustrious, that due weight may be accorded to it. He proposes that it should be led by the Earl of Crawford, Lord High Admiral; the Earl of Buchan, Great Chamberlain; and the Earl of Mar; also, of the Lords Spiritual, the Bishop of Dunblane and my humble self, duly supported by a knightly company . . ."

"How may we be sure, my lord, that such embassage would be safe from molestation?" the Bishop of Dunblane interrupted. "If the English are prepared to waylay and capture Scotland's heir to the throne and now monarch, will they be more gentle with this company, however illustrious?"

Greenlaw looked at the Duke.

"Ambassadors, even in time of war, are protected in all Christian nations," Albany said. "But we shall seek a safe-conduct. If he grants it, even Henry could scarce dare to break it." He paused. "I should not be sending my second son into his hands, who already holds my first, were I not assured on this."

That seemed convincing, and the thing was accepted, Jamie for one recognising that the inclusion of Alex in the embassage was a clever move and could well be viewed with suspicion. It might to some extent close his lips, yet he would be established as less important than the new Earl of Buchan, the Great Chamberlain. It would embroil him in Southern affairs, which might lessen his influence in the North.

The Chancellor went on to ask parliament to renew the mutual-aid treaty with France, due to expire shortly; and this, which had become almost the corner-stone of Scots foreign policy, was passed without dissent. There followed three or four routine matters concerning trade, customs dues and claims for royal burgh status, which were unproductive of dispute. Then, with Greenlaw gathering his papers together and Albany clearly preparing to announce adjournment, Alex rose to his feet again.

"I have a matter with which, I believe, this parliament should be concerned," he said. "I am surprised that it has not already been raised or remarked upon, since it concerns persons here present and one who should have been. I refer to the slaying of Sir David Fleming of Biggar and Cumbernauld, at Lang Herdmanston in Lothian, who had escorted the Earl of Carrick, now King James, to the Bass Rock, and was thereafter waylaid and murdered. I say that parliament should receive details of this outrage and learn what steps have been taken to bring the offenders to punishment."

If hitherto the assembly had had its moments of drama and tension, these were as nothing to the effect of this bombshell.

Few there did not know that this killing had been perpetrated by Sir James Douglas of Abercorn, nicknamed the Gross, next brother to the captive Earl of Douglas himself, and therefore acting head of that so potent house. Moreover it was accepted that it had been done at Albany's instigation, as indication of the Governor's disapproval of the secret move of the young prince from St. Andrews. So that, in publicly raising this issue, the Earl of Mar was in effect challenging both the Regent and the house of Douglas, the two greatest powers in the land.

"Your man is no faint-heart, I will say that for him!" Will Douglas murmured to his half-brother.

"I am glad that my lord of Mar has raised this matter," Bishop Wardlaw supported, rising. "I should have done so, myself. Sir David Fleming was my good friend. More important, he was a leal and true friend of our late King, of our present King, and of his brother the late Duke of Rothesay. His murder was a most grievous crime against the King's peace and the King's interests — which I call upon the King's Regent and government to punish."

In the hush that followed, the Chancellor spread his hands, eloquent of non-involvement and disassociation.

Albany took his time about speaking, as the silence became almost a living thing. "I know of no such murder or crime," he said evenly. "The Earl of Carrick, my nephew, had been removed from his place of safe-keeping at St. Andrews secretly, by stealth, without my authority or knowledge, and conveyed to this barren rock of the Bass, and there held — by this Fleming of Cumbernauld. I would have failed in my plainest duty, as Governor, had I not made due enquiry. I requested Sir James Douglas of Abercorn to find Fleming and bring him to me, for question. Sir James did find him, riding from the Lothian coast to Biggar, but he refused to accompany the Douglas. Indeed he drew a sword, and in the resultant mêlée was unfortunately fatally wounded — a mishap wholly of his own making. No blame attaches to Sir James Douglas." Almost as though exhausted by this, for him, lengthy disquisition, the Regent sat back in his throne, eyes closed, the matter finished with.

Alex and the Primate eyed each other, waiting one for the other.

"My lord Duke," Wardlaw said, after a moment, "with respect, there are one or two relevant points which require to be

196

stated, on Sir David Fleming's behalf, since he cannot make them himself. You say that the prince was removed from my castle of St. Andrews without your knowledge and authority, by Sir David. I would point out, however, that it was done on the authority, indeed at the direct command, of the King's Grace, father of the prince. Secretly, yes, for the best of reasons. Sir David, therefore, was carrying out his liege lord's orders — as was I in permitting the prince's removal. No blame can attach to him."

"Then, sir, he should have yielded peaceably to Sir James Douglas's request, and come to explain the matter to myself."

"Perhaps he had no opportunity to do so, my lord Duke."

"Explain yourself, sir."

"He may have been . . . silenced!"

"May have been . . .! Perhaps . . .! This is a parliament, sir, not a churchmen's chapter! We are here concerned with facts, not suppositions. You will not impute motives to others which cannot be substantiated."

"My lord Chancellor," Alex intervened, comparatively mildly. "Sir James Douglas of Abercorn is here present. Let him speak, and tell us the circumstances in which Sir David died."

"No! Douglas will *not* speak," Albany rapped out. "He was obeying my orders, as Governor, to bring Fleming to me. I will not have this parliament's time wasted with base calumnies and aspersions."

"Nevertheless, my lord Duke," Crawford put in heavily, "the allegation has been made publicly that Sir David Fleming — who was *my* friend also — may have been silenced. Surely it is this parliament's concern to learn what caused the Primate-Bishop to make such allegation?"

"My lords," Henry Wardlaw declared, giving no time for any ban to be pronounced, "Sir David spoke to me before he left my castle, with the prince. He told me that I would be wise to send the young Henry Percy, Hotspur's son, and heir to Northumberland, off to France with the prince. He said that there was a plan to deliver up the boy — who was also in my care — along with his grandfather, the Earl of Northumberland, the Lord Bardolph and the Bishop of St. Asaph, who took refuge in our realm from King Henry's spleen, to the English — in exchange for the Lord Murdoch, Earl of Fife. I said that I could not do this without higher authority. But I did send here to Perth, to warn the Earl of Northumberland and the others,

197

here resident. I understand that they have . . . departed."

Another prolonged silence.

"If the Bishop of St. Andrews is finished with his hearsays, prittle-prattle and clerks' clishmaclavers, I shall now rule that this parliament be spared further waste of time," Albany said sternly. "If, on the other hand, he has any true *evidence* to support his extraordinary allegations, if he will submit it to me in due course, I shall see that it is laid before the Privy Council or other suitable court of law. I should but add that had these addle-pated plans for the removal of my nephew not been put into practice, the prince would still be safe within my lord's palace of St. Andrews, and my brother the late King no doubt still on his throne. I leave you all to consider that well. My lord Chancellor — adjourn the session."

Without waiting for the further formalities, Robert Stewart rose from his throne and stalked from the chamber, banner-bearers hurrying behind.

The parliament of 1406 was at an end — which meant that talking had had its day and the rule of law began, the Regent's law.

XIII

IT WAS DIFFICULT to maintain any suitably sober and dignified air for the Scots embassage, however illustrious, as the brilliant company trotted down through the fair English countryside at its summer finest. They were on a grimly serious mission in a traditionally hostile land, and they represented an angry nation. Yet they were in the main young men, clad in their colourful best, presently released from their normal day-to-day duties and responsibilities, on a prolonged flag-waving expedition in a strange country. It would have been unnatural had a holiday spirit not prevailed. Even if some of them did not rely too entirely on King Henry's safe-conduct, with their escort of seventy they were secure enough from anything but major assault. They did not dawdle but nor did they indulge in any unseemly rush; a steady forty miles a day was the target — something of a daunder for some there, though sufficient for the two bishops no doubt. This permitted ample time for sight-seeing, wine and women sampling and appreciation of the good life generally.

The two young Stewart earls very much set the tone and tempo of the venture, for though David Lindsay, Earl of Crawford and Lord High Admiral, was nominally the senior member of the delegation, he was now an elderly man and had become somewhat quiet, almost morose, with the years; and Bishop Greenlaw, the Chancellor, although an able administrator, was no leader and somewhat out of his depth with lively young men — while the other Bishop, Finlay Dermoch of Dunblane, likewise a creature of Albany's, was so much in awe of the company he now kept as to be an embarrassment. For the rest, both John and Alex Stewart had vied with each other in bringing along a cheerful crew of youthful gallants, in the interests of prestige — although Jamie Douglas would certainly have excepted himself from such description, and Sir Alexander Forbes of that Ilk, in his early forties, scarcely qualified either. The former had been included simply because Alex desired his company and support, the latter, ostensibly as one of the senior vassals of Mar but in fact so that his master might have an easier mind as to the activities of the Countess Isobel in the interim. Whatever feelings of rivalry existed inevitably between the Stewart cousins, no sign of it was revealed; they made a gay, handsome and attractive pair, and the embassage very much took its character from them.

They went by Berwick-on-Tweed, coastal Northumberland and Newcastle — and for Jamie at least it was an odd experience to be riding peacably through territory over which he had campaigned, sword in hand, so frequently. By Durham and Cleveland and York they rode, and so down into the English Midlands, new country for all save Crawford, putting up at abbeys, priories and monkish hospices, where the bishops' presence assured them, if not welcome at least sustenance and shelter — the English lords and landed gentry eyeing them very much askance. Ten days of this and, beyond the endless level lands flanking the Fen country, they came by Peterborough and the one-time Scots-held earldom of Huntingdon and St. Neots, to the broad vale of the Thames — although it was unlike any vale, dale or strath they knew in Scotland — and approached their goal.

London appalled, affronted and yet exhilarated them. Indeed they could scarcely take it in, so overpowering was the impact, in size, noise, smells — above all, smells. Extremes were the rule here, extremes in numbers, in quality of building, with magnificence and tumbledown hovels side by side, in riches and poverty, in splendour and filth, in music and laughter, screams and groans, in the variety at least of the stenches. The Scots were used to towns and burghs, to crowded narrow streets and tall tenement lands and burrowing closes and wynds; but even in the greatest cities like Perth, Dundee and Aberdeen, there was nothing to compare with this teeming, throbbing, deafening, stinking ant-hill of humanity. Although ant-hill was quite wrong — that was part of the trouble. There was no least hill of any sort worth calling even a brae, to relieve the endless sprawl, the ranked and serried clutter of streets and lanes and alleys, of dark arched vaults and tunnels and vennels. Scots towns were usually built around a fortress or castle, which almost always perched proudly on top of a hill or rock, with the streets climbing towards it or clustered under its walls. Here, although the dread of the famous Tower of London was known to all, it presumably did not sit on any upstanding rock — at least it could not be seen to do so from the stifling huddle of the causeways. The buildings were no taller than those at home — less so, often, indeed — but they tended to extend outwards over the streets, one storey projecting above and beyond the next in extraordinary fashion, so that with the roadways narrow enough in the first place, the two sides often nearly met at the top, leaving the merest strip of sky to be seen, and daylight at street-level only a pale memory. Down there the causeways were all but choked with the refuse thrown from windows or pushed out from the doorways and closes, or else deposited by the poultry and even pigs which roamed and proliferated everywhere. The flatness, lack of hills and vistas, and tight huddle of buildings, all kept out the air and sea-breezes which made the Scots burghs tolerable. In the height of summer, the resultant odours hit the newcomers like a blow, a continuing hail of blows. They rode on in a sort of stupor of noise, of fetor, of claustrophobia. Yet the sense of vigorous, teeming, pulsating life was such as they had never before experienced.

In less time than it takes to tell they were quite lost in that chaotic labyrinth, at a loss which street to take, which way to turn. There was no lack of people to direct them, but their requests were singularly unproductive of result, their Scots voices being as little understood apparently as were the Londoners' answers — although they had made themselves understood well enough all the way down through England. But here not only their accents but their very appearance, it seemed, was a source of wonder, indeed of general hilarity. Laughter, jeers, even occasional hurled refuse, tended to greet their enquiries — though most of the reaction was not probably intentionally ill-natured, however disrespectful. Young lairds, unused to such behaviour, were inclined to drop hands to sword-hilts, but their leaders sternly commanded restraint. Their mission must not be started on the wrong foot.

Eventually, after much time-wasting and casting around, they reached the riverside and a sudden widening of vistas. They could at last see a considerable distance up and down stream. Ahead of them, still a distance off but now eye-catching, beyond a bend of the river, rose the massive white walls of a huge, slab-sided square keep, with four angle-towers topped by onion-like domes, and surrounded by high curtain-walls, set apparently at the edge of Thames. Amongst all the welter of buildings, of gables and turrets, spires and steeples and roofing, this could only be the redoubtable Tower of London itself. Crawford said that the monarch no longer dwelt there but in the palace of Westminster, attached to the abbey. Amidst the innumerable churches visible from here, the tall triple towers of one larger than all the others stood out plainly, not far from where they had emerged, again near the river, almost certainly the Minster. It was sixteen years since Crawford had been here, and he had forgotten how he had reached the palace, it having been a private visit. But, evidently, by keeping to the waterside, they could make directly for it.

When the visitors reached the great cathedral-like church, it was to discern little sign of any palace, only the lengthy ranges of the abbey's monastic buildings, purlieus and cloisters linked to a great hall of ecclesiastical aspect. Yet Crawford declared that this was indeed the place — and certainly there was much coming and going around its environs, with none wearing monkish habits and some indeed clad in fine scarlet-and-gold livery. On Jamie's asking one of these if this was indeed King Henry's palace of Westminster, the fellow looked him up and down, pointed within the courtyard arch with a pitying gesture, and hurried off. It seemed that this was journey's end.

Dismounting in a wide courtyard, watched by a multiplicity of guards but no guides nor welcomers, the Scots leadership decided to make for the largest doorway. Here, halted by the crossed halberds of the guard, Crawford announced that they were the Scots embassage come to treat with the King of England, and seeking His Grace's hospitality. From the many interested onlookers an officer came forward, the statement was repeated, and this man, shaking his head doubtfully, turned and made his way within, leaving the visitors standing on the doorstep, still facing the crossed halberds.

They had to wait some considerable time there, with proud Scots tempers rising. At length the officer returned, told Crawford to follow him and waved back the others. As curtly, the remaining Scots leaders informed him that they were not going to be left waiting like beggars at the door, and marched in behind the Lindsay.

Conducted by this disappointing guide through long corridors and across inner courts, they gained little better impression of this as a palace than they had done of London as a whole, considering it but a poor sprawling place compared with the towering royal strongholds of their own land. Admittedly those parts which were furnished seemed to be richly plenished, with a great deal more of hangings, tapestries, floor-coverings and the like than they were used to, but the effect was still of a converted and overcrowded monastery.

They were brought eventually to a lobby in no very splendid portion of the rambling establishment, where an overdressed individual of middle years awaited them. To him Crawford repeated, rather stiffly his statement of identity and purpose.

"Were you looked for, sirs?" this gentleman asked.

"*Looked* for?" the Earl barked. "We have come here from the Regent of Scotland, under your King's safe-conduct and invitation. I should say that we are looked for!"

"Perhaps. But did any here know of your coming?"

"God's sake, man — why ask *us* that? King Henry well knows of our coming. What arrangements he has made is his business, not ours."

"The King's Grace is not here at this present, sir. He is hawking on the marshes of Erith."

"Then find someone who knows the King's business, sirrah. Who are you?"

"I am Sir Everard Bacon. Deputy Master of the King's Wardrobe."

"Saints a' mercy — a wardrobe master!" Crawford exploded.

John Stewart intervened. "Sir Everard, I am Buchan, Great Chamberlain of Scotland. The Earl of Crawford is Lord High Admiral. This is the Earl of Mar and Lord of Garioch. This is Bishop of Dunblane. And this the Bishop of Aberdeen, Chancellor of Scotland. Since your King is absent, our accommodation would seem to be a matter for his Chamberlain. Kindly inform him of our presence."

"The Lord Chamberlain, the Earl of Kent, is not here, sir, er, my lord. He is with the King's Grace."

"Then go find somebody who is here, Wardrober, of some rank and position," Crawford exclaimed.

"*I* am in charge of the palace meantime, sir," the other said shortly.

"God's eyes — is this how Henry of Lancaster manages his

household! Be off, fellow, and find someone who may decently receive us, and suitably bestow us. Or I swear your King will be needing a new deputy papingoe!"

Flushing hotly, the other turned and stalked off.

Seething, the older Scots huffed and puffed, although Alex and John Stewart counselled patience. It was all no doubt a mistake, some foolish misunderstanding.

"Do you mean to tell me that Henry Bolingbroke is so ill-served with spies and informants, to say nothing of his flunkeys here, that he knows nothing of our progress down through his realm, these ten days?" Bishop Greenlaw cried. "It is a calculated insult!"

"Scarcely that," Alex demurred. "More probably mere mismanagement and poor manners."

"They are barbarians . . . !"

Again they were kept waiting, this time for even longer than before. At last the same Sir Everard Bacon reappeared, now supported by quite a phalanx of liveried guards with halberds, all looking aggressive.

"I have been able to have word with the Lord Chancellor himself, sirs . . . my lords," he declared, almost grandly. "The Lord Henry, Bishop of Winchester. He says that you are to be bestowed in the Tower, meantime. I will send a guide to conduct you there, to the Governor."

"The Tower? You mean — the Tower of London?" Crawford got out, all but choking.

"Yes."

"By the Rood — this is too much! It is a prison!"

"Not so. Or not only so, sir. It is a house of His Grace. Much used. Besides, I would have thought that you would wish to bide there — since the youth, your so-called King, is lodged there! Sergeant, convey these Scots lords to the Tower. Present them to Sir Thomas Rempton."

"The King . . . ? James? In the Tower . . . ?"

But the Deputy Master of the Wardrobe had turned and hurried off. The visitors were left with the glowering guards, the sergeant of whom was gesturing for them to follow him.

Angrily the assemblage stamped out.

* * *

Within the gloomy portals of the Tower of London there were further delays. It proved to be a vast citadel, almost a city in itself, the tall foursquare central keep, visible from afar, only the grim heart of it, with its inner and outer moats, its tiered curtain-walls, its baileys and wards, its proliferating lesser towers and gatehouses, its barracks and armouries, stables and yards. The Scots' escort of seventy men-at-arms would have made a major mouthful for most establishments to swallow; but here they were absorbed without difficulty, even if equally without cordiality. It took a considerable time for the sergeant to find the Governor, however, so that the men-at-arms' betters had to kick their heels, in mounting ire and frustration, in an inner courtyard.

There, after a while, a curious coughing, grunting sound, allied to a new smell, animal, throat-catching, attracted their speculative attention, and eventually their physical presence, towards an archway and vaulted passage opening from a corner of the yard. Pushing along this stone-flagged way, they came to a great open well of a place below the main White Tower walling, sunk below general ground level — but not below the underground dungeons obviously beneath their feet, over the gratings for which they trod in that passage, and from which unpleasant sounds and more smells arose at them. But it was not this which drew them. The large sunken central pit was subdivided by heavy iron bars and partitions into sundry cages of varying sizes; and in these up to a score of lions and leopards paced and wheeled and padded, snarling, in a sort of terrible, ritualised, contained and hopeless rage. A keeper with a great steel trident over his shoulder, paraded his own monotonous circuit of the pit's terraced perimeter gallery, whilst two boys, at the far side, sought unsuccessfully to interest a huge, dark-maned lion in a piece of red meat dangling on a line.

It was Jamie Douglas who recognised one of the lads as their new monarch. Oddly enough, despite the fact that the two Stewart earls were his first cousins and Crawford his uncle by marriage, few there really knew James Stewart, who had been brought up very much away from Court, almost as much a recluse as had been his father. Jamie, however, through his service and friendship with the late David, Duke of Rothesay, the boy's elder brother, had known him quite well.

"That is the prince," he called. "James — the King. With the thin-faced wiry boy."

The party of nearly a dozen went hurrying round the rim of the pit.

The lads, looking up, watched their approach with interest. The younger was an attractive, sturdy boy, not tall but well-made, with good regular features, dark-eyed and dark-haired, but with a wary, self-contained expression, twelve years now though looking older. The other, a year or so his senior, was bony and gangling of build, dark also but intense. Neither was dressed with any distinction.

As the visitors approached, James's eyes widened and lightened. "Jamie!" he cried. "It is Sir Jamie Douglas!" And thrusting the meat on its string at his companion, he darted forward, hands out.

Jamie, glancing at his betters, went to drop on one knee before the boy, and taking one of those slender hands between his own two, in the gesture of fealty, kissed it. "Sire," he said, "Your Grace's leal and humble servant."

"It is good to see you, so good!" James exclaimed, eagerly. "Have you come to take me home?"

The Douglas swallowed. "I . . . ah . . . not yet, Sire, I fear," he said unhappily, rising. "But soon, no doubt. I . . . we rejoice to see you also. Here is Your Highness's uncle, my lord of Crawford. And my lords of Mar and Buchan, your cousins . . ."

The kneeling and hand-kissing proceeded, as each of the visitors, in order of precedence, murmured allegiance, the boy seriously and with unassumed dignity, acknowledging each token. When it was finished, he turned to the older lad.

"This is Griffith Glendower, my lords, son to the Lord Owen Glendower, the true Prince of Wales. He is also held hostage here. He is my friend."

They all bowed to the Welsh boy, who smiled brilliantly.

It was to Jamie that the boy-King turned. "My father is dead," he said, biting his lip. "But the Bishop? The good Bishop Henry. All is well with him, at St. Andrews?"

"Yes, Sire. He is greatly concerned for your welfare . . ."

"As is the Regent, your royal uncle," Greenlaw put in. "He sends greeting, Sire."

The boy eyed the Chancellor levelly for a moment, and then turned back to Jamie. "You have come all the way from Scotland? To see me?"

"Yes, Your Grace. Bringing the love of all your people. We have come also — or these great lords have — to seek negotiate your release."

"I do not think that King Henry will let me go," James said flatly. "Do you, Griff?"

"No," his friend agreed.

The visitors exchanged glances.

Alex cleared his throat. "Do they treat you well, Sire, in this fell Tower?"

"Oh, yes. We have sufficient to eat. I have a dog the Governor gave me. And there are these lions, and leopards. There are bears too, in another part. They had a bull-baiting in the tilt-yard a few days ago . . ."

A cough, other than that of the brutes below, turned all heads — although perhaps it should not have done when their monarch was speaking. A tall, handsome, soldierly-looking man stood behind them, with the sergeant.

"A good day to you," the newcomer said, from thin lips, with the briefest of bows. "I am Rempton, Governor here. You will be the deputation from Scotland. I would prefer it if you do not have speech with this boy save with my express permission."

"You do, damn you!" Crawford gave back. "I'd have you to know, sirrah, that this boy, as you call him, is our liege and sovereign lord, James, King of Scots, and we shall not seek any permission save *his* before we speak with him. In our presence, at least, you will refer to him as His Grace."

"Indeed I shall do no such thing. My lord King and only Grace, as yours, is the Lord Henry of England and France, who is also Lord Paramount of Scotland. I take instructions only from him. As, if you are wise, will you. Boy — be off. And Glendower with you."

"Your Grace — be pleased to stay with us a little longer," Alex said, mildly enough. "We have come a long way to see you."

"Aye, Sire — if you will," John of Buchan added. "You, sir — leave us. We shall send for you when we are ready."

"That you will not! I have my orders and I shall obey them. James Stewart, go to your chamber. Or shall I send for the guard?"

"Sir Thomas," the boy said, his voice quivering just a little. "These are great lords in my country — my cousins, and uncle, and the Chancellor of the realm. Pray speak them more . . . heedfully. My lords — I will leave you now. We shall speak again. There is much that I would have you to tell me. Come, Griff."

207

The Scots bowed low as the boys hurried off, the Governor and the sergeant not at all.

"You, sirrah, may bear the knightly style, but you are as ill-reared and upjumped a lout as that papingoe Bacon we saw at Westminster! Has your prince never taught you how to behave? Or does himself not know? I am Crawford, Earl and Lord High Admiral of Scotland. These lords similar. See that you do not forget it. Now — convey us to our quarters."

Rempton began to reply, but thought better of it. He turned to the sergeant. "Fetch the Captain of the Guard to take these Scots lords to Byward Tower, where their chambers are prepared for them." He stalked off without another word.

"So we were expected here, at least!" Jamie observed.

*   *   *

The Scots found that they had a single flanking-tower of the Byward allotted to themselves, with a basement dining-vault, damp and chill, where food was brought to them from some central kitchen, and four upper chambers for sleeping — which meant that none might have a room to themselves, even the bishops — who protested strongly. It was scarcely the accommodation for high-born ambassadors; but, as Alex pointed out philosophically, it was good by campaigning standards. The food provided proved to be adequate, plain but plentiful enough, presumably the same as that supplied to the garrison, possibly even to the state prisoners. There was ale, but no wine.

Whilst they were eating, and discussing their reception, a stranger arrived, a fine-drawn elegant man of early middle years, pale, with a thin dark moustache and only the hint of a beard, almost Spanish-looking but announcing himself to be Henry St. Clair, Earl of Orkney. Crawford had once met him, although none of the others knew him — but then he was scarcely to be considered as a Scot, seldom appearing at Court and looking across the sea to the King of Norway, of whom he held his island earldom, as liege lord — which was why he had been chosen to escort the prince to France, as diplomatically safe — an evident misjudgement where Henry of Lancaster was concerned.

After greetings, he told them that he feared that they had come on a fools' errand.

"Henry will never let our young King go, now he has him," he asserted. "He went to sufficient trouble to get him."

"You mean . . ." Alex said, "you mean that this capture of James, at sea, was more than just chance piracy?"

"To be sure. It was no chance. This shipmaster, Hugh-atte-Fen, is no common pirate. He is a large merchant venturer, out of Great Yarmouth, Norfolk, with two other ships besides the *Kingfisher* which captured us. They were waiting for us, off the Yorkshire coast, knew who we were when they boarded us. And sailed straight for the Thames with us, captive, to bring us to King Henry. He knew just what he was at."

"You are saying that Henry planned it all?" Buchan demanded.

"Yes. No common shipmaster or merchant, much less a pirate, would have acted so, brought us straight to this Tower, not even returning to his own haven first. I tell you he was waiting for us. He said that he had been looking to welcome us for days. And he called the prince by name. Think you that Henry, having gone so far, will let James go again?"

As they digested that, Crawford spoke. "What does he want, then? Some great ransom?"

"I think not. He is sufficiently rich without your Scots siller. Besides, like all the Plantagenets, he is a man concerned with power rather than riches. He has refused to ransom Douglas, the most powerful lord in your kingdom. Also Murdoch of Fife. Others likewise. Now he has better even than he planned — since he could not know that this would kill King Robert. Now he holds the monarch, the most valuable of all."

"To what purpose, man? If it is not to ransom them?"

"He calls himself Lord Paramount of Scotland. As did Edward First and Second. I believe that he intends to be so, in fact, not just in name. And these are steps on that road."

"My God — then he will have to be taught differently!" Crawford cried. "Will these English never learn?"

All down the table these sentiments were echoed with angry vigour.

"Do not underestimate the man," Orkney warned. "This Henry may be a usurper, but he is clever. He is not of the stature of Edward Longshanks, but he is shrewder, cunning. He uses his head, rather than just his fist — and might gain more in Scotland with the one than the other."

"What then do you suggest?" Alex asked.

"I do not suggest anything, my friend. I but warn you."

"May I ask my lord of Orkney how does he think King Henry

knew of our prince's being on that ship?" Jamie Douglas said.

"I know not. I have thought long on this. We were a month roosting on the Craig of Bass, awaiting this *Maryenknyght*. I can only suppose that word of us being there got out. The Bass is but two score miles from the Border."

"But to know the right ship to assail?"

"I cannot tell you, sir. I have seen Henry but the once, and he was scarcely forthcoming! He made it seem that it was but a chance encounter, mocking us."

Grimly the leaders of the Scots embassage regarded each other.

No word came to them that evening, from Westminster.

All next day they waited for a summons to the royal presence. By early evening, with none forthcoming, they hotly demanded an interview with the Tower's Constable. Even that was difficult to attain. When at last they saw Rempton, it was to be informed coldly that they must wait their turn, that the King's Grace had much to attend to, that he was aware of their presence here and would no doubt summon them when he was ready and pleased so to do. And not before. Meantime, they had sufficient victual and comfort, did they not?

The day following was equally unprofitable and frustrating. As the time passed they decided that they must assert themselves somehow, and should find their own way back to Westminster, there to make their presence felt. But they discovered that they were not permitted even to leave the Tower, every gate held against them. Their vehement protests met with the reply that this was for their own good. His Grace could not ensure their safety from the populace if they wandered the streets, Scots being less than popular. It was unsuitable that their armed escort should parade London's streets. They would, in due course, approach England's sovereign lord under *English* escort. They must learn a modicum of patience. Had they any cause for complaint? The open spaces of the Tower Hill and garden was available to them for exercise if such they required, the tilt-yard and bear-garden likewise, a dozen acres no less, within the walls. No, it would not be possible for them to speak again with the boy James Stewart, without the King's express permission.

Feeling extraordinarily helpless for men accustomed to wielding authority, the ambassadors fretted and fumed.

Most of yet another day passed before the Deputy Constable, one Davies, came to inform them that they were to repair at once

210

to Westminster. The King would see them. There was, however, no reason for a dozen of them to go; half that would be more than sufficient. When Crawford once again burst out with indignation, Alex Stewart explained patiently that the embassage, in the Scots fashion, was carefully composed, of great officers of state, lords spiritual and temporal, and knight nominees, as representing the realm and parliament of Scotland; all should take part. Davies declared that the King of England did not grant audiences to regiments. But, with tempers rising again, he conceded that they might all go, at least as far as Westminster. Who actually entered the royal presence would be a matter for the proper authorities there. This was no time for debate. They must move at once. His Grace must not be kept waiting.

Arriving at the outer bailey, however, the Scots leaders discovered that, despite all this sudden haste, no horses were forthcoming. They were expected to walk to Westminster. Hot protests had no effect. They either walked or did not go at all. Horsed foreigners were not to be considered in the narrow streets, would be much resented. Besides, they would be quicker walking, in the congestion. Crawford all but refused to go, under these conditions, but the others persuaded him, for the sake of their young monarch.

So, in most ill humour, the illustrious envoys set out, tightly hemmed in by a strong guard of liveried spearmen and halberdiers under a peremptory captain, more like a troop of prisoners than the representatives of a sovereign power, marching at a pace unusual for bishops and for an elderly earl. Admittedly their guards were very effective at clearing a way for them through the crowds, pushing the populace aside ungently with the butts of their spears from the crowns of the causeways; but nothing prevented the filth and ordure of the kennels and cobbles from soiling and splashing the marchers feet and legs, much to their offence.

It was a full two miles from the Tower to the palace, by Eastcheap, St. Paul's Church, Blackfriars and the riverside, and though the younger members of the party were glad enough to stretch their legs after three days of cramped confinement, their elders were not appreciative. They went, barked at by dogs and shouted and jeered at by the citizenry — who no doubt took them for captives on their way to a well-earned hanging.

At Westminster they were handed over to the palace guards

— who betrayed no increase of interest or favour, but who at least made no attempt to divide up the party. A functionary was found at length to take charge of them, wielding a wand of office, who conducted them through a different selection of passages and corridors than heretofore, these becoming ever fuller of folk as they progressed. A series of ante-chambers and assembly-rooms followed, before they came eventually to a stone-arched lobby from which opened a vast hall, larger than any of the other former monastic apartments, through the open doors of which they could see it full of people, diners sitting at long tables waited on by hurrying servitors, with much noise of music, talk and laughter coming out in gusts. The hall was certainly one of the finest any of the visitors had ever seen, stone walls hung with arras and tapestries, a magnificent hammer-beam roof, dark with smoke, minstrel-galleries high on both sides. The tables were arranged lengthwise just out from the walls, with the usual dais-table crosswise on a raised platform at the other end of the chamber, leaving the central rush-strewn area free. Here an entertainment of leaping, vaulting tumblers was in progress, to music from the galleries, Eastern-seeming men, stripped to the waist, their brown bodies gleaming with sweat.

The usher told them to wait, and stepped within, bowing low, to move off round the walling. The Scots sought to wipe their feet and legs with the floor-rushes, with appropriate comments.

"It seems that we are to be dined, tonight, rather than listened to," Alex said. "Or first, leastways."

Their man with the stick came back, and signed for them to follow him again.

Once more, within the doorway, he bowed, lower than ever. Up at the centre of the dais-table what was presumably the King of England was paying no least attention, nor were those flanking him. The visitors were more moderate in their genuflection.

The entertainment still proceeding, the Scots were led not directly forward up the centre of the hall but round the right side behind the tables there. Few accorded them more than a glance. As they neared the far end, they could see that the central figure lounging at the dais-table did wear a slender gold band round his brows and the shock of straw-coloured hair. He was a heavily-built, red-faced man of about forty, in aspect more like a yeoman-farmer than any monarch, hulking of shoulder, broad of feature, with a square thrusting jaw. He appeared to have finished eating, platters pushed away from him, and was toying with a wine-cup, listening casually to a smooth-faced, richly-clad prelate who sat on his left. Between them a great deer-hound, larger than usual, sat with its shaggy head resting on the table.

It occurred to Jamie Douglas that the Stewarts, whatever their faults, at least looked royal. This Henry Plantagenet, although he was grandson of both Edward the Third and Henry, Duke of Lancaster, gave no such impression.

About a dozen others, all men, sat at the King's table, at one side only, and facing down the hall. But there were two other and smaller tables on the dais, at right-angles to the main one. That at this side was empty; at the other half-a-dozen men sat, one of whom Jamie was quick to recognise as his own chief, Archibald, Earl of Douglas. Beside him were Thomas, Earl of Moray, Murdoch, Earl of Fife, and other major captives of Homildon Hill battle four years before. These at least were watching the new arrivals.

It became evident that the visitors were being conducted to the empty table facing these last, to the left of the main one. As they mounted the dais steps their guide sank on one knee once more, signing to his charges to do likewise. They contended themselves, however, with fairly businesslike bows. This time the King did glance briefly in their direction, but without change of expression, and continued to talk with the cleric.

It made a distinctly tight fit for the Scots to seat themselves at their table, which was clearly not intended for a dozen; but they crowded around it, since it seemed that no other was provided. It meant that the lesser men, Jamie included, had to sit with their backs to the King — which might be considered unsuitable but which could scarcely be helped. Jamie sat opposite Alex and John Stewart.

"Think you this King Henry is but a boor?" Buchan wondered. "Perhaps always acts thus? Or does he behave so to humble us?"

"They say that he is a clever enough man. No boor, I think," Alex answered. "So I fear that he does all this of set purpose. Our friends over there would be able to tell us, no doubt — Douglas, and your brother . . ."

"My *half*-brother," Buchan corrected. It was no family secret that John had little love for Murdoch of Fife.

"The fact that they are here at all may mean something,"

213

Jamie suggested. "I would not think that this King has his captives to dine with him."

"You think that they are here further to humble us? Or themselves be humbled?"

"Both, belike."

Servitors brought them food and drink, and the entertainment proceeded, with dancing bears, jugglers and a choir of singing boys. King Henry seemed as little interested in these as with the Scots envoys.

At length the monarch abruptly pushed back his chair and rose. The singing died away, and everywhere the diners got to their feet. Without sign of acknowledgement Henry Plantagenet turned away and stalked to the guarded dais-door, and out. The cleric and some of the others from his table followed him, one of whom Jamie recognised as George, Earl of Dunbar and March, the renegade.

Men resumed their seats and the singing continued.

"The manners of a hog!" Crawford growled, sufficiently loud for all around to hear. "Why were we brought here?"

He got no answer to that.

Presently Murdoch Stewart rose and came strolling across the dais to their table. He was dressed, or over-dressed, in the dandified height of English fashion, in parti-coloured clothes, his hose green and red, such as he never would have worn in Scotland. Even his carriage seemed to have changed, so that he all but minced.

"Ha, Johnnie," he said. "On my soul, 'tis good to see you! Grown into a man, after all!" The voice was an unsuccessful attempt at the higher-pitched but languid English overlaying the broader Lowland Scots.

"Would that I could say the same for you!" his brother gave back, not rising. "For all that you seem to thrive on captivity."

"Captivity?" Murdoch repeated. "Scarce that. Henry treats me as cousin and guest."

"Better than he treats your liege lord, then!"

The other raised his eyebrows, and shrugged. He turned to nod to Crawford. "My lord." He gestured airily with a hand at the two bishops, gazed blankly at his cousin Alex — whom he had never met, but as to whose identity he had undoubtedly been informed — and moved on to look down at Jamie. "Ah — Sir James Douglas! Last seen departing from Homildon's field with much celerity!" which was at least more than he would

214

have been able to get his tongue round in the days before his sojourn in England.

Jamie inclined his head but did not attempt an answer. Rising, he looked at his own earls. "With your lordships' permission, I shall go pay my respects to my lord of Douglas," he said.

He crossed the dais and bowed to his chief, then to Moray and the rest.

"So, Jamie — we meet once more in less than happy case," Douglas said. "I had not expected to see you here. You were better hiding in your Hielands, man."

"It would seem so, my lord. But some effort had to be made, on King James's behalf."

"No doubt. But why you? I fear that you will gain little for your pains. Henry is a strange man. Devious."

"More devious than the Duke of Albany?"

"Ah, now there I am sweert to judge! They make a pair, I think. I see that you have his other son, there, John Stewart."

"Now Earl of Buchan — and a man to be reckoned with."

"So? I scarce know him. His father ever kept him at arm's length."

"No longer. Not since my lord of Fife was captured. He has brought him on notably. He is now Great Chamberlain and Lieutenant of the North, as well as Earl. But he is able, and well disposed. Though not one to cross, either."

"Chamberlain . . . ? That Albany kept ever to himself. The office carries considerable revenues, does it not?"

"No doubt. But I understand that my lord Duke keeps these to himself. As yet."

"That sounds like Robert, yes."

"My lord," Jamie said. "How are you treated, here, by these English?"

"None so ill so as we do as we are told! We are never allowed to forget that we are captives, to be sure. Henry blows hot and cold. And the others follow his lead. We have all had to give our word, of course, not to attempt escape. Some it irks more than others!" He looked, with his one eye, across the dais, to the colourful figure of Murdoch of Fife.

Jamie nodded. "Do you know, can you tell us, anything of King Henry's intention towards *us*? The embassage has been mocked and made light of ever since we reached this London. We are in the Tower, as good as prisoners. It can scarcely be without the King's knowledge. What does he intend for us? He acceded to our coming. Granted us safe-conduct. And now, this. After much waiting, he summons us to this hall — and then ignores us."

"Do not ask me, Jamie, what Henry Plantagenet is at! He never ceases to surprise me. But . . . he will rule Scotland one day, if he can. That is certain. All is to that end . . ."

One of the English lords who had left with the King emerged from the dais doorway and came to the embassage table, a tall, handsome man with a noble brow and less noble mouth, prominent pale eyes seemingly set in an unblinking stare, implicit with arrogance.

"That is Edmund Holland, Earl of Kent," Douglas said, "the King's cousin. He is Lord Chamberlain here. You had better go. Beware Kent, I advise you."

The newcomer all but overlooked the Scots in that he appeared to stare just above their heads, and with every aspect of distaste, the Earl of Fife discreetly sidling away.

"His Grace commands your presence," he jerked, briefly.

They eyed each other doubtfully. But clearly they could not refuse even this peremptory summons into the presence they had come four hundred miles to gain. Led by Crawford, they followed Kent to the door, Jamie tacking himself on at the rear.

In the ante-room Henry stood fondling his deer-hound, backed by his lords all laughing at apparently some royal witticism. The Scots perforce bowed again, however stiffly.

"Ha — Lindsay, is it not?" the King said genially, but as though he had only just recognised Crawford. "Sir David Lindsay! Whom we have had the pleasure of seeing in London once before. Long since, I think?"

"Yes, Sire. In 1390, it would be. Although now I am usually called Crawford! We respectfully salute Your Grace. Here are my lords the Earl of Buchan, Great Chamberlain; the Earl of Mar; the Bishop of Aberdeen, Chancellor; the Bishop of Dunblane; and representatives of the Scottish realm and parliament."

"Almost the *entire* Scottish realm and parliament, no?" Henry observed, to loud laughter from his companions.

The emissaries stood silent.

"Shall I eject the, the surplus, Sire?" Kent asked. "Although, dammit, I scarce know where to begin!"

"No, no, Edmund — let them be, now they are here. So be it they do not all wish to speak!"

216

Crawford opened his mouth, and then shut it again, as though he did not trust himself with words. Alex Stewart spoke instead, pleasantly enough.

"Your Grace, it is the Scots custom to mark the importance of such a mission by the number as well as the quality and representative position of those forming it. Here in England you may do otherwise. The Earl of Crawford, as well as being uncle to our King, is Lord High Admiral of Scotland — since matters on which we seek to treat include piracy on the high seas. The Chancellor is chief minister of the kingdom. The remainder of us represent the lords spiritual and temporal and the baronage and parliament of our liege lord's realm."

"Indeed. Then I perceive that I must consider myself flattered that so large and distinguished an array has descended upon my poor Court, sir. But, correct me if I mistake — as I am sure that you will do, being Scots! — but it seemed to me in your so helpful explanation, that you used certain words in error. Words which cannot apply here, such as treat and piracy. Or did I mishear?"

"I used those words, yes, Your Grace."

"Then it is your turn to be instructed, friend. I do not treat with any save equals, certainly not with such as owe me allegiance. And no question of piracy arises."

There was a moment or two of silence.

"How would Your Grace describe the waylaying and attack at sea of a peaceful trading vessel by another, but armed, trader, not a King's ship? And the forcible removal of passengers?" Crawford growled.

"That might conceivably be piracy, sir — but it does not describe the circumstances. Hugh-atte-Fen, of Norwich, the shipmaster, bore letters of mark and reprisal from me, as privateer. He was entitled to act as a King's ship. Vessels from the Low Countries and France have been preying on our English shipping. His duty was to intercept and investigate any such in our waters. This *Maryenknyght* was a Danziger. The passengers he found aboard were such as owed allegiance to me, as Lord Paramount of Scotland, who were travelling forth of my realms without my permission or safe-conduct. Rightly the shipmaster brought them to me."

Another silence.

"Lord Paramount of Scotland is not a phrase which we in Scotland recognise or accept," Crawford said heavily, "save

217

insofar as it may apply to our own liege lord, King James."

"Then you are ignorant, if not contumacious, sir. If not worse, indeed. Since it has been a style, designation and lawful status of the Kings of England for over a century, adopted and established by my great-great-grandsire, Edward the First, of blessed memory. And held by his successors in inalienable right, and to be so held for all time coming, God willing."

Helplessly the Scots eyed each other.

"Self-assumed and self-styled, Your Grace," John of Buchan said, quietly but firmly.

"Acknowledged, admitted and confirmed by charter. By John Baliol, sub-King of Scots, and sworn to in allegiance by all the whole nobility and community of that realm, sir. As by John's son, Edward Baliol, sub-King."

"John Baliol was a puppet, Your Grace, nothing more. His son a usurper," John returned, strongly. "The good King Robert the Bruce, *my* great-great grandsire, made that truth amply known to England, as to Scotland. Would Your Grace name *him* sub-King?"

"Young man, I would advise you to watch your tongue!" Henry said, almost gently. "My friends," he turned to his lords, "what shall I do with a guest at my table so ill-disposed as to declare the King of England liar to his face? And to seek deny him one of his rightful styles and positions bestowed on him at his coronation?" That was mock-sorrowful.

There was a chorus of wrathful advice. "Back to the Tower with them! Hold them in chains! It is treason! Bring them to trial . . .!"

"No, no, my lords — let us be merciful. Our guest is young. As is this other who spoke — I misremember the name. Although Sir David Lindsay and these bishops ought to know better! We shall bear with them, this once. So be it there is no more such unseemly contradiction of my words. I would advise, Sir David, that you or your Chancellor be spokesmen. With, I hope, the wisdom of years. Proceed."

When Crawford stood silent, but breathing deeply, lips tight and brows black, Bishop Greenlaw cleared his throat.

"My lord King," he said, picking his words, "we come from the Duke of Albany, Regent for young King James and Governor of the realm of Scotland, to seek renew the truce between the two realms, due to expire in four months time. And to ascertain Your Grace's terms for the release of our liege lord James. Also, if it please you, the release of the Earls of Fife, Douglas and Moray, as of other captives held by Your Grace."

"*Release*, Sir Bishop? Do I hear aright? Release does not come into it. The Earls of Fife, Douglas and Moray are prisoners-of-war, yes, on parole. And I shall decide, in due course, their destination. But the boy James Stewart, Earl of Carrick, is in totally different case. He is not a prisoner. He is my guest, dwelling in a house of mine at my expenses. Cared for by my servants. How can you speak of release for such as he?"

Greenlaw swallowed, audibly. "You, Your Grace will allow him to leave?"

"To be sure. In due course. When it seems good and proper — for him."

"To return to Scotland?"

"As to that, I shall have to consider well. For the boy's weal. He is, to be sure, sub-King to myself, as Lord Paramount. And he was fleeing from Scotland, secretly, was he not? With reason, it is to be presumed. He believed himself to be in danger of his life, I have learned. As did his father, whom God rest. Would not I be most unkind, harsh, cruel, to force him to return to this dangerous realm of Scotland? The more so with his father no longer there to protect him?"

"But . . . but he is now King, Sire. All is changed. Not that he was ever in danger . . ."

"The Earl of Orkney, who accompanied his flight, believed him to be so, sir. As did others. Some of whom died thereafter, I heard! Who, then, am I to believe? You, Sir David? Do you say the boy was in no danger?"

Crawford glanced at his colleagues doubtfully. "I know not," he said. "He may have been — then. I am not fully apprised of the matter, at that time. I was in Angus. But now, certainly, he is in no danger in Scotland. He is the monarch."

"I rejoice to hear it, friend. But even monarchs may be in danger, amongst their own folk, I have heard!" It was Henry's turn to glance at his companions, who duly indicated their appreciation of this remark from the man who had toppled and allegedly slain King Richard. "You will understand, however, that I shall have to ascertain, to my fullest satisfaction, the assured safety of this my young vassal prince, before I could advise him to leave the security of this my own Court and realm."

As neither Crawford nor Greenlaw appeared to know what to say to that, Alex elected to raise his voice again.

"I may be young, Your Grace, but I am a fully accredited member of this mission of a sovereign nation, and accordingly entitled to speak to its purpose. I would point out that the said mission is here for the very purpose of satisfying you on the desire of that Scots nation to have its King back amongst his people. As is proper. That is why we are so large and representative an embassage, of all manner of opinion in Scotland. Your Grace cannot have greater assurance of King James's safety than is given by the present company."

"Indeed? Yet all here were in Scotland when the lad *was* in dire danger, were you not? I fear that I shall require greater assurance than this, my friends."

"Then — who is able to give you that assurance?"

"That I will have to consider. The Duke of Albany, perhaps? Fortunately I have the pleasure of his heir's company here! It may be that this will facilitate such assurances — who knows? But, see you — until I am so assured, I shall advise James Stewart to remain here where he is safe and well cared for. He was being exiled to France, was he not? For his further education, he tells me. I vow that I am competent to educate the lad as well as any Frenchman!" He nodded at them, with a half-smile. "I think that is all, my Scots friends."

The visitors looked from one to the other. Was this, then, the end of their audience? Was this what they had come all the long road to achieve? Precisely nothing.

Alex spoke up once more. "My lord King — are you sending us away thus, with no more than this considered? Nothing gained — on either side. We were sent to treat in the matter. You say that you will not treat with Scots. Yet treat you have done, each time the present truce has been negotiated and renewed."

"That is not treating, sir. That is conceding — no more." Henry was frowning now, the superficial bonhomie gone.

Alex inclined his head, non-committal. "May we discuss these other matters, Your Grace?"

"No, you may not. There is naught to discuss. The release of the prisoners-of-war is no matter for discussion, but my own decision only. When I deem the time ripe, I shall consider it. As to this truce, I continue it for the space of one year from this day. You may so inform your Duke of Albany. Now — you have my permission to retire."

"But . . . but . . ."

"Young man," the smooth-faced prelate said, cold-voiced, "whatever you do in Scotland, no man gainsays the King of England. Hold your peace, sirrah! My lord of Crawford — retire, with your company, from His Grace's presence."

"We had, indeed have, certain proposals to put to His Grace . . ." Crawford began, when his words were overborne.

"Precious soul of God!" the Earl of Kent cried hotly. "Do these cattle not understand plain speech? Out, Scots — out!" He strode forward, hand pointing from them to the door. Behind him some of the other English lords moved forward threateningly also.

Henry watched, with a half-smile.

Crawford glanced at his colleagues, and shrugged. He bowed to the King, and the others followed suit, features strained, lips tight. But as Alex Stewart straightened up, the Earl of Kent, scarcely by accident, in his hectoring advance, cannoned into him, all but knocking him over.

Hotly Alex turned on him, hand beginning to rise automatically. He restrained himself from striking the other only by an effort.

Kent made no such effort. He reached forward and grabbed the still slightly raised arm, and jerked its owner round. "Out, oaf!" he exclaimed. "All of you — be off!"

White-faced, Alex wrenched his arm free, and with a strangely deliberate action, slapped the Englishman across the face, left cheek and right.

The two slaps, small sounds as they were in all the stir, might have been the loudest of explosions, in their effect upon the company. Immediately all was still, silent.

"Christ God!" Kent got out, at length, hand up to his face. "Struck! You . . . you shall die for that!" he whispered.

"My lords . . .!" the Bishop of Winchester said.

"You may attempt my death, by all means, sir," Alex returned, tensely. "I presume you are knight? Can offer knightly satisfaction?"

"You will receive my cartel forthwith, lout! And pay for your base effrontery in full."

"It shall be my pleasure to teach you otherwise."

A snort from behind them halted this exchange, as King Henry decided to assert himself. "Fiend seize me — as well that I did not perceive this scuffle!" he cried. "Brawling in the royal

221

presence! Edmund — you may leave us. And you, Scots — begone! While still I retain my patience."

The embassage backed out, without another word.

On the main hall dais, they paused, to eye each other, wordless still. Then, without waiting for escort, Crawford led the way down and through the still crowded and noisy apartment, whence they had come.

XIV

EDMUND HOLLAND WAS as good as his word. His cartel and formal challenge was delivered to the Scots' quarters in the Tower, by an esquire, that very evening. It consisted of a demand, in high-flown terms, for Alexander, styling himself Earl of Mar, to meet him, Edmund, Earl of Kent, two days hence, the Feast of St. John the Baptist, at noonday at London Bridge, in knightly and mortal combat, mounted, armed *cap-à-pie* in due armour, with lance, sword and dirk, the joust to be *à l'outrance*, that is, to the death. Since the said Alexander Stewart would presumably not have come equipped for such contest, the Constable of the Tower would offer the resources of the Armoury there, the best in all England, whilst he himself, Edmund of Kent, would provide a destrier or war-horse, fully trained and armoured, exact match of his own.

Alex expressed his thanks to the esquire, agreeing to the meeting, the venue and the conditions, declaring that he would look forward to the occasion.

The Scots reacted to the affair with very mixed feelings. *À l'outrance* was the grimmest of contests, with the two contenders not to be content with unhorsing or disarming, but fighting on until one or other expired. The fact that Kent had chosen to go to such drastic lengths indicated, presumably, that he was an expert jouster and supremely confident of success. Whereas none there knew anything of Alex Stewart's abilities in this respect — but they feared the worst. The fact that he had been reared in the Highlands where chivalric tournaments were unknown, was unhopeful. Heavy full armour would be strange to him, and a trial, seldom indeed worn in the North; and however good the horse provided, it would not know him and his touch, and so be less swift to react — which could make the

223

fatal difference. As well as these personal forebodings, there was the general annoyance that they had to wait another day and more as part-prisoners in this Tower. Their mission totally unsuccessful, their pride affronted, their tempers on edge, all were anxious to get away from London and home to Scotland just as quickly as possible. None wanted any further contact with the English Court, indeed Londoners in general. They none of them blamed Alex Stewart for what he had done; but they all could have wished it undone.

That night, in the cell-like chamber he shared with Alex, Jamie voiced his more particular doubts and fears to his friend.

"Pride, Alex, honour and the like, are all very laudable and to be expected from such as yourself. But we can pay too high a price for it. This folly could well result in your death. Indeed, it would seem almost likely, dear God! That Kent is a hard man, and not like to have challenged you thus unless he was very sure of himself. The Earl Douglas warned me to beware of him."

"He is perhaps *over*-sure of himself," Alex observed easily. "So he seemed to me. A bullyrook and braggart."

"Perhaps. But fighting on his own ground, at his own trade, on his own horse with his own weapons. You could have objected, not have accepted all so readily."

"For why, Jamie? I am not afraid to meet him on these terms. I am younger than he is. And have less belly — which means a better wind. Important in such a ploy. And I am not just a babe at this business. I know how to joust with lance and sword."

"Fighting the Earl of Kent will require more than but knowing how, man!"

"True. But perhaps you have forgotten, Jamie, whose son I am? The Wolf of Badenoch, see you, was renowned for more than his misdeeds. He was also Earl of Buchan, one of the finest jousters in Scotland. He won tourneys innumerable, in his day. Think you that he did not seek to pass on something of his skills to his sons? Even in the barbarous Highlands! We used to tilt together on a terrace of Aitnoch Hill, above Lochindorb. We were never as good as he was, but we learned the way of it. We did not use heavy destriers, to be sure — I doubt if there is one above the Highland Line. But we rode the heaviest garrons we could find. Just as, in this contest, I do not intend to use Kent's chosen destrier."

"What, then?"

"Why, my own grey stallion, on which I rode south. It is a

good beast, strong, well-winded. It is not trained for the tilt-yard. But it will be a deal lighter on its feet, faster, more swiftly turned, than any clumsy war-horse. Kent can scarce object, since he has had the choosing of all else."

Jamie remained doubtful, but his friend settled to sleep apparently with a quiet mind.

The day following was a trial for them all, long hours of a summer's day to be got through in restricted quarters, with the feeling on all that they should be somehow preparing themselves for the morrow, doing something at least to make ready, to seek to even the scales somehow. But there was nothing that they could do — save for Alex himself who spent some time in the Tower Armoury, extensive indeed, selecting and trying on plate-armour, shirts-of-mail and helmets, and trying out swords and lances for weight and balance.

Next morning they were hustled off much too early — on the principle, presumably, that they must not keep Kent, the King's cousin, waiting. Once again they were not permitted to ride through the streets, nor use their own Scots escort. Alex was allowed to lead his grey horse, with another led beast behind burdened with his armour and equipment.

This time they found crowds flocking in the same direction as themselves and in holiday mood, and realised that they, in fact, were today cast in the roles of entertainers, providers of spectacle and amusement. At least there was a less hostile atmosphere. And the journey was less long, London Bridge lying no great distance west of the Tower.

When they reached the place, through the dense network of crowded narrow streets and lanes of the waterside, the smells atrocious this warm morning, it seemed a more extraordinary venue for any sort of passage of arms than even they had anticipated. It was indeed quite the most strange bridge that any of them had seen, more like a village spanning the broad river, the bridge itself, raised on nearly a score of piers, lined on both sides by tall tenements of housing, projecting outwards as they rose. It was, in fact, merely another long and narrow street stretching across the Thames, little different from all the others. It was already packed with people, who crowded the causeway, filled the booths on either side and all but spilled out from the windows and balconies at various levels above — and this apparently all the way along the bridge, which seemed to imply that the contest was to be staged, not at some open space at a bridge-end, as the Scots had assumed but on the cobble-stones of the crossing itself. These certainly had been covered with some inches of new-looking sand for a considerable length.

The Tower party was, of course, much too early. They had to wait, near the north bridge-end gatehouse, within their circle of guards. All of London appeared to be converging on its curious bridge that forenoon — this proving to be one of the city's many holidays, John the Baptist's Day, and possibly had been chosen by Lord Kent for that very reason. Alex remained calm if a little withdrawn, although his stallion was restive with the noise and crowds.

At length the gentry and nobility began to arrive, in colourful, laughing droves, the women dressed as though for some festive occasion. Though they eyed the Scots curiously, these offered no greetings. Eventually, half-an-hour before noon, Edmund Holland himself appeared, at the head of a glittering company, mounted, with horsed musicians playing a stirring air on flutes, horns and drums as they came, to the cheers of the populace. Behind, grooms led two massive war-horses, like great cart-horses indeed, thickset, ponderous, splendidly turned out as though for a show, even their mighty shaggy-topped hooves painted with the blue and white colours of the house of Holland. They were followed by a heavy, lumbering cart, bearing armour, weapons, mantling in vivid hues, and heraldic shields.

Kent did not so much as glance at his opponent as he passed. But one of the grooms with the destriers peeled off with his charge and led it towards the Scots. The cart stopped.

"For the Earl of Mar," the man said briefly.

"I thank you," Alex called. "But I prefer to ride my own beast. Less handsome, no doubt, but . . . more fitting."

The groom blinked. "That . . . ?" he said, pointing at the riding-horse.

"That, my friend."

"But — that will not carry this 'ere h'armour, m'lud. Too big for it, too 'eavy."

"I am aware of that, and shall make do without. My thanks to your lord. But I require nothing of his."

Staring, the man bobbed his head and went off with the destrier, after his betters, signing to the carter to follow. A buzz of talk rose from the watchers.

"I hope that you are wise," Jamie said flatly, at Alex's side.

He was to act esquire and aide to his friend. "I cannot think so."

"You were ever a prophet of woe — before the event, Jamie. Perhaps the bridge will collapse under the weight of yonder pounding destrier, and my challenger go right through and drown! Look on the bright side, man!"

"I am looking! As did Kent — and as must you! Presently. Southwards, into the sun! You will perceive that the Englishman has passed on — a plague on him! Leaving you at *this* end. So that you will face south, the sun in your eyes. That is the chivalry of him!"

"I noticed, yes. Let us hope that he requires that advantage."

There seemed to be no provision made for a viewing-place for the Scots party, and all reasonable stances had been fully occupied before ever they arrived. They huddled where they could — and were left in no doubt when they might be obscuring the prospect of those already in the booths lining the bridge. No sort of pavilion was provided, either, for Alex to don his armour, as was usual at a tourney; it was certainly the oddest venue for such a contest. Jamie was for forcibly ejecting some of the on-lookers from one of the booths, and using it as both dressing-tent and viewing-stand; but Alex said just to wait until they were told what to do. If the proceedings were held up thereby, that would be no fault of theirs.

Information eventually arrived in the person of a gorgeously-garbed herald, who announced that he came from the Earl Marshal of England himself, and sought Sir Alexander Stewart styling himself Earl of Mar.

"I am Alexander Stewart," Alex conceded. "But why do you say 'styling himself'? I *am* the Earl of Mar. Does Edmund Holland likewise only style himself Earl of Kent?"

"No, sir. My lord of Kent is belted earl. You, it is understood, only assume the style in the right of your wife."

"Ah, is that it? So you know more about us than you pretend! I was not aware that our Scots custom was so different from yours, in this. Was not the King's father only Duke of Lancaster in courtesy of his wife? However, my earldom was confirmed and ratified by the King of Scots and his parliament. Is that not sufficient for you, Englishman?"

"I but bear the Earl Marshal's instructions, Sir Alexander."

"Then I could send you back to your Earl Marshal to have his instructions amended, sirrah, before we proceed further. Since in an affair of honour identity is important, is it not? But I

227

suppose that I should be thankful that my knighthood at least is acknowledged!"

"Were you not accepted as knight, sir, my lord Earl could nowise cross swords with you," the herald pronounced stiffly. "May I proceed?"

"You make yourself, and your masters, sufficiently clear, Sir Herald. But continue, yes."

"The Earl Marshal informs you, and all others, that by the command of the King's Grace, the proposed joust *à l'outrance* is forbidden. His Grace will not have the death of an envoy on English soil. The jousting therefore will be as in any tourney, with blunted lances and swords. Dirks will not be used. Is it understood?"

If Alex was distinctly relieved, as was Jamie Douglas, and others there also, he gave no sign of it.

"This is disappointing, sir," he said conversationally. "I had intended to relieve this realm of England of one of its more unpleasing encumbrances. Many, I am sure, would have thanked me. But I can understand your King Henry's concern for his cousin — for, I think, it is that rather than any fear for foreign envoys, which accounts for this. But I shall abide by his royal wishes, to be sure — and seek only to teach my lord of Kent a lesson, and better manners."

The herald seemed to be having difficulty with his breathing. "You will abide by the terms of the contest, sir, as laid down by the Earl Marshal, sole authority for such in this kingdom. In the event of a broken lance, that contender may elect to fight on with the sword. But no requirement lies on his opponent thereupon to abandon *his* lance. In the event of an unhorsing, the unhorsed may yield him, or may choose to fight on afoot. But no requirement rests on the other to dismount. Disarming of both lance and sword constitutes defeat. If a contender falls and remains fallen for sufficient time for the other to place his foot on his neck, that is defeat. Is all understood?"

"It is. But how shall I do? I have here only a sharp sword and a pointed lance."

"My lord of Kent has spare weapons. I shall have lance and sword sent down. Thereafter, at sound of trumpet, you will ride forward over this bridge, to a bar, where you will salute the Earl Marshal and the Earl of Kent, and at my signal will return to your starting-point two hundred paces back, there to await a further trumpet, which will commence the joust."

"Understood."

Nodding abruptly, the herald stalked back whence he had come.

"Thank God that King Henry at least showed sense," Jamie said, as he began the elaborate process of aiding his friend into his armour, piece by piece.

"You are less than flattering," Alex protested. "As well that I am armoured in faith, even better than in this steel! But I have this to thank God and King Henry for, at least — that I need not now wear the chain-mail under the plate, and shall be a deal more comfortable. And possibly agile."

"I would watch that Kent, nevertheless," his ever-suspicious friend advised. "Blunted weapons or none, he will seek to injure you if he can, that one. There has many a man died in a jousting that was not *à l'outrance*."

"I am warned," the other nodded. "Tighten that greaves-strap, will you?"

Presently the herald returned with a man bearing a nine-foot-long wooden lance, and a two-handed sword, cutting edges blunted.

"The Earl Marshal is displeased that you have refused the destrier," he announced.

"I grieve for the Earl Marshal," Alex returned. "But prefer my own horse."

"You understand, sir, that it is to your own disadvantage? This beast will tire quickly, under the weight of the armour."

"That I realise. I must see to it that the joust is not unduly prolonged."

"It makes the contest less . . . even."

"My lord of Kent does not conceive it to be even in any degree, does he? Or your Earl Marshal? Or indeed your King? In their eyes, I am beaten before I commence, am I not?"

The other did not attempt an answer to that, but strode off.

Alex, fully accoutred save for the helmet, was standing by his stallion when the trumpet blew for the first time. Jamie held out a hand to grip the steel gauntlet, wordless now, while the other Scots called their good wishes — and spectators offered light-hearted advice, largely to the effect that the Scotchman would be well advised to turn in the other direction entirely and not stop his nag until he got back to Scotland and safety. Lance high, Alex, helmet within his shield-arm, waved to all and sundry, and rode his horse off over the bridge at a trot, Jamie and Sir

229

Alexander Forbes, acting as esquires, coming along behind, on foot.

London Bridge was built in three sections, with a drawbridge-like raising portion two-thirds of the way across on the south side, coinciding with the deepest part of the river's channel, so that shipping could pass upstream. The chains for this lifting section were housed in slender towers on either side — and there were, of course, no houses here. The centre of the longer main stretch for this contest was railed off today with hurdles for most of its length, covering about three hundred and fifty yards or four hundred paces. This length, two hundred paces on either side, was important, being estimated to be just sufficient for a heavy war-horse to attain major if not maximum speed — not a gallop, which it would never reach under any circumstances, but a lumbering canter — impetus being a vital factor naturally, although not necessarily the most vital. Midway in this four hundred paces a cord in the Kent colours was stretched across the sanded causeway. Here stood the herald, a trumpeter, two mounted marshals in half-armour, and a resplendent gentleman in Court clothing whom Alex recognised from two nights before at the King's table, presumably the Earl Marshal himself.

Cheers from all around heralded the arrival of Edmund of Kent as he rode up from the south side, at the head of a large and laughing group of sauntering knights and esquires. At least as far as tournaments were concerned, he appeared to be a popular figure. Certainly he looked the part. Indeed, the contrast between the two protagonists was very marked, almost laughable. Kent was clad in the most magnificent armour, gleaming with black lacquer, gold inlaid, bearing in the crook of his arm a great helm of similar design, crowned with the crest of a silver demi-lion guardant arising from a flourish of tall ostrich-feathers, blue-and-white for Holland. His shield was vivid with the quartered device of his house and earldom, in contrasting colours. A silken scarf around his neck presumably represented the favours of some lady other than his wife, being different from his own in hue. His charger was as splendid. Pure white but clad in matching black armour on head and body, over this it bore heraldically painted linen mantling, very colourful, whilst from between its steel-guarded ears sprouted more ostrich-feathers. The harness and trappings were of rich maroon leather studded with precious stones. The total effect was overwhelming, perhaps just a little overdone.

Alex Stewart, on the other hand, inevitably was without any such display. His armour, chosen from the Armoury for effectiveness and as much suppleness as was possible in such commodity, was entirely plain and unpolished, not exactly rusty but dull and dented as was the long shield and uncrested helmet. His mount, looking positively fragile beside the massive, thick-legged destrier, carried no plate armour at all and certainly no plumes. The only gesture Alex had made was to drape the blue-white-and-gold fesse-chequey banner of Stewart, with its bend sinister, brought south only for identification purposes, round his stallion's chest and withers.

At the rope barrier both contestants reined up, facing each other, their horses' noses almost touching. They inclined heads stiffly, and then each turned in the saddle and raised his lance in salute towards the Earl Marshal. Nothing was said. That magnate bowed in return, and waved a hand.

Kent, as challenger, leaned forward and extended the butt of his upright lance to tap Alex's shield, twice; and as he sat back, Alex made the same gesture.

A chorus of groans and shouts arose from the spectators near enough to observe these moves. It was the indication that the joust was not to be to the death, as had been said, and great was the disappointment. The populace felt itself to be cheated, having come to see blood shed.

At a nod from the herald, the contestants reined round and with their supporters headed back to their starting-places, accompanied — at least as far as the Scots were concerned — by catcalls and insulting comments from the crowd. A mounted marshal followed each.

Two hundred paces back, at another marked spot, Alex turned, and put on his helmet, visor still up, clamping it secure. Jamie and Forbes made a final check of all accoutrements and fastenings, and signed their satisfaction to their principal.

It was as Jamie was moving back to his own new stance at the side of the starting-line that, his glance lifting, he saw amongst the many other faces watching them from the booth behind one which riveted his attention. It was an extraordinary sensation — for it might almost have been a trick of his vision, some sideslip of timing. The features could have been those of Alex Stewart, save for some slight blurring of outline and a difference of expression. For a moment Jamie floundered, mentally. Then he realised that he was looking at a face he knew. He had not seen

Sir Duncan Stewart of Loch-an-Eilean for many a year, but he had no doubt as to his identity now. Alex's brother was here in London, and had come to see the fight.

As recognition came to the Douglas, the other's glance locked with his own, and for a long moment they stared at each other, the fair man and the dark. Then quickly, almost furtively, the former ducked away behind the spectators next to him, and was gone.

Jamie's first impulse was to push his way into the booth, through the press, to grab and hold Stewart. But the briefest thought told him that this would be foolish, even if practicable. It could only distract and upset Alex at a time when he required all his concentration. Duncan Stewart would not submit tamely, that was certain, so there would be trouble, disturbance — and the crowd was scarcely friendly anyway. He turned away, doing nothing. He did not even make a sign to his friend.

A trumpet-blast sounded from mid-bridge, and the mounted marshal beckoned.

Alex Stewart snapped down his helmet's visor, lowered his lance to the level, and leaning forward, kicked with his heels his beast's flanks.

Two hundred paces, on a horse, is no great distance, especially on a spirited riding-horse. But it was quite sufficient to get the grey up through trot and canter to a gallop. On the other hand, although the distance did mean more to the slower, heavier destrier, it still did not allow it to attain quite its fullest impetus. As a consequence, Alex reached the central barrier considerably before Kent did. But the rope was withdrawn now, and there was nothing in the rules to say that the contestants must remain on their own sides of the division. He pounded on over the sanded cobbles. The sun in his face, striking through the slits of his visor, was a major handicap, barring his vision in confusing dazzle and shadow.

His opponent was thundering towards him on the most determined of collision courses, carrying more than twice his weight and strength. Orthodox jousting tactics were for the two to meet head-on, lance-tips aimed at wherever each deemed to be the most vulnerable spot, with the object of smashing the opposite number right out of his saddle and to the ground, if possible — where he might well be stunned by the impact or by the battering effect of his own plate armour. It was not a delicate or precise operation, the precision lying in the handling of the horses, the timing of the strike, the aim, and of course the ability to withstand the shock and keep in the saddle.

Since any such headlong collision would almost certainly result in Alex's overthrow, his methods had to be less than orthodox. Yet no mere dodging, by-passing and, as it were, skirmishing, would serve or be acceptable, as against all the laws of chivalry. His opportunity to manoeuvre was strictly limited.

He continued, then, on his head-on course, the yells of the crowd loud and echoing within his helmet. A corner of his mind noted that Kent had transferred the silken scarf from his neck to his lance-head, where it streamed in confusing fashion — an allowable device but one which could mask, even for a moment, the all-important point of aim.

With less than a dozen yards to go, their squared-off lance-tips only about seven yards apart, Alex acted. Fiercely he dug in his spurs, at the same time jerking up his beast's head. The stallion responded nobly, leaping forward and upward with an abrupt access of speed and change of level. The scarf-tied lance-head wavered in instinctive reaction. Even as the grey's forefeet touched down again, Alex pulled to the left. Only a trained, agile and light-footed horse could have conformed sufficiently swiftly. The beast swung off to the side before Kent's lance could adjust, and the scarfed tip missed by inches. Alex, on the other hand, who had so planned it, was able to bring his own lance to bear. Because of the angle, and turning away, it could not be the sort of major thrust which might have unseated his opponent; but he managed to strike a glancing blow. Kent was able to deflect it on his shield, and scarcely even rocked in his saddle. Nevertheless, it was a hit, the first point to the Scot.

They hurtled past each other, to the yells of the onlookers.

Alex did not even draw breath before flinging himself and his mount into the next move. Urgently he reined back and back, and snorting violently the grey reared high on its hind legs, staggering forward on two feet for half-a-dozen paces, its forelegs pawing the air even as its upper half turned in response to the furious tugging to the right. By the time its forefeet touched sand again, it was half-way round, and in an involved but remarkably well-adjusted side-stepping dance of the hindquarters completed the turn. Seldom if ever could the spectators have witnessed so rapid and complete a reversal of course, at speed. Spurring hard again, the Scot went pounding after the destrier a mere dozen yards behind.

Kent was not seeking to rein up or round. His obvious course now was to get well to the other, northern end of the lists before swinging round in a wide arc, both so as to maintain the fullest possible impetus on his war-horse and to avoid putting himself directly into the sun's dazzle. Unfortunately for him, he did not know that his antagonist was on his heels — his helmet prevented any part-backward view and the thunder of his own charger's hooves allied to the deadening effect of his armour, drowned the sound of the chase.

The grey stallion was infinitely faster, and swiftly overtook the destrier. Alex could not, of course, attack the other from the rear. So just as Kent began his swing round to the right, the other pulled off in the same direction. The Englishman must have been astounded suddenly to discover his enemy rearing to another pawing turn directly in front of him. And surprise would not stop at that. For the Scot had in fact tossed away his lance, and drawn sword instead. That Kent was unready for instant action went without saying. His lance was half-raised. If he could have brought its nine-foot length down to bear in time, with the necessary velocity, he would have had the other at his mercy and hopelessly out-ranged. But those instants he was not given. Alex plunged at him, sword high, and as the lance came down to the couched position, but before it could be aimed, drove down his steel upon it with maximum force. Edge blunted or none, the weight of the massive blade snapped the wooden shaft of the lance clean through. Kent was left with only the stump.

Raising his sword high again, in mocking salute, the Scot reined round and trotted off towards the south end of the lists.

The howls of the crowd were angry now. However unusual, there was nothing improper in what Alex had done. Nothing in the rules insisted that the lance must be used in preference to the sword. It normally was, of course, because of its greatly longer reach. But that was little to the crowd's taste; undoubtedly the inevitable wagering was heavily on the Earl of Kent.

The situation was now much transformed, and in Alex's favour. Kent it was who now faced the wrong way, into the sun. And the heavy destrier held no advantage for swordery.

By mutual consent the contestants waited a little, giving their mounts rather than themselves some small breathing-space. But no lengthy pause was permitted, and soon the trumpet blared again. Both plunged forward.

This time Alex did not urge his grey to a gallop, or even a

canter. He trotted out in no hurry at all. Kent, however, drove his animal at the same earth-shaking charge, sword outstretched before him as like a lance as possible.

Alex was well aware where both danger and opportunity lay. Sword-fighting was close work, inevitably; and at close quarters the great destrier could be lethal, its weight and strength overwhelming. Struck by it, cannoned into, the grey could be easily knocked over and trampled. However close the fight, therefore, the horses must not touch. On the other hand, manoeuvre, speed, agility, were far more important with the sword than with the lance. Although, of course, clad in armour as they both were, delicate and intricate swordsmanship was neither possible nor productive, the use of the weapon limited.

Now, by deliberately going slowly and holding back, Alex allowed the other to gain almost maximum speed and momentum, so that to suddenly change the course or deflect the hurtling monster would be all but impossible. He had to hold his stallion hard in and on its straight course, for the beast was all too well aware of the menace beating down upon it. Then, as Kent almost crashed upon them, the Scot jerked and kneed his grey to the left and, thankfully and just in time, the creature almost leapt sidelong out of the way. It meant, to be sure, that Alex could not use his sword. But, as he plunged past, the Englishman lashed out in a furious back-handed swipe. It missed the man by inches, but the tail-end of it struck the grey's croup near the tail, causing the brute to rear and whinny with pain and fright. The lack of horse-armour was being paid for.

Then they were past. To Kent's slight advantage — but only apparently.

Alex was reining round immediately. But now he had a hurt and alarmed mount to cope with — and quickly knew the difference. The stallion, agitated, responded much less swiftly and effectively, side-stepping, dancing, head-tossing. Nevertheless its rider enforced his mastery, seeking to reassure by word and hand — although a steel gauntlet is scarcely made for gentling — but at the same time forcing the beast round with rein and knee and spurring it on. Training, familiarity and reliance told. They plunged on after the destrier.

Now Alex's problem was two-fold. He wanted to retain the advantage of the sun, and at the same time close with his opponent at a moment of the destrier's minimum impetus. He pulled over to the right therefore, to the west, as widely as he

235

might, so as to circle round to actually confront the other. Kent was seeking to rein-in his charger for the turn.

Alex was scattering the spectators lining the western side of the bridge, for there was precious little space for his manoeuvre in this the most constricted lists he had ever known. His aim was to get as far to the south as he might, and for the other to see him doing so, despite his helmet-restricted view, and to turn in that direction to meet him.

Alex ran out of space, of course, at the end of the marked-off area. He had to pull south-eastwards, cursing the narrowness of the bridge — even though, as bridges went, it was broad. Fortunately Kent, of intent or otherwise, had drawn over to the other, east side, and was now turning, speed reduced to a ponderous trot. Alex spurred in at him, yelling "A Stewart! A Stewart!" little like him as this was.

There were only a few yards available, little time to muster significant speed; but the situation was a deal better for the Scot than for his enemy. Kent was almost stationary, in a corner, and facing south-westwards, so that the sun slanted in through his left-hand visor-slits.

Deliberately forcing his grey to rear and plunge and sidle right in front of the other, Alex leaned forward in his saddle, blade as nearly flickering as was possible with a heavy two-handed sword. All but dancing his beast there, he sought to feint, confuse, aid the sun's dazzle. Kent, restrained from making any mighty lunge by the need to parry, his mount at a standstill now, had been forced to a defensive posture.

This play could not be kept up for any time, the weight of those great swords, meant for double-handed work, being too sore on the wrist. Because of their shields, neither could use the left hand to aid the right. But Alex was the younger man, and, not being a courtier, almost certainly the fitter. He cherished his advantages, kept his horse sidling and his blade weaving.

When he recognised that his own wrist would stand little more of it, he chose his moment to make a direct lunge for the throat when the other's sword was flagging after a mid-body parry. The only way Kent could cope with this was by an instant reversal, a directly upward stroke. This only by a great effort. It was achieved, at a price. Alex, expecting it, swung his blade away to the right, as though to smash down instead on the other's left shoulder, above the shield, pausing fully extended thus for an instant. He was entirely vulnerable at that moment, had his opponent been in a position to take advantage of it. But Kent's awkward upward sweep could nowise be altered to any sort of forward thrust. It had to reach its full height and then come down through sheer weight and muscle failure. The man chose to bring it down in an attempt to parry the wavering point threatening his shoulder. Which was what Alex had manoeuvred for.

Jerking back in his saddle at last, the Scot drew back his weapon just in time to avoid that slashing downward cut — which nothing could bring up again quickly. Then, kicking his beast nearer, with all his strength remaining he lunged forward his blade in a fierce but controlled thrust to the throat again. Or just a little lower, directly at the base of the gorget, where the helmet joined the body-armour. With all his concentration he guided the blunt, flattened-off sword-tip right in under the flange of the helmet, slightly upturned to reach in. And then, with a final explosion of that weary wrist, he jerked the whole weapon up, from the hilt. With a snap the leather strap securing the helmet to the rest burst at Kent's right side, and over the helmet itself toppled, to hang, still held by the strapping on the other side, over its owner's left shoulder, resting on the shield-top, and leaving the man bareheaded, blinking open-mouthed and gasping, sweat running down into screwed-up eyes.

For a long moment Alex held the sword poised above his opponent's unprotected head; then, as the other's blade came up automatically, he slashed down on it, driving it aside. Pulling back, he flung his own weapon down on the sand in front of his defeated foe — for to be unhelmeted was as final a verdict as any — and raising gauntlet in salute, reined round and went trotting back over the bridge, whilst the populace and spectators groaned, shook their fists and roared their disappointment. He paused to bow briefly to the Earl Marshal and herald, in passing, but received the merest nod of acknowledgement.

Jamie and Forbes ran out to greet the victor, shouting their congratulations and admiration, scarcely able to express their delight and relief. Alex took off his helmet and gave it to Forbes, smiling, and shaking a shower of sweat-drops from brow and plastered fair hair, generated by the heat inside that steel box.

"I would not have believed that you had it in you!" Jamie, tactless as ever, cried, leading the grey back towards the other waiting Scots. "You are a notable jouster, man. That was a joy! You had him all ways."

"I but recollected what my great ancestor, Robert Bruce, did at Bannockburn, at the first onset," the other replied, still panting a little. "You'll mind, he was caught on but a palfrey against de Bohun's charger — yet won the day. His tactics I used. He was my great-great-grandfather, after all."

The reception by the Scots party of their champion was in marked contrast to that of the crowd round about them. Since, apart from the sword Alex had brought with him originally, they were none of them armed save with dirks, the two bishops were not alone in urging that the sooner they removed themselves from the vicinity the better. Their escort, provided by the Constable of the Tower, looked as though it might be less than enthusiastic in their defence from a mob's anger. Jamie and Forbes, therefore, with all speed aided Alex in divesting himself of the armour, the officer of their guard looking apprehensive.

It made a distinctly hurried and undignified departure from the scene of triumph — but already some missiles and filth had been thrown at them, and fists and sticks shaken. Whether the Earl Marshal would feel any responsibility to protect them the visitors were not prepared to wait to discover.

It was as they were moving off from the bridge-end, Alex leading his stallion and in his own clothing again, that Jamie felt a tug at his elbow. He was prepared to turn and defend himself against attack, hand on dirk, but discovered there only a middle-aged individual, grizzled and tough-looking, in the garb of a man-at-arms. Although he had a hand on a short cavalry sword, he was nodding his head in greeting.

"Sir James? Sir James Douglas, is it no'?" this new arrival said, in a strong Lowland Scots voice. "I jalouse you'll maybe could do wi' a bit mair steel handy, in this pass? I'll bide wi' you, a whilie."

"Why, thanks, friend. You could be right. This crowd looks ugly. You know me, then?"

"Aye, I do. I'm Rab Douglas, frae Peebles. I was wi' you at yon stramash at Preston, against Hotspur Percy. Aye, and I was at Otterburn, forby. I was wounded at Homildon, and taken prisoner wi' the Earl. He should ha' done as you said, man. I've been wi' the Earl these four years. But, och I'm wearying for hame, mind."

"That I can believe. Is the Earl here today, then?"

"No' him. Forby, he'll wish he had been, when he hears. He said he didna want to see decent Scots gien mair ill usage and

238

mockery. Little did he ken! Sakes, Sir James — your man fair skelpit yon baistard Kent!"

"Aye, it was a bonny fight. The Earl of Mar is no bairn at the jousting."

"He was the Earl o' Buchan's son, was he no'? I've seen his faither at the same ploy, one time — at a tourney at Stirling. He was an awfu' man that — but a right stark fighter!"

They dodged, as a handful of dirt was thrown at them. Cursing, the new arrival whipped out his sword and flourished it threateningly.

"Dirty low swine!" he snarled. "Have you no' a guard? Decent Scots, no' this Englishry?"

"They are still at the Tower. We were not permitted to bring them. The English have sought to humble us, ever since we came."

"Och, you should never have come, at all. Anyone could ha' tell't you that."

"We had to come. To seek the young King's release. Scotland could not just leave her liege lord a prisoner. Not that we have achieved anything."

"Nor would you. Anyone here could have tell't you that same, too. The laddie will never be loosed. When they went to siclike pains to get him."

"How mean you — pains?"

"Trouble, man. Siller. Plotting."

"How that? James was captured at sea, on his way to France. A mischance . . ."

"Nae mischance! They kenn't he was in that ship, and lay wait for it. We a' kenn't, here aboot the Court, what was to do."

"What mean you? How could you know? James was a month on the Craig o' Bass, waiting for that ship."

"Aye, we kenn't that, forby. A messenger came to this King Henry, frae Scotland, wi' the word o' it. Killing beasts to get here in haste, they said."

"A messenger? From whom, man?"

"Whae'd tell the likes o' me that? But I've heard it said it was one o' the Governor's men."

"Lord — Albany!"

"Aye, that's the whisper amongst the English lords' servants. That the Governor sold the laddie to Henry. The price I dinna ken. But he's no' like to hand him back, I'm thinking."

Appalled, Jamie did not speak for a little. It was scarcely

believable. And yet, and yet . . . Was it not logical enough? If Albany had murdered Prince David, and threatened young James's life sufficiently for his father to send him to France, would he boggle at betraying him to the English? Was it worse than starving to death, poison, or the knife? And if it was true, what likelihood was there of James Stewart ever coming back to Albany's Scotland? Instead of astonishment should he, James Douglas, not be blaming himself for having failed to think of it?

"Did you ever see this messenger of Albany's?" he asked presently, heavily. Before his mind's eye there had arisen the features, so like Alex's, of Duncan Stewart hiding amongst the throng in that saddler's booth, to watch his brother.

"No."

"Does the Earl of Douglas know of this?"

"It would be unco strange if he didna, Sir James."

Thereafter, wending their way through the narrow streets, Jamie was notably silent, considering it all and wondering how and when to tell Alex Stewart. Not in front of the others, certainly. Presently, with the Tower in sight and the disappointed tourney crowds far behind, the Douglas man-at-arms left them, with good wishes and handshakes. Jamie gave him no message for his master.

When the Tower gates clanged shut on them, Crawford and Buchan went to inform the Constable that they would be leaving for Scotland at sunrise next morning.

*   *   *

Although they were prepared for delaying tactics and general obstruction from the Tower authorities, in this matter as in all others, the reverse in fact applied, and speeding the parting guests was the theme. Indeed, the Scots were requested to leave, not at sunrise but an hour before it — this again to ensure that mounted and armed foreigners did not make unsuitable appearance in London's streets. They were nothing loth to comply. Apparently King Henry and higher authority had no further interest in their presence.

So they made a very early start, their Scots men-at-arms even more thankful than the leadership to be on their way — for, of course, their seventy-strong escort had been cooped up in cramped quarters ever since arrival, to their great resentment. It was on the whole, therefore, a cheerful company which, despite the hour, shook the dust of London from their feet and headed northwards for home.

The Earl of Mar was the exception. Since Jamie's revelations of the evening before he had been in an unusual withdrawn mood of abstraction and reserve; if not depressed, certainly distressed, grieved, angered. Clearly the thought of treachery such as was indicated towards their young prince shook him to the roots of his being, both from the dynastic and the family standpoint; and that his own brother was probably the means by which that treachery was effected hurt most of all. As well as this, a sensitive and friendly man, he had been much galled throughout by the deliberate discourtesy shown to them all by Henry and his Court, and especially by the unchivalric behaviour at the tourney the day before and the utter ignoring of them after the victory. Respecting his friend's state of mind, Jamie maintained a fair degree of silence himself, something he had an aptitude for.

They were over a dozen miles on their way, crossing the rolling hunting country of Enfield Chase when there was an unexpected interlude. Shouts from their rearward turned all heads. Behind them a hard-riding company of perhaps a score pounded after, two large banners at the head. It did not greatly tax the Scots' English heraldic knowledge to recognise the colours of the earldom of Kent and the house of Holland.

"How think you? A recall by Henry?" Buchan wondered.

"He would have sent more than this," Crawford said. "He knows our numbers."

"He would require to send an army to turn us back now!" Forbes declared. "We have had sufficient of English hospitality!"

So said they all as they trotted on.

As the newcomers caught up, Kent himself was seen to be leading them. He actually smiled, something they had not seen before, as he flourished a feathered and bejewelled velvet bonnet at them.

"Greetings, my lords," he cried. "Whither away this fine morning, so early? Do not say that you are on the road to Scotland, so soon? Without the courtesy of a farewell?"

His hearers' gasps were audible, none finding words easily to match such effrontery.

"We heard but an hour or so back that you were gone," the other went on. "I rose with all haste."

241

"Why, sir?" That was Alex Stewart, baldly for him.

"For sufficient reason, surely, my lord? To pay my respects and to wish you God-speed, if naught else."

"The first belated, the second unexpected!" Alex jerked.

"Come, come, my lord of Mar!" Kent reproved, reining nearer. "You did not wait to allow me to congratulate you on your, your prowess yesterday."

"I gained no notion that such would be forthcoming, sir. And the crowds scarcely encouraged delay."

"Pooh — wagering losses, nothing more. They showed me little love, either. But you should pay no heed to such cattle. What made you think, sir, that I would not acknowledge your superior . . . cunning?"

"Cunning?"

"To be sure. Cunning, wits, artifice, wile, sleight of hand. Which gained you the victory."

"You are suggesting, my lord of Kent, that it was by cunning contrivance that I gained the advantage yesterday? Rather than by knightly skill and honest fight?"

"Did you not make that sufficiently evident to all, man? You rejected fair matching, refusing equal horses. You mocked the accepted terms of fight, playing at horsemanship instead of jousting. You discarded the lance without informing me, the true tourney weapon, and deliberately broke mine. And then you used the sword merely to unhelmet me and gain a cheap end to it all. Had I known that we were to engage in jugglery and hall-floor entertainment, I would have come prepared, sir."

Alex drew a deep breath. "*I* came prepared to fight to the death, my lord — as you had challenged. *You* chose the terms, the weapons, the place, the time, the sun even. Henry of Lancaster forbade *à l'outrance*, not I. If I used my head to redress the balance, you have no call to complain, I say. I broke no rules. I fought fair."

"You fought like a jester, a mountebank, sir — scarcely a knight. But if you will agree to meet me again in honest jousting, anywhere, equally mounted, equally armed and armoured, to abide by knightly custom, I shall rejoice. And perhaps show a different result."

"I see no virtue in anything of the sort," Alex returned. "I never desired such contest in the first place. Let it be, my lord."

"So — you choose not to meet me in fair fight?"

"I would choose not to meet you again in any circumstances,

sir! Fair or otherwise. I have seen enough of you." Alex's voice quivered a little. Despite his generally equable and courteous disposition, he did not lack the spirited Stewart temper. "But if ever we do encounter each other, it will be my earnest endeavour to do more than unhelmet you!"

"I see, then, why you are in such haste for Scotland! You will be secure there from test, to be sure. Unless my Cousin Henry decides to show his barbarous northern realm the weight of his hand. In which case it will be my pleasure to seek you out."

"We shall await your coming, sir. And thereafter continue your education in jugglery and hall-floor entertainment! Your Cousin Henry's, likewise. Tell him so, if you please. Tell him also that the price for pirating and holding captive our young King may prove more expensive than he bargained for with his friend north of the Border! Tell him, likewise, that more than usurping a throne is required to make a true king. A good day to you, sir."

Alex reined round and rode off, followed gladly enough by the other Scots.

The Earl of Mar returned to Scotland a different man from he who had left it.

XV

THE HIGHLAND HARVEST over that autumn, Jamie Douglas
was summoned to a meeting at Aberdeen. He had stayed
on at Lochindorb, where he was useful, kept pleasantly
busy, and where Mary and the children were happy. Reported
conditions in the South, under the Regent's complete sway now,
were not such as to entice him to leave Badenoch. His brothers
were looking after his lands of Roberton, Stoneypath and
Baldwinsgill for him, and he was well enough content superficially, however much he seethed in his inmost heart over the
state of Scotland, its mismanagement and what he considered
to be the triumph of wickedness and bad faith. He got on well
with the Highlanders, was learning the Gaelic, and was gradually
becoming something of a minor power in his own right in
Braemoray and Badenoch. He saw Alex at intervals and continued to enjoy their association but recognised that his friend
had become a preoccupied man, in some measure at war with
himself, and not as prepared to be forthcoming about it as was
usual. Also that he was still not altogether happy about his wife
and her activities.

The Aberdeen summons, in early October, was to meet at the
provost of the burgh's change-house in the Shiprow; which
struck Jamie as a strange rendezvous for the Earl of Mar. He
was surprised at the composition of the party assembled, likewise. Apart from Sir Alexander Forbes of that Ilk the others
were merchants, burgesses and shipmasters. Their host, Provost
Robert Davidson, was a big powerful man of about forty, with
a ruddy, weatherbeaten face unlooked-for in a townsman; he
had been a shipmaster himself until a few years before, when he
had inherited his father's merchanting business and quayside
inn, and thereafter by his drive and energy had quickly made

himself a powerful figure in Aberdeen, now being its chief magistrate and spokesman of the merchants' guilds.

With beakers and flagons of excellent wine before them the company of about a dozen sat around a long table in a handsome panelled upstairs room, richly if soberly furnished, which would have bettered many a lord's hall, overlooking the busy fish-market and quays of the port. Alex sat at one end and his host at the other. Jamie was intrigued by the composition of the party, never having had occasion to sit down with a roomful of burgesses before. They seemed substantial, shrewd men, in their own way formidable, and clearly somewhat suspicious of such as himself. For his part, he had no least notion as to the reason for this assembly.

Robert Davidson, deep-voiced, almost grim, opened the proceedings. "My lord Earl of Mar has a matter of much import to put before us," he said, in a strong and unmistakable Aberdeen accent which gave no hint of his Highland antecedents — the Davidsons were, of course, a branch of the great Clan Chattan of Badenoch. "It could concern us all. My lord — we are listening."

"Mr. Provost and my friends," Alex said pleasantly. "What I have to say may not be approved by you all. Or indeed, by any. In which case you will tell me. But I have come to you because I believe that if you *do* approve, together we can strike a blow for our realm and our young King. And also for your own interests. You are all merchants, shippers, traders with foreign lands, France, the Low Countries, the Baltics and the like. And you all have been suffering grievous losses in your shipping at the hands of English pirates, losses for which you can obtain no redress."

Throaty growls of agreement for this, at least.

"As no doubt you are aware, I have recently returned, with Sir Alexander Forbes and Sir James Douglas and others, from an embassage to England, to London, to the Court of the usurping King Henry, to seek negotiate the release, by ransom if need be, of our rightful King James, shamefully taken by English pirates from the Danzig ship *Maryenknyght* chartered by the King of France, in which our liege lord was on his lawful way to France. We were most rudely used by King Henry and his servants, who refused to consider the release of our sovereign and who said openly to us that the ship which took our prince was no pirate but a privateer under letters of mark and reprisal

245

from himself, the King. And this in time of signed truce between the realms. That ship, the *Kingfisher*, of Great Yarmouth, under Hugh-atte-Fen, is a notorious pirate, as you all know too well."

As his hearers scowled and muttered, Alex leaned forward over the table.

"You perceive what this means? It means that King Henry is himself involved in piracy. He encourages these English shipmasters to attack and rob on the high seas, and divides the spoil with them. This is why you have had no redress, no response to your complaints. The King of England is chief pirate!"

General exclamation broke out round the table. Alex gave it its head.

Presently he went on. "You are angered, as was I. But . . . Henry Plantagenet, by that admission, gave us the means to strike back. If he can employ privateers, so can we! He can have no lawful complaint if we trade with him in his own coin. And that, my friends, is what I propose to do. With your help."

There was no doubt now about the company's rapt attention. However doubtful most of them looked, they all sat forward eagerly.

"Henry mocked and ignored our embassage. He is a man who heeds only deeds, not speeches. So we will give him deeds. And seek to regain our young King's liberty by means he cannot fail to understand. I intend to charter and fit out a stout ship, here in Aberdeen, and sail her against English shipping, under letters of mark."

Alexander Forbes slapped the table delightedly and roared his approval. Davidson was stroking his chin thoughtfully. Jamie Douglas, however, when he could make himself heard, undoubtedly spoke for more than just himself.

"Where, my lord, would you get the said letters of mark? Not from the Regent Albany, I think!"

"Not from Albany, no. But from his son."

"What! But . . . ?"

"Jamie — hear me. This is more than a device. These letters of mark and reprisal are issued by the government of a realm in the name of the King. Who governs this northern portion of King James's realm? Not the Duke of Albany, but John, Earl of Buchan, Lieutenant and Justiciar of the North. I have spoken with him. He is ready to give me such a letter. He misliked our reception, and Henry's manners, as much as I did. Wait, man!

I know that such a letter would be unlikely to stand good in an English court of law. But — would any? Henry in his arrogance claims that he is Lord Paramount of Scotland. Would he accept any letter of mark from whomsoever in Scotland? Albany's or other? I say he would hang us as pirates, out-of-hand — if he caught us. So we must not be caught. But the letter will serve well enough for anything less than Henry's warships. And it is not his warships that we go to assail, but his traders — as he does with us. Aye, and his privateers."

Noisy debate arose around that table. It was clear that it was not the ethics of what was proposed which was preoccupying the company, but the likelihood of being captured by the English king's ships. At least none doubted Alex's verdict that any captured sailors would hang.

"My lord of Mar," the Provost said presently, "none of us will question the worth of this ploy, if it is possible. Nor the need for some stroke against these pirates. Nor, indeed, your lordship's good heart in proposing this. But to have any success, we would have to be able to out-sail not only the English privateers but their king's ships, forby. And I know of no vessel like to do that, in Aberdeen or elsewhere."

There were murmurs of agreement.

"Surely we do not wholly lack for fast ships in Scotland?"

"Sufficiently fast for this — yes, my lord. Craft that could out-sail ships of war have to be built to do so. Our ships are for trading, carrying goods, cargo. They have to be right stoutly built to withstand stormy seas, and of bulk to carry sufficient cargoes over long voyages. Heavy vessels."

"Are the English privateers not the same?"

"Not so. They use lighter, narrower craft, not made for long voyaging. These dart out from their ports of Kingston, Yarmouth, Harwich and the like, to prey on vessels using the seas off their coasts on their way to France and the Low Countries. They do not have to make long voyages, and can choose their weather. So they can be fast and light — aye, and sleep in their own beds of a night! We build no such craft."

"But we *could*, could we not? Build a vessel to outmatch these pirates. For that purpose?"

The merchants eyed each other.

"How long would you be prepared to wait, my lord. One year? Two?"

"So long . . . ?"

"Does Scotland hae nae ships o' war o' her ain?" one of the others demanded.

"Few, if any, I fear, sir," Alex said. "And if such there are, they would be under the control of the Duke of Albany, who would not allow that they be used against Henry, I wager!"

There was silence for a little.

It was Jamie who broke it. "I am not assured that this project is altogether sound," he averred, frowning. "Although I am as strongly in favour of teaching the English a lesson as any here. But . . . in this matter of fast ships, it seems to me that we need not look further than the galleys and birlinns of the Islesmen."

"Galleys, 'fore God!"

"Yes. They are the fastest craft that sail, I was assured by shipmen in the West. Long and lean as wolfhounds, driven by thirty-six long oars, two men to an oar, besides their square sails, they can outpace and overreach anything that floats. When I journeyed, yon time, from Ardchatten Priory to Dumbarton, to see King Robert, my ship was challenged more than once by the robber galleys of the Islesmen. The Priory's flag saved us. But I saw the speed and power of these ill craft."

"A notion, Jamie, bless you . . . !"

"That was in the sheltered Hebridean seas, Sir James," Davidson objected. "Galleys would not serve in our stormy main."

"They get swifter storms and steeper seas there, shipmen told me, than anywhere. Because of mountain winds and the fierce currents . . ."

"Nevertheless, sir, their galleys are not the craft for our great main seas. They are open vessels, men exposed. There is little decked-in cover, cabins or holds. They could not make long voyages, as would be required. Fast they may be, but they are cockle-shells compared with our sea-going carracks and the like."

"Yet, it was in vessels like galleys that the Norsemen crossed your same main, Provost, to raid our land long ago," Alex pointed out. "I understand that the Islesmen's galleys are but improved Viking longships."

Davidson shrugged, obviously unconvinced.

Another shipmaster spoke. "Thae light galleys couldna hold the cargoes they might pirate frae the English ships," he pointed out. "Sae where'd be the guid o' that?"

Jamie intervened again. "Why not use *both* kind of ships,

then? In partnership. Your heavy but slow trading-vessels to act as base, a floating haven, well out to sea, and the galley to make the attacks. Like cavalry and foot, in a host. Might it not serve?"

They all considered that for a few moments. Alex was smiling beatifically. Gradually the others nodded, scratched heads, or grinned.

"It is just possible, sir," the Provost admitted. "Forby, the ship, the proper ship, would be at risk all the time — from king's ships, whilst it lay off."

"Possible, man — it is more than possible," Alex cried. "It is the answer. Trust Sir Jamie! Cavalry and foot — to be sure!"

"It is only a notion," Jamie pointed out, embarrassed a little. "As to this of the large ship being at risk as it lay off, it could do with a light cavalry screen, like any infantry host. Another galley, always with it, for protection. If we could find one galley, we could find two."

"Excellent!"

"You would require crews," Forbes said, "for the galleys, trained oarsmen. Aye, and men used to fighting from such devilish craft. You would need Islesmen, many Islesmen. And the Islesmen scarce love you, my lord! Or any here."

"Not only Islesmen have galleys," Alex contended. "Every Highland chief in the West has his birlinns, which are but smaller galleys."

"It is not the Islesmen who are our enemies, my lord, but their chief, Donald of the Isles, and his brother Alastair Carrach. And not all Islemen owe Donald MacDonald allegiance," Jamie pointed out. "Some hate and resist him, I have heard, notably the MacLeods. The Campbells also, to be sure — although they could be kittle cattle to herd with! Others. The Mackenzies are ever at war with the MacDonalds. And all their palms itch for good siller."

"Sir James is right," Alex exclaimed. "We will get our galleys, I swear, since I think that I may find a little siller — and the men to sail and fight in them."

"My lord, the English king's ships — aye, and some of their privateers forby — carry these new bombards, cannon, using gunpowder. They can throw a great ball or bolt far. Much further than any siege ballista or catapult. To smash a vessel's timbers, and men," Davidson reminded. "I have seen it. To such, a galley would be no more than an egg-shell."

"But a lively egg, friend! An egg that would not stand still to

249

be smashed! I have heard that these cannon are ill things to serve and aim, even on land. On a tossing ship, to hit a speeding galley might tax such not a little. Nevertheless, we must seek to gain a cannon or two for ourselves — although it may not be easy. Perchance two can play at that game."

"It will all take time, my lord. When do we start?" Forbes asked.

"We start our preparations forthwith. We cannot sail, with hope of success, until the winter's storms are over. So we have until the spring. But much work to be done before then, in finding, equipping and victualling the vessels, mustering and training the crews, planning our warfare!" Alex raised his wine goblet. "Here's to the spring of Our Lord's year fourteen hundred and seven, my friends! Are we all agreed?"

However doubtful some of those present, none failed to drink to that. It was not every day that an earl of Scotland offered Aberdeen burgesses such a toast.

Outside, on their way to the stables behind the inn, Alex threw an arm around his friend's shoulders.

"What a man you are, Jamie Douglas!" he said, shaking his fair head. "You are a black-frowning, thrawn, suspicious devil! Yet you have the wits of us all, and the keen and far-seeing eye. You are a joy to me, lad — and the finest friend a man ever had!"

The other scowled. "For an earl, and a Stewart one forby, you talk great havers!" he accused.

"Perhaps. But you, now, for so chary an adventurer, talk all others into that adventure! By the sheer worth of your proposals."

"I but spoke of simple facts."

"Quite. Facts, however which others had not thought of. But now we must turn your simple facts into a plan of action, Jamie. I shall come back to Lochindorb with you, for we have much to discuss and settle. Before we head for the West and your MacLeods."

"We . . . ?"

"To be sure. You do not think that you are not in this matter up to the hilt, my Douglas friend? If you did not want to go travelling again, you should have held your tongue between your teeth back there! Dunvegan, is it not, in the Isle of Skye, where MacLeod roosts . . . ?"

XVI

THE GREAT VENTURE was set to commence on St. Serf's Day, 20th April, Serf or Servanus being a notable Celtic saint much experienced in voyaging, and his day an auspicious one for sea-going. Despite sundry inevitable hitches and delays, all was ready, or as ready as it would ever be, a couple of days before, and Aberdeen in no small excitement. Some seventy of its seafaring men were involved, to crew the substantial carrack *Greysteel*, of three hundred and eighty tons, captained by Provost Davidson himself, who had agreed to relinquish both his burghal and inn-keeping duties for a while, having debts to pay in southern seas. His prominent adherence had been of the greatest value to the entire enterprise, of course, much facilitating the support of others, the enlistment of a first-rate and experienced crew and the provision of the best equipment. Other shipmen and merchants had rallied round, and the result was this fine sea-going vessel, Aberdeen-built and formerly chartered by the Abbey of Deer for trading with the Baltic ports and Muscovy. The MacLeod galleys had been obtained also, without too much difficulty but at great cost, with the necessary large complement of rowers and fighting men to the number of over three hundred, no less; but it was considered inadvisable to let loose this host of wild Gaelic-speaking warriors on the decent burgh of Aberdeen, in the interests of continuing goodwill, so that the galleys — which, being shallow-draught vessels, did not require deep-water quays and anchorages — were meantime waiting in the shelter of Nigg Bay, a mile or two to the south, having arrived from the West nearly a week early, to the embarrassment of all.

Alex had held a farewell banquet the night before, in the Town House, graced by his Countess, at which were present most of the city's notables as well as officers of the *Greysteel* and the various higher-born adventurers whom Alex had persuaded to take part. It had been a noisy affair, and Jamie Douglas's head still ached. Now, at last, they had reached the final leave-taking, the Dean of Aberdeen and the Abbot of Deer had ceremonially bestowed their blessing upon ship and company, and all was ready for casting off.

Mary Stewart was clutching her husband's hand tightly. "Do not think that *I* am calling down blessings on this stupid venture!" she told him — as though it was news. "I have let you go on all too many ploys, without protest. But this is nonsense, quite unnecessary, the pair of you behaving like bairns. I mislike the sea, have never trusted it. You are knights and lairds — not pirates. You will either hang or be drowned, and I shall never see you again!"

"Yes, my dear."

"You will take great care, Jamie? Remember that you are not on a horse, this time. Do not go jumping from one boat to another. You all but fell in, at the quayside here — so what you will do on the sea I do not know."

"Yes, my dear."

"Do not stand there saying 'yes, my dear'!"

"No, my dear."

"You should never have allowed yourself to be talked into this. You said yourself that you doubted the wisdom of it. Because Alex is eager to get away from his wife, that is no reason for you to do so!"

"Hush, lass . . ."

"Why should I hush? Is anybody else hushing? I am fond of Alex. But he is being foolish. He should never have married that woman. But if he must put distance between him and Isobel of Mar, there is no need to go to sea to do it, or to go pirating against the English. Are his Highlands not sufficiently wide for him? *She* would not chase after him, I warrant!" And Mary nodded her comely head towards the Countess.

That woman stood laughing in the midst of the group of young lairds enlisted for the venture, in mid-deck — John Menzies of Pitfodels, Alexander Irvine of Drum, Alexander Keith of Grandholme, Alexander Straiton of Lauriston and Patrick Leslie Younger of Balquhain, all Mar vassals. She certainly did not look upset at the imminent departure of her lord. Alex himself, with the younger Forbes of that Ilk, was busying himself with superintending the charging of the two small cannon which he had managed to hire at great expense, and which were presently to fire a blank-shot parting salute.

"Like a bairn with his toys!" Mary insisted.

"Let him be," Jamie said. "He has worked long and hard on this project. It means much to him. And he is our good friend."

She was silent.

Isobel Douglas's throaty but uninhibited laughter prevailed.

At last the cannoneers declared themselves satisfied, and Alex called out that all was ready, and that those who lingered longer must needs sail with them. From the poop Robert Davidson shouted for warps to be readied for casting off.

Mary flung herself into her husband's arms. "Oh, Jamie! Jamie!" she cried.

"Hout, lass — this is not like you," he said, stroking her hair. "What ails you?"

"It is the sea. You have never gone sea-fighting before. I hate and fear the sea."

"You did not hate or fear it one time, at Aberdour, I mind!"

"That was different, different altogether. Promise me that you will take heed for yourself, the greatest heed . . ."

"I will, yes — for I am a careful man. Anyone will tell you so."

She shook him in exasperation, but allowed herself to be led to the gangway and quayside.

There Alex was ushering his Countess ashore likewise, assisted by her bevy of admirers. Their embrace was fairly brief, formal.

"I require a shipload of the best that England can provide," Isobel proclaimed, to all and sundry. "Do not come back until you have it, I charge you!"

Mary muttered uncharitable comments towards her sister-in-neglect, kissed Jamie hurriedly, and broke away.

Alex sensibly cut things short, by waving to his trumpeter to sound. Amidst cheers the great banner of Mar was run up to the mainmast-head, that of Stewart to the mizzen, and the saltire flag of Scotland to the foremast, whilst, at Davidson's commands sails were unfurled and ropes cast off.

With the stern warps still holding and the *Greysteel*'s high bows gradually beginning to swing out from the quay, Alex signed to the cannoneers up on the forecastle. These had their fuses ready and smouldering. Blowing them lustily into a red glow, the chief man on each piece applied his to the touch-hole at the base of the wide-mouthed, short-barrelled clumsy horn-like device made of wrought-iron bars bound together by steel hoops. The port-side piece flashed immediately and mightily, a vivid red flare singeing the cannoneer's beard and hair and sending him and his assistants staggering back — but unfortunately making no desired report. Its partner did, a moment or two later, bang loudly however, setting all the gulls screaming and sending a peculiar ball of smoke rolling out over the harbour waters, to the mixed admiration and alarm of the onlookers. The plan had been to have a small succession of salvoes; but, concerned for the state of the crew of the first gun, Alex signed for no more, and hurried forward to look to and condole with his humiliated artillerymen. Most there shook their heads over this new-fangled invention, which clearly never could be relied upon, as the carrack's stern warps were cast, her sails began to fill and she moved out into the brief estuary of the Dee. Gradually the cheers from the shore died away.

Alex Stewart's private war had started.

Rounding Girdle Ness beyond the estuary, they came to Nigg Bay. Warned by the cannon-shot, their two galleys had hoisted sail and were driving out to meet the carrack. They were extra-ordinarily different-looking craft from *Greysteel*, long, slender, graceful in a menacing fashion, low in the water, each with a single great square sail painted with the black bull's head crest of the Siol Tormod, the senior line of the Clan MacLeod. They were not of equal size, one a hundred and sixty feet long, with thirty-six great oars in two banks, the other a hundred and twenty feet, with twenty-four oars, but both no more than twenty feet wide. Each had a fierce, upthrusting, high prow, to finish in an outstretched eagle's head, this sharp prow sheathed in steel to form a savage cutting-edged ram. In the stern was a raised platform, on which stood the commander, pilot, helms-man, boatswain and other leaders, and beneath which were scanty sleeping quarters. The bows also had a smaller platform, with a little storage accommodation below. The oarsmen, two to each sweep, sat their thwarts open to the sky, with a gangway down the centre of the craft between the seventy-two or forty-eight men. Beneath them the vessels were decked-in to provide a very shallow hold. Because the oar-teams were duplicated for continuous rowing, where necessary, a lot of men had to stand

and sit around in notably restricted space. Davidson's comments about galleys being unsuitable for long-range voyaging could be seen to be valid.

The two strange craft came out of the bay at a speed which had to be seen to be believed by more conventional sea-goers, amidst a cloud of spray from the flashing oars, which drove in long, rhythmic strokes in time to a curious chanting, throaty, angry-sounding, unending, which rose and fell, every other beat punctuated by something between a gasp and a growl, as the rowers expelled breath and took the strain, with on the poops, oarmasters or boatswains beating the time. Out they swept, to drive fore and aft round the carrack — and nothing could more plainly demonstrate that they moved at more than twice the speed of the bigger ship. Out to sea they sped, presently to curve back, leaving long white washes, to take up position astern of *Greysteel*. Now they rested most of their oars. Clearly they were going to find keeping that position as tedious as it was difficult.

"Wolfhounds you named them, that time, Jamie," Alex commented. "Myself, I would say wolves, and be done with it! How think you we shall manage these expensive allies we have acquired?"

"I would not think that we *could* manage them, at all. Work with them we must, and may learn much, gain much."

"I would not like to be in one of those in a storm," Davidson said.

"Yet storms are frequent in their own Hebridean seas," Alex answered. "They must be seaworthy. I think that we should pay our Islesmen friends a visit. It would be civil. How do we go about it?"

"I can heave to and lower a wherry, my lord . . ."

"Why trouble?" Jamie asked. "These galleys can do all that your wherries can do. Hail them alongside. That is their custom, is it not, when they board vessels?"

Waving and shouting brought the galleys up without any difficulty, one on either side of the carrack — and without the latter even having to shorten sail — the nearside oarsmen raising their long sweeps vertical, the offside ones sculling expertly to hold their craft in position, upper bank working against lower. Grinning half-naked Islesmen were about to toss up grappling-hooks on chains, but Davidson stopped them with oaths, concerned for his decking, and ordinary ropes were thrown down to them instead, then rope-ladders. The smell of sweating men came up on each side, chokingly.

Alex told Sir Alexander Forbes, who was a Gaelic-speaker, with one or two others to go down into the smaller galley, whilst he and Jamie climbed carefully down the swaying ladder to the larger. Both then cast off from the carrack.

On the galley's crowded tiller-platform they were greeted by a cheerful red-headed young man in faded tartans and long pie-bald ponyskin sleeveless waistcoat, with sword-belt — as indeed were most of those present, save the actual rowers, who were stripped to the waist above short kilts. Only the fact that the sword-belt was jewel-studded distinguished this individual from the others. He was John MacLeod Younger of Dunvegan, known as Ian Borb, elder son of the fifth chief of the name, William Achlerich. *Borb* meant fierce or furious, and *Achlerich* meant the cleric; but this young man gave no special impression of ferocity, and his father, whom Alex and Jamie had negotiated with the previous November, had looked anything but clerical.

"Greetings, sir," Alex said heartily. "Sir James Douglas you know? We rejoice to have you join our venture. And we much admire your two fine craft, and how well you handle them. An excellent augury. The speed at which you came out to join us impressed us all."

"Speed is it, whatever? That was no speed, friend." There was never any my-lording amongst the Islesmen, who accorded no-one that title save — and the MacLeods only grudgingly — the Lord of the Isles himself. "We shall show you speed, if you would see it." Without waiting for agreement he slapped Alex on the back, and turned to the oarmaster, who as well as beating time and leading the chanting, carried a bull's horn slung at his side. A wailing blast on this drew the attention of the other galley — which seemingly was called the *Clavan* or Hawk (this one being the *Iolair* or Eagle), and was commanded by a natural brother, one Ruari Ban, or the Fair. Ian Borb made some energetic signals with a clenched fist, which seemed to be understood, for they were answered by a great shout from the *Clavan*, and a distinctly derisive horn ululation, clearly a challenge.

There followed a pause, as flagons of whisky were passed from rower to rower, men spat on their hands, and Ian Borb, the pilot and the boatswain held a brief conference. In these galleys the overall commander was not the shipmaster, or pilot, but the leader of the fighting men, usually of chieftainly status. Then the horn was blown again, loud and long, to be answered from across the waves, and what evidently was to be a race was on.

The oarmaster, a brawny, almost bald-headed character of middle age, with a great paunch but no hint of flabbiness, raised his mighty voice to a bellow, at the same time lifting a short broadsword high above his head. Every rower's eye on him, tensed, ready, his shout maintained. Then abruptly ending his cry on a single explosive word, he brought down the sword on to a large bronze gong-like object, set on legs like a table and barbarically carved. The booming clangour coincided with the deep first powerful thrust of every oar, and all on board, from commander downwards, took up the outlandish but exciting, pulsing chant. At each stroke the sword clanged down, and gradually the intervals between lessened and lessened, the rowers soon dispensing with their contribution to the singing, save for the regular punctuation of coughing grunt which was synchronised breath and effort. The sweeps creaked in their sockets, the blades splashed and feathered in unison, the bow-waves creamed back hissing, and the wind whistled in the rigging.

Jamie Douglas, sober man, had seldom experienced such sudden exhilaration. The sense of power, united effort and determination, of tension, the clanging of the gong, the vehement singing and ever-increasing speed, was heady in the extreme. Even the almost overpowering smell of sweating humanity wafted back on their own wind added its own measure to the excitement.

The oar-strokes had gradually changed character, the blades dipping less deeply and at a different angle, with much shorter pulls in the water, to enable them to quicken tempo dramatically, seeming almost to skim the waves. So dense was the curtain of spray around them now that they could only intermittently see the other galley a quarter-mile to starboard. The visitors had neither of them realised that man could move so fast save on horseback.

Ian Borb, yelling encouragement, kept gazing to the right and frequently shaking a fist towards his half-brother's vessel. They seemed to his passengers to be running neck-and-neck.

"How can they keep up with us?" Alex shouted. "They have fewer oars, and men."

"Och, in a light sea . . . such as this . . . *Clavan* has some advantage," the other panted. "Less weight. Sits higher in the water. Shorter oars . . . ten strokes to our eight. Heavy weather, *Iolair* gains. But . . . we will beat them, by God!"

It seemed impossible that the rowers could maintain their herculean efforts, purple in the face, arm-muscles bulging, sweat streaming, mouths wide. Yet that slamming sword and the relentless chant went on and on, so that it became, for the visitors at least, almost a physical pain to watch, their own tensed muscles aching in sympathy.

"This . . . this is faster than a horse could gallop!" Alex exclaimed. "They will burst their hearts!"

Jamie nodded, but pointed over to the right. "We are drawing ahead, I think."

"Praise God!" He peered through the spray. "Yes, we are." Turning, he grasped Ian Borb's shoulder. "We are winning, man. It is enough. Call a halt, of a mercy! They will kill themselves!"

The other laughed, shaking his red head, and shouted mixed abuse and encouragement to his men the louder.

At last, when it was amply clear to all that the *Clavan* was indeed being left behind, Ian Borb threw up his hand, and signed to the boatswain who, reluctantly it seemed, blew on his horn a prolonged blast. As though it had slain them all, the rowers collapsed forward over their oars in heaps, the singers changed to cheering — such as could summon the breath — and the poop party beat each other about the back and beamed on their guests with simple joy. An answering horn-call from across the water signified acceptance of victory and defeat.

In the sudden relaxation and comparative quiet, Alex actually mopped his brow, although he had done nothing more exhausting than hold his breath.

"I would not have believed it," he said. "It is beyond all. Such speed. Every man, on both ships, shall be rewarded, I promise. If they live! Jamie — this, in a sea-fight, could give us untold advantage."

"Aye — if these craft can twist and turn at a like pace."

"Can you, man — twist and turn?" That to Ian Borb.

The other shrugged, and jerked a word or two to the bald boatswain. That man bellowed for a change of oar-crews. Now all the singers began discarding shirts, jerkins and plaids, and went to replace the panting heroes on the thwarts, the whisky flagons going round once more.

While this was going on, Jamie pointed away astern, where *Greysteel*'s sails were just to be seen.

"We came further than I had known, as well as faster. How many miles have we outdistanced our ship?"

"Lord knows! Jamie — we shall have to consider all this with much care. In planning our warfare and sallies. To use it all to greatest advantage . . ."

The new rowers in place and anxious to show their prowess, *Iolair* swung hard round, to make for *Clavan*. Nearing her, Ian Borb hailed his half-brother, in mocking condolence over the evident age and decrepitude of his crew and his misfortune to command such a lumbering wash-tub, before declaring that they were now going to show these Lowland Sassenachs a few tricks, chasing their own tails and the like.

Thereafter, the great sails run down, followed a highly alarming interlude, as breathtaking as the other had been breathless, with the two galleys weaving and circling, describing figures-of-eight, turning at speed, reversing stern-first, cavorting on the waves like frisky colts, even going through the motions of ramming each other with those cruel steel-shod prows, and only pulling aside at the very last moment, with oars swiftly raised high and dripping, to avoid a splintering crash. Time and again it seemed that nothing could save them from disaster, but always most skilful steering and oarsmanship prevailed. Time and again, likewise, Alex cried out that it was enough, that he was more than satisfied; but there was no stopping their gleeful allies. One bank of oars countering another, starboard oars countering port, helm aiding, tempering or reversing, the dangerous, crazy sport continued. To his employer's protests, Ian Borb declared that this was nothing compared with dodging strewn reefs and skerries of the West in a Hebridean storm. From ever having to experience such, then, his passengers prayed that they might be delivered.

At length, with *Greysteel* drawing near, the demonstration was called off. But before returning the visitors to their own ship, Ian Borb had one more piece of galley-craft to display. The spare crew was set to unlashing and raising tall poles which lay along the low bulwarks, and which proved to be spare light masts, to be set into sockets in the stern and fore platforms. Extra small square sails were then hoisted, along with the mainsail, to give additional power when there was a suitable following wind. It was explained that this was only really useful in special conditions, since it tended to alter the trim and steerage of the craft and could confuse the rowers.

Alex invited Ian Borb and Ruari Ban aboard the carrack for a meal, loud in his praise. But as they surmounted the rope-ladder, he murmured to Jamie.

"We are going to have problems with these people, I fear. Do you see them obeying my commands?"

His friend shrugged. "Possibly not. Unless you can make them love you. But — you are good at that, Alex. Otherwise, we could be out-pirated, I think!"

"My own thought, whatever. We shall have to consider this, too. But, by the Mass, they are bonny seamen!"

"Yes. When we start fighting, I would wish to be in that galley."

"Aye, man — so would I . . ."

*   *   *

Greysteel led a course almost due south-east. They wanted to get, and remain, well out of sight of land. Also Alex did not wish to become involved with North of England shipping; his quarrel was specifically with King Henry, the Earl of Kent and the East Anglian privateers. So it was the open sea for them meantime. But leading the way did not necessarily mean that the carrack was followed as though by obedient dogs at heel. The galleys sometimes were there, one or both, sometimes were not, ranging about near and far, frequently not even in sight. Clearly it was difficult for them to adjust their speed to the slower vessel; but more vitally it was a matter of the mind — these Islesmen not being of the sort patiently to follow anyone, independent to a degree.

The second day out, the weather broke, with rain squalls, gusting winds and angry seas. Conditions in the galleys must have been highly unpleasant, and it was the turn of the Aberdeen crewmen in *Greysteel* to laugh and look superior. But despite their slender, rakish appearance, the smaller craft proved themselves to be surprisingly good sea-boats, however exposed their companies to the elements, riding the seas like ducks rather than ploughing through them as did the carrack. Low-set as they were, frequently they were out of sight in the wave-troughs, to reappear at odd and even alarming angles. Most of the oars were shipped in these conditions, and the remainder used more for steerage and balance than for propulsion. In consequence, the Islesmen tended to fall far behind now, or else swing off on different courses altogether in their running battle with the seas. There was the minimum of contact with *Greysteel*.

For two days and nights the half-gale continued, from the south-west, the carrack stolidly beating its way south-eastwards through the cross-seas. Inevitably they were blown quite a lot further east than intended, when at length wind and seas moderated and fair visibility returned. Robert Davidson reckoned that they might be as much as one hundred miles off the North Yorkshire coast. Many of his passengers were, however, too seasick to care greatly.

Neither Jamie nor Alex were troubled that way, thankfully, and their concern was for the galleys, nowhere to be seen on the empty, tossing horizon. Some distinctly anxious hours passed, with Alex suggesting that they should put about and go back to look for their missing associates, and Davidson declaring that this would be a pointless exercise, with no least indication as to where to search in hundreds of square miles. However, just before midday the fourth day out, a look-out on *Greysteel* reported the galleys fine to starboard, due westwards perhaps eight miles off and coming up fast. It was not long before this was evident to all; and soon the Islesmen were milling around the carrack in fine style, evidently not only none the worse for their battering but in lively, indeed challenging mood, shouting across to the effect that did the Sassenachs know not that they were nowhere near where they ought to be, leagues out of their course? They had been hunting the seas for them.

Davidson's comments were unrepeatable; but Alex was much relieved.

This content did not last long, nevertheless — a bare couple of hours, in fact. Then, soon after the Aberdeen look-out spotted a single sail hull-down far to the north-west, suddenly, without permission or warning, their MacLeod friends swung around both galleys and went streaking off in that direction, oars flashing. No amount of shouting or signalling from *Greysteel* had the least effect on them, and after a while both they and the hull-down ship disappeared over the horizon.

Again there was debate as to whether to turn and go after them; and again Davidson pointed out that it would be useless, since they could nowise catch up. Alex's concern that North of England vessels should not be interfered with made him angry.

"They are like ill-trained hounds!" he declared. "Chasing any game that moves."

"Wolves, you decided, not hounds," Jamie reminded. "And wolves hunt at will, not at command."

Davidson muttered darkly.

It was early evening before the truants returned. They came in high spirits, obviously, dashing up with horns trumpeting and much waving. Alex beckoned for *Iolair* to come close alongside.

"MacLeod!" he shouted down. "That was . . . unfortunate. A mistake. A mistake, I say . . ."

"No mistake, friend. And excellently fortunate!" Ian Borb waved towards a stack of casks and barrels on his poop. "Have you a taste for French wines? Brandies? Lower a net and you shall have your share. And, look you — catch this! A gift, just." And he tossed up a handsome silver goblet which Jamie managed to grasp. "Would you wish for a jewelled sword? A toy, but pretty . . ."

"I thank you. But . . . it is not a matter of booty, man. I told you, my quarrel is with the English king and the Southerners. Not these of the North. And if we rouse the North against us, behind us, it could be the worse for us later."

"I do not hear you, friend."

Alex sighed, and raised his voice to a shout. "Do not attack in these northern waters. Do not attack, I say. Save on my orders."

The MacLeod did not comment on that, other than by a wave of his hand and a wide grin.

"You will never hold these devils!" Sir Alexander Forbes said. "They are but sea caterans."

"Perhaps. But we may be glad of them, nevertheless, before we are done."

The Earl's orders were not put to the test thereafter, for they sighted no more sails that day or the next. They were, of course, deliberately keeping well away from land, and most shipping tended to keep within sight of the coastline. They had reached a point which Davidson reckoned to be about seventy miles east of the Thames estuary by the following evening. At last they were ready for action.

At first light, next morning, after cruising quietly westwards all night, Alex and his lairds transferred themselves to the two galleys. Land was still not in sight, but the low-lying shores of Essex and Kent could not be more than twenty-five miles off.

Greysteel was to beat up and down at this range, waiting, whilst the galleys went in search of prey.

Jamie found a holiday atmosphere prevailing on *Iolair*, the whisky flagons already circulating. He judged that most of the scanty storage space beneath the rowers' deck must be loaded with barrels of the fiery spirit. Ian Borb welcomed Alex and himself like old friends unseen for long, and they set off westwards without delay.

They spied their first sail in only a short time; but the general opinion was that it was only a small, low-set Netherlands smack, little more than a heavy sailing-barge, of the sort used for carrying hides, grain and suchlike bulky cargo across the narrow seas, not worth attacking. Then, with land beginning to show as a dark line ahead, they saw, somewhat to the north, a group of half-a-dozen dark sails, fairly close together. These also were small, however, and almost certainly a fishing-fleet from one of the outer Thames havens. The galleys swung away south-westwards.

It was mid-forenoon, and men becoming restive, before they saw their first tall ship, heading north-by-west as though for the Thames. Even if Alex had decided not to intercept, it is doubtful if he could have restrained the Islesmen. As though slipped from the leash, the galleys darted forward on a converging course. Each lowered its sail, now, for better manoeuvrability.

The vessel proved to be a large three-masted bark, flying the red cross on white of England. The galleys made a wide circuit of it at speed, and the *Iolair* drew in close, the *Clavan* lying off at the far side.

"What ship is that?" Alex cried. The bark's rail, high above, was lined with suspicious faces.

"I am the *Clara*, of London. Master, Peter Holden. But — what is that to you?" a hoarse voice answered.

"Sufficient. I am the Earl of Mar, out of Scotland. On my King's business. Heave-to — I am coming aboard."

"That you are not! I heave-to only at King Henry's orders. Be off, Scotchman, or it will be the worse for you."

"Indeed, sir? How could that be?"

"I will sink your oar-boat, sirrah — earl or no earl! I have cannon aboard."

"Unfriendly, Master Holden. Prepare to be boarded."

"Two cannon," Jamie reported. "Not large. One on the poop, the other at the bows."

"Easy, just," Ian Borb commented. "We go in and keep below them." He raised his voice, to bark orders at his crew.

Thereafter everything happened at great speed. Oars shipped on the near side, *Iolair* was swung in directly under the bark's port side amidships, timbers actually bumping. There she was quite safe from the cannon at least, which could by no means be depressed sufficiently to shoot down at them. Men, stripped to the waist, were already climbing up the rigging of the galley's central mast, to loosen booms which swung down and outwards, over the *Clara*'s deck. The booms were suspended from a circular platform, something between a fighting-top and a crow's-nest, two-thirds of the way up the mast. On to this spearmen clambered, to hurl down javelins upon the Englishmen, to provide cover whilst their colleagues swarmed out along the booms, to drop on to the bark. At the same time grappling-irons on chains were being flung up, to hook on to the other's deck, binding the ships together. Before these could be detached and tossed down again, more men were streaming up the chains, scaling the bark's side like monkeys, swords being thrown up for them. In almost less time than it takes to tell, a score and more of the Islesmen were aboard, steel in hand.

Trained fighting-crews on king's ships might have managed a more effective defence and created casualties amongst the boarders; but these were ordinary merchant seamen, and such tactics quite beyond their experience. Ian Borb himself was one of the first up the chains and, sword in hand, took vigorous charge. The English shipmaster and his mates did their best, but were wholly outclassed by their experienced attackers, and very quickly isolated on the high aftercastle, without having been able to strike a blow.

It was at this stage that wild shouts and the sound of bagpipes from the other, starboard side of the *Clara*, heralded the arrival of the *Clavan*'s contingent of boarders. Ruari Ban appearing up on the aftercastle itself. That was more than sufficient for the skipper. Throwing down his sword, which he had held in less than accustomed fashion, he folded his arms and so stood, waiting and chewing his lip. His people were thankful to follow his lead. By the time that Alex and Jamie had clambered up on to the deck of the bark, all was over, in only a few hectic minutes.

"Skilful work, MacLeod," Alex commended. "I think that you are scarcely new to this practice! I would not like to sail your Western Sea lacking your safe-conduct!"

"Yours for the asking, friend. Any time, whatever. What shall we do with these?" Ian Borb gestured around. "Cut their throats?"

"Not so. They have yielded decently. Our quarrel is with their masters. They have two wherries, I see. Lower them, and they can row to land. It is within sight. Master Holden — my sympathies. But your king should not have pirated mine, and held him prisoner. If you have opportunity, tell him so. Tell your betters that they will continue to lose ships until they release King James. You have it?"

Wordless, the unfortunate shipmaster nodded.

"Very well. Get your men into the wherries and be off. You should make land in but a few hours. You will take nothing with you but your lives."

As the Englishmen hastily lowered their boats, the Islesmen were already scouring the ship for what they could find. The cargo proved to consist of woven cloth and linens, bale upon bale; also carved ironwork, clearly for church furniture, glassware packed in straw, great cheeses and innumerable bundles of furs. The MacLeods found this exceedingly disappointing, although the cheese they appeared to appreciate and the furs they were prepared to appropriate. The master's and crew's belongings did not add up to much, either — so that, to the Islesmen at least the *Clara* was poor reward for their expertise.

"Sink her, whatever," Ruari Ban recommended.

"No, burn her," his half-brother said. "Near land, as here, a burning ship will bring others to investigate. Smoke will be seen far off. Further pickings, see you. It seldom fails, I tell you."

"Perhaps not," Alex objected. "But this is a fine ship, in excellent order. Our Aberdeen friends have lost many such to English pirates and privateers. It would be folly and a wicked waste to destroy her. We shall send her back to join *Greysteel*. These two more cannon I covet."

There was some demur, but at this juncture shouting from above sent the two young MacLeod chieftains hurrying up to the deck.

"This cargo could sell for much in Aberdeen," Alex said. "And Holy Church would be glad of much of these plenishings. I have found it ever advisable to keep the churchmen my friends!"

Jamie nodded. "These Islesmen have different values. Let them have the furs and cheese, and what else they want, if they will sail us back to *Greysteel*. And praise them, Alex — much praise. They like it. They are like bairns . . ."

When they returned to the deck, it was to find the situation changed. Another sail had hove in sight to the west, and Ruari Ban MacLeod, envious of his brother's success, had hurried back to his *Clavan* and gone off alone to intercept. He was already a mile away.

In the circumstances Ian Borb accepted that it would be unwise to set the *Clara* alight meantime. He agreed to provide a small crew, under his navigator, to sail her back to *Greysteel*. As he conceded this, his eyes were on his brother's receding galley. Clearly he was anxious to be after him.

Hastily, then, a dozen men under the *Iolair*'s pilot were detached to man the captured bark as best they could; and MacLeod and the rest swarmed down to their galley and cast off, Alex and Jamie, with the other lairds, electing to stay on *Clara* meantime.

The prize-crew were not used to handling full-rigged ships, of course; but they were good seamen, and the moderate breeze and sea enabled them to control the vessel sufficiently to steer a fair course, if slowly. Indeed, after the galleys' speed, it seemed painfully slow.

So the lairdly party had opportunity to watch what was happening to the west. Far beyond the two small wherries, now looking as tiny as water-beetles as they pulled clumsily for the land, both galleys had come up with what seemed from this distance to be much like a lighter version of *Clara*. They were too far off to see details, but all three vessels were massed as one, and if not halted were moving very slowly. The reports of two cannon-shots came booming across the water, but no effects therefrom were evident. Presently, however, with the scene of action almost hull-down, a dark cloud of smoke began to mount above the ships. The Islesmen, it seemed, were trying out their burning-decoy theory.

"It seems to me that there is little need for us in this venture!" Jamie observed, grimly. "We could sail back to Aberdeen and leave all to the MacLeods!"

"Somehow we must bring them under control," Alex agreed. "But how? Though, see you, they are serving our cause excellently well. So long as they do not make our name infamous, by savagery."

"Are there degrees of piracy, my lord?" Forbes asked.

"We are privateering, not pirating. Under letters of mark. There should be a difference."

"Convincing the MacLeods of that will be difficult, I think."

It took them some time to find *Greysteel*. Davidson and the other Aberdonians were delighted with the *Clara* and her cargo, however bored with beating up and down the empty seas in idle waiting. They felt even more useless than did the lairds.

They waited, that evening, for the Islesmen to turn up, lookouts high on the masts of both ships. But when darkness fell there was still no sign of the galleys.

That night Alex held a council, in the low-ceilinged main cabin of *Greysteel*, aware that morale demanded it, allowing all, leading shipmen and gentry, to say their say. Jamie felt distinctly guilty. It had been at his suggestion that the galleys had been hired, and although their effectiveness had been amply proven, it was as evident that mixing Islesmen in an East Country expedition was of doubtful wisdom. The men's respective attitudes and characters were incompatible, their outlook and code quite different. But such recognition was late in the day. They were here now and must make the best of it — although there was one train of opinion to the effect that they would not see the galleys again anyway, and could forget the problem; the MacLeods, having flexed their muscles and been brought to the hunting-grounds, would now go their own way. Both Jamie and Alex contested this view, claiming that the Islesmen had their own loyalty and would respect the bargain made with their chief back in Skye.

Meantime an effective strategy had to be worked out, if they were not going to become mere onlookers at their impulsive allies' activities. It was decided that *Greysteel* should provide a prize crew for *Clara*, not just to sail her but to fight her, cannoneers on both ships and Sir Alexander Forbes in command. They would go hunting as a pair, irrespective of what the galleys might do.

Next morning there was still no sign of the Islesmen, although they gave them some hours of daylight to find this waiting area, At length, disappointed, Alex gave the order to abandon their beating-up-and-down stance. *Greysteel* leading, they headed off under full-sail south-westwards.

Towards midday they spotted two sails at once, although on different sectors of the horizon — for now, of course, they were coming into the main trade routes between the Low Country and French ports on the one hand and London and the English east coast havens on the other. Deciding to intercept the nearer and larger of these vessels, they altered course, preparing for action, cannon charged, fuses burning, boarders ready.

As they drew near, however, they perceived that the ship, a fine carrack somewhat larger than *Greysteel*, was flying a banner bearing the Lilies of France. At first, balked, Alex was for making a polite signal and then veering off to look for something they could legitimately attack. Then he changed his mind and asked Davidson to move in close, *Clara* to stand off.

Greysteel stood about, to gain a parallel course with the Frenchman on her windward side, and then drew in to within hailing distance — her people staring into the open mouths of French cannon at the ready. Alex, on the aftercastle, took off his velvet bonnet and waved it.

"A good day to you, messieurs!" he called, in fair French. "I am the Count of Mar, in Scotland. Greetings from one ally to another. May I ask whither you are bound?"

"Your reasons for asking, monsieur? And your right?" came back thinly.

"On the King of Scots' business, friend. I hold letters of mark against English shipping. You understand? Letters of mark?"

"Privateer? You are privateer, Monsieur le Comte?"

"Yes. But only against the English, who have captured our King James, on his way to your country, on *your* King's invitation. You are bound for an English port?"

"For London, yes. On our lawful business. *St. Barthemely* of Etaples. What do you wish of us? You have no right to trouble us . . ."

"No, monsieur. I desire only the courtesy of your assistance, as ally of Scotland. When you reach London, will you be so good as to inform the English officers that the Earl of Mar is happy to permit *your* passage, with his compliments. But English shipping will continue to be assailed until such time as King James is released. To tell their King. You understand, monsieur?"

"Yes. If it is your wish, I shall tell them. Is that all?"

"Why, yes. I am indebted to you. We wish you well. Pray, proceed." Alex flourished his bonnet again, and turned to wave Davidson on.

"What will that serve, my lord?" young Irvine of Drum wondered.

"It will reach King Henry's ears the more surely, and swiftly. And foreign shippers' likewise. The English will mislike this, on their very doorstep, almost more, I think, than losing a ship or two."

The second sail which they had spotted earlier was now too far off to be worth following up, so they continued on their prowling progress in a south-westerly direction. They saw no more shipping for a considerable time, to the frustration of all. When a sail at length did appear, it proved to be only a small coasting lugger scarcely worth the chasing. Nevertheless, with his colleagues eager for some action, however modest, Alex acceded.

They had no difficulty in running the craft down, which, when challenged by two larger vessels, promptly and discreetly hove-to, with the minimum of fuss, and did not obstruct a boarding party. She proved to be the *Gillyflower*, of Deal, in Kent, with a smelly cargo of untanned hides. Despite the disgust of the Aberdonians, Alex was interested in this, questioning the unhappy master closely. Had he any dealings with Edmund, Earl of Kent? Was Deal connected with the Earl's domains? Had he any hand or interest in Kent trade? The shipman said that he had never seen the Earl, but that he was of course overlord of all the region, as was his father before him, every village, farm and field owning him as superior. Where had these hides in the cargo come from then, he was asked? From Kent's farms and fields? The other agreed that this would be so, although they were really the Earl's *vassals'* property. They were being sent to Rye for tanning. Satisfied, Alex ordered the lugger's crew into their small boat, to row for the shore, there to send word to the Earl of Kent that his vassals' hides were at the bottom of the sea. Then he allowed the *Clara*'s cannoneers to try out their armament by sinking the lugger. This was achieved after much misfire, noise, smoke and waste of powder and shot — but providing much-needed practice. It all did not represent much of an achievement and no glory, but might have its own repercussions.

It was decided that they were getting too far to the west, into the mouth of La Manche, the Channel, and they turned on a reverse course, on the look-out for their galleys. They were fortunate, just before darkness came down, to come up with a large and heavy vessel, from Greenwich bound for Danzig which, being slow and lumbering, made little attempt at flight, and hove-to obediently whilst the letters-of-mark announcement was made — but had the spirit to put up something of a fight on being boarded, which enabled the Aberdonains to regain their self-esteem somewhat and get rid of mounting frustration. The prize, the *Maid Mary*, had no cannon and was not really a very adequate adversary. But it had a rich cargo of salt, always valuable, especially in Aberdeen where fish-curing was important; casked ale, always welcome; ironware pots and cauldrons; and handsome horse-harness and saddlery. Transferring all this to *Greysteel* and *Clara* would be a lengthy process and must await daylight. The English crew were battened down below, therefore, and the three vessels lay-to for the night. They were approximately twenty miles off the North Foreland, Davidson said, although the south-westerly breeze and the current would inevitably drift them a considerable distance northwards.

Daylight revealed no sign of either land nor sail. The work of transferring the cargo went on apace, the Englishmen being forced to labour, however unwillingly. It took a long time, even so, in open sea conditions.

Sail was sighted just before midday, with the task nearly finished. Two full-rigged ships were reported by the look-outs, close together to the north-west; and presently a third, somewhat smaller but in the same vicinity. Davidson did not like the look of this, and said so. Trading vessels did not usually sail in convoy, and two of these were large ships. If they were king's ships or privateers it could be serious. There had been ample time for word of their activities to reach London.

Alex did not dispute it, and gave orders to abandon the work on *Maid Mary*, its crew to take to the boats forthwith, and gunpowder to be used to set the vessel on fire quickly. This might possibly distract the attention of the newcomers.

This could not be done in a few minutes, and before the Scots ships were able to draw away, leaving the other blazing at various points and sending a black column of smoke into the air, the three strange sail had halved their distance. It seemed clear that they were making directly for them, too.

"I fear they *are* king's ships," Davidson said. "Do we run or fight, my lord?"

"Run if we can, fight if we must!" Alex answered.

Greysteel and *Clara* headed due eastwards now, to gain searoom — and fairly quickly the approaching vessels reacted. The two larger, both bigger ships than *Greysteel*, swung on an intercepting course, whilst the third and smaller, a galiot by the look of it, proceeded on towards the burning *Maid Mary*.

"No question but they are king's ships," the Provost decided grimly. "They have come looking for us. This will be less easy than picking off unarmed traders. Eagles, not barn-door fowl!"

"To be sure. But perhaps more satisfying!" Alex rejoined cheerfully. "Can you out-sail them? Or must we come to grips?"

"We can try. But I am no' happy about yon *Clara*. Manned by a crew no' used to her."

"We cannot abandon her. And have no time to transfer her people to this ship."

Davidson shrugged, and ordered an alteration in course southwards.

So commenced a curious chase, anything but straightforward, with continual tacking, gybing, twisting and veering away, *Greysteel* making the running, concerned to keep distance between herself and the Englishmen but at the same time not to outsail *Clara*. It became evident, fairly quickly, that although the newcomers were probably able to sail faster than *Greysteel* they were less manoeuvrable and unable to lie so close to the wind; but that they outdid *Clara* on both counts. The Englishmen were frequently near enough, despite all the dodging, for their great banners of the Leopards of Plantagenet and the St. George's Cross of England, to be distinguished. Also, unfortunately, that each had at least a dozen cannon. Keeping out of range of these would have to be a major preoccupation for the Scots.

Clara, of course, was given the first taste of the medicine, one of the enemy opening up with her four port-side armament in a notably ragged salvo. Cannon were a comparatively new development in warfare at sea, their effectiveness as yet far from perfected, their standard of handling seldom high. Indeed their usefulness was probably very largely in the sphere of morale, their noise, flame and smoke being apt to have more impact than their shot — save in siege warfare and battering at castle walls. Flash-backs and misfires were frequent, and could be very dangerous for the cannoneers.

In this case one of the weapons misfired, one ball plunged into the sea only a few yards away, one went wide astern and only one fell close to the target. This amidst impressive expolsions and vast smoke. *Clara* fired back with one cannon —

presumably the other misfired — and was no more successful in scoring a hit.

"I say that we should forget these toys!" Jamie snorted. "They are for scaring bairns, just."

"Not forget," Alex returned. "When they do hit they can do much hurt. But we should not let them frighten us, I agree, cause us to feel inferior, or to change our tactics."

"What *are* our tactics, my lord? Other than seeking to keep our distance?" Davidson demanded. They were standing in a group on the poop, beside the *Greysteel*'s helmsman.

"We are hampered by *Clara*," Alex said. "But . . . we must fight, eventually. Look for our best opportunity."

"Board them, you mean?"

"What else . . . ?"

He was interrupted by a banging of cannon-fire from the Englishman nearest to themselves. Five booms there were, in an uneven succession — but well before the last Davidson had his helm hard over and they were bearing away to starboard putting them stern-on to the enemy, to minimise the target. One ball made a neat hole in one of their sails, another a mighty splash to port, as total result.

Alex shouted to the stern cannoneer to open fire. But he had had his weapon facing the enemy over the port rail, and his men had to man-handle the heavy, clumsy contraption round at right-angles. By the time he was ready to apply his glowing fuse, the ships had drawn considerably further apart and the shot fell hopelessly short.

"At least it will show that we can hit back," Alex muttered.

Jamie was watching the gunners at the reloading process, thoughtfully. It took a considerable time. The touch-hole and breach had to be cleared out with cloths, a fresh charge of powder carefully ladled in per measure, and tamped cautiously down, then a wad of tinder packed in on top, to channel the explosion and prevent a flash-back. At the same time a stone ball had to be selected, pushed down the gaping muzzle and rammed firmly home with a ramrod. It could not be done hastily, even when the cannon were cold. They got scorchingly hot after two or three shots, and then handling became slower still — and with the added danger of premature explosion.

As *Greysteel* swung again on to a different tack, and her cannon had to be moved once more to face the enemy, Jamie was calculating.

"Timing," he said to Alex. "Timing is the heart of the matter, if the English are no quicker than these. They have their cannon at the sides, port and starboard. Where we, with only two, have them fore and aft. So they must turn their ship around, after each volley, to use the other side while the first reloads. Whilst they are turning they cannot fire. Nor can they fire the same cannon without this delay."

"Yes. You mean . . .?"

"I mean that here is the measure of their weakness. If we can keep them having to turn, firing at an awkward line or angle, and getting their cannon over-hot. Keep ourselves as much as possible bows-on or stern-on. Close in. Close range does not matter, if they cannot bring their bombards to bear. Then, whilst they are reloading, directly after a salvo, move in, fast, to board . . ."

"Aye — something of this was coming to me, also. You hear, Davidson man?"

"Boarding?" the other said, at his Aberdonian dourest. "These are king's ships. Bigger than this. More men than have we. Men-at-arms . . ." He broke off to shout a change of helm.

"The more their surprise," Jamie contended. "They will scarce expect to be boarded. And they may not be such bonny fighters, depending on all those cannon. How often will they have had to fight off boarders, think you? I tell you . . ."

His voice was drowned in more gunfire as the second English ship made another attack on *Clara*. They were the best part of a mile away now, and details were difficult to see, but it looked as though at least one hit had been made. Then their own adversary opened fire with his starboard armament on themselves, *Greysteel* swinging violently away — but not before a ball smashed into them amidships with a splintering crash of timbering, seemingly between rail and waterline. Their stern cannon fired in return, but again the shot fell well short.

"Out-ranged!" Alex exclaimed. "They have bigger pieces. Davidson — we have no choice. We must go in, as Jamie says. Can you steer for the Englishman? As near bows-on as you may? But not midships. So that he must shoot at a slant. You understand? He will be coming about, now. Jamie — prepare the boarders . . ."

So instead of circling and twisting, *Greysteel* turned directly in for the enemy. Directly only in the broad sense, however, for Davidson was concerned both to present as narrow a target as

273

he might and to present that target at as acute an angle to the other's broadside as he could. Only an expert master and an experienced crew, in a sufficiently swift-helmed vessel, could have attempted it. Fortunately the wind was consistent, fresh without being strong, reducing the complications.

The Englishman was neither laggard nor fool, and after some initial and understandable — but very valuable — hesitation, did all that he could to counter the tactics of the suicidally-inclined Scot. But it took him almost half as long again to effect any sharp change of course, and he was always just sufficiently behind to leave the advancing *Greysteel* with the initiative and a fairly consistently favourable angle of approach. He did manage to fire off both port and starboard armament once, but because of the slantwise aim involved, this was ineffective. On the other hand, *Greysteel*'s own forward cannon was able to fire almost directly ahead, at ever-shortening range, and scored two hits despite two misfires. The stern weapon could not be brought to bear.

The final stage of the approach had to be timed to a nicety. It was essential that they should run alongside the enemy on the flank from which a salvo had just been fired — which meant that they would be at very close range when it *was* fired, the most dangerous stage of the tactic. Fortunately for them, this seemed to coincide with the realisation by the Englishmen that there was actually an intent to board them — with disconcerting effect. Cannoneers were particularly helpless and vulnerable against a boarding foray, not concerned with hand-to-hand fighting. At any rate the shooting, which could have been the most telling of the battle, was the feeblest and most erratic yet, resulting in only one spar and minor sail being brought down.

Robert Davidson's handling of his ship thereafter was beyond praise. It is no easy matter to lay two sailing ships alongside smoothly at sea, even when both so desire it. When one is seeking to turn away, so as to bring its alternative armament to bear, a very high standard of seamanship is called for. But the thing was achieved, at the second try, scarcely smoothly but fairly speedily. Timbers grinding and creaking, the vessels came together, amidst wild shouting and cheering.

The strategy for such an engagement had been planned and gone over, on *Greysteel*, times without number, and every man knew his part. First into action were men who had climbed the rigging and mast-stays with blazing torches and

274

pitch-soaked tow tied to javelins, to cast down, lit, on to the Englishman's deck. This was more to cause confusion and alarm than anything else, smoke as important as flame — although with tubs of gunpowder beside every cannon, there were fair chances of an explosion. Needless to say it was at these that the aimers directed their blazing brands. None actually ignited a barrel, but some fell very close. This again had the effect of upsetting many of the enemy crewmen who, well aware of the danger, pushed away from the vicinity urgently. At the same time, grapnels, hooks, ropes and scaling-nets were being tossed up on to the taller ship. Or, more accurately, the heavy nets were cast *down* from *Greysteel*'s fore and aftercastles into the other's well-deck amidsmips, whilst archers and spear-throwers endeavoured to keep the English from casting these off again. The two Scots cannon were set to firing as regularly as they might at point-blank range directly into the enemy's hull, this being possible on account of the bigger ship's decking being some eight feet higher than their own. The cannons' wide mouths were capable of little elevation and no depression, so they could fire only straight ahead; but the Scots could pump balls into their opponent's timbering, which could not be reciprocated. It might not do much real damage at that level, but the effect on morale could be considerable.

The boarding-party, of course, was the principal assault, but this had to wait until the ropes, nets and ladders were in position. Then, led by Alex and Jamie and the other lairds, they swarmed up.

The English, needless to say, were not inactive meantime. But their defence, at this stage, was less coherent, co-ordinated, than it might have been. Undoubtedly they had never anticipated being boarded, and had not made adequate plans to deal with it. Bugles blew, commands resounded, but confusion raged. A group of archers on the high aftercastle were fairly effective, causing a number of Scots casualties; but at that short range they were within throwing distance of javelin-men on *Greysteel*'s poop, their position very exposed.

Once aboard, Alex's policy was to try to put out of action the enemy leadership, which also was mainly concentrated on the poop or aftercastle. In the swirling smoke-clouds, swords slashing, they hacked and thrust and parried their way aft, at last engaged in the task they had come to perform. They had the distinct advantage in that these young lairds were all trained swordsmen, experts, and fighting ordinary men-at-arms and sailors; and the fact that they were few in numbers was of little account on the narrow crowded deck where only a small proportion of the defenders could actually engage them at any moment. Jamie, shouting "A Douglas! A Douglas!" drove steadily onwards, unquestionably the most veteran fighter present.

A sudden violent explosion, much greater than the intermittent banging of the *Greysteel's* cannon, swept the deck with its blast and forced a temporary pause in the swordery as men were knocked over, shaken and distracted, One of the powder-barrels had blown up, turning a small fire quickly into a large one.

The effect was immediate and obvious — and a deal more noticeable on the defenders than on the attackers. Nobody likes being on a burning ship; but it is much worse when it is one's own ship and the enemy has a means of escape — and when there are other barrels of gunpowder all too close at hand. It would be too much to say that demoralisation set in, but undoubtedly the English rank-and-file now had only part of their minds on the fighting.

To the Scots, on the other hand, the effect was to some extent the reverse. It made them anxious to finish off the engagement before worse might befall and the entire ship become an inferno. With redoubled fury they renewed the attack.

Alex and Jamie had fought their way to the foot of the poop-stairway, and were faced with the difficult task of mounting this against opposition, when there was a new development, another convulsion. Not an explosion this time, but a concussion. The entire ship jarred and shook, knocking many off their feet. At the same time, there was much shouting from the direction of *Greysteel.* In the subsequent second pause, the Scots had opportunity to glance over their shoulders — and were dismayed at what they saw through the drifting smoke.

The second English warship had abandoned its assault on *Clara* and come to the aid of its partner. The bump had been this vessel laying itself alongside *Greysteel,* at the other side, the impact transmitted through the Scots ship now sandwiched between the two. Englishmen were already beginning to pour across the intervening deck to assist their fellows.

Now, of course, the situation was transformed, with the Scots facing attack from the rear and their original opponents gaining new heart — even though the fire tended to preoccupy all. Jamie shouted to form a schiltrom, a sort of back-to-back hedgehog, an admittedly defensive device. There was little alternative meantime.

There followed a period of major confusion, with the main Scots boarding-party as it were under siege but two smaller detached groups seeking to aid them, and Davidson and such of his crew as remained in *Greysteel* fighting their own battle. The English on the aftercastle were now exploiting their lofty position, and the lairdly group seeking to edge away forward from under it. The smoke and crackle of flames made an ominous and distracting background. The Scots cannon had ceased firing.

There was no question but that the Scots position was now serious. They were greatly outnumbered, their ship wedged between the others and the enemy's nerve recovered, even though the fire's progress was in all minds. Help from the *Clara* scarcely could be looked for — where she was or what her state was not evident. Jamie almost wished for another and larger explosion, which might injure the enemy more than themselves. Or the fire to cause an abandonment of the fighting. They were suffering mainly from the javelin-throwing now. Most of the boarders wore half-armour, the lairds having shirts-of-mail also. But javelins cast down on them from the aftercastle could find chinks and joints in the steel-plating, and injure below, even if they did not actually penetrate, the chain-mail.

Desperate situations may demand desperate remedies, and Jamie was beginning to consider the possibilities of seeking to cut their way back, in a fighting-wedge, first into the sandwiched *Greysteel* and then over on to the second English ship, in an attempt to take it over, only part-manned as it would now be, and to sail clear — this, when, in all the noise, clash and shouting, his ears heard a new sound. It took moments, in his preoccupied state, for the significance to sink in. Then his heart lifted in a great bound. It was the skirl of bagpipes on the wind. Panting, he raised his voice.

"The Islesmen! They come! Listen — pipes!" he shouted. "The MacLeods! The MacLeods!"

From scores of dry and weary Scots throats strangled, gulping cheers arose and new strength surged into flagging arms. The Englishmen were less affected — as yet.

The sworders were far too busy to see their allies arrival, but they certainly heard them come in no uncertain fashion, pipes shrilling, horns ululating, men yelling. Like one of their own Highland rivers in spate the half-naked MacLeods came pouring over the various decks, irresistible, terrifying.

The English, appalled and clearly out of their depth in face of this savage horde, fought on bravely enough, but with defeat implicit almost from the start. It was all too much. Fairly quickly the boarders from the second warship came to the conclusion that they would be better back on their own vessel, and began to disengage as best they could and straggle off. Another explosion expedited matters, and gave even the Islesmen pause for a little. The shipmaster of the enemy vessel took the opportunity to cast off in haste, and stood away in no hesitant style, however many of his men were left behind. Seeing this, the commander of the burning ship wisely decided that he had had enough. He shouted that he surrendered, ordering all his people to lay down their arms, and sending men to strike their flag.

Only the Islesmen seemed disappointed that the battle was thus suddenly over.

The *Greysteel* party had suffered heavy casualties, nine dead and almost all wounded in some degree, a number seriously. Both Alex and Jamie were slightly hurt, the former with a flesh-wound in the thigh, the latter with a grazed and bleeding brow where his helmet had been knocked off.

Three distinct movements commenced, each little concerned with the other. The *Greysteel* people sought to get themselves, their dead and severely wounded, back to their own vessel and such attention as was available. The Islesmen, who had never had so large and impressive a ship to loot, even if part aflame, set about despoiling it with a will, before it was too late. And the English crew, finding nobody now very interested in them, and recognising also that time was probably short, began to lower their small boats at the poop, to pile in, taking their own wounded with them.

The fire was growing apace, even though the MacLeods had tossed overboard the remaining powder-barrels on deck.

At length even the acquisitive MacLeods decided that it was better to be content with what they had than to die getting more and, heavily laden, retired to their own galleys. Ian Borb and his brother came aboard *Greysteel*.

"I do not know whether to fall on your necks, thanking you for coming to our aid, MacLeod," Alex said, having his leg dressed and bound, "or to curse you for deserting us, in the first place! Where a God's name have you been, man?"

"Och, we have been doing well. Very well, friend," the other assured cheerfully. "Taking many ships for you. No trouble, at

278

all. But, you — you left your place, whatever! We have been searching for you, for long. Had it not been for the smoke of that ship you fired yonder, we might not have found you in time. Foolish, just."

Alex's gasp was the only rejoinder he allowed himself.

Jamie did his best for his friend. "My lord of Mar was scarcely required to lie idle, awaiting *your* pleasure, sir! He commands this expedition, does he not? We waited a night and a day for you to return to his authority. If all had ended in disaster, the fault would have been yours."

The Islesman seemed amused rather than contrite. "Disaster? You were near to disaster? Without us? As well we saw the smoke, then. You have a sore head, friend?"

Helplessly they gave it up.

The situation at large seemed now to have resolved itself. The second English king's ship was off at best speed west-by-north, clearly making for the mouth of the Thames estuary; and her smaller colleague, which had never joined in their fight but had apparently taken over the assault on *Clara*, was now in full sail after her. *Clara* herself was in a poor state, one of her masts down and listing somewhat to port. The Greenwich *Maid Mary* was now but a smoking hulk on the horizon.

Decision fell to be made, and swiftly. Once those fleeing warships reached the Thames, there could be little doubt but that a major hunt would be mounted for the raiders. King Henry would have many such ships and privateers at his disposal, and it would probably be a fleet which would come seeking them. Such they were in no state to face, whatever the MacLeods' reaction. A move should be made at once, north-by-east, homewards. The question was what to do about *Clara*? The Islesmen were for abandoning her, as only a handicap, and Alex tended to agree. But the Aberdonians were concerned to hold on to her, both as a useful prize and on account of the rich accumulation of booty with which her holds were now stuffed. And since it was the Aberdeen contingent which had had the greatest casualties and the least joy out of the whole expedition, he felt bound to humour them. They might *have* to abandon *Clara*, but meantime they would make her as seaworthy as possible and head eastwards, in convoy, for the open sea. With the night before them, and no chase likely for a full day, at least, they ought to be able to lose themselves in the wide ocean.

While this decision was being taken, a series of internal

explosions rent their late foe, toppling her masts and leaving her a sorry sight. With mixed feelings, the Scots limped from the scene.

*　　　*　　　*

It took them almost two weeks to win home to Aberdeen — long before which they had lost the galleys, the MacLeods going off on their own one evening and just not returning. No doubt they considered their duties to be over, and sped back to Skye, laden with loot.

Fortunately, *Greysteel* did not sight a single ship-of-war or privateer throughout, and the weather being fairly kind, *Clara*'s jury-mast and patched-up state were not severely tested. Wounds, in healthy young bodies, healed up quickly, in the main. In a general way the expedition was voted a success. Certainly they had done more damage to English shipping than could have been anticipated. The effect on Henry remained to be seen.

Aberdeen greeted them warmly, as returning heroes. Bishop Greenlaw himself, the Chancellor, came down from his palace, a notable sign of favour. But, after a word or two, he drew Alex aside, and changed tone.

"My lord," he said, lowering his voice, "I have ill-tidings for you. A grievous matter. Your lady-wife, the Countess . . ."

Alex schooled his features. "She is a, a woman of spirit," he said.

"She was," the Bishop agreed. "She has gone to other . . . activities, in the providence of Almighty God. I grieve for you, my son."

"Gone . . . ?"

"Gone, yes. She died, two weeks past. Fell from her horse, whilst hunting, at Balquhain Castle. Broke her neck. Death would be painless . . ."

"Good God! Isobel . . . !"

"God is good, yes. And this is the will of God, my friend. Accept it."

Alex was much distressed. Although whether he was actually heart-broken Jamie Douglas was uncertain. He remained very silent on the matter.

The company broke up, and these two friends parted, for Kildrummy and Lochindorb respectively, Jamie at least a richer man than when he had set out. He was longing to see Mary and the children again.

PART THREE

XVII

ALEX STEWART AND Jamie Douglas could hardly have
anticipated being anxious to see their MacLeod friends
quite so soon as the following mid-November of 1407,
sufficiently to be travelling in person across the width of
Highland Scotland for the purpose. But since their return from
their privateering venture, events — or better, the shadow of
coming events — had so loomed and developed in Albany's
Scotland that clarification and some planning ahead had
become vital if so much that these two stood for was not to be
overwhelmed. And since the most immediate threat appeared
to be from Donald of the Isles, some illumination on the
Hebridean scene was necessary, and scarcely to be obtained
without personal contact. Hence this secret journey to see
William Achlerich MacLeod of Dunvegan, in Skye.

It was, of course, hardly the best time of year to be making
such an expedition. But they had little choice in the matter; any
offputting now would delay them until mid-March at the
earliest. The weather, if not good, was at least not impossible,
windy and cold but with little rain, or worse snow, to make
the rivers, bogs and passes impassable — the major hazard in
Highland travel. Even crossing the high watershed of Scotland,
the Great Glen and Glens Moriston, Cluanie and Shiel, they
had seen no snow — although the savage mountain-tops were
consistently veiled in low cloud and might be white-tipped.
Now, down the shores of the long, linked sea-lochs of Duich
and Alsh, weed-hung and rocky, they had come to the narrows
of the Kyle of Lochalsh, with the Isle of Skye looming mightily
only half-a-mile away across the slate-grey, white-capped waters.

They sat their garrons considering the situation in the fading
light of a dull afternoon, their two gillies behind. They were

inconspicuously dressed and with only this pair as escort, for the last thing they desired was to draw attention to themselves, here in the Highland West where Donald MacDonald was the major power. The small castle of Dunakin soared on a fang of rock at the other side of the narrows, dominating the passage. There were other crossings than this to Skye, for it was a very large island; but those further south led into the MacDonald territory of Sleat, and last time they had come to see MacLeod, to arrange the hire of his galleys, they had crossed there, from Glenelg to Kylerhea, and been all too much involved with MacDonalds. Further north the crossings were much longer. That castle opposite, Dunakin, belonged to MacKinnon, not a MacDonald nor yet a MacLeod — but the lands west of his were MacLeod's. They had heard that MacKinnon was at odds with Donald of the Isles.

Before them was a jetty but no ferry-boat. Beside the jetty was a low-browed thatched cottage, little more than a turf-hut, heather-roofed, from the black doorway of which a plaid-wrapped man was watching them heedfully. As they reined closer, this man spoke in the soft lisping Gaelic.

"It is none so poor a day, friends, and not that cold, at all," he declared conversationally. "Good enough for travelling. Och, yes."

"As you say. We would cross over to Skye. Are you the ferry-man?"

"Sometimes just, sometimes. Och, yes. For the time of the year I have seen it worse, mind."

"No doubt. And we are thankful for it. But — the ferry?"

"There is many a time when it is not possible to cross the water at all, no. Wild it can be, just wild."

"I am sure of it. But — not today. How *do* we cross, friend? Where is the boat?"

"Och, the boat, yes. MacKinnon has the boat. Your name now, will be . . . ?"

"My name is MacAlastair," Alex said, with exemplary patience. "How do we get MacKinnon's boat?"

"MacAlastair is it? Och, yes — MacAlastair. Which Mac-Alastair would that be?"

"*My* MacAlastair! Now — do we cross this ferry, with your aid? Or with the aid of some other?"

"None cross to Skye save at MacKinnon's pleasure, whatever."

"Not even MacLeod? MacLeod of Dunvegan."

"MacLeod . . .?" The man's voice and attitude changed noticeably. "Och well, MacLeod . . ."

"Yes. We travel to see MacLeod, at Dunvegan."

"Yes, yes, MacAlastair. MacLeod it is. William Achlerich of Dunvegan."

"And Ian Borb and Ruari Ban likewise."

"Surely, surely. MacKinnon will be glad, just, to put you over on your way to MacLeod, MacAlastair." The man ducked back within his low-doored hovel.

"A mighty to-do to cross a ferry!" Jamie commented. "You might think this carle a chief at his castle gate!"

"In the Islesmen's West we must do as they do. The stresses and strains here, between MacDonalds and MacLeods, MacKinnons and MacKenzies, perforce make us to walk warily. But it seems that MacKinnon supports MacLeod."

The man emerged with a blazing torch, with which he set alight a bundle of pitch-soaked rags hanging in a chain from a sort of gibbet. It was not long before an answering flare showed as a red gleam from the castle across the dark water. They were informed that it would be no time at all before they were on their way to MacLeod.

As they waited the man enthused carefully on the power, puissance and potency of William Achlerich MacLeod of Dunvegan, fifth chief of the Siol Tormod — at the same time trying hard to discover the identity of MacAlastair. The MacLeod, he declared, was a mighty man of valour who had slain his hundreds, despite his name — Achlerich meaning the cleric, he having been intended for the Church but, God be praised, had been spared from that fate by the death of an elder brother. The travellers knew all this well enough, but preferred to encourage their informant to talk rather than continue his devious but probing questions. At length a large flat-bottomed scow, propelled by four oarsmen, arrived at the jetty, and the young man in charge — who proved to be a son of MacKinnon of Dunakin — after a muttered conversation with the beacon-lighter, announced himself as agreeable to carry them across the kyle — at a price. Embarked, he too began, almost at once, to seek to establish just who they were and whence they had come.

As they were pulled slantwise across the choppy narrows in the fading light, horses standing uneasy in the heaving boat,

Alex was glad to divert the conversation by pointing to a massive seaweed-hung chain which, anchored to a great cairn of stones on this east side, sank away gradually out of sight into the water.

The young man laughed. "That is MacKinnon's Sword-Belt," he explained. "No ship passes through these narrows without paying tribute to MacKinnon. The chain lies just beneath the water, and can be raised or lowered from the castle. None may pass Dunakin."

"Save, I think, MacLeod? Or should it be Donald of the Isles?"

The other looked at him sharply, and then shrugged. "Only these, yes."

"MacKinnon must do well, then — if he demands as much tribute from shipping as he does for his ferry! But perhaps shipmasters avoid your Sound of Sleat, in consequence?"

Young MacKinnon laughed again. "They dare not. They must sail round this side of Skye, or the other. This side they pay only *our* tribute. The other side, Donald takes them — and demands more than tribute!"

"I see. Who would be a shipmaster in the Isles?"

Lachlan MacKinnon of Dunakin, chief of the name, a tall old hawk of a man, greeted them with a sort of wary arrogance until he ascertained that they were bound for Dunvegan. Then he was all hospitality, although his small, rude castle's facilities were of the most primitive, it being merely a stark square tower of three storeys and an attic, one chamber to each floor, with nine-foot walls. He pointed out that Dunvegan was two days journey to the north-west, fifty miles, at the other side and other end of the island, and darkness was falling. They must be his guests for the night — his house was theirs. But although Alex still did not wish to divulge his identity, not being sure of MacKinnon's allegiances however much he might approve of MacLeod, he found it impossible to put him off with the pseudonym of MacAlastair against no devious probings but a direct demand.

"I am loth to give you my name, MacKinnon — for fear that it could be to your hurt to know it, and you befriending us," he said carefully. He took a chance. "I am friend to MacLeod, you see — but scarcely so to Donald of the Isles."

"Donald is it? Devil burn his bones!" MacKinnon cried. "I am your better friend if you are Donald's foe. He executed my

286

own father — or had Maclean of Duart do it for him — and then stole our lands in Mull, wide lands. Yet MacKinnon had always supported his line."

"Ah. Then I understand your feelings for him, sir. And I accept that my name is safe with you. I am indeed MacAlastair — *Alastair MacAlastair Mor-mhic-an-Righ*, Earl of Mar and Lord of Badenoch. And this is Sir James Douglas, son to the Lord of Dalkeith."

"God in his heaven — Mar! Who was Justiciar? Buchan's son — the Wolf?"

"The same." Alex found himself actually embraced.

"Your father — I knew him. A man after my own heart, whatever!"

"M'mm. Not all would say that, I fear, MacKinnon! I thank you."

"Now I know why you are seeking MacLeod. His son, Ian Borb, did great things with you against the wretched English, we heard. You want more of him? My own sons would be happy to have a hand in that noble work."

"I thank you again. But it is scarce that. I am here to seek to watch and contain Donald. The English yes — but they can wait. Donald first, whom we have found out is in league with them. And intends invasion."

"Ha! Then you will be for Ireland?"

"Ireland . . . ?"

"Ireland, yes. Have you not heard? Donald is gathering a great host to go to Ireland, to Ulster. To aid the English king in his trouble there, who is faced by an alliance of the Irish princes. These have recovered most of Ulster and much else. They boast that they will throw the English into the sea. Donald is to go to the help of the English."

His visitors exchanged glances. "So-o-o! We heard nothing of this. What we heard was . . . otherwise." Alex explained the situation more fully to Jamie, whose Gaelic was not yet sufficient to cope with these details.

"If true, this could change much. Explain much. But it could be no more than a feint, a bluff to put us off our guard." Jamie was ever cautious. "Ask him when? When is this Irish expedition to be?"

MacKinnon did not know that, but assumed that it would be in the forthcoming campaigning season, from April onwards. Indeed he could give them little further information. It was all

287

only hearsay. But he could confirm that there was much activity, much coming and going of island chiefs at Finlaggan Castle on Islay, Donald's main seat, and a great repairing, refurbishing and preparation of galleys and birlinns up and down the entire seaboard. All of which left the main question as to destination open.

They retired that night to couches of heaped deerskins and plaids in the draughty attic of the tower — having gratefully declined the offer of suitable female bed-warmers of unspecified identity — wondering whether in fact their journey had been necessary.

They were awakened in the morning by the strains of Mac-Kinnon's piper parading around the small castle's constricted parapet-walk in a smirr of rain. After a breakfast ambitious enough to last them all day, not to mention whisky offered by the flagon, their host would not hear of them setting off forthwith on their journey to Dunvegan. He wished them to meet sundry of his MacKinnon notables, would have them go hunting stags in Strathsuardal, even to demonstrate the sport of salmon-spearing in the Anavaig River, seemingly an Isles specialty. When Alex regretfully declined, pointing out that they still had a long ride ahead of them and time unfortunately precious, the other had to reveal that they would not in fact be riding at all — which was no way for gentlemen to travel in the Isles; they would go by water, infinitely more swiftly. When his guests eyed the chief's birlinn, lying at anchor in the lee of the castle-rock, with no sign of crew or activity about it, MacKinnon was forced to admit that it would be a MacLeod boat which was coming for them, that he had indeed sent one of his many sons hot-foot through the night for Dunvegan with the word. Why this, instead of despatching them onward in his own vessel Alex was too polite to ask. Probably the MacKinnon had sent his messenger before learning of his guests' true identity, and was merely passing the responsibility to MacLeod.

So they went salmon-hunting in a rushing crystal-clear river under the shadow of thrusting Beinn na Cailleach, and saw young MacKinnon transfix two fine fish, although they themselves failed miserably to overcome the refraction of the water combined with the darting speed of the quarry, try as they would — this from a series of tiny jetties built at an angle to the current beneath various runs and rapids. Both keen fishermen, they were much put out at being found so ineffective at the business, but decided to practice it in their own more peat-stained waters in due course.

When, at dusk, a smallish sixteen-oared birlinn arrived at Dunakin from the north, it proved to be under the command of Ian Borb himself, who greeted the visitors with every appearance of simple pleasure, clearly anticipating a new pirating expedition for MacLeod co-operation. However, he swallowed his disappointment, expressed himself delighted to see his former co-heroes, and, in an evening's great drinking and talking, entertained the company to a highly-coloured account of their exploits in English waters in which the visitors scarcely recognised their own parts. Here obviously was a saga in the making. It was no occasion for questioning as to the state of affairs in the Isles. The hospitality, liquid in especial, was such that coherent thought, much less meaningful converse, was all but impossible, to say nothing of the fiddling, piping, singing, dancing, story-telling and the like. Eventual bed, even with sore heads, was something of a relief.

But on the morrow, on their spirited way up the widening Inner Sound of Skye, with the lesser islands of Scalpay and Raasay on the one hand and the mainland mountains of Applecross on the other, now glistening and gleaming in watery sunshine, now hidden in driving rain-storms, they had ample time to learn something of what they required to know, from Ian Borb, as his oarsmen thrashed their way north-about round Skye's long and spectacular east coast in fiercely proprietorial style. They learned that Donald MacDonald was undoubtedly preparing to mount a major expedition to Ireland where, as well as aiding the English, it seemed that he had his own feud with certain Ulster princelings. He was actually seeking to hire galleys and men for this from chiefs who were not normally his supporters — presumably with English gold since he was not believed to have overmuch of that commodity of his own. When Alex wondered whether this could be a ruse, a blind to disguise the mustering when in fact his host was destined for an invasion of mainland Scotland, MacLeod was sure that it was not so. For there was considerable coming and going with Ireland, allies being sought in Ulster. His own father had been approached to co-operate, through third parties, with rich pickings promised, although normally Donald's foe. There seemed no doubt that Ulster was the destination and early summer the planned time.

They learned also why MacKinnon had not sent the visitors

to Dunvegan in his own birlinn. Donald, it appeared, resented the lesser chief's enterprise, not so much in putting his chain across the Kyle narrows as in charging a lower scale of tolls for shipping to pass it, and so undercutting his own barriers and toll-gatherers and causing much trade to use the inner channel past Skye. He threatened, in consequence, to sink any vessel of MacKinnon's found in the outer seas. MacLeod, scorning such pedestrian methods of producing an income, did not compete in the matter — and anyway was strong enough for Donald not to challenge without major cause.

Ian Borb's craft always seemed to move at top speed. The birlinn was scarcely so fast as a full-sized galley, but its sail and sixteen oars drove it along in stirring fashion, to the usual chanting and sword-clanging; and in just over three hours they were passing the dramatic heights of the Quirang and rounding the cliffs of Rudha Hunish at the northern tip of the Trotternish peninsula and moving into the very different conditions of the open Sea of the Hebrides, to head south-westwards now into the long Atlantic swell, the disadvantages of winter-time voyaging becoming quickly more evident to the travellers. What had been merely a keen, chill breeze developed into a fierce, piercing half-gale, steep short seas overlying the swell and the birlinn pitching and rolling in the cross-seas in highly uncomfortable fashion, flying spray soaking all continuously. However, the oarsmen appeared to be in no way distressed, skilfully adjusting their strokes and rhythm to suit the troughs and summits of the waves. Ian Borb remained his usual cheerful self, the whisky flagons going the rounds.

Twice they saw other craft, the second time two larger galleys together, their sails painted with the black lymphad of the Isles; but when these drew near enough to discern the black bull's head of MacLeod on the birlinn's sail, they veered off discreetly. It was clearly a matter of dog not eating dog.

Passing presently another great headland at the tip of the Waternish peninsula, they turned in at the mouth of six-miles-long Loch Dunvegan, a fairly narrow fiord but island-dotted, at the head of which reared the MacLeod castle, crowning the usual rocky bluff, an oblong keep larger than most in these parts, with irregular flanking curtain-walls outlining the rock's summit, and a beetling sea-gate entrance. A fair-sized township clustered around the skirts of the rock and a dozen galleys rode at anchor in the basin of the loch, *Iolair* and *Clavan* amongst them.

The visitors discovered themselves to be highly popular at Dunvegan, the booty brought back by the temporary privateers not forgotten and the prowess attributed to the entire Mar expedition by no means fading with time and repeated telling. William Achlerich treated them distinctly differently from on their previous visit, more like dear kin long lost. He was a plump, rubicund, smiling little man, smooth of feature, all bows and gestures, unlikely-seeming sire for his clutch of stalwart sons, yet with a martial reputation of his own to outdo any of them. He too was disappointed that they had not come to hire more galleys and fighting men for further adventures; but rejoiced to find them inimical to and suspicious of *Mac Dhomhuill*, as he called Donald of the Isles. Anything that they could contrive against that man and his whole house would have his whole-hearted co-operation.

Mightily fed, warm and relaxed around the long table in Dunvegan's blue peat-smoke-filled hall, antique but capacious drinking-horns to hand, the visitors found that they were expected to give as much information as they got — with William Achlerich both more interested and knowledgeable about mainland affairs than they had assumed. Why were they so expectant of an Isles invasion of Scotland, he wanted to know. It must exercise them greatly to have brought the great Earl of Mar himself all this road to Skye?

"We have had sure word from London, from King Henry's own Court," Alex told him. "A letter to myself from the captive Earl of Douglas. It reached me some three weeks back. The Earl, Sir James's chief, is an anxious man, and with reason. He fears for the whole future of his great house. But he fears for Scotland too. Fears so much that he is prepared to take most drastic steps. Captive as he is, he has agreed to swear to be Henry's man, to support him and his sons against all, save only the King of Scots himself!"

"God Almighty — then the man is a traitor, whatever!" MacLeod exclaimed.

"Scarcely that, I think — although it is an ill choice. But it was the only way he could gain temporary release. To come home to Scotland for a time. To see to Douglas affairs and to try to counter the Duke of Albany's moves. Albany is playing a strange double game. With Henry . . ."

"But Douglas was Albany's man, was he not?"

"Not truly. He has supported Albany when he thought it best.

Against Prince David, who insulted his sister. Against others."
That was Jamie speaking. "I do not say that he is always wise
or far-sighted. But I do not believe that he is Albany's man.
Indeed I think that he much dislikes him. And he is no traitor —
that I swear. But Albany has allowed Henry to send back the
Earl of Dunbar, who *is* a traitor, to Scotland. Douglas's enemy.
Dunbar acting as go-between for Henry and Albany can only
mean trouble for Douglas — and Scotland. I say that this swear-
ing to be Henry's man, ill as it is, may be something of a warning
to Albany, something of a declaration of war!"

"All because of this of Dunbar?"

"More than that," Alex said. "Albany has gone much further
towards the English. He has offered his daughter to marry
Henry's son, the Prince John. And, in order to get his captive
son Murdoch of Fife released, he has offered to send up his
second son, John, Earl of Buchan as hostage instead — without
Buchan's knowledge or agreement. For Buchan is critical of his
father. *I* let my cousin know of this — and he will not go, if he
can help it. But it means that Albany is playing a deep game —
and Henry perhaps deeper."

"For why?" MacLeod demanded. "What does he seek, your
Albany?"

"I think to ensure that young King James is not allowed to
come home. Either that he should be kept captive in England
indefinitely, or else disposed of otherwise, so that Albany can
perhaps assume the throne himself. So Douglas thinks. There is
more to it — but that is the heart of the matter."

There was silence round the table for a little.

"What has this to be doing with Donald, then?" their host asked.

"Albany is not the only one who sees opportunity in the boy-
king's plight. Donald, remember, is the King's cousin, his
mother a sister of Albany — as of my father's. He could see
himself on the throne."

"Donald — King!" MacLeod hooted at the notion.

"It is not so far from possible," Alex pointed out. "A successful invasion, and Albany and his sons disposed of — and who
else is there? The Lord Walter of Brechin, whom Albany has
now made Earl of Atholl, is a drunken sot, whom none would
support. And all the rest of the royal women are wed to
Douglases. Anyway, Donald also has been dealing with Henry
Plantagenet. Did you know that his nephew, Hector Maclean of
Duart, has been to London?"

"God in heaven — Maclean! Red Hector! That, that . . .!"

"Yes. He has been negotiating with Henry, Douglas writes. He believes that a full alliance is planned. He says that Henry will have Scotland one way or the other. While seeming to work with Albany, he plans for Donald to raise most of the Highlands and the Isles against Lowland Scotland, while Henry himself prepares to attack from England. Dunbar's return to Scotland is to work so that there will be a large and strong party in the Lowlands to support such double attack. Now do you see why the Douglas was prepared to pay so high a price to return home?"

William Achlerich shook his round head. "This is beyond all!" he said. "Treachery on every hand."

"When a crown and a kingdom are at stake treachery is seldom absent. Henry knows that, if any does. Consider how he usurped Richard's throne. Nobody can teach Henry Bolingbroke about guile and plotting and double dealing — even Albany. Myself, I think that Donald is the innocent, in this. Ambitious, yes — but not a match for these other two. But dangerous, in that he can field thousands of men and hundreds of ships. Henry will use him, and discard him. Henry will win, whoever loses. If we, the rest of Scotland allow it. Henry has sent envoys to France, to offer a new peace treaty. On condition that the old alliance with Scotland is broken. So Douglas comes home — paying the price. He believes that *I* can rally the North against Donald, and only I. It may be true. I must try, at the least. So I must know what Donald plans — and when."

There was another long pause as they eyed each other. "This of Ireland?" MacLeod wondered, at last. "I swear that Donald aims at Ireland, not Scotland. All the signs are there. It is no cheat, no stratagem, to be sure. Ireland will be invaded — that I am sure, whatever."

"I rejoice if it is so. For it will give us time — time we need greatly. It could be that this is part of the bargain with Henry. Ireland first." Alex frowned. "Henry is known to be in trouble in the Irish North, many of his garrisons wiped out, occupied towns in revolt. It could be. So that Henry could withdraw many of his troops to England — for his attack on Scotland later. Yes, it could be."

"Would Donald be prepared to play that game?" Jamie demanded. "To fight two wars, not one? On Henry's behalf?"

"On his own, Jamie, it could be . . ."

"Och, Donald is much concerned in Ulster, mind," MacLeod pointed out. "He has had two of his younger brothers to wed heiresses there, moved them across the Irish Sea. Ian Mor the Tanist is wed to the only child of Bisset of the Glens of Antrim. Marcus MacDonald wed to much of Tyrone. See you, if he could land and take Tyrconnel, with these other two he could have most of the North in his hands. Use this to extend his sway over O'Neill and the other Irish princelings — with the help of the English, from the south. He would be overlord of Ulster. God — he has been after dabbling in that water for years, the man! Could he be . . .? Could he be . . .?"

"Aye!" Alex breathed out. "It could be, indeed! High King of Ireland! As well as King of Scots! Donald, King of the Celts, one day! Dear God — it is possible! That could be where he lifts his eyes."

"Save us — that, that turkeycock!" Jamie exclaimed. "That island bog-trotter!" Recollecting the company he kept, the Douglas swallowed.

"He is no bog-trotter, man," Alex reminded. "He is a deal more learned than any of us. He studied at the University of Cambridge. He speaks many languages. History he dotes on, they say. The history of the Celtic peoples, in especial. Aye, it could be. And, as well as being grandson of Robert the Second, he comes of the ancient line of the Kings of the Isles and of Man. Do not underestimate Donald in this. Seeing the disunity and treachery in all the lands concerned, he may see his opportunity."

MacLeod had become very thoughtful. Clearly this new conception shook him — as it would shake all the Celtic polity. His own house had supported the Isles lordship loyally enough. It was Donald's claim to the earldom of Ross and overlordship of Skye which had aroused his fears and enmity, since these implied vassal status for himself. When Donald, or at least Alastair Carrach his brother, had heavy-handedly emphasised the claim a few years before by descending upon Skye with a sizeable force, burning, sacking and rounding up cattle, as some sort of tribute-taking, William Achlerich had risen in wrath, assailed the invaders near Loch Sligachan and roundly defeated them. Since then the feud had intensified. Oddly enough, however, Ian Borb and his brothers were less concerned; indeed they, whilst declaring no love for Donald, had in fact been toying with the notion of taking part in the Irish expedition, in which the pickings were almost certain to be substantial.

There was another aspect of the situation on which Alex desired elucidation — the attitude of the other mainland seaboard clans towards an invasion by Donald. After all most of the West Highlands, right down to the Clyde estuary, had once been part of the ancient Kingdom of the Isles. On how much support, or otherwise, could Donald rely, not against Ireland but against Scotland?

William Achlerich was reluctant to commit himself on that. He pointed out that Donald was not popular, and his brother who had been doing most of his fighting for him, was less so. But on the other hand, if there was a triumph in Ireland, and a vision of renewed greatness for the Celtic peoples generally, with English assistance assured, anything might happen. The situation was intricate, he reminded — reminded at length, proceeding to give as example the position of Clanranald, the great house of Garmoran, mainland neighbours of MacLeod — whose attitude must necessarily affect his own, if it came to hostilities. Their chief, the late Ranald, had in fact been Donald's elder brother. Their father, John, Lord of the Isles, had led a fairly united principality and married Amy MacRuarie, heiress of Garmoran — the vast province which included mainland Moidart, Knoydart and Morar, as well as the island Uists and Barra — herself the descendant, like John, of the great Somerled, King of the Isles. Then, in a fatal political move, John had divorced Amy and married the Princess Margaret, eldest daughter of Robert the Second of Scotland, and raised a new family of whom Donald was the eldest — although he had three sons already by Amy. He had thereafter declared the second family to be senior to the first, a folly for which all the realm was to pay. Donald was made heir to the lordship of the Isles, while his elder-born Ranald was made to sign a deed of resignation and given instead his mother's lands of Garmoran — or some of them. Godfrey, the eldest of all, was driven out because he refused to sign, made landless. Ranald himself, however resentful, had never rebelled against father or step-brother, being content to found his own lesser branch of the house, known as Clanranald. But he had died a few years before this, and his sons Alan and Donald were otherwise minded and positively hostile to Donald senior. So the Lord of the Isles by no means led a united patrimony.

The visitors had to take what comfort they could from that.

MacLeod would not forecast reactions. They went to their couches thoughtful indeed.

After three days at Dunvegan they took their leave of William Achlerich who promised to keep them informed of any significant developments, and were rowed back to Dunakin in Ian Borb's birlinn, to pick up their horses for the long ride home to Badenoch. The cold rain and blustering winds emphasised that the sooner they were safely back across the high spine of the mountains, the better — for the tops, when they could be seen, were already gleaming white.

"How say you?" Alex demanded, when at length they rode away eastwards from the grey waters of the Kyle of Lochalsh. "We came a long way — for what? Much trouble, for what achieved? Was our journey worth the making, Jamie?"

"I say it was," the other answered. "We have learned much of value, I think, which we needed to know — and which we would not have learned otherwise. We have learned that Earl Douglas was wrong — that this alliance between Henry of England and Donald is not against Scotland but Ireland — at least in the first instance. Later, who knows? So we have time. We have learned something of Donald's weaknesses. Strengths, too. But the weaknesses we can seek to exploit. We have learned that he may have much greater ambitions than we thought. That he may be looking a deal further ahead. But, again, that gives us time. I say that it was worth coming."

"Agreed. Donald is still a threat, yes. Perhaps a greater one. But not immediately so. The immediate and principal threat remains as it was — my uncle Albany. Who, the saints be praised, is Donald's enemy also! The house of Stewart, my friend, may almost be left to defeat itself!"

"I wonder . . . ?" Jamie said. "Robert Stewart of Albany will survive, I swear, whether Donald does or no. Leave *him* out, at your peril!"

Alex Stewart nodded as they rode on.

XVIII

GAZING WESTWARDS FROM *Greysteel*'s forecastle rail towards the hazy line that was the last of the Scottish coast, off Angus, it seemed scarcely credible to Jamie Douglas that he should be so doing, within six months of their Hebridean journey — more especially with his arm around the shoulders of his wife Mary Stewart. Nothing could have seemed less likely even that Yuletide. Yet now, in early May of 1408, here they were, heading south-eastwards once more, and in fine style — although this time with no accompanying galleys. The fine style included ladies advisedly, for on this occasion they were on no privateering expedition — even if *Greysteel* was again well equipped to deal with any attackers they might encounter. They were bound for France.

Alex came strolling forward to them. "Mary, my dear Aunt," he said, "does it stoun your heart to see your native land fading from your sight? You have never left Scotland before, I think?"

"Not so," she replied cheerfully. "So long as I come back before too long. I am rejoicing in this, Alex — to feel as free as my dear husband, for once! To come and go. The going is no hurt, believe me, provided I come again — for I have left two bairns hostage back yonder at Lochindorb."

"We shall return, never fear. I am no more for exile than are you. Or Jamie here. This is but a flourish, a demonstration."

"As well an absenting," Jamie added dryly.

"That too, yes."

They were both right, although the absenting had taken precedence over the demonstration originally. The fact was that John of Buchan had come to see Alex, just after Yule, and strongly advised him to leave Scotland for a while, in his own

297

interests. He had it on good authority that a trap was being set for him, all in due process of law. Albany, as Regent representing the Crown, was commanding a Privy Council enquiry into the proper destination of the earldom of Mar — which would be rigged against Alex, of course — legal niceties were being concocted and marshalled and a major sitting of the Council was scheduled for June, before which Alex would be ordered to appear, to state his case. This he could scarcely refuse to do, without hopelessly prejudicing his position by defying the Crown in Council — as distinct from Albany himself — and making an official outlaw of himself. In which case, naturally, the earldom would be found to be rightfully destined for Sir Robert Erskine, the claimant. On the other hand, if Alex did appear, he would be admitting the competence of the hearing to rule against him, would find the majority of the Council already decided for Erskine and might well be arrested thereafter on the old charge of murdering Sir Malcolm Drummond and forcing the Countess. If, however, he should be out of the country at the time, the hearing could scarcely be held, or if it was, its findings could be contested as improper and not binding. All would fall to be delayed — and in the present turbulent conditions, delay might well mean never. It was the Earl of Douglas, back on the Privy Council, who had conveyed this advice to Buchan for onward transmission, and suggested France as an excellent objective for the traveller.

Alex's first reaction had been outright rejection. He would not run away, to France or anywhere else. He would remain in possession in Mar, and challenge Albany and the Council to come and eject him. But it was pointed out that, though he might be successful in this, it was again to put him outside the law. The case would be adjudged against him as having refused to contest Erskine's claims; and for so long as he could remain holding Mar it would be as an embattled outlaw. Much better to be outwith the realm, prepared to come back at short notice if indeed an attack on Mar in force was made — which seemed unlikely. Moreover, France would give him an excellent and legitimate excuse for travel — on young King James's behalf. He had been prominent in the official embassage to Henry on this subject — to say nothing of the privateering enterprise. What more natural than that, as the King's cousin, he should go seek the King of France's aid in obtaining James's release? To urge the French not to renew the truce with Henry unless James was freed — who had been on his way to France. Albany could scarcely declare publicly hostility to this mission, however unofficial he named it; and the Council would at least have to acknowledge it as a noble gesture, and so be disinclined to take active proceedings against him in the interim. Who could tell, he might succeed with King Charles?

So Alex had been persuaded. But he would make it all a flourish, a demonstration, as much to Scotland as to France. He would not go like any fugitive or minor applicant for help. He would go as a prince, the King of Scots's cousin indeed, a great earl of Scotland, would spend his all on it if need be. It would be an embassage worthy of Scotland, even if unofficial. Fortunately he was given time, for he was not to be sent a summons to appear before the Council until close to the due date, so that he should have no time for preparation. There had been opportunity to charter *Greysteel* once more, and to fit her out in much finer style, as regards accommodation, than on the privateering trip, and to assemble quite a glittering company to sail in her. No fewer than eighty knights, lairds or sons of lairds were included, and three other ladies besides Mary Stewart — Lady Margaret Forbes, mother of Sir Alexander; the Lady Straiton of Lauriston; and Lady Melville of Glenbervie. There were two chaplains; also a full company of musicians and singers. Even Sir Andrew Stewart, the eldest of Alex's awkward brothers, had been persuaded to come along — more to ensure that he did not get into mischief in the interim than anything else. Mariota de Athyn had declined to take part, saying that she was too old for such cantrips and would stay at home and look after the young Douglases. John of Buchan himself would have liked to have joined the company, but as Lieutenant and Justiciar felt that he could hardly leave the North for so long. No summons by the Council had arrived at Kildrummy before Alex left. Also well before they started he had heard that Donald of the Isles had indeed sailed for Ulster with a large galley fleet, so clearly there was no threat to Scotland meantime.

Although *Greysteel* was well armed with cannon and had a sufficiency of fighting men aboard, they sought no engagements with the English on this journey and were to follow a dog's-leg course which would take them south-eastwards at first, well clear of the English waters before turning south-westwards for Sluys, the port for Bruges. Robert Davidson was acting ship-master again. He was combining the role with that of merchant, in a joint trading venture with Alex which, it was hoped, would help to defray some of the costs of this ambitious project.

Fortunately their voyage proved uneventful and reasonably speedy, with a fair breeze maintaining and no challenges from English shipping. They saw sundry sails, at a distance, but only single ships and none greatly larger than themselves. And the seas were never rough enough to upset the travellers to any degree. Six days after leaving Aberdeen they beat into the West Scheldt estuary, at the head of an inlet of which Sluys lay, on the level Flanders coast, so different from the last upheaved land they had seen. Now, in the estuary there was shipping in plenty, for this was a busy waterway and haven indeed, the port for perhaps the greatest trading centre in Christendom. The low flatness of the land struck them all, with the buildings, churches, houses, windmills, seeming to tower everywhere, the only objects to dominate that strange featureless and all but treeless landscape.

They met with no difficulties in docking and disembarkation, for the Flemings' entire economy was geared to international trade, and foreigners were as common in the streets, wharves and lanes of Sluys as were natives. They continued to use the ship as sleeping quarters whilst arrangements were made for their onward journeying. Horses were hired — over one hundred of them, no less, for riding and pack animals — guide-interpreters engaged, messengers sent ahead to smooth the way and announce the coming of the illustrious Earl of Mar, and so on. Sluys was linked to Bruges by canal, but *Greysteel* was rather too large to use this.

Two days later they moved on to Bruges, the Flemish capital, about ten miles inland, in a quite impressive procession, all in their finest clothing under an array of heraldic banners, Mar, Badenoch, Garioch, Stewart, Forbes, even Douglas, and with their mounted instrumentalists playing stirring music in the rear, the two priests in full canonicals. This was all an exercise in public relations to try to ensure the right reception in Paris eventually.

They did not have to complain about Bruges's reception, at any rate. The Flemings had strong links with Scotland, with many trading colonies settled therein. They were not a warlike people, although sturdy in defence of their own interests, and scarcely looked upon the Scots as allies, as the French did — more as business partners, which perhaps was a sounder and

300

more enduring relationship. They traded with England also, of course — but relations were less happy with that dominant nation which was ever concerned with overlordship, military threats, special terms and the like, and whose privateers took indiscriminate toll of all shipping. It turned out that the Earl of Mar's own naval exploits against *English* shipping the year before had made a great and exaggerated impact upon the Flemings. Bruges now hailed him as hero, sea-warrior and benefactor. The Burgomaster, masters of the merchant guilds, and magistrates came to meet them outside the principal of the seven gates of the city, to make speeches of welcome and to conduct them to the governor's palace — on the way to which the Archbishop of Bruges waited for them outside his great cathedral of St. Sauveur, to give them his blessing and an episcopal stirrup-cup. The visitors were pleasantly surprised.

They were surprised at more than this welcome. Save for Robert Davidson who knew it of old, they had had little idea as to the size, wealth and importance of this Flemish metropolis and centre of the Hanseatic League. It was, they were informed, at this time the largest city in all Christendom, outdoing Paris, London, Rome, Lubeck, Genoa and Venice, and certainly the greatest merchanting centre. There were said to be over two hundred thousand inhabitants, almost one-third of the population of all Scotland. Although the prevailing flatness spoiled it somewhat for the Scots, they could not fail to be impressed by its extent, the richness and variety of its buildings, churches, monasteries, hospices, palaces, towering tenements, cloth-halls, warehouses, market-places and the rest. They were amazed at its network of canals with their innumerable fine bridges — that is what the name Bruges meant — the public statues, the soberly rich dress of much of its population, the notable lack of beggars and all the other signs of long-continued prosperity. It all made Aberdeen, Dundee, Perth, Stirling, Edinburgh seem poor places — save for the scenic qualities of the Scots hills and castle-crowned rocks, their trees and orchards. Although they reckoned that St. Andrews, the Scottish metropolitan see, could probably rival it in the magnificence and number of its ecclesiastical buildings, if not in size.

Outside the huge and ornate cathedral, as Alex bowed his fair head for the Archbishop's benediction, Jamie could not help conjuring up before his mind's eye the scene before that other splendid cathedral at Elgin, Scotland's pride, eighteen years before, in blazing ruin, sacked and set alight by this man's father, a younger Alex torn by dire distress. Like many another, Jamie was apt to forget, in the assured and courteous leader he had become, whence Alex Stewart had sprung and the dramatic background to his upbringing.

In procession they moved on over the bridges to the governor's palace. The government of Flanders, part of the Empire, was in a curious state, for the Count of Flanders, under the Emperor, had died, and his daughter's husband was the French royal prince, Philip de Valois, Duke of Burgundy. He had acted heir to his father-in-law; and dying, his son John the Fearless, Duke of Burgundy, became ruler, although an uncle of the French king, so frequently at war with the Empire. The Duke at present was, it seemed, absent in Paris — indeed he usually was — and his brother, the Lord Anton of Brabant, was deputising for him. He it was who greeted the Scots with a strange mixture of haughtiness and flattery, a curious, pale slight man in his late thirties, overdressed and very slightly deformed, with burning eyes and features which gave the impression that he was racked with pain. However, he handed over a wing of the vast rambling palace, which itself bridged two canals, to the visitors, regretting that he could not entertain them, at such short notice, in the manner to which they were no doubt accustomed; but the Burgomaster and guild leaders would do the honours in the Hotel de Ville, and the next day it would be his pleasure and privilege to offer the hospitality to such close relatives of the King of Scots.

So in due course they all moved across to the Town Hall. But before doing so, Alex came to Mary Stewart and Jamie in their palatial if distinctly gloomy chamber.

"My dear," he said, "tonight I would wish you to act the princess. This Anton of Brabant is clearly a man much concerned with rank and standing. His brother, the Duke, is one of the two most important men in France, highly influential at the French Court — where he is at present. It will be to our advantage to make much of our royal blood, however illegitimate, I think. *I* shall be very much the King's cousin — and you must likewise act the King's aunt — which you are. On what side of the blanket you were conceived is little to the point, in this issue. But it would be best for you to *be* the Princess Mary Stewart. You understand?"

"But I am *not* a princess, Alex!" she protested. "I am Robert the Second's natural daughter, yes — like many another! But I have never looked on myself, or called myself, a princess. The nearest I have come to that was to be maid-of-honour to my sisters Gelis and Isabel — and I am able to be that no longer, being wed to this, this Douglas bastard and outcast here!"

"Nevertheless, Aunt, you will much oblige me by allowing yourself to be treated as your father's daughter whilst on this ploy. A princess of Scotland will, I swear, serve our cause a deal better than just Jamie Douglas's goodwife, however comely!"

"You have depths of deceit in you hitherto unsuspected, Nephew!" she accused. "But — do not overdo it."

In the event they were entertained not in the Hotel de Ville but in an extraordinary composite building nearby called Les Halles — this because there appeared to be no apartment in the former sufficiently large to accommodate all who were to attend the banquet, other than the great council-chamber itself which for some reason could not be got ready in time. Les Halles was a vast square range of building on an island-site, incorporating an enclosed market surrounded by the guild halls which the name implied, some of these of great size. Out of this far-flung extravaganza in stone, of arches, buttresses, crenellations and pinnacles, soared a mighty clock-tower and belfry in three tiers like some enormous wedding-cake, overdecorated and over-whelming, rising to no less than three hundred and fifty-three feet, they were assured, and apparently the pride of Bruges. From it bells jangled in a deafening cacophony to welcome the distinguished guests.

Installed in one of the largest of the halls, that of the Lace-makers' Guild, some four hundred sat down to a feast. It said much for the power, wealth and organising ability of the Bruges burghers that they could, at one day's notice, produce and mount such a repast, lacking nothing in quantity, quality or variety, even if something heavy for a warm evening of May. Mary, addressed by all as Princess, found herself seated at the centre of the topmost table between the Lord Anton of Brabant and the Burgomaster, with Alex at the latter's other side and Jamie well down the board. As the interminable meal pro-gressed, she began to wish that she was safely at her husband's lowly side, for the Lord Anton had a roving hand as well as a burning eye, and she had frequently to discourage its exploratory ventures whilst maintaining a polite conversation on the iniqui-ties of successive Kings of England and the rebellious nature of the lower classes — in which she rather gathered Anton of Brabant included their hosts for the evening.

Unlike Scots banquets, great eating was very much the prime preoccupation here, with drinking — at least at this stage — very secondary, and no distracting entertainment the while. Never had most of the Scots seen such eating, such determined demolition of endless provender, or heard so much slurping, munching, champing and belching.

It was a relief, especially to Mary Stewart, when at length the succession of viands began to tail off and musicians made their appearance, with the advent of serious drinking. Unfortunately the music and the wine had a rousing effect on the Lord Anton, who had been inclining towards the soporific; and presently, in desperation, speaking across the nodding Burgomaster, Mary was urgent in suggesting to Alex that they should volunteer a demonstration of Scots music and dancing, in which they all might take part — in especial herself. Alex was glad to agree, and in the announcements and arrangements, the temporary princess was thankful to escape.

The Scots dancing went down very well, with members of the resident Scots colony in Bruges taking part, inspiring some attempts at emulation — although by no means all the company were in a condition to react positively. Fortunately, the Lord Anton did not feel called upon to take part; fairly clearly he thought it was no way for people of birth and breeding to behave.

When they were finished, Mary would not hear of returning to her place at the table and the further gallantries of the Governor's brother. She insisted on being taken back to their lodging in the palace, in sufficiently royal fashion, and the other Scots ladies were well content to accompany her. She also declared that if Anton of Brabant was himself to give them a banquet the next day, she for one would be indisposed. If this was the price for being a princess, the sooner she reverted to a humbler status the better. Jamie escorted them back to their quarters gladly enough, emphasising to her the pleasures of freedom and foreign travel.

Next forenoon Alex informed the Lord Anton that, grateful as they were for his proposed hospitality, time pressed and it would be advisable for them to be on their way to Paris, still some two hundred miles off. Their host, who appeared to combine an appreciation of economy with that of feminity, made no real protest. The good burghers of Bruges were very much more loth to see the Scots go. Robert Davidson remained behind. He was to negotiate a cargo of Flemish goods and ship it back to Scotland, returning to pick the others up again in ten or twelve weeks' time.

The cavalcade rode southwards over the level lands of Flanders, where every community stood out from the flats abruptly, as though only recently dropped there ready-built — although many of the villages and towns seemed ancient enough at closer inspection. At every sizeable place they passed their musicians played and Alex acted the gracious prince, even bestowing largesse and paying bountifully for their entertainment. Despite what he had said about time pressing to the Lord Anton, they did not hasten — deliberately — for Alex wanted word of their style and repute to reach Paris before them.

Crossing an unending pattern of canals, ditches and meres, by innumerable bridges and causeways, gradually, imperceptibly, the ground rose and dried out beneath them, until eventually they rode on land of sufficient altitude to reveal an actual valley ahead, however shallow and wide, down which a sluggish river coiled and twisted — the Lys, a principal tributary of the Scheldt. This they crossed, and presently came to the upper Scheldt itself, up which they turned, westwards, by Roubaix, Valenciennes and St. Quentin. They put up at abbeys and monasteries each night, being consistently well received. There were great numbers of such religious institutions, which had clearly gathered much of the wealth of the countryside into their hands, many of them having cloth, lace and tapestry weaving manufactories attached.

When they crossed into France from Flanders, at Cambrai, it was remarkable how quickly the entire face and character of land and people changed. Instead of husbandry, manufacture, prosperous towns, field cultivation and drainage, was neglect of land, forest and scrub, swamp, bad roads and everywhere the signs of local warfare. The villages and towns were poor huddles of houses, in the main — but many were the proud castles, châteaux and mansions of counts and barons, something but little seen in the Flemish plains. The abbeys and religious houses were less frequent, but still larger and more splendid. But elsewhere were all the signs of poverty and oppression, beggars abounding, gallows with their rotting fruit at every cross-roads and market-place — in monastery yards likewise. It was much more picturesque country, with much woodland and some undulation to the landscape; but there was a fear and sadness about it not seen hitherto. The peasants scurried into hiding at sight of the cavalcade, instead of thronging and waving; agriculture was wretched and hunting appeared to be the preoccupation of those with leisure.

The Scots began to wonder whether their ancient allies of France were all that they had believed them to be.

Across the Picardy plain they followed the River Ouse to its junction with Seine, still resting at religious houses but on the whole with less satisfaction and at greater expense. The evidences of the internecine warfare which was splitting France, the indiscipline of the nobles and the sheer anarchy which prevailed, began seriously to worry the travellers, not for their own safety — for they made a sufficiently strong company — but for the value of their mission. They had known that King Charles the Sixth was lacking something in his wits and strength — but they had not realised that he was now quite mad, and that the factions of his two cousins, the Dukes of Burgundy and Orleans, with that of the Archbishop of Paris, were at each other's throats and tugging the monarch — or, more important, the Queen — this way and that. They had as guide and interpreter one John Duncan, a member of the quite large Scots trading colony in Bruges, who told them hair-raising stories about French affairs. It became fairly clear why France had proved something of a broken reed as an ally against the English.

They came to the Seine at St. Germain, with only thirteen more miles to Paris. They were still travelling deliberately slowly.

If Alex had expected a similar reception at the French capital to that at Bruges, he was disappointed. He had sent messages ahead, of course; but there was little sign of them having had any effect. No deputation awaited them at the city gates, from Court or municipality, no crowds lined the streets, and even though their musicians played their best, they aroused little more than a passing interest from the citizens — who no doubt were entirely used to nobles' cavalcades parading the town. They gathered a vociferous tail of urchins, and that was about all.

Even apart from the lack of reception, Paris did not impress them, certainly not as Bruges had done. It was, as a whole, dirty, smelly and airless, more like London. There were fine buildings, especially palaces, but many of these were shut up and with an appearance of neglect — and the squalor of the town came right to their doors. There were many great and fine churches and religious houses, the Sainte Chapelle quite lovely, shrine for Christ's alleged Crown of Thorns; but these tended to give the impression that they were scarcely part of the community, turning their backs on the streets, as it were gathering their skirts from contact, the monasteries behind high walls and barred gates like lesser fortresses. There was no lack of inns, hostelries and wine-shops however, in the narrow alleys and lanes, seemingly largely patronised by innumerable bands and groups of men-at-arms in a great variety of lords' colours, many of these drunken and noisy. Beggars, the maimed, loose women — who made their profession notably plain — and yapping dogs abounded.

The Scots' hearts sank. They had come a long way for this.

Since no offer of quarters seemed to be forthcoming from the authorities, Alex was certainly not going to present himself at any palace-door begging for hospitality. With a princely image to maintain, he consulted their guide, seeking some hostelry sufficiently large to accommodate the entire party, and sufficiently near the royal residence of the Louvre to be convenient. Duncan, a dealer in tapestries and wall-hangings, whom they had chosen because he made frequent business visits to Paris, after consideration suggested that they try an establishment in the Ile de la Cité rejoicing in the designation of At the Sign of the Tin Plate, almost under the walls of the cathedral of Notre Dame, which was in fact a former monkish hospice of a serving order where the poor had been given shelter and fed on tin plates. The monks had gone but the name had stuck. Now it was a very large inn, indeed a sort of caravanserai.

They made their way across bridges to this establishment therefore, to the sound of music, yelling boys and barking dogs, and found it in what was almost a town within the city, on an island site, within the precincts of the towering cathedral, in a great bend of the river. It was a sprawling place, somewhat decayed, but with ample accommodation, yards, outbuildings, stables, even an overgrown orchard. The innkeeper was quite overwhelmed by the size of the company and the work involved in catering for them — but his shrewd and businesslike wife was not long in convincing him that all could be managed — and in striking a notable bargain with the visitors. Alex, in pursuance of his chosen role as illustrious envoy, had come prepared to spend money — he had, after all, married one of the richest earldoms in Scotland and had made considerable profits from the privateering expedition — and he agreed to take over the entire hostelry meantime, with suitable servants to be found, food and drink to be provided in abundance, and cost no object. He required for it considerable cleaning-up, however, without delay. A judicious disbursement of silver coinage reinforced his demands, and worked wonders.

The next step was something of a problem. Foreign envoys normally proceeded to present their credentials to the ruler of the state concerned; but they were not official ambassadors and had no letters of introduction to present. Private persons could not just thrust themselves into the presence of a monarch, even a partially mad one, requiring a royal summons — and none such seemed to be forthcoming, as yet. The innkeeper's wife informed them that King and Court were in fact presently at the royal hunting palace of St. Germain-en-Laye — which they had passed nearby — but were due to return to Paris two days hence it was said, to celebrate the Feast of Saint Boniface — Queen Isabella of Bavaria being notably pious. The King, of course, might not come, being much more interested in killing things than in worshipping; but the Queen would — and it seemed that it was the Queen who counted in France now. Or, at least, the Duke of Burgundy and the Orleans faction who sought to influence the Queen.

Alex decided to wait.

The next day the Scots spent finding their feet in Paris. They nearly all spoke French fluently — after all, it was not so long since it was an everyday language for the gentry in Scotland — and they found the common people friendly enough, much more so than in London, although in the main they seemed desperately poor and ragged, with an extraordinary proportion homeless, diseased and deformed. For the rich capital of Christendom's Most Christian King, this seemed strange; but presumably misrule and constant warfare, national and feudal, along with a sort of endemic indiscipline, were responsible. Even Albany's Scotland, by comparison, was beginning to look less shameful.

All this poverty and obvious hunger stirred Alex on to making a gesture, partly politic, partly out of a kind heart. Calling on the city's mayor, he announced that meantime at least the former hospice of the Tin Plate would revert to one of its earlier roles, with food and drink available for all comers, gratis, the poor to be provided for in the stableyard at the rear, open house for the better sort at the front, all at the Earl of Mar's expense. Jamie thought this a wild extravagance, and said so; but his wife reminded him that Alex was a Stewart, and the Stewarts were always notable for large gestures and seldom did things by halves. And it would certainly make his name and fame ring throughout Paris. So the Scots found themselves thrust into the role of caterers, suppliers and general benefactors — and were all but bowled over in the rush. It was amazing how swiftly the word swept Paris and the crowds converged, not all content peaceably to await their turn, either at the back door or the front. Dealers in meats, victuals and wines flocked in on them also. Few gestures could have been calculated so to move the city.

The day following it was confirmed that the Court was indeed returning to the Louvre Palace, and should arrive in mid-afternoon. Leaving the noisy crowds besieging the hostelry for food and drink, the Scots, arrayed at their finest, rode off northwards again.

The metropolitan seat of the French monarchy was an extraordinary establishment by any standards, almost a separate fortified town. It stood nearly a mile down-river from Notre Dame, in many-towered splendour, occupying a vast area of ground within outer and inner baileys and high curtain-walls, the entire many-acred site cut off from the city by a broad moat diverted from the Seine, with an enormous detached gatehouse range at the riverside, itself almost another palace. There were eighteen major towers around the double perimeters, and a legion of lesser ones. Enclosed in all this and flanking many courtyards, was the royal palace itself, but also other buildings by the score, lodgings, government offices, barracks, armouries and the like. Also kitchens, allegedly a round dozen, breweries, bakehouses, laundries, warehouses, blacksmith's forges, even a slaughterhouse. The stables were said to accommodate five hundred horses. So vast an establishment was quite beyond the visitors' experience — indeed it was some considerable time before they were fully aware of its dimensions and ramifications.

This first day they took up their stance on the broad riverside avenue at the north-east corner of the gatehouse range, where the main drawbridge crossed the moat near its junction with the Seine. Here, watched somewhat askance by guards at the bridge-end and tower, but not interfered with, Alex drew up his company in an orderly formation, dismounted meantime, and set the musicians to play. He sent his brother Andrew and two others to keep watch at the approaches beyond their view from the north, to give them warning of the royal arrival — in particular as to whether royalty was accompanied by its own music.

Thus they waited, whilst an admiring throng gathered.

It was some time before Sir Andrew Stewart rode back, to say that a large horsed company was not far off, apparently not accompanied by musicians. He had had to wait until they were fairly close before he could ascertain this last, so they would be in sight very soon. Alex ordered all to remount, and the instrumentalists to redouble their efforts in a rousing marching tune.

An escort of the sovereign's guard, all gleaming armour and tossing plumes, trotted into sight some three hundred yards off, and drew rein at sight of the Scots phalanx, obviously at a loss. Alex rode out a little way to meet them as two of their number came spurring forward.

"What is this?" a haughty officer demanded. "*Parbleu* — who are you to stand in the way of the King of France? His Majesty approaches." He had to shout loudly to make himself heard above the orchestration.

"I am the Earl of Mar, cousin to the King of Scots, sir. With an illustrious Scottish company, including His Grace's aunt, come to greet His Most Christian Majesty of France, our ancient ally," Alex returned.

"Scots? An embassy? But . . . but . . . ?"

"We but seek to bask in the sun of His Majesty's presence for a moment, as he passes to his house, sir. As the humblest citizen of this town may do."

"But . . . this noise, Monsieur le Comte!"

"It is our Scots custom, friend. Music for those we would honour."

The officer looked undecided, glanced back, saw the main royal cavalcade now in view and almost on top of the halted escort and, calling something to his colleague, reined round and rode back at a canter. Alex returned to his former stance at the front of his carefully marshalled company, between Mary Stewart and Lady Forbes, flanked by his brother, Jamie Douglas and Sir Alexander Forbes. The band of fiddles, lutes, flutes, trumpets and cymbals continued to play loudly.

310

The new arrivals came on now, almost warily for so splendid and authoritative a company. The escort, now doubled in size by bringing forward the rearguard also, rode up ahead, to take up protective positions flanking and opposite the Scots. Then the front ranks of the main procession drew level, slowing to a walk, all eyes on the strangers. Foremost were four gorgeously clad riders, three men and a woman. And just behind, in a fine two-horse litter with canopied and heraldic fittings, lounged an extraordinary trio, a middle-aged man dressed all in white, but slovenly, stained white, with sprawling at either side of him a girl and a boy, each perhaps ten years or so of age and both stark naked. Behind rode rank upon rank of men and women, the proudest and fairest in France.

Alex doffed his bonnet with a flourish, and all the Scots bowed from their saddles — and behind them the musicians reduced their notes to the merest background murmur, trumpets and cymbals silent.

"Your Majesties of France and my lord Duke and other lords — most humble and respectful greetings! We hail you in the name of James, High King of Scots. I am Alexander, Earl of Mar and the Garioch, Lord of Badenoch. And here is the Princess Mary Stewart, sister of our late liege lord Robert and aunt to King James. And others of renown from Scotland."

The reaction of the new arrivals was varied. The lady in front, a handsome woman in her late thirties, somewhat massive as to build but upright in carriage and dressed entirely as a man in hunting green, conferred with her magnificent companions. The lounging man, who was scratching in his unusually long and lanky black hair, paid no least attention, whilst the naked children sat up interestedly.

One of the men in front, a florid, well-built man of about Alex's own age, notable for his remarkably heavy eyebrows, spoke.

"Her Majesty is interested to meet the renowned Comte de Mar," he said. "She bids you welcome. Also the Princess." He bowed. "I am John of Burgundy. And this is the Archbishop of Paris and the Comte d'Armagnac." He glanced back over his broad velvet-clad shoulder. "His Most Christian Majesty. We, ah, heard that you were in France, monsieur."

"Yes. We had the honour to be entertained by your brother, the Lord Anton, at Bruges, my lord Duke." Alex bowed again towards the Queen and then the reclining King. This was rather

311

difficult. He could scarcely carry on a conversation with Burgundy in front of the monarch and his consort. "We greatly rejoice to see Your Majesties, and to convey to you the good wishes and greetings of all Scots. But . . . we most certainly would not wish to seem to delay Your Majesties thus in your progress. Only to salute you in passing. You will be wearied with your journey. Perhaps you would be sufficiently gracious as to grant us audience, in due course?"

The older of the two other men with the Queen, stocky, stern-faced, of middle years, dressed wholly in purple and white lace, frowned. "Her Majesty cannot stand thus, waiting," he said, looking sourly at Burgundy. "Madame, let us proceed."

"No haste, Archbishop," the Queen suggested. "Monsieur de Mar and his friends have had the civility to wait upon us. And to provide pleasing music for our ears. Strangers from another land — although renowned. The least we may do is to thank them. And welcome them to Paris." Isabella of Bavaria had a light, lilting and very feminine voice, like a girl's, markedly at variance with her present somewhat masculine appearance — although, the mother of five sons, she was no girl.

"Your Grace is most kind . . ." Alex began, but the third man with the Queen broke in. He was younger than the cleric but slightly older than Burgundy, and brilliantly good-looking, tall, broad-shouldered but slender, with very fair wavy hair and a flashing smile but no hint of weakness about him. He bent in the saddle, to murmur close in the Queen's ear, and then spoke more loudly.

"Her Majesty is ever kind. No doubt she will consider your request favourably, monsieur — at some more convenient occasion." He reined round his horse, as to ride on.

"Not so fast, D'Armagnac," the Duke of Burgundy said, strongly. "You are ever impatient. Her Majesty finds the music pleasing, even if you do not. Because you have no ear for music, there is no reason why we all should be deprived. Perhaps Monsieur de Mar will oblige us with a further rendering of his Scottish airs? I cannot think that Isabella is so wearied after but a mere fifteen-kilometre ride."

Brows raised, the Queen glanced from one to the other. "Peace, you two," she pleaded. "But, yes. If Monsieur le Comte will be so good. Some short piece, from Scotland."

Very much aware of this cross-play, Alex bowed, and waved to his instrumentalists. "*Hey Tuttie Taitie*," he called. This was

Bruce's marching-song at Bannockburn, a tune to stir even the most sluggish blood.

With an admirable minimum of delay the musicians broke into a spirited version of the traditional air. Although the Archbishop frowned and the Count d'Armagnac stared away expressionlessly, most of their hearers appeared to be appreciative. The Queen nodded her head, smiling, and the Duke John beat time vigorously. King Charles seemed to be quite unaffected, and was fondling the naked boy beside him in preoccupied fashion.

After three verses, Alex signed to his people to finish. There was considerable applause, led by Burgundy, who seemingly was requesting an encore. Alex, in some doubt, was looking at the Queen when a loud cackling laugh rang out — and all eyes abruptly switched to Charles de Valois. He had sat up in the litter in a crouching posture and was pointing a shaking finger at Mary Stewart, grinning crazily. He continued to point, gabbling incoherently through his laughter, which sank to a chuckle and then to a mere giggle, Mary seeking not to show her alarm. Then suddenly he changed expression to a fierce glare, and jerking his hand, now pointed forward with a repeated jabbing motion, eloquent enough. Immediately all his company turned to urge their horses into movement, Queen, Duke, Archbishop and Count included — for this was still the Most Christian King, supreme ruler of all France.

"We shall send for you, Monsieur de Mar," Queen Isabella called, as she rode on. And, shrugging and grimacing, John of Burgundy waved to them.

The musicians played the long royal procession past with more of *Hey Tutti Taitie* by way of encore.

As the Scots presently trotted back towards Notre Dame, Jamie asked, "That was a strange business. Are you satisfied with what you achieved? This is going to be no simple mission, I think. If we gain any good here, I shall be much surprised."

Alex shrugged. "We may do better than might appear. The Queen seems well enough disposed. We shall get our audience now. And Burgundy is clearly for us."

"And therefore the Archbishop and that d'Armagnac against us. They sharpen their dirks on each other — that I swear! And pull the Queen between them. This D'Armagnac — how has he so much influence?"

"The Counts of Armagnac have long held powerful sway in

313

Gascony. This one, Bernard, was friend to the Duke of Orleans, whom Burgundy was instrumental in having slain — slain horribly. Indeed, his daughter is wed to Orleans' son, the new Duke — both but children. It is whispered that D'Armagnac was formerly lover of the Queen — as was Orleans. For she is. ... generous! The Count has allied himself with the Archbishop of Paris, who also hates Burgundy. But Burgundy, the King's first cousin, is still the strongest voice at Court, and moreover favoured by the citizens of Paris — which seems to be important. Though the other faction is said to be growing in strength. In matters of state the Queen has to heed him most. She must be much beset."

"Poor woman," Mary put in. "Consider having that king as a husband. I all but swooned with fright when he pointed at me, with his crazed laughter. I vow I shall keep out of his sight hereafter — if I can! And those poor children — the shame of it!"

"For a princess, you are too easily shocked, my dear. Remember that the Lord's Anointed are never to be judged by everyday standards!"

"Nor the Lord's Anointeds' wives, either, apparently!" Jamie added. "From what I have heard, Queen Isabella finds ample compensations for her deranged husband . . . religious or otherwise!"

*　　*　　*

They did not have to wait long for their audience. The very next forenoon a messenger came to the Tin Plate with the Queen's command for the Comte de Mar, the Princess Mary of Scotland and a few of their company to wait upon her that evening after vespers.

When, with his four ladies and half-a-dozen of his lairds, Alex presented himself at the Louvre, it was to discover that Isabella of Bavaria had her own wing of the enormous palace, where she maintained an almost separate establishment. Conducted thither across no fewer than five courtyards, the visitors were brought to a great apartment, a salon rather than a hall since it was unlike any hall they had ever seen, vast, lofty, the walls lined with tall mirrors of polished brass and silver, as well as of glass, interspersed with magnificent tapestries and vivid mural paintings of eye-catching immodesty and religious themes mixed, all illuminated — although it was still bright daylight without — by

314

thousands of candles in huge hanging chandeliers, their light reflected to infinity by all the mirrors. All was set for a great banquet, and many courtiers were already present, chatting, laughing, strolling on the rich Eastern carpets. These eyed the Scots with frank interest as they were led, through a further doorway into an ante-room and there left for a space.

Presently ushers came to announce Her Illustrious Majesty the Queen of France. Isabella entered with a minimum of fuss, accompanied by a splendidly dressed group, which again included the Duke of Burgundy, the Count d'Armagnac and the Archbishop. If the Queen had worn masculine clothing before, now she was sufficiently feminine with a velvet and pearl-sewn gown cut so low as barely to contain her fairly heavy bosom. She moved over to a throne-like chair, but there, instead of sitting, she paused, and seemingly on impulse came forward to the visitors and held out her hand to Alex, who dropped to one knee to kiss it. She raised him up in more than mere token fashion, her generous person very close to him. Then she turned to Mary.

"And this is the Princess? Marie, did I hear? Your cousin, monsieur?"

"My aunt, Majesty. Wife to Sir James Douglas, here."

"*Mon Dieu* — is that possible? Aunt — so young? And so charming!" Isabella leaned forward again to embrace Mary, who was all but smothered.

"Scarce that, Your Grace," she got out. "I have a son of sixteen years! And I am a princess only by courtesy — since my royal father omitted to wed my mother!"

The Queen tinkled a laugh which, like her voice, was a deal more girlish than her appearance warranted, but cheerfully unaffected. "Splendid! You and I are going to be friends, I think, Madame Marie. I like an honest woman."

Alex presented the rest of his party to the Queen, who then returned to her chair and sat, while the Duke John introduced the remainder of the royal group, including two countess ladies-in-waiting, the younger of whom, besides being strikingly beautiful, with odalisque eyes and raven-black hair, was additionally eye-catching through wearing a satin gown, the bodice supported at one shoulder so that the other breast hung free, aureole and nipple painted scarlet. There was no sign nor mention of the King.

"We have heard much of Scotland, our ancient friend and ally in the North, and rejoice to welcome so distinguished a company to the Court of France," Isabella went on, in more formal tones. "We trust that you will much enjoy your stay amongst us. Are you the bearers of letters which I may pass on to my royal husband, who is somewhat indisposed? Or is your visit a private one?"

Alex spread his hands in rather French fashion. "No letters of credence, Majesty. Nor yet our visit entirely private," he said carefully. "We do not come as representing my uncle, the Duke of Albany, Regent of Scotland, since he is in truce and treaty with the King of England. Whereas we are concerned — as of course is he — for the release of our young liege lord King James, shamefully taken on his way to your Majesties' Court here, and held prisoner in London. Such concern has to be expressed in private visit rather than by official embassage."

"I see — and perceive the difficulty. We are all, to be sure, distressed at the situation of King James, and at the sad death of King Robert. But, of course, we too are in truce and treaty with King Henry of England. There is a twenty-eight-year truce, of which fifteen years are still to run. And so we recognise the wisdom of the private nature of your visit."

"Your Grace is understanding . . ."

"Majesty — may I ask Monsieur le Comte a question?" the Archbishop intervened heavily. "If his visit is that of a private citizen of Scotland, should not his concern for the state of the King of Scots be equally private, and not voiced thus openly to Your Majesty? Since it affects the relations between the states of France, England and Scotland?"

"What say you to that, Monsieur de Mar?" the Queen asked.

"Forgive me if I mistake, Highness, or unknowingly trespass upon your French usage. But I would have thought that a cousin of an unlawfully imprisoned boy, monarch though he is, might legitimately, indeed suitably, express his concern in public or private — and especially before the royal lady to whose house and care he was bound when piratically captured?"

"Well said, monsieur!" Burgundy cried.

"How say you to that, my lord Archbishop?" Isabella asked mildly. "Does it not sound reasonable?"

"So long as he does not seek to embroil Your Majesty in activities to which King Henry could take exception," the prelate declared flatly.

"God's Blood! Would you have the Crown of France seeking

316

the permission of Henry Plantagenet for what it may or may not say or do?" John de Valois exclaimed.

"Not so, my lord Duke. Only to observe the proper and accepted procedures between sovereign nations. It is my simple duty to remind Her Majesty, and all others, of this."

"His Beatitude has the rights of it," Bernard D'Armagnac put in, but in a lighter tone, and with a faint smile on his handsome features. "Private views should be kept private and private visits eschew public policies. But let us not mar a pleasant occasion, with Monsieur de Mar and the Madame Marie!" And he waved a hand to emphasise his stress of the first syllable of that last name.

The loud laughter helped to dissipate the tense atmosphere which had developed. And Isabella further added to this, by saying, "You will perceive, Monsieur le Comte, how well I am advised and guided, on all hands! But enough of this, for the moment. We hope that you had an untroubled journey? Clearly you were more fortunate, on the sea, than your royal cousin James! If the good Archbishop will permit such comment."

Again the laughter.

"We came well prepared, Highness," Alex answered genially. "Having, as it were, spied out the land, or the ocean, a year previously!"

"Ah, yes. We heard of that, monsieur. A notable . . . excursion!"

"A gesture, Majesty. We made sure that no French ships suffered, nor Flemish either, my lord Duke." As Alex said it, Jamie Douglas hoped devoutly that none of the Islesmen's unspecified targets had been French or Flemish.

"Piracy at sea is no matter to laugh over, monsieur," the Archbishop observed severely.

"No, sir. I agree. But privateering is rather different, is it not? We had letters of mark, you understand? And operated only against English east coast shipping. Since it was from thence that our liege lord had been attacked. Our object to bring King Henry to release King James. Which he has not done, unfortunately."

"On a *private* visit, Monsieur Priest, should you be pronouncing upon the Scots policy of privateering?" Burgundy demanded.

There was mixed laughter and frowns at that sally.

Again D'Armagnac intervened. "Our Scots friends' progress here has aroused much admiration, we have heard. Monsieur de

Mar has been . . . open-handed. Much liberality and distribution of largesse. Even now he holds open house here in Paris, I am told. For good reason, no doubt?" Despite the smile, there was no hiding the barb in that question.

"To be sure, my lord," Alex nodded, "I took much wealth from the English ships. Not on my own behalf. To distribute some of it to your humbler compatriots, while we are pilgrims in France, seemed only suitable. Many, it seemed, could do with it! You do not object?"

A titter of amusement greeted that.

"Ah, no. No, monsieur — but so much liberality might be expected to have a purpose?"

"It has. I seek goodwill, in this fair France. Their Majesties', yours, that of all present here. A little liberality may help, with the humble. For those more illustrious, I can only proffer my unworthy self. And, to be sure, the excellencies and charms of the Princess and others of our company."

"Good! Spoken like a proper man! Bernard, you are answered." The Queen rose. "But enough of this talk. Come, Monsieur de Mar — you will escort me to the table." And she held out a quite formidable arm.

As Alex hurried forward to take that arm, the Duke of Burgundy stepped over, to bow to Mary and offer her his. Others of the royal party, male and female, selected partners — and Jamie, to his embarrassment, found the younger Countess with the exposed bosom choosing himself, presumably finding his sombre and rugged good looks to her taste. She placed herself on his right, taking his arm enthusiastically, so that when they moved off after the more illustrious pairs, the man was all too vividly aware of the warm, bare and shapely breast which brushed and quivered against his wrist in time with the lady's animated talk. She had to sustain the burden of the conversation, it is to be feared. Jamie's wife, on the other hand, further forward, was almost equally perturbed lest the Duke of Burgundy should come to display social behaviour similar to that of his brother, the Lord Anton of Brabant.

The royal column moved into the great salon amidst general bowing and curtsying, to take seats at the top table. There was no dais here, as in a castle's hall, but the Queen's table ran transversely across the apartment, at considerable length, whilst the others were placed lengthwise. Mary found herself on Isabella's left, with the Duke at her other side. This she found reassuring — for surely Burgundy would scarcely engage in any embarrassing exploration which would be obvious to the Queen. Alex was on the royal right. Jamie, considerably further down the table, for his part found some relief also, in that he perceived that the Countess Eloise was not quite so kenspeckle as he had supposed — for the company was now seen to contain quite a number of bare breasts, some indeed in pairs; and even when not actually fully displayed, most bosoms were apt to be distinctly evident, owing to the fashion of bodices being open down the front and laced up criss-cross, seldom tightly or with any infilling. He felt considerably better for this recognition, and in fact began to acknowledge a more healthy appreciation of his companion's various endowments.

The repast which followed was such as none of the Scots had ever previously experienced, in scale and magnitude, sumptuous assortment, exotic variety and ingenious presentation. Courses came and went, over a score of them, in bewildering profusion, cooked in every conceivable fashion, garnished and supported with every extravagance to titillate the palate and the eye, hot and cold, delicacies, savouries, fish and shell-fish, fowl, game, red meats, confections and dainties. There might be starvation in the wake of war in much of France, but there was no hint of it here.

The Queen appeared to have a hearty appetite, and advised Alex as to what he should try and what not, very much as a man might do. She did not neglect Mary either, and was indeed notably friendly; but she concentrated her attention upon Alex.

"What is your name, monsieur?" she asked, presently. "I cannot continue to call you that, if we are to be honoured with your presence."

"My friends call me Alex, Highness. I am Alexander Stewart, knight, at your service."

"Then Alex you shall be. You have not brought a wife with you?"

"My wife died a year past. She also was named Isobel."

"Ah. And you were desolated?"

"I was much saddened, Highness. It was through her that I gained the earldom of Mar. She was a woman of much spirit."

"I see. You did not inherit the earldom, then, from your father?"

"He was Earl of Buchan, King Robert the Second's third surviving son. He had no lawful children — and I was his eldest bastard. From him I got the lordship of Badenoch."

"So! You Stewarts are clearly a virile race, Alex! Which of

319

the ladies you have brought with you is your mistress? Not your aunt, here?"

"None of them, Majesty."

"None? And you widowered for a year? Here is a strange state of affairs. Do not tell me that you are one who prefers men to women? You, with those eyes and that way with you!"

"No, Highness. I find women very much to my taste. In especial, strong women! Rather than dainty misses and simpering girls."

"Ah!" The Queen moved distinctly closer, her ample charms prominent. "When we are speaking together thus near, Alex, call me Lady Isabella. It is less stiff, is it not? We shall have to find you a strong woman, then, shall we not? Of . . . experience!"

"I am in Your Majesty's capable hands!" he said, mildly.

Smiling, Isabella turned to speak with Mary — who was finding the Duke of Burgundy little trouble, a determined trencherman rather than an amorist evidently. Alex turned to the Count d'Armagnac, on his other side.

"You seemed concerned, my lord, that I should be offering liberality to the poor," he said. "I should be interested to hear why."

"Tell me, monsieur, why you do it — and I will tell you why I am concerned," the other answered.

"It is simple enough. I am here to seek French aid in the Scots' struggle to gain the release of our young King. But I am not here as a beggar. Scotland has much to offer France, as closer ally and also in trade. On the seas, especially. So, I demonstrate that we are no beggars. No more than that."

The Gascon looked at him keenly. "You are either very frank, monsieur — or very cunning!"

"I have no reason not to be frank. Our mission, although not official, is open for all to know. And I have no other concern or ambition here — save friendship with the French monarchy and people." Alex paused. "Now, my lord — *you* tell me why you are concerned at the alms-giving."

D'Armagnac took his time about answering. "The situation here in France is . . . delicate," he said, at length. "As you must know. The country is split in two great factions — Orleans and Burgundy. King Charles is . . . handicapped. I shall not speak at length on our differences. But they are deep, the more so since Louis of Orleans was murdered. I am of the Orleans persuasion, my daughter married to the young Duke."

"And this, my lord, is affected by the Scots liberality to the poor?"

"It could be, monsieur. In the north and east of France, Burgundy is most powerful; in the south and west, Orleans. In any question of power in France, Paris is ever important. Burgundy makes friends of the people here, woos them shamefully — the guilds, the merchants, the Lombards, even the Jews. And you — you come here from Flanders, Bruges, which he rules, distributing largesse to the people also."

"I see," Alex said slowly. "So you believe that I do this on the Duke's behalf? Or, at least, to gain his aid and support?"

"Why, yes. And he appears to favour you, monsieur."

"I had hoped that you *all* might favour me, favour my mission. May I assure you, my lord, that I have no least enmity against Orleans and its cause? Indeed, I do not understand your differences with Burgundy."

"I am glad to hear it, monsieur. May it continue. But . . . let me warn you against too great friendship with John of Burgundy. Me, I would prefer that one as enemy rather than friend. As he is! For he is dangerous, a man of blood. Do not trust him."

Alex toyed with his swan's leg, seethed in wine. "I have heard well of him, my lord. Is he not John the Fearless, who led a Crusade against the Infidel some years ago? A noted general."

"An incompetent general! And coward. Fearless for other men's lives! That Crusade of 1396 was a disaster. His whole army captured, almost without a blow struck. Did you know that the Sultan Bajayet had ten thousand Frenchmen and Flemings decapitated before Burgundy's eyes — ten thousand! At Nicopolis. Yet Fearless John returned to France unharmed!"

Alex swallowed — and was grateful that the Queen was once again turning to him.

"Your delightful aunt tells me that you are a musician, Monsieur Alex. A noted performer on the lute, likewise a poet. I am the more intrigued."

"My delightful aunt should hold to stricter truth, Lady Isabella! I strum a lute on occasion, yes — but feebly. As for my rhyming, it is but heavy stuff, uncouth versifying . . ."

"That I shall believe when I hear it. You shall write a song, for myself, and sing it to me, with your lute. Then we shall see who is the liar, your aunt or *you*, my friend! And that is a royal command." She lowered her voice huskily. "What has Bernard been telling you so seriously?"

"He, er, spoke of France's difficulties. Between the houses of Burgundy and Orleans. I fear that I am very ignorant."

"No doubt. And difficulties there are, the good God knows! But — do not believe all that Bernard tells you. He is a good soul. But on Burgundy he is scarcely to be trusted." She shrugged those fine white shoulders so near to his own. "For that matter, my friend, do not believe all that John of Burgundy tells you either. Of Bernard or of Orleans. If you are wise, Alex, you will heed all — but believe only *me*!"

"Ah! And wisdom, Highness, is enforced on us by Holy Writ, is it not . . .?"

Alex was interrupted by a commotion at the far end of the salon. Men were pushing back their chairs and benches and rising to their feet, some women curtsying, everywhere people turning to look.

"So!" the Queen observed. "His Serene Majesty!" She laid a hand on Alex's arm. "No need to rise yet."

The odd figure of the Most Christian King took some time to appear from behind the standing guests, for he was making what might be termed a halting progress. Charles de Valois was quite alone, and moving along between the tables, pausing here and there to stare, to grin or frown, to stroke or fondle or slap, apparently indiscriminately, to take food from this platter or that, sometimes to sample, sometimes to throw away. After he had passed them, men and women sat down — although sometimes they had to rise again, for the monarch was just as apt to turn back as go forward. Once he grabbed somebody's goblet, drank a little, grimaced, spat out the mouthful, threw the half-empty goblet to the floor, and swinging round abruptly struck its owner across the face before lurching on.

"A pity," the Queen murmured. "Wine is good for him — it sends him to sleep! But he does not greatly like it, usually. Fear nothing, Alex — there is little real harm in him. He has returned to being a child, that is all. Although, even so, he can be acute still. Rise only if he comes near."

The Queen's 'if' rather than 'when' was revealed to be valid when presently her husband, pausing beside an overdressed gallant, suddenly pushed the young man roughly aside and sat down in his chair, turning to pull down beside him his curtsying partner. This lady was under- rather than overdressed, in the same fashion as Jamie's Countess Eloise, with particularly thrusting and pointed breasts, one of which projected proudly independent, ringed in red paint. This the King began to play with enthusiastically, and quickly leaned over to wrench the bodice off the other shoulder, to reveal and compare its partner, the lady simpering but not unhelpful. Charles himself was scarcely overdressed, wearing stained white satin breeches with an old and tarnished military style long tunic, fastened askew.

"Good," Isabella commented. "He will be content for a little. If she will ply him with wine, all will be well."

The lady's escort discreetly removed himself elsewhere.

For once Alex was at a loss for suitable and courteous words. "Your Highness is . . . very understanding," was the best that he could do.

"My Highness has to be," she answered. "But we do none so ill. France has greater problems than Charles de Valois!"

The meal went on, with its interminable succession of courses, now mainly sweetmeats and most elaborate sculpted confections, the King spooning up a bowl of mixed fruits in honey in between fondling, squeezing and even sucking at his chosen partner, a sticky proceeding.

"Charles by no means always honours us," the Queen explained. "He has his own apartments and company. Peculiar company, as you may guess! He may well have left his own banquet to come here. Who knows why? And may return."

In France, evidently, as in Flanders, the entertainment took place after the repast was over, not throughout as it was apt to do in Scotland. And here it was not dancers, jugglers, fiddlers, performing bears or cavorting gipsies, but troubadours, wholly — or approximately — masculine, who sang stylised love-songs, soulful, sad or passionate, often to their own accompaniment on the lute, sometimes in close company of good-looking youths, with gestures romantic and semi-dramatic. Most of the performers were themselves courtiers, members of the dining company, not all unaffected by wine. It was a new experience for the Scots — who tended to find it slightly embarrassing and insufficiently robust.

Apparently King Charles was not a troubadour enthusiast either, for quite quickly he seemed to have had enough, and tiring of the lady's mammary delights and honeyed fruits both, got up to resume his perambulations — occasioning again considerable up-rising and sitting down. This time, after a wandering start, he came directly to the Queen's table — and all save Isabella herself rose to greet him. Charles ignored their bows

323

and curtsies, his strange dark eyes fixed on Mary Stewart. Moving round the end of the long table, he came straight for her, with his odd stumpy walk.

Mary was no shrinking maid; but she tensed nevertheless as Majesty came up, her curtsy sketchy, her glance wary. Further down the table, Jamie Douglas had clenched his fists, his brow blacker than ever. Alex watched them all, carefully.

Charles stood beside Mary, chuckling, face close to her's. He reached out a not overclean hand — and hooted as involuntarily she started back. The hand went up to her head. She was not wearing the tall steeple-like headdress nor the lace-hung horns sported by many present, but was bareheaded save for a scatter of Tay pearls threaded on gossamer silk, as a sort of coif. The King stroked her hair, fingering the pearls.

As the hand strayed down towards the bare neck and throat, and Mary's smile grew fixed, Jamie stood back from his chair abruptly — despite the Countess Eloise's restraining hand on his arm. Up the table, Alex coughed warningly, and bowing to the still-seated Queen, moved behind her to the King's side, and Mary's.

"Sire," he said genially, "are not these pearls pleasing? Their colours? They grow only in one of our Scottish rivers. My aunt, the Princess, would perhaps present them to Your Majesty — as a token of our great esteem."

Mary's hands were up to disentangle the gossamer net of pearls from her hair before ever Alex had finished speaking, to thrust it at the monarch eagerly.

Charles took it with alacrity, holding the delicate thing up so that the pearls caught and reflected the light from the chandeliers, turning them this way and that to reveal the colours so much more pronounced than in normal pearls. He made a sort of crooning noise, his delight evident. Then he tried to put the net over his own lanky hair — but of course could not see it there, and snatched it off again.

"With your permission, Sire, allow me," Alex said. And taking the coif, held it against the straggling and honey-soaked royal beard, with most of the network hanging down the front of the stained tunic.

This seemed to please; but unfortunately there was no obvious way of keeping the thing in position. Mary solved the problem by reaching up again and extracting two slender bone pins, stained so as to be all but invisible in her own hair, used for keeping the coif in place. She handed them to Alex. Showing them to the King, deftly he affixed the net to the beard, smoothing the rest to hang like a cravat, so that Charles could look down and admire it. Intrigued, the Most Christian King stroked and chortled.

Greatly bold, Alex took the preoccupied monarch and manoeuvred him to his own chair beside Isabella — who aided by ecstatically admiring her husband's new acquisition. Mary forgotten, Charles sat down happily.

With all seating themselves again, Alex would have moved away to find a seat elsewhere, but the King reached out to grasp his arm, continuing to hold it. Then, with the other hand grabbing Alex's goblet from the table, he gulped a mouthful before holding it up for his benefactor to drink likewise. Still he clung to his arm.

So Alex remained standing at the royal side, drinking draught for draught, with servitors hurrying to refill the goblet. The troubadours resumed their entertainment.

Presently, as Isabella had foretold, the wine sent her royal spouse to sleep. And once asleep, it seemed, he remained asleep. At the Queen's command, he was carried off to his own quarters, snoring.

In the commotion this entailed the Scots took the opportunity to request permission to retire. This was graciously granted — save for one reservation. Isabella insisted that Alex Stewart remained behind, at her side. He would be escorted back to the Tin Plate in due course. The night apparently was yet young.

Bowing their way out, Mary murmured to her husband. "I think that Alex will require to defend *himself* against royal favours hereafter! Believe you he will be so instant on his own behalf as he was on mine?"

"Perhaps not. He admires older women, with minds of their own. But — thank God he dealt with that Charles as he did, back there! Another moment and I would have been taking a hand. And less . . . delicately! *Lèse majesté* or none."

"Yes, I feared that — what fear I had to spare! You might have been locked in some cell by now. And I also — for I could not have borne his handling."

"Aye. God — and Alex — preserve us from a mad king!"

"Amen! At least, Jamie, my curious half-brother Robert does not behave so!"

Her husband grunted.

XIX

So STARTED A stay in Paris of almost twelve weeks. The
duration of their visit had been undetermined from the first,
dependent upon various factors. Most important of course
was the achieving of results, the object of the mission, the gaining
of aid towards the release of young King James. In the peculiar
governmental state in which they found France this was obviously not easy of attainment. Had King Charles been entirely
insane it might have been simpler, in that the rule would then
have been taken right out of his hands and exercised either by a
regent or a council of State. But though mad in some respects,
reverting to infantile and fatuous ways much of the time, he
had periods of comparative lucidity if not normality, even a kind
of cunning and shrewdness — and he had, after all, been quite
a good and able monarch prior to his mental collapse, popular
enough with his people to have gained the title of Charles the
Well Beloved. He still ruled his country after an erratic fashion,
pulled this way and that by competing interests, his wife, the
Church, and the Burgundian and Orleans factions. All these
Alex sought to influence, with varying success—although he made
little progress with the churchmen. But in the nature of things,
any real decision, or even consideration, was hard to
attain.

Another factor affecting the length of their stay was the news
from Scotland. Alex had arranged, as far as was possible, for a
relay of messages to reach him, via Aberdeen vessels trading
with the Low Countries; and fairly regular information did
arrive by this means. There was no permanent Scots ambassador
to the Court of France, meantime, the system being to send
special envoys as required; but there was considerable coming
and going of churchmen to and from Avignon — where Pope
Benedict the Thirteenth, recognised by both Scotland and

France, was established, in opposition to Pope Gregory the Twelfth at Rome — and these were a further source of information. From both sources they learned much of interest. First and most important, that the Privy Council had had to defer consideration and decision on the earldom of Mar, in the Earl's absence — postponed until September. That the Earl John of Buchan had become betrothed to the young Elizabeth, daughter of the Earl of Douglas — clearly a match of policy since the child was only nine years old. On the same theme, the said Earl of Douglas had finally broken his parole with King Henry, refusing to return to captivity in England, and sending instead a ransom reputed to be of fifty thousand merks, presumably the value he set upon himself — Henry's reaction not specified. Douglas had declared that he could not possibly leave Scotland whilst his old enemy and rival, the turncoat Earl of Dunbar and March, was welcomed back by the Regent. Yet the same Douglas was reported to have entered into a mutual support bond with Albany, and been given Dunbar's great lordship of Annandale in return. In the light of all this, the betrothal of his daughter to Albany's son John might have especial significance. Other news was that the Regent's nephew, Donald of the Isles, was said to be involved in heavy fighting in Ireland, with fair success but objectives unclear.

All this, although interesting, did not add up to any urgent requirement for Alex to return home; indeed, clearly any return before the autumn's meeting of the Council was inadvisable. But there was another factor to be taken into account regarding the length of their stay, and that was money. Alex did not want to draw in his horns, seem to tarnish the princely image he had been at such pains to build up, by any evident economies. But maintaining the large company and keeping up open house at the Sign of the Tin Plate, was digging deeper and deeper into even the large funds he had brought. And siller, or the lack of it, might eventually cut short their visit — however galling this might be in the midst of all the wealth and extravagance of the French Court.

Meantime, however, the situation was not without achievements and gains. Alex's success with the Queen, perhaps was not to be wondered at, good-looking, personable and attractive to women as he was. But his impact on the King was scarcely to be expected. Nevertheless, from that incident of Mary Stewart's pearled coif onwards, he became a favourite of the curious

327

monarch, embarrassingly so. The very next day he received a command to attend on the King, and thereafter had difficulty in escaping. Charles found him understanding, patient and companionable — though courteously firm when the monarch became too indecent or outrageous, and surprisingly was then usually heeded. Isabella, indeed, rather ruefully admitted that he had a better influence on her husband than had any other at Court, herself included. And fairly clearly Charles tended to be on his best behaviour when Alex was present — which was all too often for the latter's comfort. The King had a besetting fear of being poisoned, not unnatural perhaps considering what had happened to so many of his family, which was one reason for his habit of drinking from other people's wine-cups and eating from their plates; and he appointed Alex to be an extra Cup Bearer, requiring him to stand or sit at his side at meals, when he frequently fed him tid-bits once they had been duly passed as edible by his new friend. Fortunately Charles slept a great deal, otherwise Alex's life would have been restricted to the point of desperation; his abnormality seemed to tire him excessively, and not only wine made him sleepy. Once his eyes were closed he was apt to sleep for hours, like a child, scarcely wakenable — as often as not now clutching the pearled coif.

At least, Alex felt, if he could persuade others to help with King James, King Charles would not withhold royal permission.

His endeavours to convince the real rulers of France were only partially successful. The Queen was fairly sympathetic but played him along, emphasising the divided state of the country, the inadvisability of foreign adventures at present, the dangers of English reprisals. The Duke of Burgundy was encouraging but vague, indicating general agreement but never committing himself to actual plans. Count d'Armagnac temporised and showed no enthusiasm. And the Archbishop was consistently hostile. All dreaded the English power, clearly, with Henry still claiming much of France as his own, despite the extended truce. The divided country was in no state to take on an aggressive Plantagenet.

It was during one of their many forenoon discussions of this intractable problem at the Tin Plate — Alex being apt to be elsewhere of an evening and night — that Jamie Douglas mooted a new approach.

"I was speaking with a captain of the King's Scots Archer Guard. He told me that some years ago he took part in a French expedition to aid Owen Glendower's rising against the English.

They landed in Wales and fought with the Welsh for two months, winning as far as Worcester. Glendower was defeated, to be sure, and the French returned home. But — it gave me a notion . . ."

"Wales? I fear that horse is dead, Jamie . . ."

"Not Wales — Ireland. See you, the French would *like* to strike against the English, for they know that Henry intends to attack France sooner of later. But they dare not mount an invasion of England. You will never get that, Alex — or even the threat of it. But Ireland, now — that might be a different story. Ireland is the weakest link in England's chain, ever in revolt, a quagmire for English blood and treasure. A French expedition to Ireland could be a grievous threat to Henry. Yet a deal less costly than any attack on England itself."

"True. True — but Henry would conceive it as such, and retaliate in the same fashion."

"I think not. For one thing, as we learned in London, the English nobles are weary of fighting in Irish bogs, where they gain nothing and lose much. But, more important, it could be made to seem no attack on the *English* themselves. But aid for the Irish against Donald of the Isles! Donald is laying waste in the North, we hear — no doubt at Henry's behest, as part of the price to gain English aid for his later attempt for the Scots throne. But meantime it is but an Islesmen's invasion of Ulster. O'Neill, or other of the Irish kinglets, could appeal to France for aid — or be said to have done so. A French force could land in the North of Ireland — and not, on the face of it, seem to be aimed at England at all. Though Henry would not fail to see the threat. But his nobles would not feel bound to act. And this would suit Scotland very well, would it not? Keeping Donald engaged in Ireland, instead of troubling us."

"Dear God, Jamie — you are right! That black head of yours is shrewdly set. This is something to work on. We might persuade the French to *this*. A limited endeavour, not costly — but a major threat to Henry nevertheless. And Donald given pause in his ambitions. Yes, I like that. If only . . . if only my siller will last out, whilst I seek persuade them! My purse is running low. These Paris burghers have vast bellies! Keeping them filled costs more than I had bargained for."

"Need you continue with this expense, man? This keeping of open house here? It has served its turn. You are close to the King — if not closer to the Queen!"

"No. I would not wish to stop this liberality, Jamie. It has paid us well, got us where we are, proved that we are not beggars. It has enabled me to ask aid, openly, as a prince would. Lacking any mandate from the Scots Regent and Council, I require to make such gestures. To stop them now would be unfortunate, much commented on. It might cost our cause dear."

Mary, who had been listening to all this, spoke up. "I know naught of statecraft and war, of how to persuade the French to aid you in that," she said. "But in another way, I think, they might do so. John of Burgundy tells me how besotted they all are here with tourneys and displays of knightly prowess. The other side of this languishing troubadour nonsense. The King, in especial, dotes on such contests. Burgundy says that Charles offers goblets of gold pieces to the winners of bouts, on occasion. You, Alex, are proficent at this, I believe? And have the King's ear. You can scarce ask him for money, but you might *win* it."

"Ah!" that man said thoughtfully.

"You unhorsed the English Earl of Kent, did you not? Something of a champion, was he not? Would these Frenchmen prove more difficult?"

"M'mm. I cannot seem to fight for money, Mary. I would have to have a reason for jousting. To challenge or be challenged. Dispute for a lady's favours would serve. But . . . I can scarce choose any other than the Queen, in this present pass. And I could by no means challenge any openly for *her* favours! And, too, I wish to make no enemies here, while our business is unresolved."

"A pity that Holy Church does not go in for jousting!" Jamie observed. "That Archbishop has been against us from the first. No risk of making a new enemy there. You will just have to seek opportunity to make a challenge, Alex. That D'Armagnac should not prove difficult!"

"No. I must not offend the Orleans party any more than the Burgundian. The Italians, now, are scarcely popular — over this Papal dispute. Perhaps I could find a Lombard to fight, or a Florentine. Or for that matter a Castillian. But . . . he would have to be a man of repute in arms . . ."

In fact, this aspect of the problem solved itself only two days later. The Queen announced to Alex that an envoy had arrived from England, the Earl of Warwick, on a mission concerned with Henry's claim to the revenues of the duchy of Aquitaine — an unpopular subject, naturally. He would be given an official audience the next evening. She suggested that some of the Scots might be interested to attend. The usual banquet would follow.

So Alex and some of his party joined the splendidly-dressed throng waiting in the Throne Room of the Louvre the next afternoon, to see how an *official* ambassador was received. The royal couple came in, to the usual flourish of trumpets, flanked by the Archer Guard, Charles finely clad for once but eating an apple, Isabella's arm firmly tucked through his. They seated themselves on the two thrones on the low dais — although the King almost immediately got to his feet again, to peer around him. Mary Stewart involuntarily drew in behind her husband.

Then, after a pause, another door was thrown open and a herald announced the presence of the most illustrious Monsieur Henry Beauchamp, Comte de Warwick — he pronounced it Vark — Envoy Extraordinary of the King of England, seeking audience of His Most Christian Majesty. Long live the King!

Warwick stalked into the Throne Room, escorted by two more Archers, bowed stiffly, advanced three more steps, bowed again, and advanced to near the dais. He was a heavily-made man of early middle age, clean-shaven, square-featured, indeed square-built altogether, with a stumping short-legged walk. He had a reputation as a soldier and looked the part, with a distinctly aggressive mien and determined mouth. He looked in little doubt, likewise, as to the unpopularity of his mission. Charles sat down and eyed him somewhat askance, spitting apple-skin on the floor.

From behind the thrones the Archbishop, who was acting Chancellor, spoke. "His Most Christian Majesty graciously welcomes your lordship to his Court. And would scrutinise your mandate from his royal cousin, Henry of England."

Warwick nodded, stepped closer, drawing from his doublet a heavily-sealed roll of parchment, and making a gesture of dropping on one knee, held this out to Charles.

"With this, Highness, I bring warm and cordial greetings from my lord King Henry," he jerked. He spoke clipped but clear French — for he had spent years of exile in France, with Henry, when the latter was Earl of Derby and banished from Richard the Second's England.

Charles found the great seal of interest, peering at both sides of it. But he did not unroll the parchment. Nor did he say anything.

The Archbishop came forward to take the roll. But frowning, the King clung to the seal, and at a tug the two parted company.

331

Coughing, the prelate drew back, and unfolding the document, commenced to read its contents aloud. It was in fair French, to the effect that Henry, by the Grace of God King of England, High King of Ireland, Prince of Wales, Lord Paramount of Scotland, Duke of Aquitaine, warmly greeted . . . and so on.

Charles quickly wearied of this, and rising to his feet the better to scan the company, soon identified Alex Stewart. Grinning happily, he stepped down from the dais, brushing past Warwick without a glance, and hurried to Alex's side, England's seal held out to show him. Isabella raised resigned shoulders, the courtiers, used to this sort of thing, merely smiled discreetly, and the Archbishop went on reading the credentials. But the Earl of Warwick frowned darkly, toe tapping on the tiled floor.

Alex made a point of examining the beeswax seal at much length, to give the prelate time to finish, Charles pointing out details. But it was a particularly long-winded document of introduction, concerned to make it entirely clear that in sending this eminent envoy to negotiate payment of his Aquitanian revenues, Henry was in no way admitting or conceding His Majesty of France's lawful superiority, rights or concern in the matter, Aquitaine being a Plantagenet fief, independent of the Crown of France.

Charles de Valois was not long in having enough of this also. Taking Alex's arm, he turned and pushed through the bowing throng, for the door. Sighing, the Queen rose, held out her arm to the affronted ambassador, and followed her lord. The Archers hurried to take up some sort of position, theirs a difficult and unpredictable task.

The King made for another huge salon, even larger than that in which the Scots' first banquet had been held, all set for the feasting, with servitors waiting. All but dragging Alex, he went directly to his place at the centre of the top table, and sitting down clapped his hands for service to commence. He pointed for Alex to take the seat at his right; but that man carefully stood back.

The Queen came up, with a glowering Warwick, and took her chair, two to the right of her husband, and indicated for the Englishman to take the seat between — the same to which Charles had gestured Alex.

Warwick sat down and Alex remained behind the King's chair.

Charles looked up at his friend, and then glared at the envoy. Leaning over, he pushed at Warwick, telling him to be gone in no uncertain terms.

332

Urgently the Queen spoke. "Charles — this is where King Henry's representative *should* sit, at this audience banquet. Alex may sit at your other side. Or here, next me."

The King scowled.

Alex bent to his ear. "Sire — I would prefer to stand here. At your back. To serve you the better. I can see better that all is well."

Charles stared from him to Warwick, made a face at the latter, and then pulled the Scot forward so as to place him, standing, between the two chairs. Thus he hid the Englishman — to whom he had clearly taken a powerful dislike — from his sight.

So the repast proceeded, Alex plying Charles with food and drink, eating and drinking little himself, ignored by Warwick, frequently smiled at by Isabella.

In due course the King fell asleep and was carried off, as usual. Alex was able to sit down in the vacated chair, Warwick pointedly turning a square shoulder towards him.

Presently, with the time for the entertainment arrived, at the Queen's command, Alex led off by rendering, troubadour fashion, the song he had composed about Isabella:

> One thousand three hundred and four-score year
>> After the birth of our Lord dear,
>> The dark Ysabel of Danubius' banks
>> Was matched to the heir of all the Franks;
> A child of wit and elegance,
>> At the age of twelve she came to France;
> Like an alpine rose of high Bavaire
>> She bloomed anew in a lowland fair;
> Changing Danubius' banks for Seine,
>> To live and love and charm and reign . . .

And so on, pedestrian stuff enough but redeemed by flashes of humour, drollery and eloquent expression, the man accompanying himself on the lute. He had a fine tenor voice, and if he sang with less than the usual languishing sentimentality, he made up for it by his allusions, extravagances and near-comic postures, whilst always skilfully remaining the Queen's worshipful gallant. He soon had his hearers laughing delightedly, Isabella most of all. He was rewarded with much applause, a warm royal embrace and powerful kiss, on his return to his place.

The plaudits were not joined in by Henry Beauchamp, however. Continuing to ignore his neighbour until a break in the proceedings, preparatory to a change over to dancing, allowed him decently to seek and obtain the Queen's permission to retire, he turned at last to Alex.

"You, sir, are, I understand, the notorious freebooter, Earl of Mar so-called, who has been pirating our English shipping and attacking King Henry's interests?" That was bluntly said.

"Say privateering, my lord," Alex answered, as lightly as he might. "It scarcely becomes your good King Henry to complain of pirating, moreover, after his waylaying, capture and imprisonment of the King of Scots. But . . . perhaps we might discuss this elsewhere, at another time?"

"That boy, sir, is safer in the Tower, as you know well, than in his own barbarous realm. And I hope that I may be spared any further discussion with you at any other time."

"You have my sympathy, in the last. The first, however, is but your contention. I contest it, my lord. But, might I remind you that King James would have been *here*, not in Scotland, had Henry not unlawfully and in time of truce seized his ship?"

"He is very well, in all respects, where he is — pirate!"

"Ha! So you would challenge me, my lord of Warwick?"

"Not I. I challenge only my peers! I but name you what you are — a pirate, a rogue and the bastard of a rogue!"

The smack of Alex's back-handed slap across the other's square face resounded through the hushed salon.

"Then *I* challenge you, Warwick! Eat your ill-mannered words. Or support them before all, with lance and sword, so soon as you may."

"Curse you, oaf!" The older man's clenched fists and quivering voice testified to his tight-held fury. "You shall weep blood for that! Ill-begotten bastard's blood. I will teach you not to strike an earl of England!"

"I shall look forward to the lesson, sir. So soon as it can be arranged. With Their Majesties' royal permission. Meanwhile, we both should humbly seek Queen Isabella's gracious clemency for our boorishness in her presence." Alex spread his hands wide, to the Queen. Belatedly Warwick jerked a nod, and turned to stride to the door.

Isabella, frowning, looked regally displeased. But when, after a moment or two, she came closer to him she looked anxious rather. "Alex, my dear, I may perhaps forgive you the ill behaviour — since you were much provoked. But . . . was that wise? I have heard that man is a noted warrior."

"Ah, but you must not believe all that you hear, Highness —
you told me so yourself! After all, the same has been said about
myself, I am told — despite my bastard blood! And . . . once
you have forgiven me for the behaviour, you will thank me for
the sport to come, no?"

She did not answer, but took his arm to lead off the dancing.

*   *   *

It took almost a week to organise the joust — for, of course, the
opportunity was taken to turn the occasion into a full-scale
tournament with numerous lesser contests supporting the main
event. It all aroused great enthusiasm and heavy wagering,
King Charles in especial waxing gleeful and, in theory at least,
superintending all. The lists were set up in the huge parade-
ground and archery butts of the royal bodyguard, and large
quantities of soil and sand brought in and strewn on the ground
— peat being little known here — and pavilions, awnings and
tentage erected, with floral and heraldic decorations. One side of
the four-sided enclosure was reserved for the populace. Fortunately it had not been necessary tactfully to prime the King on
the subject of chalices of gold pieces, he volunteering these
prizes from the first, with a specially large one for his *cher ami*
Alex, apparently whether he won or lost.

It was a steamy hot late-August afternoon when the trumpets
sounded and the royal party arrived. To, as it were, warm up
the great company, comic jousters first took the arena, to clown
and caper mock battles wherein lances bent and snapped,
sword-hilts parted from their blades, armour fell off to reveal stark
naked heroes, and ancient bony nags competed against tiny ponies.

The spectators suitably humoured, an introductory bout was
staged between two groups of sword-fighters, wholly armoured,
four a side, Gascons against Normans, who were to fight it out
to a finish, the side with one or more remaining on their feet at
the end winning. It was, to be sure, a fairly unedifying spectacle,
of slow-motion banging and clanging, with little of finesse or
skill demonstrated or possible — since men totally sheathed in
steel cannot wield heavy swords in any other than a ponderous
and hacking fashion, the motion indeed growing slower and
slower as weariness set in. Sheer percussion and shock within
the armour-plating represented success since no penetration was
likely and one by one the contestants dropped, stunned, or lost
the use of numbed limbs, until there were only two left upright,

335

both Gascons — who possibly were less affected by the heat than were the Northerners.

This triumphant if exhausted pair, egged on by the crowd, then turned on each other, to slog it out, until one's sword dropped from nerveless grasp and he sank down creakingly on all fours on the soil and so remained, and the victor went staggering off towards the royal box in zigzag style to receive his prize. When he removed his helm, before the excited monarch, it was to reveal, surprisingly, the bald head and sagging cheeks of a man in late middle years. The cheers were loud and long.

Then it was the turn of the principal contenders, and a change in the entire atmosphere became evident. The procedure was now formal and deliberate. Trumpets preceded a royal herald who announced in measured but ringing tones that the illustrious Henri, Comte de Warwick, of England, envoy of the King of England himself, would meet the equally illustrious Alexander, Comte de Mar, of Scotland, cousin of the King of Scots, in full battle on a field of honour, with lance and sword, the challenger being the Monsieur de Mar. Let the best knight win. Then, from opposite ends of the lists the champions rode out, fully armoured and accoutred, helmed but visors up, to meet in the centre, bow stiffly in their saddles, and turn to salute the royal pair, lances raised, before pacing slowly back to their own bases, where their respective banners hung limply over their supporters. Both were splendid in polished, gleaming steel-plating and chain-mail, borrowed necessarily, but with the breast-plates and shields painted for the occasion with the colours and emblems of their houses.

It was not Alex Stewart's fault that what followed was anticlimax, that he was prevented from demonstrating to a keyed-up and critical audience that he was his father's son in this at least and a match for any England, or France itself, could throw against him. It was not really Warwick's fault either — only unfortunate circumstance and ill luck. For, despite the fact that Alex had sent him information beforehand that he intended to use a light horse, in the Scots fashion, recognising that the other would choose what suited him best, the Englishman had elected to borrow a huge and most massive mount from the royal stables. This, covered in the conventional plate armour also, made a mighty and impressive sight, which caused Alex's ordinary riding-horse, fine Barbary stallion as it was, with only

336

linen, lion-rampant-painted trappings, to look like a whippet before a mastiff. The crowd did not fail to draw uncomplimentary comparisons.

These changed their tune however once the trumpets blew again, and at vastly differing speeds now the antagonists rode at each other, lances levelled. Alex, meeting his opponent more than two-thirds of the way to his base, proceeded to demonstrate all the advantages of pace, lightness, manoeuvrability and a familiar mount, feinting, veering, rearing away, making rings around his enemy, in a fashion which soon had the spectators laughing almost as much as at the clowns' efforts. If Warwick had been content to stand in one place, pivoting his destrier round on its rear hooves, horse and rider secure behind their armour-plating and all but unassailable, he might well have tired out his spirited attacker and remained fresh for a final powerful thrust. But instead of doing so, he lost his proud temper at this wretched display of monkey-tricks, and lashed out savagely but ineffectually time and again, forcing his ponderous steed to twistings and turnings and labourings for which it was quite unfitted. As a result, the brute not only tired first and quickly, but soon became totally unmanageable. It eventually lumbered to the side of the lists, where it stood immovable, despite all its rider's frenzied efforts. Alex ranged to and fro for a little, concerned at this ridiculous and utterly tame outcome; but as the crowd's jeers and epithets rose to a crescendo, drove in from the flank and swiftly, simply, unseated the unhappy and all but helpless Warwick, who crashed to the ground. Here, at the listside where no real fighting had been anticipated, little soil or sand had been spread. The impact was accordingly heavy. Henry Beauchamp lay still within his fine armour.

Men came running, Jamie Douglas from Alex's own support team amongst them. They loosened and removed Warwick's helmet, to reveal an unconscious man, purple of face and breathing stertorously. Raising his own visor Alex shrugged, saluted his fallen adversary, and to mixed jeers, laughter and cheers, reined round and trotted off towards the royal box.

He received a rapturous and uncritical welcome from Charles de Valois at least, and rather more than the traditional queen-of-the-tournament's salute from Isabella. Also the so-necessary chalice of gold pieces, to which was added a gold chain and jewel as keepsake from the Queen. But nothing could make it a triumph or a credit to anyone, Alex was the first to assert.

337

Few were the sympathetic enquiries for the Earl of Warwick, symptomatic of contemporary French hostility for England — although Alex himself made a point of ascertaining that the other was not seriously injured.

A Scots stay of a week or two longer in Paris, was paid for. But it was necessary to make such stay productive.

* * *

Try as he would, Alex's success remained only partial. Perhaps he should not have expected more, in the then state of France. He obtained agreement to the principle of an Irish expedition, limited in size but to be mounted soon, before winter set in. If it proved effective and successful, the small French expeditionary force could be reinforced in the spring, as greater pressure on Henry. The Duke of Burgundy it was who accepted responsibility for this — although he could not commit himself to personally leading the venture, since he could not afford to leave France for any length of time lest D'Armagnac and the Orleans faction took advantage. The Queen added her acceptance of this. And that seemed to be as far as they were going to get.

The Scots decided that it was time to be gone. But breaking loose was not easy, with King and Queen both urgent for them to stay — at least, for Alex to stay. Their popularity was now something of a disadvantage.

The disengaging process lasted for a full week longer than they had intended, and lack of funds was again beginning to loom large when, at length, they were able to close up their over-successful establishment at the Sign of the Tin Plate and make their farewells. Alex was able to use as excuse the information that apparently the bulk of Burgundy's proposed Irish force was to come from his province of Flanders, and the advisability therefore that he himself should go there in person to help whip up enthusiasm for the venture, time now being pressing, with September already upon them.

The farewell Louvre banquet was a notable occasion, prolonged until dawn on the day of their departure — although long before that time King Charles had been carried off, not so much asleep as unconscious, and indeed Isabella and Alex himself had been unseen for some time.

With sore heads, empty pockets but a distinct feeling of relief, then, the unofficial Scots embassage rode out of Paris north-eastwards, leaving behind multiple promises to return when possible, the Auld Alliance most certainly the firmer for their visit. Some, at least, were longing to be home in Scotland.

The journey back through Vermandois and Picardy to the Flanders plain, however, with its contrasts of war, anarchy, ruin and near-famine, renewed their doubts as to the reliability and effectiveness of a regime which could so mismanage a fair land.

At Bruges they were faced with unexpected problems. They found the great city in a stir, and far from being in a position to muster troops for any Irish adventure. It was involved, albeit unwillingly, in raising forces for a military confrontation much nearer home — something John of Burgundy had omitted to mention. It seemed that the peculiar Lord Anton of Brabant, amongst his other responsibilities, was eager to assume episcopal ones. He had indeed had himself elected Prince-Bishop of Liège — by what electorate was not entirely clear, and the fact that he was not in holy orders apparently no handicap. The bishopric, admittedly, was no ordinary one. It had enormous revenues and carried with it a princeship of the Holy Roman Empire and the title of Duke of Bouillon, also the suffraganship to the arch-bishopric of Cologne, which was one of the Electors of the Empire and probably its greatest eccleciastical power. Unfortunately for Anton, the citizens of Liège, egged on by the diocesan chapter and canons, had elected a different nominee as Bishop, in the person of one Heinrich Horn, who was daring to contest the Lord Anton's right. This might have been dealt with in suitable summary fashion, had it not been for the fact that this Horn's father was a rich and powerful lord, with his own influence and support within the Emperor's hierarchy, as well as in Holy Church: moreover the latter had obtained for him the backing of Pope Gregory the Twelfth, in Rome — whereas, of course, Anton was a supporter of and supported by Pope Benedict the Thirteenth, at Avignon. So there was nothing for it, apparently, but to settle the issue in the only really effective way, by the sword. Anton, as it happened, was not much of a soldier and though besieging Liège, was not achieving much thereby, and calling for ever more troops. In the circumstances, Bruges was not in a state to take recruiting for any Irish expedition very seriously.

As well as this, a spell of unseasonably bad weather had hit Northern Europe, and the *Greysteel*, which should have been waiting for them at Sluys, had not put in an appearance. The Bruges authorities were as hospitable as ever, but advancement of the travellers' plans was annoyingly held up. Endless eating and drinking was beginning to pall on the more frugal Scots.

They all summoned up what patience they could muster.

With still no sign of Robert Davidson in *Greysteel* a week later, they were surprised by the arrival at Bruges of the Duke of Burgundy himself, in some style. And it did not take him long to reveal the reason for his journey from Paris. It was to persuade the illustrious Earl of Mar and his renowned Scots knights to go to the aid of his brother Anton outside Liège. Their military ability and prestige was famed all over Europe, it seemed, and nothing would more quickly bring to an end this ridiculous and wicked rebellion, he contented, than their appearance in his brother's camp.

Needless to say the last thing that Alex desired was to get himself involved in a military campaign in Flanders at this stage — even though the prospect of some more spirited activity appeared to commend itself to some of his younger lieutenants, after too much courtiership, feasting and the like. He made known his reluctance very plainly, whereupon the Duke, in the friendliest possible way, pointed out that the troops with Anton represented his main available forces, and until they were free of their commitments at Liège they would not be available for adventures anywhere else.

This, naturally, greatly upset the Scots, Jamie in especial. It was sheerest blackmail, and he said so in no uncertain terms. They all resented being tricked and made use of, thus.

But Alex pointed out, in his reasonable way, that if the Irish expedition was indeed dependent upon a quick finish to this Liège controversy, and their involvement could aid in that, then it might not be too high a price to pay. It all required thought and discussion.

To assist in this process, John the Fearless brought in reinforcements in the shape, the voluptuous shape, of his sister, the Duchess of Holland, a large lady of ample proportions and major curves, supported by a bevy of beauties — whose duty clearly was to convince the Scots that it would be well worth while lingering for somewhat longer in Flanders. It seemed, indeed, that all this pulchritude was intended to accompany the warriors to Liège, warfare here evidently being conducted on a different scale and tempo from the Scottish custom — which perhaps helped to account for the Lord Anton's lack of any swift success in his endeavours.

Whilst all this was being coped with and debated, *Greysteel* arrived at Sluys, and Robert Davidson came on to Bruges, cursing the weather and declaring that he had been blown across almost to Norway. The main items of his news from Scotland were that the Privy Council had still not sat to decide on the Mar earldom case; and that Donald MacDonald was said to be back in his Isles, but he had left most of his force in Ulster under his brothers Alastair Carrach and Ian Mor, presumably to winter there — which seemed to imply that there might well be a seasonal lull in his campaign for Irish hegemony, to be resumed in the spring.

The effect of this information on Alex was somewhat to relax the pressure on him, both for any speedy return to Scotland and for the need for haste over the Irish-French project. The immediacy of requirement, for a start before the winter storms, was removed, making a larger and better-organised spring campaign more practical. He did not tell the Duke this meantime, however, since clearly he was a man who required no encouragement to put off action. In the circumstances, the Liège interlude might not be so objectionable.

Jamie Douglas was otherwise minded. They were being tricked and used, and to his more uncompromising mind, that ruled out any co-operation. Moreover, Mary wanted to get home, and so did he. *He* had a family at Lochindorb, even if Alex had not. Their womenfolk should not be dragged off on a warfare adventure, to Liège or elsewhere. Moreover, Donald of the Isles could not be assured to lie quiet until the spring.

The other accepted the force of much of this; but believed that if he could indeed put Burgundy much in his debt over Liège, one of the main objectives of their entire expedition would be brought much nearer fruition. It was not often that these two disagreed. But at length a compromise was worked out. Jamie and some few of the older Scots would return, in *Greysteel*, with the womenfolk, forthwith, to Scotland. And Alex with the others would go assist the Lord Anton to gain his bishopric — and with it apparently, the vitally important electorship of the Empire — thereafter to return home when Robert Davidson could bring his ship back for them, hopefully before Yule.

Not everybody was happy about this — especially the Scots ladies, who viewed the Duchess of Holland and her entourage with grave suspicion.

XX

IT WAS GOOD to be home amongst the great heather hills of
Braemoray, so much more dramatic and satisfying than the
level landscapes of the Low Countries and France. It was a
joy, too, to be with the young people again, now in lively
adolescence and requiring their parents — even if they gave little
impression of realising it. Mariota de Athyn rejoiced to see them,
and Mary at least declared that she had had enough of foreign
lands and foreign ways to last her for the rest of her days.

Jamie, however, was inconsistent, according to his wife. It did
not take him long to be almost wishing that he was back with
Alex and his friends in Flanders. He recognised that this was
folly, that he was so much better here, that this was where he
ought to be. But his mind constantly was drawn over the seas to
what might be going on at Liège and Bruges and Sluys. Not that
he lacked for work here, and useful occupation, or failed to
appreciate the satisfaction of a full, ordered and family life.
But . . .

He was by no means housebound at Lochindorb, either. He
got in touch with Earl John of Buchan, gave him some account
of their doings abroad and gained in return a summary of the
present situation in Scotland. Albany his father, Buchan said,
was growing ever more concerned about the activities of Donald
of the Isles, which he had seemed to dismiss for so long as of
little account. He was not actually seeking to interfere in the
affairs of the North, but was urging on his son the need for
constant vigilance and the drawing up of plans for mobilising
men at short notice and in major numbers. He had little faith in
the Highlanders themselves as any bulwark against attack by
the Islesmen; but the low country lairds of Angus, the Mearns,
Aberdeenshire, Buchan, Banff and Moray must be warned, and

ordered to have their maximum forces ready. The Earl of Douglas was similarly making mustering arrangements in the Borders, to be in a position to repel any English invasion timed to coincide with Donald's. These considerations, with the financial ones attendant upon supplying and maintaining large armed forces, was tending to preoccupy the Regent's government to the exclusion of others, and there was little else of importance going on apparently. The Highlands themselves were now alive with rumours of Donald's intended descent upon them, as never before; and certainly threats were being spoken of on all hands as to what would happen to Highland chiefs who opposed, or even failed to support, the Islesmen.

John Stewart thought that it was high time that his cousin Alex came home.

Jamie, for his part, did what he could towards readying forces for mobilisation. But his influence with the Aberdeen and Moray lairds was slight, and with the Gaelic-speaking clans of the glens less so. He made some impact on various of the Clan Chattan federation chieftains such as Macpherson of Cluny, MacGillivray of Dunmaglass, Shaw of Rothiemurchus, and the Cattanach — all very much within the orbit of the lordship of Badenoch; but with the Captain of Clan Chattan, the Mackintosh himself, a kinsman of Donald's and making hostile noises, it was difficult for a lowlander to achieve much. It was even reported that their former MacLeod allies, Ian Borb and his brother, were lining up on Donald's side, despite their father's disapproval. It was that sort of situation which was developing in the North and West, houses divided against themselves; and it would be a bold stranger indeed who would seek to intervene. Actually Mariota de Athyn's influence was much more effective than Jamie's. She was a Mackay of Strathnaver, her name but an Anglo-Normanisation of Mac Aodh, the Sons of Hugh. She sent warnings and urgings to her own people in the far North, in Caithness, Sutherland and Ross, and obtained encouraging assurances.

Winter closed the passes and the seasonal sort of hibernation set in over the Highland scene, at least insofar as travel was concerned. Yuletide passed pleasantly enough, but without any sign of Alex Stewart. Robert Davidson had taken *Greysteel* to the Low Countries once again, in November, complaining about weather conditions and the hare-brained schemes of lordly ones with insufficient to do; but had not, so far, returned to Aberdeen. It was, in fact, a Flemish shipmaster trading with Aberdeen who brought the letter from Alex. It was addressed from the Castle of Duffel, in Brabant.

It read:

I fear, Jamie, that it will be after Yuletide before you receive this, if receive it you ever do. I shall not be home so soon as I thought. Much has happened to delay me. For one, I am wed again. You will not approve, I swear, my sober friend. Indeed, a whisper in your ear, I am beginning to have some doubts my own self, in a small way. The lady is the Countess Marie of Duffel, and I have no complaints as to her person and attractions. The difficulty is otherwise. She is most handsome, and by no means unkind in her body. She was one of the Duchess of Holland's ladies, and indeed the greatest heiress in the dukedom. You may remember her. When at length we won for them the Liège battle — of which I shall tell you hereafter — nothing would do but that I must have this lady and her wealth in reward. It cost the Dukes nothing. All call Liège a notable victory, and Alex Stewart's fame as general resounds through the courts of Europe, I am assured. I was to be a rich man, in consequence, and Count of Duffel forby.

Alas, I am not certain whether or no I am even Count of Duffel, and as yet none the richer. For my lady, who was but recently widowed, from one Baron Thierry de Lienden now whispered to have been poisoned no less, it appears omitted before that to gain a bill of divorcement from the earlier husband, the Count of Beveland. Some confusion, with this problem of the two Popes, at Rome and Avignon, the divorcement by way of falling between them. So I can scarcely claim to be wed, after all. And the lady's family have close fists and are loth to loosen their grip on her fortune.

I can, I think, now hear Black James Douglas muttering that if he had been there none of this folly would have been allowed to happen.

There is more to it than this, I fear. The Dukes knew of it all, to be sure, and it was all but another trick, a ruse. This Count of Beveland, the true husband still as I must believe him, despite my Archbishop's wedding, is a notable scoundrel and thorn-in-the-flesh to the Dukes of Burgundy and Holland and all the Low Countries. He is indeed a pirate, preying on the great shipping of this coast. And it so happens that most of my Marie's — of his Marie's — wealth is in shipping and trade, in the Dutch fashion. And this

344

Beveland has kept his hands on it all, and uses the ships for his pirating ventures. So you will see why I had to be wed to the lady. My reputation as a pirate matches his. And, they considered, I ought to be disposed to out-pirate this wretch, slay him, recover the lady's wealth, save the coastal trade, and so cause all to rejoice.

You, my friend, may well conceive my state when I but lately made discovery of all this. I was for coming home so soon as Robert Davidson could carry me. But second thoughts have prevailed. I have decided to play these French and Netherlanders at their own game. I shall indeed go and seek pirate this pirate, and take his treasure and ships if I may. But I shall endeavour not to slay him. I shall leave him truly wed to my deceiving Countess, and sail home with such of his loot as I can stow in Greysteel. You, Jamie, will at least approve of this ploy, I think.

Liège, although called a great victory, was to my mind a sorry business, and I hope never to see such another. They say that 25,000 died, and I believe it. In these lands a general's fame is counted by the numbers slain in his battles. So I am much esteemed — for that Anton left all to me to achieve, save the slaying afterwards. In truth nearly all the dying was done after the fighting was over, when I had gained Anton and the Duke's entry to that unhappy city. Men, women and bairns, the streets running with blood, the town set afire. I was sickened. I shall tell you how we won it, when I see you. For the rest, I had rather forget it.

I hope to be back in Aberdeen, in Greysteel, in not many weeks after you read this, God willing. Also, God willing, the richer — though the poorer of a wife.

I ask that you convey my affection to my good mother and my fair aunt. To you, my sure friend, my much esteem.

At the Castle of Duffel, Brabant.
ALEXANDER STEWART

There was a sufficiency in that letter to keep Jamie Douglas thinking, and his wife commenting, for long.

Later, they heard through Buchan of the great victory of Liège, which Alex had won for Burgundy and his brother, and the Duke of Holland, who seemed also to have been involved. Albany's informants on the Continent all wrote of it. Whatever the victor's own modest assessment of the affair, his fame as a commander, rather than as just a privateer captain, seemed to be established. No word of pirating activities, however, were as yet forthcoming.

It was March before *Greysteel* arrived back to her home port, and in fine style, laden with the richest of booty, and Alex in excellent humour. It transpired that they had achieved a surprise attack on the awkward Count of Beveland, in the shallow sand-banked coasts of the eastern mouth of the Maas, more or less ambushing the Count's squadron of ships laden down with the fruits of a trading-cum-pirating expedition to the Baltic lands and Lower Muscovy — including a great hoard of gold, silver, jewellery, church ornaments, ikons, silks, rich furs, liquors and the like, not to mention chestsful of coinage of various realms and dukedoms. Never had the Scots seen such treasure. They had set the Count and his crews ashore on one of the innumerable sand-islands, to fend for themselves — so that the Countess could not claim to be truly widowed again; and they had handed over the captured ships and the bulkiest part of the treasure to the authorities at Bruges, for the Countess, the Dukes, and the Flemish and other merchants who had suffered loss for so long. Then, without waiting for embarrassing meetings or the inevitable arguments over the division of the spoils, they had slipped out of Sluys, for home. Although he did not admit as much, Alex appeared to have more or less given up hope that Burgundy would honour his commitment to send an expedition to Ireland. Although perhaps the very threat of him proposing to do so might have its effect on the well-informed Henry Plantagenet.

At any rate, Alex came home rich indeed, and so in a better position to encourage the maximum effort on the part of his northern compatriots to rise to resist Donald of the Isles, when and if the time came. Jamie was the last to contest the theory that gold and silver could be a major aid to patriotic endeavour.

It was good to have his friend home again.

PART FOUR

XXI

"MUCH AS I love my nephew Alex, I must say that I have come to dread these messengers of his, from Kildrummy," Mary Stewart declared, to her husband. "They ever presage some further headstrong venture, of much flourish but little need, which will remove my helpmeet and support, father of my bairns, far from my side. This will be just such another, I swear! If Alex would indulge in his cantrips on his own, I would have no complaint. But he seems to be unable to move more than a few steps from his new door without Jamie Douglas by his side. To *my* cost!"

"I left him in the Low Countries, to come home with you," Jamie reminded.

"Nor will you ever let me forget it! You came home because you *wanted* to."

"And Alex did very well lacking me, did he not? Moreover, some of what you name his cantrips have proved profitable, my dear — to us, as to others. Do we not all live the more comfortably therefor?"

"We could live comfortably enough without that. And better to our liking. At least, to mine. You, I do declare, enjoy these flights away from your wife and children. Leastways, you never say no to him, do you?"

"This may be nothing of that sort," he protested. "It is but a request for me to attend him at Kildrummy, for an important meeting, in which he seeks my counsel. I may be back in a night or two."

"Do not be a hypocrite, Jamie Douglas, as well as a shameful wife-deserter! You know very well what happens after Alex's important meetings. You disappear from my ken, north, south, or furth of the realm, on some ploy, usually dangerous. And I am left to weep alone."

349

"Weep! You? When did I last see Mary Stewart weeping?"

"You are never here to *see* me weeping, wretch . . .!"

It was June. Mary perhaps should have been grateful that she had had eight months.

Despite all this, the man rode off quite cheerfully to Donside.

The first person Jamie saw at Kildrummy was Gilbert Greenlaw, Bishop of Aberdeen and Chancellor of Scotland — which seemed sufficiently significant. Then he recognised none other than Sir Robert Erskine of Balhaggarty and Conglass, the claimant of the Mar earldom, still more unexpected. When he heard that Alex was closeted with the Earl of Buchan, Justiciar, it became evident that some major development was projected. Mary's fears might even be substantiated.

Presently, alone with his friend, Alex explained. "We have become acceptable, Jamie," he announced cheerfully. "My Uncle Robert deems himself to have need of my services. So all is forgiven! For which we have to thank my Cousin Donald."

The other looked predictably suspicious, unimpressed.

"He has, apparently, been getting ever more ominous reports as to Donald's activities, intentions and ambitions, and has at last recognised the menace. He now accepts that Donald's Irish venture was merely a prelude to a major invasion of Scotland, to coincide with an English assault from the South, from Man, possibly from the Dublin Pale. It has taken him a long time to reach this conclusion. But now he is much concerned. Since Crawford's death and Douglas's failure at Homildon, he finds himself and the realm singularly lacking in soldiers — or, at least, in commanders. And he has gained the notion that I might have my uses. Especially as I have the reputation of being able to raise large numbers of Highlandmen, and ships, galleys. In token of which he sends the Chancellor, as messenger, and Sir Robert Erskine as bribe, to inform me that he will drop the Mar claim if I will agree to work with them, and I can remain earl for life. And his son John, to reassure me of his sincerity in the matter and my, h'm, safety."

"I still would not trust him," Jamie said bluntly.

"No doubt. But, since we are of a mind to stop Donald anyway, is there any reason why we should not do so aided by the Regent's authority, arms and siller?"

"The day I see that, Albany offering arms and siller — or *providing* them — I shall sing a different tune, Alex!"

"We shall see. He desires me to go south, to discuss all with him, of my goodwill. And *I* desire you to accompany me, old friend, as adviser. If you will."

"My advice you can have now. Do not go. If he needs you so badly, let him come to you."

"He is an old man getting, Jamie. This must be his seventieth year. Moreover, there are others I would wish to sound, on this. Your chief Douglas, for one. The new Crawford. And . . . would you not wish to see your father again? He too is getting old."

"You are satisfied that you, we, will return safely?"

"John of Buchan pledges his word on it. I trust *him*. He has never failed me yet. He will come with us. And we can take a fair company. To show our dignity!"

"You have made up your mind?"

"Yes. I see no ill in it — and possibly much good. Authority, the Regent's authority, could serve us well, even lacking other aid. Remember our letters of mark, how valuable these can be. This is of the same sort. We can call on men to aid us, aid the realm, everywhere. Instead of merely buying them with our siller. You will come, Jamie?"

"If you are set on it. When do we go?"

"Soon. So soon as may be. They believe that there is urgency in this . . ."

So Mary was right, as usual. Three days later a quite impressive cavalcade set off southwards through the Mounth passes, out of the security of the Highlands.

They did not have very far to go into the Lowlands, for Albany had come to Perth, from his castle of Doune in Menteith.

The meeting, however significant, was scarcely dramatic — Robert Stewart was never a man for drama. In the company of Buchan and the Chancellor, Alex was led to a small study in the Prior's quarters of the Blackfriar's Monastery, where the Regent sat alone at his papers, wrapped in a furred robe, spare, ascetic, the picture of a dedicated scholar rather than one of the most ruthless and unscrupulous rulers in Christendom. His cold grey eyes narrowed momentarily at sight of Jamie Douglas — but thereafter he totally ignored him. He greeted Alex with thin affability.

"Ha, Nephew — it is long since we foregathered, although I hear much of your doings, from near and far. Notably that you have been distinguishing yourself in France and the Low Countries. Cup-bearing to King Charles, instructing his Consort, teaching the Earl of Warwick how to joust and the Duke of Burgundy how to treat rebels. Aye, and marrying again — after a fashion!" That was a long greeting for Albany; and Jamie, for one, marvelled at the man's information — as no doubt was the intention. He also noted how much older the Regent looked; it was years since he had seen him in the flesh, however frequently he had been in his mind's-eye. But, though more brittle-seeming, stiffer, thinner, there was no least impression of any diminution of mental powers and will.

"You are well served by informers, Uncle," Alex answered. "I am flattered that you find my poor doings of sufficient interest to warrant such attention. I hope I see you in good health?"

"Fair. Although weary with overmuch of the weight of government — requiring some younger shoulders to relieve me of some part of it." He laid down his quill. "You are namely for putting down of rebels, it seems. We have some nearer home, worthy of your attentions, I think."

"You refer to your nephew and my cousin Donald, sir?"

"I do. The Chancellor and my son have explained matters to you?"

"They tell me that you now accept what I have known for long."

"M'mm. That is as may be. Yet, if it is so — you went away to France and left this danger behind, which you knew of so fully. For others to face."

"I believed the danger to Scotland to be not yet. Ireland first. And have been proved right. Sir James Douglas and I made a journey in the Hebrides before we sailed for France, to seek learn the truth."

"To MacLeod of Dunvegan. I know of that. MacLeod told you that Donald aimed at Ireland first?"

"Not only MacLeod. That was the general belief in the Isles. For two reasons. One, to ensure that his rear was secure, when he came to invade Scotland, that there would be no attack on the Isles, from Ireland. Also, possibly, to make a claim for the eventual high kingship of Ireland, a stepping-stone in his ambitions. And two, to prove to King Henry that he was a sufficiently sound and effective ally, fit to be ruler of Scotland, under the English. Before, he had always sent Alastair Carrach to do his fighting for him. This time, he went himself."

"No doubt. Yet *you* went to France. For more than a year. In costly style."

"I went to France, sir, for good purpose. To seek French aid for the release of our liege lord James. Since *you* would do naught in the matter."

"How know you what I do or have done, young man? In this or other matters. I do not shout all from my castle parapet! Forby, you would win no aid for James from France. That I knew well."

"I gained the Duke of Burgundy's agreement to send a force to Ireland in the spring, against Donald and the English forces. He has not done so yet. But . . ."

"John of Burgundy will agree to anything — and perform nothing! You wasted your time, Alexander. We shall have to do better than that, against Donald."

"I, my lord Duke, always intended so to do. But you — what do *you* intend to do?"

"I intend to protect this realm and throne. I have two flanks to protect, possibly three. For, as well as an English attack across the Border, there may well be an assault against Galloway and Carrick from the Isle of Man and even the Irish Pale. The Earl of Douglas commands in the Borders, as is his right and duty. Montgomerie of Eaglesham will command in the West. My son John, here, is Lieutenant of the North. But he is as yet inexperienced in war. You, I would place in command there, to act with him. How say you?"

"In command? What does that mean? Save that on me would fall the task of halting Donald's main array and strength. Who would I command? What are my forces? Would my lord of Buchan be in a position to over-rule me? What moneys, arms and supplies would be at my disposal?"

"All Scotland north of Clyde and Tay would be at your disposal to levy men and moneys. My son John, as Justiciar as well as Lieutenant, would have the fullest authority to supply you, aid you. But *you* would have fullest control of the forces of the Crown in the field. And in return, Robert Erskine would waive his claim to the earldom of Mar, the lordship of Badenoch would be confirmed in your name, and all outstanding issues between yourself and the Crown remitted."

Alex was silent for a moment. "You must fear Cousin Donald greatly, I think, Uncle!" he said then.

"Fear? I fear no man, only almighty God," the other assured, with a chilly certainty which robbed the words of their pomposity. "But I perceive that my foolish sister's son may pose the greatest threat to this ancient realm of Scotland since Edward Plantagenet. He claims only that he would be Earl of Ross. But it is my information that he has boasted that he will be King of Ireland and King of Scots both. And he is willing to put Scotland in thrall to England, to gain his ends. In that day, to be sure, the fool will be cut off — so!" Albany made a vicious chopping motion with the side of his hand on his table. "And Henry alone will rule all three. But meantime, Donald can raise scores of thousands of men, from his Isles, from the mainland clans, from Ulster — who knows, perhaps even from my enemies here in the Lowlands. The threat is great, and growing. I do not fear, young man — I *know*! Henry has found a monkey to pull his chestnuts out of the fire for him!"

"Henry, with whom you deal! To whose son you offered your daughter!"

"Henry, with whom I *have* to deal, fool! Can I choose who is King of England? Can I make him other than he is? You speak like a child. In statecraft a ruler faces the possible, not what he desires. Something you should have learned ere this. So — do you accept this command, or do you not?"

Alex glanced from Jamie to Buchan. "I shall have to consider it, sir, consider it well. Give me a little time."

"Do not take too long. Time may be short."

"One matter. You said that all outstanding issues between us would be remitted. I would expect this to apply also to my friends and lieutenants. Sir James Douglas, here."

His uncle picked up his quill again and inclined his grey head briefly. "Even Sir James," he said grimly.

Alex did not really require time to make up his mind, since he had more or less decided before ever he came south. But it looked better; and allowed him to take soundings, interview others and test opinion. Jamie took the opportunity to go to Dalkeith and see his father and brothers; also to Edmonstone, where he was distressed to find the Lady Isabel ill and looking almost an old woman, although she greeted him with a pathetic warmth and wept at his departure. He feared greatly that she was not long for this world. The others were eager to hear of his adventures overseas, having heard garbled and exaggerated tales. The general belief now, indeed, was that he was very rich, on the proceeds of piracy, trade and foreign adventures. He was even approached for a loan by Sir Robert Stewart of Durrisdeer, to initiate a foreign trading venture. His brother Johnnie, sadly, had died while he was away in France, and Aberdour was his own again. He did not visit his Lowland properties, however;

stewards were managing them satisfactorily, his father assured. One day, his son David would inherit a fine patrimony.

There seemed to be little of alarm or despondency at large over the Islesmen's threat. Donald had been a bogeyman for too long.

Alex saw the Earls of Douglas and Crawford and a few other nobles, and gained little impression that they were greatly concerned or doing anything very much about the situation meantime. As Chief Warden of the Marches, as well as the greatest landholder in the Borders, Douglas always had his ear fairly close to the ground, and had heard nothing to suggest that the English were preparing any especial activity. Since the Battle of Bramham Moor, when the Percys had finally been brought low, there had been a fair measure of peace in the North of England and little cause for armed comings and goings. Henry kept a military presence at York, but there was no indication that this was being reinforced or otherwise activated.

None of this convinced Alex that he and Albany were being unnecessarily fearful. Henry Plantagenet was a wily character and would not be apt to reveal his plans a day earlier than was necessary. Moreover, it would be entirely in keeping if he held back deliberately, allowing Donald to do all the major fighting, and only moving in over the Border when success was assured.

At any rate, nothing that they heard or saw convinced Alex and Jamie that they ought to reject the Regent's offer of co-operation. They returned to Perth, signified Alex's agreement to accept the official command of the realm's forces in the North — forces not yet in being — and received an authoritative document under the Great Seal to that effect. Albany, showing no sign of pleasure in the decision, told him that his latest reports put Donald back in Ulster, holding a great meeting with Irish kinglets and chiefs. He was still shipping troops to Ireland, however, so it looked as though there would be no Scottish invasion this year before the campaigning season ended. So they had some months, at least, to prepare. Incidentally, there was no indication of any troop movements out of France, to Ireland or anywhere else.

If, indeed, a marked inactivity seemed to characterise the entire international scene, Albany at least believed it to be only the lull before the storm. Others might scoff and shrug, but for once both Alex Stewart and Jamie Douglas agreed with him.

They headed north thereafter determined not to emulate this apparent inactivity.

XXII

ALBANY'S FORECAST THAT they would be granted a few
months' grace was fulfilled. Donald did not return from
Ireland until the late autumn, announcing to all concerned
that he had concluded a treaty with his friend the King of
England whereby each would support and protect the subjects
of the other — first step towards the independent ruler status.
He was now affecting royal style, in employing uniformed
heralds in his entourage, the Islay and Ross Heralds and the
Kintyre and Dingwall Pursuivants. All that winter and the following spring the Highlands were agog with rumours of the
mustering and massing of hosts, on Islay, Mull, Skye and the
Outer Isles, from every corner of the Hebrides and much of the
west mainland also, and later from Antrim, where Ian Mor,
Donald's brother, was being called his viceroy. Galley-fleets
were assembling, in alarming numbers. Word of fence-sitters
amongst the Highland chiefs being cajoled, pressed, threatened,
was brought to Alex almost daily — even as near home as his
own Badenoch, where the Mackintosh himself was alleged to be
under strong pressure, friendly with Alex as he was. Donald was
waving the flag of Highland dominance in Scotland, instead of
Lowland, something unknown since Malcolm Canmore's Queen
Margaret had effectively contrived the southern supremacy, a
powerful incitement for the clans. The hegemony of the Celts
was being held out as practical politics, at long last, with Ireland,
other than the English Pale, brought within the scheme of things.
With no effective King of Scots to be rebelling against, King
Henry giving his support, and Donald himself nephew of the
late King, the thing was possible as never before.

Alex, aided by John of Buchan, did all that he could to counter
this pressure. He sent his emissaries, Jamie Douglas amongst

them, all over the Highlands, warning, directing, commanding, exhorting. He sought to gain promises of contingents for his army, requiring each sheriff to raise his quota, in the name of the Crown; but quickly was made aware that it was one thing to be lent men to fight against Lowlanders, the English, or even in private feud, but altogether another when it was a matter of defeating a demonstration of Highland independence. He came to the conclusion before long, that, commander-in-chief and Lord of Badenoch or not, friendly as he was with many of the chiefs, he could only rely for his fighting-force on the eastern lowlands of his area — Mar, Angus, the Mearns, Buchan and Moray, and the cities of Aberdeen and Elgin. No help came from the South in all this, Albany having passed on the responsibility to Alex and leaving him severely alone. There was no doubt as to who would get the blame if things went wrong — though that might well be of academic interest in that event. Jamie even suggested that they would be wise to watch their rear when and if fighting began, with a stab in the back entirely possible.

The Douglas made more constructive suggestions than that, however. He urged Alex to form and train an officer-corps, based on their privateering group of lairds, which could assemble frequently and regularly, discuss strategy and tactics, plan for various eventualities, and learn to co-operate in the field, so that their force, once mustered, would be an effective fighting-machine with a highly-trained leadership, that what it might lack in numbers might be made up for in efficiency. In this the leading lights were those old foes, Sir Alexander Forbes and Sir Andrew Leslie, with their sons; Sir James Scrymgeour of Dundee, the Standard-Bearer; Sir Alexander Keith; Sir John Menzies of Pitfodels; Sir Alexander Irvine of Drum, and Provost Robert Davidson. Only one Highland chief was prepared to be included at this stage, Donald Og Macpherson of Cluny. Alex's brothers, Andrew and Walter, co-operated after their awkward fashion, and James, the youngest, promised aid from Atholl.

So the winter passed and the campaigning season of 1411 opened.

Messengers from the West were now arriving regularly at Kildrummy, many from old MacLeod in Skye, intimating great activity all over the Isles; but the major concentrations of men and shipping were at Islay, with its many harbours, where was the main seat of the Isles lordship, at Finlaggan. Decisive action must be soon now.

357

But still nothing happened — while Alex fretted. He had decided on his strategy, made his plans as far as was possible in advance, held almost daily councils with his lieutenants. Yet April passed, and May, with the passes clear, the river-levels falling and the cuckoos calling on all the glen-sides. Still Donald did not move. The tension at Kildrummy was acute.

And then Donald MacDonald managed to surprise, despite all their eager preparedness. From Islay his vast galley-fleets sailed at last — but northwards, not east nor south. All up the Western Sea reports came in of his progress, gaining strength all the way, through the northerly isles. This was totally unexpected, for any assault on the mainland must aim for the South eventually, and any round-about and delayed approach would only give warning and time to the defenders. Islay was almost the most southerly of the Sudreys, the southern half of the Hebrides, and to have assembled there, and then to head north, did not seem to make sense. Alex had anticipated a landing in Lochaber or Argyll, and then a swift strike eastwards across the spine of Scotland, by Laggan or Rannoch. Yet Donald made straight for the north of Skye, and this turned, landed on mainland Ross.

It became clear that his first objective was to take the earldom of Ross — which, of course, he claimed to be his in the right of his wife, the original reason for his dispute with Albany. Possibly he intended to use it as a secure base. Certainly it would provide him with additional manpower. But the personal pride and prestige aspect of it must be very great to account for this major preliminary gesture. At least, it encouraged Alex in the belief that his adversary might be a man who might throw away military advantage for heroics and superficial lustre.

Nevertheless Alex was faced with a difficult decision. To head north towards Ross, to deal with the invaders, could be dangerous, removing him from his own base and greatly extending his lines of communication. He would be fighting on Donald's chosen territory rather than his own, and his levies would be unlikely to react with enthusiasm. Moreover, he had no experience of moving, supplying and foraging large armies — nor had any of his people. On the other hand, just to wait idly whilst the other consolidated his position, and took over large tracts of the mainland, was not good either, and could be injurious to morale.

On balance, he decided to wait. At least it gave him time to gather and train more men — and now that the threat was self-evident, men were more ready to come forward.

Alex was unprepared, however, for the news that, in the midst of elaborate celebration and initiation ceremonies as Earl of Ross at Dingwall, the ancient seat of the earldom, Donald had made a sudden and vicious raid on the town of Inverness, eighteen miles to the south, sacking and burning it, with considerable slaughter. This savage move, apparently with no other purpose than to show his teeth and appease the blood-lust of his Islesmen, could not be ignored. John of Buchan, as Justiciar, declared his cousin the Lord of the Isles to be outlaw, and all aiding and supporting him equally so. The cities of Aberdeen and Elgin were proclaimed to be in a state of siege, and the magistrates thereof ordered to see that all able-bodied citizens were provided with arms, and made constant practice of their use, walls and defences to be strengthened, fire-fighting forces set up and curfews instituted. Alex moved from Kildrummy south-eastwards down the Don to Inverurie, the head burgh of the Garioch lordship, where at Thainston, the same spot in the green levels where his ancestor Robert Bruce had set up his camp before the Battle of Barra, he established the nucleus of his army. It was only a few miles from Aberdeen.

After that events moved fast. Donald set his huge force in motion — and a Highland army on the march was a terrible and fast-moving host. It was now reported to number anything between ten and twenty thousand. Word came that another force of West Highlanders under the famous Hector Maclean of the Battles, son-in-law of Donald, was marching up the Great Glen to join him. Alex assessed his own strength at less than three thousand, mainly the followings of Mar, Garioch, Angus, Mearns and Buchan lairds — plus what, at the last moment, he could persuade Aberdeen city to provide. It did not add up to encouraging odds.

Where to confront the invaders? Alex had worked out a great variety of suitable battlegrounds, with Jamie's help, where the terrain could be used materially to fight for them. With the threat coming from the north, however, the choice was much limited. And there was the question as to whether Donald intended to come seeking them out, and do battle, or only to fight if he was intercepted on his way south — which could much affect the situation. He was reported as declaring that he would burn Aberdeen more direly than he had done Inverness

— but this might be mere dramatics. Either way, to be sure, much wild and difficult country lay between the two forces. Jamie suggested — and it seemed good sense to his friend, although it might seem like a lack of spirit on the face of it — that if anybody had to expend major time and energy crossing that wilderness and the northern Mounth passes, it should be the enemy, leaving themselves fresh and in good order. In the circumstances, the nearer base the ultimate battle, the better for them.

South of Inverness, the Islesman's host, now joined by Hector Maclean of Duart's contingent, could move either directly onwards southwards, over the Moy and Slochd passes into Badenoch, or eastwards, by Drummossie Moor into the Laigh of Moray. If they were aiming for the conquest of the Lowlands, obviously the first would be the direct advance; but if seeking a speedy confrontation with the defending forces, the second course would be the choice. When an exhausted courier reached Alex with the information that, in fact, the invaders, moving notably fast now, were into Braemoray, last reported in the Barevan area, avoiding the Nairn plain and the Forres-Elgin lowlands, it seemed clear that they were looking for battle. There was no reason to believe that Donald would be any less well served by spies and informants than they were themselves. He would know who was waiting for him, and where. Also, no doubt, approximate numbers. There could only be a few days, now, before the clash, wherever it was going to be.

Jamie, no less than Alex, was put in a state of anxiety by the word that Donald was advancing through Braemoray — which might bring his host close to Lochindorb. It was not particularly near to this Barevan, but it was a noted place and Donald might consider it worth going out of his way to attack. The castle, on its island, was well nigh impregnable however, without cannon — which Donald was unlikely to have with him, on fast forced marches. So their womenfolk were probably in little real danger. But they might well be alarmed and frightened — especially as later word had come in that there *had* been opposition to Donald before Dingwall, and this had been led by Mariota de Athyn's two brothers, Black Angus Mackay and his brother Roderick, the one now prisoner, the other slain. Nothing could be done about this, however, by Alex.

Then they had news that the invaders had, oddly enough, turned seawards down Spey from Rothes, to the Enzie area near

Speymouth — which almost certainly meant that they would have missed the Lochindorb uplands. Enzie was a detached property of the Ross earldom, so evidently Donald was still concerned with demonstrating his rights — an interesting facet of the character of a man in process of throwing three kingdoms into turmoil. By the same token he would probably move on to Boyne, near Banff, another of the outlying Ross baronies. If this was so, then his onward approach to the Aberdeen area would almost certainly be by the Deveron valley and Strathbogie into the Garioch. This was what Alex had had to know, to crystallise his plans.

They reckoned that they had three days, no more. They could not ambush tens of thousands of men; but they might perhaps select a battleground which could serve them as well as a couple of thousand extra troops — and they were going to require every such help. There were a number of sites to be considered; but the choice was limited by the fact that the Aberdeen contingent, which might make a major difference, would not be horsed, and would therefore be slow-moving and not really of much use over long distances. So the battlefield must be near-at-hand. Alex sent word to Robert Davidson, and then, alone save for Jamie and Sir Robert Erskine, the earldom claimant — whose estates of Balhaggarty and Pittodrie were nearby and who knew all the land like the palm of his hand — set off northwards on a hurried tour.

They were looking for a position which would tend to negate the Highlanders' overwhelming superiority in numbers and at the same time enable them to gain the fullest benefit of their own strength in cavalry and armoured knights. Also to be able to use the hoped-for Aberdonians to best advantage. They could rule out any idea of surprising the enemy — thousands of men can neither be hidden nor taken by surprise. But they might *constrain* Donald.

According to Erskine, within reasonable marching distance of Inverurie there were five such sites possible; but inspection reduced these to only the two. One, at Manar, up the Don westwards about three miles, where the river made a sharp bend through steep bluffs and hanging woods. The other the long, low ridge of Harlaw, actually on the Balhaggarty property, a sort of whaleback in the valley of the Urie, the Don's major tributary coming in from the north, about a mile east of the Urie and parallel to it, lying north-west and south-east. It was scarcely a major feature, reaching no more than a hundred and fifty feet above the valley floor. But it was over a mile long and three-quarters wide, firm ground on a gentle curve, flanked on both sides by low-lying marshland. Cavalry could operate up there, and large numbers be much restricted. But it could be a death-trap if the cavalry had to flee, those surrounding marshes fatal for horses. On the one side, these were the usual river's flood-plain boglands; the other had presumably once been an earlier or subsidiary course of the Urie, now silted up.

"Which, then?" Alex asked. "Neither are all I would wish. But they are the best that we have seen. We must believe Sir Robert when he says there are none better within our distances. Manar would give us more constriction and a better route for retreat. But Harlaw has advantages, too . . ."

"I say Harlaw," Jamie answered promptly. "We are not really concerned with retreat, are we? If it comes to that, all is lost. We shall not be able to remuster and make a stand elsewhere — not one that could halt Donald. The Manar site is cluttered with trees, narrow, wooded, close, fine for small fights but poor for a great battle such as this must be. You require to *see* what is happening, the whole field. To move your forces as required. This Harlaw ridge will give you that. And Donald will never be able to mount his fullest strength against us — there is not room."

"He could get round, outflank us. Send some to take us in the rear."

"Yes. So we must have no rear! Like a besieged city. But our cavalry will be able to dominate that ridge, if properly used. The foot form schiltroms, strong-points."

"How say you, Sir Robert?"

"I agree with Sir James. Somehow we must shorten our front. Manar would, I fear, shorten it too much. No full battle could be fought there — so we should have to do it all again, elsewhere."

"Very well. Harlaw let it be. Unless we are faced with something unforeseen . . ."

They rode back to Thainston.

* * *

Alex sat his horse on the top of the great Bass of Inverurie, a green artificial mound, which had once been crowned by an ancient fort, flanked by the glittering array of his lieutenants and principal supporters. He was looking magnificent, and deliberately so, for morale was all-important this day, St. James's Eve of July, 1411. He wore gleaming half-armour and heraldic linen surcoat below a gilded camail, or hood of chain-mail covering neck and shoulders, plumed helmet in the crook of his shield-arm, mount splendidly caparisoned in the Mar colours. Fully a score of only slightly less resplendent figures formed a row behind him, on sidling, fretting chargers, not only his own group of tried and trained colleagues, such as Forbes, Menzies, Keith, Straiton, Leslie, two of his brothers and Jamie, but notables like Sir Alexander Ogilvy, Sheriff of Angus; Sir Robert Melville of Glenbervie, Sheriff of the Mearns; Sir Thomas Moray, Sheriff thereof Sir James' Scrymgeour, Constable of Dundee and Standard-Bearer of Scotland; Sir William Abernethy of Saltoun, a nephew of Albany; Sir Gilbert de Greenlaw, styled nephew of the Chancellor-Bishop; Sir Robert Maule of Panmure and others. Below them, on the Don meadows all around the base of the Bass was drawn up their host, in troops and companies and squadrons, standing by their horses, the lairds of the North-East with their sons, men-at-arms and fighting-tails, with a sprinkling of Badenoch and Atholl Highlandmen, mainly of Clan Chattan — although their Captain, the Mackintosh himself, was reported to be marching with Donald to whom he was related. Jamie made the grand total two thousand nine hundred — which was less than grand in relation to the task ahead, however stirring a sight they made in the forenoon sunshine. There were still some to come, however — especially Robert Davidson and his Aberdeen contingent, for whom they were specifically waiting and who could be seen as a dust-cloud shot with the gleam of steel a mile or so back along the road from Kintore.

Before the marching Aberdonians could come up, a much faster although smaller body put in an appearance in dashing style, the banner at their head showing the three green holly-leaves on white of Irvine.

"I did not think that Sir Sandy would fail us — despite his wedding!" Alex asserted.

Sir Alexander Irvine of Drum, a cheerful, ruddy-featured young man, grandson of Bruce's renowned armour-bearer, leaving his eighty or so men at the bottom, rode up on to the mound, to the laughter, cheers and ruderies of the waiting lairds. Grinning, he saluted Alex and waved and gestured crudely at them all. He had been married only the day before.

"I hope that you are not so exhausted as to be unable to wield as lusty a brand this day, friend, as you did last night?" Alex enquired kindly.

"Not so," the other assured. "God's eyes — I have a bone to pick with Donald MacDonald this day! He ruined my bridal night!"

"Sakes, man — could you not raise your standard for fear of the Islesman!" his crony, young Alexander Keith, demanded.

"Think you so, oaf? There was naught amiss with the Irvine standard. It was the socket to fit it in that was at fault! Making the wedding five days early, on Donald's account, set my lady's calculations adrift. The Islesman will pay for it, I say!"

There was a howl of mirth and commiseration. "My heart bleeds with and for Lady Irvine!" Alex said. "Deprived so cruelly."

"Aye — and how will she do if you do not return from this tuilzie, Sandy?" the irrepressible Keith, heir to the Marischal, cried. "What will she use for the standard of Irvine, then?"

"I have attended to that," his friend asserted, solemnly. "I left my brother Rob behind at the Drum Stone of Skene, the last place from which we could see my castle of Drum, on the Dee, sent him back. If I do not return, Rob will change his name to Alexander, take my new wife for his own and raise up sons for Irvine." He shrugged steel-clad shoulders. "Och, he likes her fine, forby!"

The grins and chuckles faded, at that. Suddenly the reality of the situation was brought home to them all, even the least sensitive, and the high-spirited adventure before them took on a different colour.

Alex coughed. "Commendable forethought, Sandy. Your brother will have to find his own bride, I vow, nevertheless! Now — we wait for Provost Davidson and his burgesses, yonder. Others are still to come, likewise — with perhaps less excuse for tardiness than you! But we shall not wait for them all . . ."

Shouts drew the attention of the company on the Bass to still another horsed party, coming this time from behind, from the north, skirting Inverurie burgh by the riverside. It was larger, fully two hundred strong, at its head the blue banner with three golden boars' heads of Gordon. A shout went up.

"Thanks be for that!" Alex murmured. "Now, pray God, we will learn something."

Sir Alexander Seton put his horse to the mound, a fine figure of a man in the richest armour there, black inlaid with gold, the Lothian laird who had married, three years earlier, the heiress of Sir Adam, the Gordon chief who had fallen at Homildon. He was now Lord of Gordon in her right.

"How fares Strathbogie, my lord?" Alex asked eagerly.

"But poorly, my lord Earl," the other answered. "The Hieland savages have swept down it like a heather-fire, God damn them! Brute beasts!" The new Gordon would have to learn an amended vocabulary, for the North. "Scarce a house left unburned or a woman unraped! I would have brought you twice this number otherwise."

"It was no little matter that you came at all, man. I thank you. But . . . what of Donald, now? What news have you for us?"

"The Islesmen camped last night at the Whitehaugh of Montgarrie, after leaving Strathbogie. They are now marching by Keig and the back of Bennachie hitherwards, in their thousands . . ."

"Keig, and Bennachie? Not down the Vale of Alford? Then they are making for the Urie. Looking for us! We thought they might come by Alford, Tillyfour and Monymusk."

"No. They take the north route round Bennachie. We avoided them, by Auchleven and Oyne . . ."

"Then it is time that we were moving, not waiting here!" That was Jamie Douglas, strongly, behind. "Keig is little more than a dozen miles. Ten, no more, from Harlaw. And they march fast, as we know . . ."

"A little longer only, Jamie," Alex said. "This means that we can now recall the Forbes force waiting at the Tillyfour gap." He turned. "Forbes, my friend, will you now send for the main mass of your people to rejoin us? Quickly. And now — we must welcome the good burgesses of fair Aberdeen, as is seemly. Forby, we must not all be on top of Harlaw's hill too soon, or Donald may stay down, and avoid battle up there. We have to *coax* him up. Bisset — go you out to welcome the Aberdeen men. And bring Robert Davidson to me here. Tullidaff — some music, if you please, for the burgesses."

So, to the sound of fifes, fiddles and drums the hot and tired Aberdeen contingent straightened stooping shoulders, lifted their steps higher and marched in, about four hundred strong, twenty-six burgesses of the city with their following of shop-keepers, seamen, apprentices, clerks, fishermen, a motley crew of all ages and shapes in comparison with the ranks of steel-clad knights, men-at-arms and horsemen, but well-armed and equipped. Alex led the cheering.

Walter Bisset, son of Lessendrum, Sheriff of Banff, brought Davidson, in fair armour, and his second-in-command ex-Provost Chalmers, up the hill. Alex dismounted and strode forward to greet them, hand out.

"Bless you, friends," he exclaimed. "I rejoice to have you at my side, this day. This is a sight to sing over! Who knows — I may yet put it into my halting verse! It is not every day that the Provost, magistrates and council of the city of Aberdeen march out to war!"

"There would be more, my lord, had we not had to leave the gates and walls manned, mind."

"To be sure. Master Chalmers — take the Provost's helm."

"Eh . . .?"

"His helm. Take it off, Robert. And kneel down."

"What is this, my lord . . .?"

"Do as I say. You are all soldiers now, under orders. *My* orders! Kneel, man. You are none so stiff yet, are you? I have seen you leaping about your ship's decks nimbly enough! Down with you."

As, staring, the Provost half-knelt, half-stooped, Alex drew his sword.

"As commander of this host and an earl of Scotland, as is my undoubted right, I, Alexander Stewart, knight, do now knight you, Robert Davidson, Chief Magistrate of the city and royal burgh of Aberdeen, and so honour you, your burgh and all your men." Intoning thus, Alex brought down his gleaming blade on the other's wide shoulders, one side then the other. "Thus, and thus, I hereby dub you knight, in the presence of God and this host. Arise, Sir Robert. Make your knightly vows hereafter. And remain a good and true knight until your life's end. Arise."

Surprise was so complete that it was moments before the cheers broke out. But when they did, there was no doubt as to the enthusiasm and delight, not so much on the part of the other knights and lairds, but on that of the thousands of the rank-and-file, in especial of course, of the Aberdonians. Never before had such a thing been seen. Loud and long the acclaim resounded, while Sir Robert Davidson gulped and moistened his lips and scratched his helmetless grizzled head.

Then men surged forward to shake him by the hand, and everywhere the great assembly hummed with excited comment and remark. Nothing better calculated to raise the spirit of the men could have been imagined. But Alex gave them only a few moments, then turned back to his horse, nodding to Jamie and signing to his trumpeter to sound the Advance.

Out of seeming confusion, then, the host eddied, moved and coalesced into four distinct groupings, and finally set off, to cross the Urie ford shallows east of the Bass, and then to turn northwards up the riverside, opposite the small burgh of Inverurie. Sir James Scrymgeour, Constable of Dundee and the realm's hereditary Standard-Bearer, commanded the van, with Sir Alexander Ogilvy, Sheriff of Angus, the senior sheriff. Next came the left wing, under Sir Andrew Leslie of Balquhain, styled Master of Horse to compensate for not commanding the right, which was given to his rival Forbes. Leslie's seven fine sons led his wing, with Johnston of Caskieben and Barclay of Towie Barclay. Sir Alexander Forbes, most of whose people were still at Tillyfour on the Don waiting to delay the Islesmen, should they have chosen that route, had Sir Henry Preston of Fyvie as second-in-command, his son's father-in-law, with the stern Sir Robert Melville of Glenbervie, Sheriff of the Mearns. Finally came the main body, under Alex himself, with most of his closest lieutenants around him. As Jamie had suggested, they did not use a rearguard.

They made a lengthy column, winding up the riverside meadows, however much less so than Donald's array would make. They had two miles to go to Balhaggarty, at the southern tail-end of the Harlaw ridge. There, above Erskine's small castle, whilst Scrymgeour and his van went on ahead, openly, to take up a position on the high ground, evident to all, the rest waited. His role was to be bait to draw the Islesmen up. The van would look like a comparatively small force, only a few hundreds, but larger than any patrol; therefore an outpost of the main army, holding this upland — which must therefore be important. The chances were that Donald would thereupon seek to take the position, even though he used only a small proportion of his host in the attempt. These would find a reinforced Scrymgeour difficult to dislodge, in a strong defensive site, and Donald would have to send up more Islesmen. Alex would feed up more and more of his force, until Donald must either commit his main array or give up the attempt. The Lord of the Isles' pride, however, had been sufficiently proved, and the likelihood of him withdrawing was remote. So, they hoped the battle would be fought there, on the ground of their own choosing, initiative and strategy theirs.

Alex, of course, had his scouts out, who now sent back reports as to the enemy's progress. Last word was that they were in the Logie area, a mile west of Pitcaple, which itself was a bare couple of miles west of the north end of Harlaw, all in the valley of the Urie. Donald's advance-guard must be seeing Harlaw, and Scrymgeour, now.

Hidden by the escarpment, the main eastern army waited tensely.

A messenger came from Scrymgeour to announce that a force of about a thousand Highlandmen was climbing the north slope of the escarpment towards them. They would let them get up before attacking.

Alex did not require a courier to inform him, presently, that battle was joined; they could all hear the clash and shouting, on the westerly breeze. Presently a man arrived to inform, however, that the fighting was hot and reinforcements should be sent, quickly. Sir Andrew Leslie sent up two hundred men, under one of his sons.

Donald reinforced his advance-guard. It was going according to plan.

Swiftly thereafter, Leslie and the entire left wing was despatched up the hill. That ought to bring matters to a head.

It did. In but twenty minutes after Leslie's departure, the news came that all Donald's host, thousand upon thousand, appeared to be on the move uphill along a mile-wide front.

"This, then, is the hour we have waited for, my friends," Alex cried. "All Scotland has waited for it. Today this realm's road will be decided. Pray God it is *our* road! And that we may prove worthy of the task. Come — waiting is over."

It was almost three hours past noon.

*   *   *

Up on the grassy plateau visibility was suddenly enormously extended, sight replaced imagination, reality conjecture. Far and wide the land was laid out, rising dramatically in the west to the towering conical summit of the Mither Tap of Bennachie, central landmark of all Aberdeenshire, five miles away. But sight, however welcome, was in some measure disappointing for Alex. Not in the stirring quality and excitement of the scene or even the spirit of the actors, but in the relative positioning. The northern half of the whaleback was a seething mass of men and horses all colour and movement and noise; but the entire southern half was as good as empty. Which was not as planned. Scrymgeour, once he had drawn the enemy, was to have made a strategic retiral here, Leslie likewise, so that they could all then form a unified battle, not exactly a front but a coherent and manageable array. Instead of which, the Lion Rampant standard of Scotland — presumably with the Standard-Bearer beneath it — was most evidently still pressing forward into the thickest of the enemy ranks, totally surrounded now but certainly not retiring. The same could be said of Leslie's entire wing, in a quite separate battle, over towards the west side of the escarpment. Both were obviously engaged in slaughtering as many of the saffron-clad enemy as possible in the shortest-time — but neither were doing as ordered.

"Curses on them!" Alex exclaimed. "What do they think they are at? Some clan squabble!"

"There are many fewer horses than there should be. Already!" Jamie pointed out grimly.

"You are right. That means . . ." He did not finish that. "Greenlaw — go you and command Leslie to fall back. Menzies — go tell Forbes to advance with his right wing, round the *east* edge of this scarp, to draw some of the enemy away from Scrymgeour. But not too far. Tell him to keep level with Leslie — form a line. And to watch his horses — dirkmen! Sandy — take your company and Skene's in, at the centre, in behind Scrymgeour. He's surrounded. Try to free his rear, so that he can retire. But — keep line with Forbes."

"Gladly, my lord," Irvine said. "But . . . should we not *all* go? Rescue the Constable, and then throw these Islesmen down the hill. With our fullest force?"

"Fool!" That was Jamie Douglas, at his gruffest. "Have you forgot already? Not one-third of Donald's force is yet engaged, on this hill. My lord cannot engage his main strength until he has the enemy more fully committed."

"Jamie is right, Sandy. Off with you. We have to fight this cunningly, if we are to win."

"Or to survive!" the Douglas growled.

"If you need aid, I will send Gordon . . ."

Irvine and Barclay rode off.

All the time more and more of the Highlandmen were appearing over the crest of the rise all along the northern perimeter and quite far down the west flank, this last preoccupying Leslie's wing — which was much too greatly extended. Alex and his remaining lieutenants had found a slight eminence from which to survey the field — and did not like what they saw.

"Leslie will not be able to withdraw," Jamie declared. "He is losing his horses fast, hamstrung and disembowelled. You will have to send him aid — a diversion, hard-hitting, along the edge, there. But not too many, of a mercy . . .!"

"Yes. Sir Thomas Moray — take two hundred and drive between Leslie and the lip of the hill, then back. Tell Leslie he *must* retire, or they will be cut down to a man. He thinks that he is fighting his own small war, there! But — for the saints' sake, watch your horses! The Islesmen are rushing in beneath them and dirking open their bellies. And, Sir Thomas — send me back word of Donald's main force."

Jamie was glaring around him in a fever of frustration. "This is going but ill," he declared. "If they will not obey your commands, how can you order the field?"

"The weakness of such an army. Made up of proud lords and lairds, with their own men. We did seek to train them . . ."

"These around you know their duty. It is their betters . . ."

The main mass of their own manpower was formed up in four great companies covering most of the southern end of the plateau, two of cavalry, two of infantry and bowmen, these being the Aberdeen force and the mixed contingent of churchmen, the servants and tenants of the bishoprics of Brechin, Moray and Aberdeen, under Tullidaff of that Ilk. Impatient as all were to be in and striking, there was nothing that they could usefully do at this stage without endangering their whole further strategy. Men cursed and swore as they stood idle, and at a distance watched their colleagues dying. But the supreme leadership was adamant. No move to be made until ordered by the Earl of Mar.

And men *were* dying, on Harlaw's hill, terribly and in large numbers. On both sides, to be sure — and probably many more Highlanders than the steel-clad Lowlanders. But with their vast preponderance in numbers, from a military point-of-view, this was not significant. Scrymgeour's van was but a sorry residue of its original gallant strength with barely one-third of its horses still surviving. Irvine's company was hacking and slashing to try to reach the encircled men, but the Constable had pressed much too far ahead and there was still a wide belt of axe-wielding Islesmen between them and rescue. Even as they watched, the proud Lion Rampant banner went down — and was not raised again. That could only mean that Scrymgeour himself, grandson of Bruce's standard-bearer, as Irvine was of his armour-bearer, was fallen. Fighting one of Bruce's great-grandsons, whilst another stood and watched, helpless.

Forbes, with his right wing, was moving in from the east now, in good order — he was, of course, the most experienced of Alex's lieutenants. But the Islesmen's numbers were being added to all the time and it was apparent that he, any more than Irvine, would not be able to save what was left of the van.

"I shall have to withdraw Sandy," Alex said, hammering his saddle with clenched fist. "Abandon Scrymgeour. Or he too will be surrounded, and lost. Christ pity me!"

"The burden of the commander, man!" Jamie rasped. "The loneliest man God made!" But his heart grieved for his friend. "Aye, recall Irvine. And have Forbes straighten his line. You can do naught else."

Unhappily Alex gave the orders.

Having jettisoned the costly van, and done what could be done to rescue the errant left, gradually a semblance of order was restored to the defending force. Forbes joined up with the retiring Irvine, Alex moved his main strength forward, and about one-third of the left wing was extricated, to take up its proper position at the east of the front. A twice-wounded Leslie was brought, horseless and limping, to the mound.

"Are you sore hurt, Sir Andrew?" Alex asked. And then steeled himself to say, "You much exceeded your orders. Hazarded your command. That was not well done, Leslie."

The older man stared up at him, hot-eyed but silent, grimacing with pain.

"How many have you left, of your seven hundred — for Moray to command?"

"You cannot take away my command! I am not so sore stricken."

"How many, man?"

"Three hundred, a few less. Aye, and two sons left!"

371

"Two? You mean . . .?"

"Aye. Five lie dead, yonder."

Biting his lip, Alex turned away, wordless.

"I have two more here, and myself. For vengeance!"

The first stage of the battle was over, and it had been costly for Alex. But at least he had achieved his objective in getting all Donald's forces committed to the hill-top site. He reckoned that he had lost up to seven hundred men in doing it. Was that competent generalship?

There was no break, nor even a lull, of course. The enemy, having swallowed up the last of Scrymgeour's van, came surging on in a vast, yelling mass over a half-mile front, terrible to behold. Not in any wild and unco-ordinated rabble however, but in close-packed companies and regiments, thousands upon thousands. Nothing, it seemed, could resist that tide of ferocious humanity. There were almost as many banners amongst the Islesmen as on the eastern side, mostly bearing the Galley of the Isles in some form or colour. But three larger standards, spaced out, rose above the rest — the great undifferenced black galley on white, in the centre, emblem of the Lord of the Isles himself; the yellow lion and galley of MacNeil of Barra on the east; and, on the right of the line, the red rock-stack and galley of Maclean of Duart, Red Hector of the Battles.

This charge, to be sure, had been foreseen, and all plans made for countering it as far as was possible. The foot quickly turned themselves into four great circles of spearmen, schiltroms, perhaps a hundred and fifty yards apart, front rows kneeling, inner ranks standing shoulder to shoulder, facing all round, spears thrusting out like a hedgehog; with, in the centre of each, the archers, all too few of these, who meantime were busy indeed, winging shafts in furious succession at the advancing enemy. In front of these schiltroms steep arrowheads of cavalry projected, armoured knights in front, to divide and break up the charge and lessen the impact on the spearmen — leaving the necessary gaps for the bowmen to shoot through. Even so, almost half the total remaining cavalry strength was drawn up behind the schiltroms, ready to plug any gaps, exploit any opportunities — and at the same time be prepared to turn and face the other way, should Donald send any force round the hill-foot to attack their rear. Unfortunately, the arrows did less damage than hoped for. The Highlanders were all equipped with targes, round leather shields which, held up before them as they ran, formed a fairly

372

effective barrier. Many did fall, but little difference was evident in the charge.

The impact on the Islesmen's front of their meeting with the cavalry horns was shattering, cataclysmic, a most violent disintegration, an abrupt chaos of flailing limbs, flashing steel, rearing horses and the eruption of flesh and blood — more especially blood, which spurted and splashed and sprayed everywhere. Pressed on by the weight of men behind, there was no question of the front ranks being able to halt and fight. They were flung onward like the foam of breaking rollers, dead, wounded and unhurt alike, a yelling tide being slashed at all the way by the swords and maces of the mounted men above and flanking them. On and on they were carried, to break in appalling ruin on the spear-fronted schiltroms, there to pile up in shameful masses. It was a most fearful slaughter, all along that half-mile line.

But, however shattered, the red tide was not to be reversed, the pressure behind it too heavy. On came the men of the Isles, of the mainland West, of the Antrim glens, until by sheer weight of numbers the cavalry prongs were twisted and broken up. Time and again Alex flung in aid and support, but nothing could halt the dissolution of the horsed arrowheads. The infantry schiltroms still stood firm, islands in a ghastly sea; but otherwise the battle broke up into what Alex had dreaded and sought all along to avoid, a multiplicity of separate struggles, large and small, more or less unconnected in the main — but none the less savage and bloody for that. Now he had little or no control, save perhaps over the schiltroms — but these were static anyway. Long might they remain so. For the rest, he could only try to retain a small mobile reserve and hope to use it to best effect. That, and resist the almost overwhelming urge to plunge into the mêlée, with Jamie and his close colleagues, to smite, and if need be, be smitten. It might come to that — but not yet. Admittedly Donald himself must be in almost the same position; but that was scant consolation.

He did what he could, guided by an ever-shrinking band of lieutenants, sitting their horses on the eminence, watching, assessing, sending a messenger here, a group there, a troop elsewhere. When one of the schiltroms collapsed, he was able to rally the survivors, Aberdonians all, and stiffened with some unhorsed men-at-arms, form them into another smaller hedgehog.

But this type of fighting allowed the Islesmen the fullest scope for their dire tactic of darting under the horses' bellies and slashing them open with their dirks. Once unhorsed, the armoured men were vulnerable indeed, for however protected by steel, they were slow and heavy in movement. Most of the killing was being done with dirks now, in close hand-to-hand press, with insufficient room for effective sword-wielding. And the Islesmen were better with their dirks than were the men-at-arms.

The enemy leadership strove, equally with Alex, for some control of the battle. Most effective at this was the Maclean chief on their right; and though his wing had more or less disintegrated, he had managed to gather and hold together a sizeable and coherent company, which he was using to good effect. In fact, he was fairly clearly pressing towards the eminence occupied by Alex, no doubt with the objective of destroying the eastern leadership. The menace of this became only too apparent.

"My lord," Alexander Irvine said, "we must stop Red Hector. Give me a company. I will halt him, somehow. Or we lose this position — and much else."

"He is right," Jamie agreed. "Maclean could be our ruin. On this mound he could dominate the field."

"Aye. Take half our reserves, Sandy. I cannot spare more. Lord — that will be a bare hundred! Do what you can . . ."

Irvine formed a wedge of the precious horsemen, his own banner at their head, and drove in through the struggling throng of bodies towards Maclean's colourful flag, shouting "An Irvine! An Irvine!" Quickly their momentum sank away, but still onward they pushed, swords and maces smiting to keep Islesmen from getting beneath their mounts. Dirks could not reach them effectively, up in their saddles, but the long-handled Lochaber-axes could, and not all these were parried, bringing down fully a dozen of the five score.

"What can he do?" Keith cried. "He will never reach Maclean. And if he does, he will be hopelessly outnumbered. Let me take the rest of these, to aid him."

"No. We must hold some reserve, however small," Alex said. "Your time will come, never fear! If a schiltrom breaks, these will be needed, man."

Irvine had got to within perhaps forty yards of Maclean, but looked unlikely to get much further, so tight was the throng. Suddenly he grabbed his own banner from its bearer, and turning it over, hurled it and its shaft, like a javelin, over the heads of the struggling men directly towards Maclean. In their astonishment, men around ceased their yelling for the moment — at least sufficiently for Irvine's great shout to be heard.

"Red Hector of the Battles!" he cried. "I am Irvine of Drum. And a better man than Maclean can boast! I have come for you. You are namely as a fighter. Will you hide there behind your gillies? Or come out and fight with me, man? I challenge you — show who fights Hector's battles for him!"

There was a roar from the Islesmen. But it died away quickly as Maclean raised his arm. He was an enormous man, red-haired, red-bearded, red-furred of chest — for he was stripped to the waist above a short saffron kilt, like most of his men, only the golden-linked belt showing his quality.

"Puppy! Infant!" he called, deep-voiced, but with the soft lilt of the Highland West. "Would you die so soon? Back to your mother, boy, before you come to hurt!"

"So you are craven, after all, you big red stirk! They told me you would not fight, save behind your savages."

"You should have better advisers, whatever! But there is still time to save your life, Irvine. Be off! I am busy."

"I came to kill you. But if words are all you can fight with . . .?"

The big man hooted a laugh. "Words!" He tossed his long, two-handed sword into the air, twirling, and caught it again skilfully. "Take your choice of death then, Sassenach. Sword? Axe? Dirk? Or bare hands? Either or all. We shall teach you manners. And then finish this battle."

Irvine dismounted and pushed his way through the crush. Maclean was ordering a ring to be cleared.

"Save us, he is going to do it!" Keith exclaimed. "Maclean will devour him."

"He is a fair enough fighter. But Hector is a famed swords-man," Menzies said. "He cannot win this."

"He is buying us time," Alex declared sombrely. "But — what am I to do with it? At such cost!"

Scarcely credible as it was, there in the midst of the vast con-fused battle, this private duel took place, some small percentage of the combatants breaking off their fight to watch. Mainly these were Islesmen, admittedly. Within the circle the two champions lost to time in getting down to flailing and hacking at each other with sword and dirk. There was nothing delicate or refined about this swordery. These were the heavy two-handed brands, and dirks had to be gripped between the teeth. Maclean had the height and weight and reach, but Irvine, being considerably the younger, was the more nimble, so that they were the more evenly matched. Irvine had thrown off his steel jack and tossed aside his helmet, not so much to even their state as to free his own movement. He was dancing around his opponent, thrusting and feinting, as far as such was possible with so clumsy a weapon. But that he must tire quickly was certain.

Alex and Jamie, on their eminence, could only watch this intermittently; they had all the rest of the field to consider. Another of the schiltroms was weakening, pulled sorely out-of-shape. Alex sent two-score horsemen to make a swift sally around it, to seek relieve the pressure, give them a chance to rally and re-form. But clearly they would not hold together for much longer. And the others were sadly reduced also. Time was not on *their* side, it seemed. But how to amend it? How to take advantage of what time Irvine was buying?

A messenger from Forbes came to ask for urgent aid, on the right wing. It seemed extraordinary that there was still any right wing. This was on the farthest-away part of the hill. He sent fifty men under young Menzies of Pitfodels — which left him virtually with only his personal group and those who came back from aiding the schiltrom.

Both contestants in the duel were staggering and bloody. Who had the advantage it was impossible to say; but obviously both were weary, flagging. One way or the other, it would not be long. Alex wiped away the drips from his face. He had not realised that their fine day had turned to rain.

The ailing schiltrom recovered somewhat, though lessened in size — and then its neighbour broke. This was Davidson's own. Jamie and a few other knights fought their way desperately across to the shambles of it, seeking to rally what was left, but it was hopeless. The new Sir Robert lay on a heap of dead, his head split by a Lochaber-axe. Most of the survivors appeared to be wounded. They were still fighting, resisting the tide of Highlanders, but clearly they would never reform as a unit. Jamie and his friends managed to break up the front of the attackers, for the moment. He himself got the Provost's body somehow hoisted across his saddle-bow. They escorted the sad residue of the schiltrom back to Alex on the mound.

That man gnawed his lip at the sight of Robert Davidson, finding no words. Then Keith grabbed his arm.

"Look! Maclean is down. But . . . oh, dear God — look at Sandy!"

Sure enough, Red Hector of the Battles had fought his last battle. He had fallen, not to rise again. Alexander Irvine was, however, in only little better case. One side of his head and face was so covered in blood as to be unrecognisable, one shoulder drooped and was clearly broken, and he was lurching round in ragged circles, a scarcely human figure. The Islesmen gazed, stunned at their leader's death. Then reeling, Irvine tripped over his fallen adversary, fell all his length, and so lay.

"Let me get to him! Let me get Sandy!" his friend Keith yelled. And without waiting for permission, spurred off. Alex nodded to the little group behind Jamie, who hurried after Keith.

Fortunately the Maclean clansmen were still in something of a state of shock, more concerned with collecting their chief's body than with fighting the newcomers, for the moment. These were able to pick up Irvine and bring him back, with the residue of his company. But it was a corpse that Keith carried to Alex, in choking distress.

"Rob Irvine has . . . gained a bride this day!" he gasped.

They laid Sandy Irvine's body beside Robert Davidson's, there on the mound. They were by no means alone.

One schiltrom was left, the churchmen, with the survivors of the others and various oddments forming something like another round the eminence. For the rest, the battle was merely far-flung confusion, scores of small struggles, men dying in fearful chaos — although it was to be hoped that the right wing away to the east retained some identity.

"Thank God for this rain!" Jamie jerked.

"Why? What service?"

"It will mean earlier dark. If we can hold out so long."

"You believe it . . . hopeless? Nothing that we can do, man?"

"We can always pray!"

They gained some small comfort, presently, with the arrival of the main Forbes manpower from Tillyfour, on the Don, under Sir Alexander's heir, some two hundred and fifty strong. These had been rather forgotten, in the stress. Although somewhat tired from their fourteen-mile hurried ride, after a sleepless night, they were fresh to the fight, indeed worried that they might have missed the best of it. The trouble was that their eagerness was to be with Sir Alexander rather than to be used merely as a strategic reserve. Indeed, young Forbes had even brought his father's best suit of mail, to hand over, for some reason left behind.

Alex compromised. Retaining about fifty of the newcomers, he sent the rest, with the angry Keith, to cut their way round, somehow, to the former right wing, there to command Sir Alexander to return, to rejoin them here. There was no longer any point in maintaining a separate identity and supposed threat the best part of a mile away, especially with the light failing.

Soon after they went, the churchmen's schiltrom broke. Alex used his reserve to rescue most of the survivors and bring them to build up the defensive ring around his mound. These brought with them, amongst other leaders, the bodies of William de Tullidaff and Sir Gilbert de Greenlaw.

One of the remaining Leslie of Balquhain sons came staggering in from elsewhere with the corpse of his last brother over his shoulder. That made six dead out of seven.

Alex was indeed praying now, for darkness if not oblivion. He had not been able to strike a single blow, personally, all that grievous day, while he sent so many of his friends to die.

Stragglers from all the battle kept finding their way back to the eminence, very largely wounded, weary, dispirited. For a July night it was almost dark, the rain not heavy but continuous.

The Forbes return was heartening — even though the one-time right wing was but a shadow of its original self. But, with its reinforcements, it gave the remnants of the main body some feeling, not of strength but of solidarity.

Since Maclean's fall, the Highland right wing had been less aggressive. It kept assailing the perimeter of Alex's central position, but without the fire of heretofore. Perhaps it was waiting for a new commander. At any rate, presently, with visibility reduced to little more than a hundred or two yards, when horns began to ululate from the north, this group took it as a directive to retire, and began quite quickly to disengage. Scarcely able to believe their eyes at the suddenness of it, Alex and his beleaguered residue perceived and wondered. Wondered more as the horn-wailing continued, and elsewhere, on the edge of vision, a movement backwards could be sensed.

"My God — they are breaking off, I do believe!" Alex cried. "The saints be praised — they are retiring!"

378

"Only to regroup, I swear!" Jamie said. "This rain and darkness. I hoped for this . . ."

"I *prayed* for it! To give us time, a breathing-space. And, by the Powers, we need it!"

"We cannot be sure yet . . ."

Before long it became clear to all that the battle was over for the time being. Not dramatically, not with any sort of final victory or defeat. Merely that the fighting had stopped as no longer really practicable in the circumstances of darkness and sheer weariness and human weakness.

"What now?" the Lord of Gordon, bleeding from a gashed brow, asked. "How do we retire from this hill? With all our wounded."

"We do not. We cannot," Alex answered. "Donald has the entire position surrounded. We may get a messenger or two through, that is all. To seek aid. But — from whom? I raised every man I could, before. A few more may be scraped together, here and there. But not to counter Donald's thousands."

"I could win two or three hundred more from Strathbogie, allowed a day or two."

"And I a hundred, older men, from Forbes . . ."

Not to be outdone, the wounded Leslie roused himself. "I will beat that, by God!" he growled thickly.

"Keith will find *some* more . . ."

"Aye, my friends — so be it. Brief your messengers. Brief them well. We are going to require every man and boy tomorrow, not two days hence. If we survive this night."

"And meanwhile?"

"Meanwhile we set strictest watch. We tend our wounded, count our dead. Is that not sufficient?" That was Jamie Douglas.

That was, indeed, a task more than sufficient for any man. Few indeed on that field had come out of it unscathed — but it was the legion of the seriously wounded, scattered far and wide over the plateau, that taxed the survivors. There was little that they could do for them. Even to move many was dangerous. Yet to leave them lying there was scarcely to be considered. There were equally large numbers of the Islesmen wounded amongst the fallen, of course, and often the search-parties came across groups of the enemy similarly employed; by mutual consent they ignored each other. Save once, when one of Alex's Macphersons found a son of the Mackintosh, sore hurt amongst a heap of the slain, and called to some of his own people to look to him.

The dead, to be sure, seemed the more numerous. Most had to be left where they lay. Burial was for the future. In few battles, surely, even in Scotland, was there so great a proportion of the leadership amongst the slain. Few castles and halls of the North-East would not be in mourning tomorrow. Two of the three sheriffs present were dead — Angus and Moray; and the Banff sheriff's son, young Bisset of Lessendrum. Sir William Abernethy, Albany's nephew, was slain, like Sir Robert Maule of Panmure, Sir Alexander Stirling, Sir James Lovel of Ballumbie, Sir Alexander Straiton of Lauriston, besides those already brought in, along with many lairds of the houses of Gordon, Forbes, Abercromby, Leith, Blackhall and Meldrum. And, of course, the six sons of Balquhain.

Alex Stewart never closed his eyes that evil, desolate, watchful night.

*   *   *

The rain died away in the early hours, and dawn saw a white mist over all the valleys of Urie and Don, rising high enough to thinly obscure the plateau of Harlaw. The shrunken, desperate loyalist force had been standing to arms for an hour before that — even though sentries had reported no enemy probes or approaches, other than the parties succouring the wounded. As they stood in chilled, silent ranks, watching, waiting, gradually more than daylight dawned upon them. They had the top of Harlaw's hill to themselves. Wherever Donald and his hosts were, they were no longer occupying the northern end of the plateau.

Scouts sent out quite quickly returned with the word that the enemy was not encamped down in the floor of the valley either, nor any sign of them on the moorlands to the east. Only their dead remained anywhere in sight.

At first neither Alex nor any of his people could believe it. It could only be a trap, to lure them down from this strong position. But as their scouts ranged further and further afield, it became evident that, if it was a trap, it was a very strange one, for there did not seem to be an Islesman within five miles.

When, at length, there was reliable information that the Highland host had indeed crossed the shoulder of Bennachie and was streaming back north-by-west, there could be no doubts; and the sense of relief and wonder was almost overwhelming. They, the survivors, were not going to die — for none there had expected to live through another day. Some of their wounded also would live. They could go home, to wives and parents and friends, whom they had not looked to see again. They were men redeemed, by some strange trick of fate.

It was some time before the wider aspect began to register, even with Alex. They were left in possession of the field. Despite all their losses, their failures and mistakes, they were not really defeated, after all. They could scarcely call themselves the victors, but they had turned back the menacing tide — meantime, at least. For one reason or another Donald was retiring, had lost heart. He might come again another day — but surely not soon, nor in greater strength, nor with ramifications of support. It seemed that, somehow, with God's help, they had done what they set out to do, at whatever cost.

Yet, amidst all that grim array of their dead friends and colleagues, there could be no elation, no joy. But thankfulness, yes. Perhaps that, and the relief, was enough.

There was much to do before the leaders, at any rate, might turn for home and rest. Alex, amongst so much else, Sheriff of Aberdeen, felt that he must personally convey the Provost, and its many other dead, back to the city, a dire task. Jamie, with an axe-slashed upper arm which was swelling painfully, as well as a grazed forehead, was anxious to get back to Lochindorb, to ensure that no eddy of the Isles' tide had reached that place, making or ebbing. He was going back to Badenoch with the Macpherson clansmen, and accompanied Alex's sad cavalcade only as far as the junction of Urie and Don.

"My thanks, Jamie, old friend," the other said, on parting, voice breaking just a little. "This has been a, a sore trial. A test. Out of which I feel that I have come . . . wanting. But you — you have stood firm, always sure, a rock to lean upon. Without your black Douglas strength, I doubt if I could have stood yonder all yesterday, unmoving. If I thought that I might make a general, one day, now I know differently. But you are of the stuff of generals, man. And better, of the stuff of heroes. I could not have a finer friend. Nor needed one more."

Embarrassed, Jamie looked away. "I but stood by, advised. It is easy to advise. You made the decisions. Scotland was fortunate in having Alex Stewart in command yesterday. Although whether many will thank you for it is another matter!"

"Perhaps not. But that signifies little. What does is that the Isles threat is pushed back. The Celtic dream shattered, at least for the present. And, knowing Henry Plantagenet, the English will not now invade. My Uncle Robert may not love me the more. But he must now *seem* to! And you also, Jamie. He owes too much to us to have us as foes. I think that you may walk the South again unfearing. You will never trust him, I know — nor indeed shall I. But I believe his power must wane, from now on."

"And Alex Stewart take Robert Stewart's place?"

"No. Not that. *James* Stewart, only. We must continue to work for that, Jamie, always. To bring back the King of Scots somehow. Using John Stewart, perhaps, towards that end. The house of Stewart is, God willing, due to take a turn for the better with the house of Douglas's support. Now — go back, friend, to your Mary Stewart, and to my mother, carrying my love to them. And tell them to cherish Black Sir James Douglas — for this realm needs him sorely. As do I."

They gripped hands.

HISTORICAL NOTE

THE BATTLE OF Harlaw was, of course, one of the turning-points in Scotland's story. Never again was the North and West really to threaten the South — save perhaps 335 years later, when another Stewart, Charles Edward by name, led a mainly Highland army as far as Derby, before the Stewart line went down, once and for all. Donald of the Isles did try again, the following summer; but he got no further than Argyll.

Alexander, Earl of Mar, became a major force in the land, appointed full Lieutenant and Justiciar in place of Buchan; and under his rule the North remained in fair peace and order until he died, and was buried at Inverness, twenty-four years later, where his recumbent effigy may still be discovered in an abandoned graveyard in Friar's Street — the former Blackfriars Monastery. He died much honoured, almost beloved, a strange circumstance for the son of the Wolf of Badenoch, and who had gained his earldom in such doubtful fashion. The question of his wedding to the Countess of Duffel remained unresolved, although he petitioned the Pope to have it annulled. He did not marry again. He had an illegitimate son who became Sir Thomas Stewart. His brothers set up their own branches of Highland Stewarts, Atholl and Strathdon, although Sir Duncan disappeared into the mists of history.

John, Earl of Buchan, married the daughter of the Earl of Douglas, and made a reputation for himself as a military commander, but in foreign wars. Indeed he was made Constable of France in 1421, but fell there three years later, at the great Battle of Verneuil.

Sir James Douglas of Aberdour, Roberton, etc., passes from the pages of recorded history after 1415, when he seems to have been rich enough to lend money to various people. His old father, the Lord of Dalkeith, lingered on until 1420, when he finally succumbed to the 'flu, leaving the most interesting will in Scottish records. Jamie's father left him his second-best girdle, a pair of plates and a suit of tilting armour. The legitimate line duly became Earls of Morton, and still subsists.

The Duke of Albany died, over eighty, in 1420 'of a sound mind and Christian manner', still Regent of Scotland, with King James remaining a prisoner in England until 1424, despite efforts to gain his release — not made by Albany however. When James the First did at last come home, after eighteen years imprisonment, it was to take a terrible vengeance on the Albany line. But that is another story.

There was never again any doubt as to the dynastic destiny of the house of Stewart.